Mama Six Girls and a Cowboy

Penne Poole

MAMA, SIX GIRLS, AND A COWBOY
Copyright © 2018 by Penne Poole

All rights reserved. No portion of this book may be reproduced in any form—mechanically, electronically, or by any other means, including photocopying, recording, or by any information storage and retrieval system—without permission in writing from the author.

ISBN:

Printed in the United States of America
First Printing, 2018

Cover Design: Michael Bartlett

Dedication

To women...

The mothers, the grandmothers, the aunts, the sisters, the little girls, the strong women, and the professional women, who are the rocks of this planet, the wisdom keepers, and mentors who pass on our traditions, their guidance, and love from generation to generation.

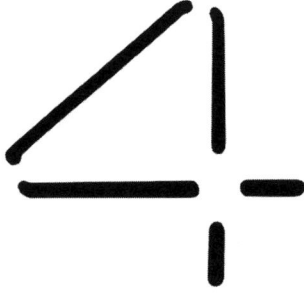

Davis Bennett's Open-4 Brand

Young Davis Bennett (engagement photo)

Catherine Connelly (engagement photo)

Left to right (back): Elizabeth and Sybil. Left to right (front): Daphne and Margaret. Not present: Nancy and Charlotte.

Left to right (back): Nancy and Margaret. Left to right (middle): Daphne and Sybil. Left to right (bottom): Charlotte and Elizabeth. (Approximately 1950)

Contents

Acknowledgments xi

❋

Chapter 1: Texas Ain't Ireland And Other Non-Catholic Discoveries 1

Chapter 2: I'll Take The Pride, You Take The Prejudice 15

Chapter 3: Take Me To The Chapel... 35

Chapter 4: Cattle, Barbed Wire, and Babies 68

Chapter 5: Dancing With Grasshoppers 95

Chapter 6: Daddy's Gone, But California Loves Me 117

Chapter 7: Rollers & Bobby Pins 158

Chapter 8: Trains, Trains, And More Trains...................................... 189

Chapter 9: Riding On Moonbeams.. 224

Chapter 10: How Do You Like 'Em—Well Done Or Over Easy? 249

Chapter 11: 10,000 Men Outside My Window 267

Chapter 12: Beyond Rainbows 294

Chapter 13: Roller Coaster Rides 321

Chapter 14: Cabin Fever 345

Chapter 15: My Boots Are Tight And I Don't See The Sunrise Anymore
.... 364

❋

About the Author 381

Acknowledgments

Without the countless hours of support, encouragement, and education into the world of writing for the public eye, I could never have accomplished this endeavor. Enormous gratitude goes to my family: my brother David and sister-in-law Donna, grandsons Connor and Patrick, and granddaughter Hadleigh, who encouraged me along the way. And to my great-aunts, who shared their personal stories. In an effort to protect their privacy, my aunts requested that I change their names and town identity. I would like to acknowledge the times and the historical events that provided such a rich background for my story.

To my friends Ginny Smith, Kathy Bradley, and Michael Bartlett.

To my beta readers, Christina Garrity, Robin McCartney, and Jessie Roderick.

To my essential support system—editors, teachers, and cover designer: Cris Wanzer, Jenny Van Velkinburgh, Donna Helmuth, and Michael Bartlett.

No one ever accomplished a project of this magnitude without a team of many hearts and hands. My endless appreciation goes to all of the above and more. Thank you.

1

Texas Ain't Ireland And Other Non-Catholic Discoveries

The Texas Panhandle, 1914

So, this is the "better life," having to beg for used pots and pans, I grumbled to myself as I trudged along Main Street, the dirt road between the buildings of the small town of Twist Junction. *I'm only sixteen...and my family and I walked 600 miles through the dust just to settle in this barren cattle town. And we aren't even ranchers! Granted, we're Texans, but boy is east Texas hill country different from the Panhandle.*

I took a deep breath to calm myself, only to choke on the dust kicked up by a flatbed wagon hauling materials for a ranch down the way. Oh, how I missed the lushness of New Braunfels. But now my new life lay ahead of me and I had an errand to complete. I turned and sheepishly went into the DeSoto Hotel.

"Is Mr. Huntington here?" I asked the first person I saw, who was an older gentleman in a neat suit. My accent was that of a Southern Texan, not an Irish brogue like my mother's. I'm sure had it been so, I would have fallen into immediate disfavor, as the Irish were not accepted in these parts. But my twinkling blue eyes won the man over, and he broke out into a wide grin.

"I'm Mr. Huntington. You must be the young lady come to collect our old cook pans for that poor Catholic Mission family."

I wanted to answer, "Well, I'd rather be here collecting books from your town's great library," but instead I said, "Yes, sir."

His kindness calmed me, and I no longer felt like the odd one out in this town of Southern Baptists and cattle ranchers. We walked in silence to the back of the hotel's big kitchen, where he gave me a small wooden crate full of used pots and pans.

"This is mighty heavy for a little lady like you," he commented, eyeing me with compassion.

"I'll be just fine. Thank you, sir," I said, and I was off, too embarrassed to linger.

I passed the tiniest building in Twist Junction, our parish Catholic church. Its white exterior siding had peeling paint, and its tilted steeple held an old bronze bell. Every other Sunday, the priest would travel by train from the next town to say the nine o'clock Mass in Latin. This Old World ritual comforted my mother, giving her a connection to the familiar, to her church and the life in Ireland that she had left behind as a girl. The foreign tongue always made the eyes of my three young brothers glaze over with boredom. I could get through the long Catholic services, but I was much more interested in the boisterous singing and clapping that came out of the windows of the big stone Baptist church on Main Street, which most of my new girlfriends attended. They had choir practice on Tuesdays, and on those days I would hurry through dinner, excusing myself by saying that I wanted to go see the coral sunsets of the prairie. But in truth, I wanted to catch the beautiful singing of the soulful Baptist hymns.

Today was Tuesday. Shifting the weight of the crate in my arms, and with the pots clanking together with my every step, I headed toward the sound of the singing voices. *Mother is still doing the after-dinner cleaning up, and all three boys are with her. Surely she won't miss me if I listen just for a minute...*

I tiptoed up to the closest open window, which was at the front of the church near the pulpit. I set down my crate as silently as possible, and was immediately lost in the beautiful sound of the men's strong voices singing "On-ward Chris-tian so-ol-diers!"

My controlled, quiet breathing gave way to an unexpected, giant hiccup. I was so startled that I let out an audible gasp, and before I could cover my mouth to stifle it, another loud hiccup jumped from my throat. I flung myself against the wall, flattened myself against the rough stone, and held my breath, trying to force the noisy chirps down into my chest.

Oh, I so didn't want to leave, but I was losing the battle against my body. At least it seemed that no one inside had heard me. No head poked out the open window to shoo me away. I closed my eyes in relief and took a huge breath, determined to stop the next hiccup that threatened to push its way up my throat. I clamped my lips tight, and my cheeks bulged as I held my breath for a moment. Then I opened my eyes to see a square-jawed young man standing in front of me, nearly bursting with laughter.

Hiccup!

We both began to laugh, but I stifled my giggles almost as soon as they started. I had been discovered.

The boy quickly contained himself. He made a friendly gesture for me to come closer to him, away from the open window.

"Miss Catherine Connelly," he said matter-of-factly.

My eyes widened with surprise at hearing my name from this handsome young man, but my mouth stayed firmly shut this time, lest another unruly hiccup waited to escape, even though it appeared that being startled by the boy had cured my affliction.

"Did your priest send you over to check up on us rambunctious Baptists?"

His wide grin gave away the playfulness of his stern tone, but I couldn't stop the blush from burning my cheeks.

"That's a heck of a technique you've got for interrupting my favorite song," he joked.

I couldn't believe my luck. Of all the people to catch me at a time like this—Davis Crockett Bennett, the young man that all my friends swooned over! He could just sing and capture the heart of any girl in town.

"I'm so sorry. I was drawn in by the beautiful singing," I hurried to explain. But seeing him standing there only a foot away from me, grinning widely, his hazel eyes staring directly into mine, gave me a kind of thrill I had never felt before. A small smile crossed my lips as I held his gaze. "I guess it took my breath away."

"Well, we wouldn't want that," he said sheepishly.

Could it be? I wondered. *Is he blushing too?*

His eyes were turned down now. He continued to grin, and I did too. He was wearing his usual dark suit with a white starched shirt, the rounded collar lying perfectly and buttoned around his neck. A breeze tousled his blond hair just enough to emphasize his boyish good looks. He looked back up at me and caught my stare.

"I'd better get back home," I said. "I have to take these things to my mother." I nodded toward the crate of pots.

"She must rely on you a lot."

I didn't have a response for that, and we stood awkwardly for a moment, but I hoped this wouldn't be the end of our conversation.

"With five of us, we need all the extra pans we can get..." I added, my voice trailing off.

His only response was a nod of understanding. It looked like that was it. He turned and walked back toward the church, and my heart sank a bit. That is, until he turned and winked at me. "Until next time, Catherine."

I don't even remember walking home that evening. I might as well have been flying. *Davis Bennett, Davis Bennett...* I kept repeating his name in my head. All the girls around town buzzed about this eligible bachelor, the youngest of fourteen children, oh so polite to everyone young and old, but never showing favoritism to any of the young women who tittered when he walked by.

I had a feeling that he had noticed me before. A few weeks earlier, when Mother and I were walking to the bank, my brothers trailing behind us, we passed a group of kids outside the general store. I made a small wave at one of the girls I knew, and just then Davis looked up from the center of the group. He may have been returning my mother's brogue-laced greeting, but it seemed like his smile was just for me.

Twist Junction didn't have many Irish girls—at least, none with curly, raven-colored hair and alabaster skin like mine. I was small framed, only five foot two, which was tiny compared to Davis's six-foot stature. I'd like to think my china-blue eyes beguiled him, but because I was shyly looking away more often than not, I doubt that's what caught his eye.

When I arrived home, I dumped the filthy pans in the kitchen and went straight to my chores, my mind racing feverishly with daydreams. Mother's sharp blue eyes noticed right away. *Nothing* got past her.

"I've never seen chores make a girl so giddy before," she said as she passed me while I mopped down the wooden floor of our modest, two-bedroom rental.

"What?" I asked, startled.

"You're humming away."

"Oh, I hadn't noticed," I said, dismissing the comment.

She stood right behind me. I dared not turn to look at her. I could never lie to my mother, and I still could not wipe the silly grin off my face.

"It's just a lovely day," I said, and focused all my efforts on getting an imaginary spot of grime off the floorboard.

I didn't have to face her to know that she was squinting intensely at me, lips pursed in concentration as she worked at unraveling my secret. She had never been one to bond over sharing emotional stories, or to give a quick hug of celebration for something as frivolous as having met a boy. Conversation in our house was for teaching or discipline.

My lighthearted comment didn't make her budge. She still stood behind me. I tried a tactic of diversion.

"Weren't there lovely days like this back in Ireland?"

"Hmm…" she said. She seemed to drift off for a moment, perhaps pondering her homeland of green grass capped by blue skies, and not a speck of Texas dust. Then she snapped back to attention, smoothed back a wayward strand of black hair, and resumed staring at me. "Yes, but this is Twist Junction and we have to focus on what we have here, Catherine."

That was Mother—stoic and never wavering in her devotion to seeing the day through to its end. I couldn't complain. She somehow always kept a roof over our heads and food on the table. Her strict frugality was what allowed us to live off the lump of money she'd gotten from selling our house in New Braunfels after Daddy passed away.

Mother and I shared a bedroom, and my three brothers crammed together in the second one. I stayed up that night as long as possible, doing every chore I could think of to guard against Mother reading my thoughts. When I finally heard her snoring, I quietly tucked myself into bed next to her and surrendered my imagination to Mr. Davis Bennett.

By morning, reality had set in and I had come down to earth a bit. Well, a very *little* bit. A tiny voice in my head reminded me that surely a good Baptist girl of English descent would fit into Davis's family far better than an Irish Catholic girl. An image of Adelaide, the daughter of the town's wealthy family claiming to hail from English aristocracy, floated through my mind and I pictured the whole Baptist congregation cheering heartily upon her saying "I do" and accepting a wedding ring from Davis. I got so worked up about this imagined disappointment that I forgot that Adelaide was a long-faced, buck-toothed girl whose constant sneer drove everyone away.

So, there I was, sulking around the house, thinking of all the obstacles that I faced in this town. Our parish was small, and there was certainly no one among it as handsome or charismatic as Davis Bennett. But it was unheard of to marry outside the Catholic Church. Mother must have noticed my gloom, because she ignored me as I did my chores, and didn't say a word.

The day was hot, and I had opened all of the doors and windows. Mother had the blessing of the angels with this rental; it had the modern luxury of screens on the windows and on the front and back doors. This allowed us to live without the bother of a hundred horse flies flitting about our heads and landing on all of our food. I had just brought in the sheets off the line and set myself up in the main room for folding when I saw a tall figure blocking the sun just beyond the front screen door.

It took a minute for my head to accept what my eyes were seeing. There stood Davis Bennett, a newly starched collar around his neck and a clean white shirt neatly tucked into his suit pants. He must have been boiling in the heat under the matching jacket.

Mother's voice cut through my thoughts. "Catherine, don't just stand there like a statue." She moved around me in her no-nonsense way and opened the door. "How can we help you, young man?"

Boy, was Mother quick! Before he could answer she had it figured out. "Come to visit our Catherine, have you?"

"Uh, yes ma'am, Mrs. Connelly. I am Davis Bennett. I would like permission to visit Catherine from time to time."

Mother looked at him for a moment, her posture rigid and almost defensive. I was so embarrassed as I stood there holding a sheet in my hands. I wanted to throw it over my head and disappear. Davis did not seem to notice Mother's protective stance. Something in his polite smile—but probably more his strength to not shrink away from this sturdy Irish woman—made Mother welcome him inside.

I was still standing in the middle of the room, unfolded sheet in hand, when Mother led him to our small, secondhand sofa.

"Catherine, please pour some water for this young man."

Without a word, I shoved the sheets back into the basket and tucked it out of the way, then dashed into the kitchen. I frantically searched for a shiny surface in which to see my reflection so I could gussy up. I thought I must certainly look a mess. I reached up and could feel my hair fraying out of its bun and the beads of sweat on my forehead. Oh, why couldn't Davis have come calling and found me sitting on the sofa, perfectly made up and in my best dress, doing an embroidery sampler?

At least now he knows I'm a hard worker and am not afraid of housework. That has to count for something, I thought.

I couldn't find anything to see myself in, so I dampened my hands with water and patted my hair down as best I could, then peeked around the corner of the kitchen to see how things were progressing in the other room. It was clear that Davis's quick, soft manner was winning Mother over. Her posture was relaxed and friendly, even though she still spoke to him formally.

I filled a glass with water, then returned to the living room and handed it to Davis. He gave a quick smile and a "thank you" to me but was clever enough to keep his attention on the conversation with Mother. I sat down across from them in the wooden-backed chair that we sometimes used for an extra person at the dinner table.

Davis was telling Mother that he came from a family of fourteen children, when Mother broke in, "Not unlike many Catholic families I know."

"Yes, ma'am. We take up the entire first two pews at the church."

"You said you are the youngest of all the children. It's impressive that all your siblings have grown and married and certainly have families of their own, yet they still come together on Sunday."

I could see exactly what Mother was doing. She was masterful at guiding a conversation to her chosen path. As soon as Davis's affirmative "oh, yes ma'am" rang out, I mouthed along with her as she repeated her familiar saying, "Loving partners create loving marriage partners."

At that moment, my gregarious, stair-step brothers burst through the kitchen door. There stood three sweaty, curly-headed youngsters; Kerrick, Dennis, and Liam. I think they were shocked at the sight of a man sitting in the parlor.

Kerrick stepped forward. "Hello, I'm Kerrick Connelly, Catherine's oldest brother. Haven't I seen you in town with all the ladies from time to time?"

"Kerrick," Mother scolded. "That's enough. Mr. Bennett is here to visit your sister, and we'll have no nonsense or impertinence from you."

Kerrick came over immediately and shook Davis's hand with an apologetic stance. "Sorry, didn't mean to imply that you were the town's Romeo."

"Kerrick!" snapped Mother.

Davis chuckled and smiled at the boy's observation.

I spoke up at that point. "You must forgive my brothers. They don't miss anything, and they don't always say things with the utmost diplomacy."

Liam and Dennis giggled in the background. Then all three boys flew out the same door they had abruptly entered through a few moments before.

Mother called out, "Grab an apple as you all leave! That should hold their appetite for a few more hours yet."

When Davis left that day, I had no worries about opposition from my mother. My only remaining fear was that he might somehow lose interest. But that fear was soon dispelled when Davis began to make formal afternoon visits on a daily basis.

The heat wore on for weeks. One evening, Mother suggested that Davis and I go for a stroll to cool off. My heart flip-flopped! I was officially stepping out with Davis Bennett. Those days were magical for me. Mother had taken on a teaching job, and while it meant that we had more food and I had a lot more responsibility around the house—especially taking care of my little brothers—I was not about to miss any time with Davis. As soon as Mother came home in the afternoons, I would have dinner on the table so we could eat and get the dishes done, leaving enough time for me to pretty up for when Davis would arrive to take me out. He was always punctual, arriving exactly at 5:00 p.m. Mother commented one time that we might as well throw away the big old cuckoo clock on the wall because it needed winding, but Mr. Davis Bennett didn't.

I don't know how many strolls Davis and I took, but we were always arm in arm, and I was so proud when we saw the other young folks around town. He always waved and said hello to everyone we knew, but he never stopped to talk. Just like me, he didn't want anything to interrupt our time together. When we reached the town's park off Main Street, he would guide us to the bench under the lonely tree at the far end, away from the clip-clop of the horses on the street and the deep-voiced chatter of the men finishing business under the portal of the DeSoto.

Many evenings Davis and I would sit quietly and listen to the nearby birds chattering before the sun set. Relaxed and comfortable together, we didn't require constant conversation. The ease of our relationship gave me the moments to fall in love with him, never mind

Mother's hesitation—or the world, for that matter. I believe we both knew from the first time we met outside the church window that we were meant to be together. Falling in love was more beautiful than I could have ever imagined. And then it came—the special moment when Davis held my hand and his soft, warm voice finally spilled out his strong affection for me.

"Catherine, you know there have been many girls who wanted to have me and hear these words, but you, dear, sweet Catherine, are the one I have always dreamed of, the one I picture in my mind in quiet times, and the one I mentally talk to as I say good morning to my day. I want to be the husband of your dreams. I want to be the father of your children. I want to support and care for you. Catherine, I cannot live my life without you by my side. Will you marry me?"

My eyes watered. My lips quivered with joy as I nodded a gentle *yes*. My body seemed to float off the bench.

His hand moved to my waist. He pulled me closer and I nestled my head against his muscular shoulder. He kissed my forehead and we both wept with joy. His mellow voice broke into a soft love song. My entire body was captured, I'm not ashamed to say.

A short while later, we meandered back to the house, and Davis officially asked Mother's permission for my hand in marriage.

"Mrs. Connelly, I have come with a humble heart to ask your consent to marry your beloved daughter, Catherine."

"Well, Mr. Bennett," Mother replied. "I have studied you for months now, and I do consider you to be a fine young man. If you and Catherine can bridge the religious differences, I believe you will make a fine couple."

"Thank you, ma'am. I will not disappoint you, or..." he looked at me tenderly, "my Cate."

As summer finally started to give way to autumn, Mother announced at dinner one day that her sisters, Aunt Isabel and Aunt Mary, were coming for a visit. Despite Mother's casual tone, this was an unusual time of year for the two older ladies to make the twenty-mile buggy trip from Channing, Texas. It wasn't a holiday, and the midday sun was still so hot that traveling would surely be uncomfortable.

Fear struck my heart at Mother's announcement. "Oh, no...is someone sick?" I said as I circled our dinner table, serving the boys some extra greens.

I caught Mother's lips curling into an almost perceptible smile. "No, dear," she said, and in her matter-of-fact nature, she was back full force. "They're coming to meet your young man. This courting has gone on long enough, and it's time to figure out the practical use of it."

I nearly swooned and had to retighten my grip on the serving bowl in my hand. My little brothers broke into a noisy chorus of "ooohs" and Liam made kissy faces at me. Mother shut that down right away.

"They will be here tomorrow afternoon."

"When Davis comes to fetch me for our walk this evening, I'll ask him if he can be available," I said.

So soon! But there was so much to do to prepare that I didn't have time to fret over whether they would like him, whether he would like them, whether they would tell me that I was too necessary to the household chores to be allowed to leave, or whether they would take one look at me and stamp "Old Maid" across my forehead.

Before I knew it, Mother, Aunt Isabel, and Aunt Mary were sitting in our stuffy little parlor, clustered in a semi-circle around Davis. It looked like an inquisition was about to start, and I caught Davis pulling at his collar more than once in the heavy silence that lay over the room.

Always the outspoken, fiery one, Aunt Isabel broke the silence, and she gave no pretenses about the purpose of their meeting. "Now, young man, you realize that you are courting our only girl of this generation. She deserves a fine home and prosperity. We won't give her up to a life of struggle and strife."

Davis opened his mouth to comment, but Aunt Isabel rolled on like a steam train, waggling her finger in the air. "Now, that's not to say that you have to have it all now. Every man makes his own way in the world, and you have to have an idea about what kind of man you will be." She was becoming quite animated. Leaning forward on the edge of her chair, she pounded her fist on her knee. "So, I ask you now, are you a doer or are you a coffee boiler? Will we find you in the north forty feeding and calving, or in the saloon, full as a tick?"

Davis's mouth fell open in surprise, but he quickly recovered. "Well, ma'am, I'm no drinker—"

"What my sister is trying to ask," Aunt Mary interrupted in a softer voice, "is how exactly do you plan to provide for our niece?"

As Davis started his answer, Aunt Mary reached out and rested her hand gently on Aunt Isabel's arm. She was always able to calm her overanxious sister, and sure enough, Aunt Isabel visibly relaxed and scooted her big, round bottom to the back of the chair.

"Oh, yes ma'am. That is a most important question. And I take Catherine's future as seriously as my own. I have started considering how much money I'll need to rent a home for the two of us, or whether I should try homesteading some of the available land out of town."

I was so proud of Davis. How calm and polite he stayed in the face of this blustery female storm! Boy, was I glad I wasn't sweating in his hot seat.

Suddenly, Aunt Mary turned to me. "Now, you have responsibilities too, young lady. This isn't all on your young man. No worthy young man will accept a panhandler as his bride."

"Oh, no ma'am," I managed to stammer, my eyes darting between Mother's stern gaze, Aunt Mary's inquisitive stare, and Davis's supporting nod of encouragement.

Aunt Isabel, however, did not seem to notice the shift in everyone's attention. I noticed her starting to squirm in her seat. Her eyes remained firmly focused on Davis and I knew she was not finished having her say. I tried to keep the wild colt inside her from busting loose again.

"Mother has already introduced me to the local families whose children need some extra help with schoolwork," I stammered. "She knows which ones need it most since she sees them on the days when she substitutes for the teacher."

Davis recognized my tactic and sought to help me further establish this calm line of conversation. "Yes, ma'am. My sister, Polly, is the schoolteacher and she can also help in getting this kind of work set up for Cat—"

Aunt Isabel shot forward in her chair, finger again wagging in Davis's face. "You do realize that we are Irish Catholics, and that means any children you have will be Catholic."

Everyone's attention focused back on her. And although she lapsed into silence after this outburst, everyone knew there was more to come. No one spoke a word.

"And," she said with theatrical emphasis, "you must—absolutely *must*—be married by the Catholic priest."

PLBBBBBBGH!

A loud fart punctuated her statement. Everyone's eyes popped wide open in surprise, but not one of us moved an inch. I caught Davis's eye, and the two of us had to look away lickety-split to keep from bursting into laughter. But these women used sheer will to force the decorum of our little group to remain firmly intact. This time it was Mother who came to the rescue.

"Well, it seems like you have a lot of planning to do, young man. We will not delay you any longer from all the work you have ahead of you."

Nodding in respect, Davis proceeded to slowly rise from his chair. "I suppose I need to be getting on with things...unless..." He sat down, perched on the edge of the seat, realizing that he hadn't been formally dismissed. "I'm sorry...I didn't mean to leave without asking if you had any further questions."

My heart sank. Was Davis running away in shock, or was he wanting to show his good intentions by getting back to work? Were my aunts' instructions making him reconsider our marriage? I was uneasy in my seat and my reticent stare seemed to read like a book unwrapped. Davis could sense me tightening up. He calmly slid his hand over onto mine, and with this act of solidarity, he confirmed, "We will do our best to make your family very proud."

Aunt Isabel responded, "Yes, we shall see what we shall see. We trust you have a busy day, young man. You had better be off. And Mary, we have a hot ride ahead of us."

Davis walked the elderly women out to their buggy and opened the door for each one.

Isabel nodded with approval.

Mary smiled. "Thank you. You are a fine young man."

And off they went, dust billowing after the buggy's wheels.

Davis stood on the curb, brushing off the Panhandle debris. "Ladies, I'd better get movin'."

Mother and I stood and waved from the shady, peeling porch overhang. I believe I finally took my first full breath all afternoon. Glancing over at Mother, I thought I sensed a faint smile of fondness on her lips as she saw her future son-in-law disappear around the corner. She ever so gently reached for my hand and gave it a little squeeze. From that point forward, I knew that Mother approved of Davis wholeheartedly.

2
I'll Take The Pride, You Take The Prejudice

"Elmer! Put down that vase and pay attention!" I said. "You know that's your mother's favorite, and I am not about to have you break it, on top of not learning your lesson."

The sullen young man rolled his eyes up at me but didn't move. His pudgy finger stayed perched on the gold-painted handle of the fine-china urn. I could envision its delicate pattern of purple larkspur smashed to smithereens on the floor as he held it precariously tilted on its base. Oh, I just wanted to smack him! No wonder he was so behind in his math studies at school. He was no better behaved in the classroom than he was at home, I was sure.

"Elmer," I said, keeping his eye. "Tell me, what is one-half divided by three?"

Silence.

Oh, this child! I was earning every penny that Mrs. Steel was paying me to get her spoiled son to do what no teacher had been able to achieve in the boisterous one-room schoolhouse. It was impossible, but I needed to feed my savings. My aunts' words still echoed in my head, and I knew Davis deserved better than an empty-handed bride.

I took a deep breath. "Fine, Elmer. I guess this one is just too hard for you. I'll tell your mother that you aren't ready for division of fractions, and we should go back to simple addition and subtraction."

Finally, I saw some spark of life in the boy's dull eyes. I had him.

"That way I can tutor you alongside your little sister," I continued. "She may only be in the first grade, but she is already up to two-digit subtraction. I'm sure you'll catch up quickly."

As I began gathering my things to leave, I heard the base of the vase wobbling in a circle and settling back into place. I dared not look around, lest the thing lost its balance and broke, which would surely make my savings disappear. I wasn't about to give Elmer the satisfaction of seeing my anxiety.

"One-sixth!"

"What?" I turned around, startled to find Elmer sitting straight up in his chair and facing me like a dutiful pupil.

"One-sixth. The answer is one-sixth," he repeated.

"Hmm. It looks like you know your math after all. I guess we can move forward to division with decimals tomorrow."

Victory had never felt so good.

I walked home with a spring in my step that I hadn't felt since Davis and I had begun meeting each evening for our strolls to the park. The last month had been so busy. Both Davis and I had taken our first jobs, and they weren't glamorous. The tutoring was trying my patience, and Davis was wearing himself out loading and unloading supplies for the general store. But we were working toward a common goal, and that made our absence from one another slightly more bearable.

We each had other responsibilities as well. I had to plan the wedding, and Davis had to get a house to bring me home to. I knew he was busy working toward a job more solid and respectable than a menial laborer, and I didn't nag him for any details. My mind, however, was constantly nagging my own heart. Why had I not yet formally met his family? His family was large, I knew, and Davis was the youngest. His mother had long since stopped trying to exert control over her fourteen children, and Davis said that his sister Polly was the one who had raised him like a mother, from as far back as he could remember.

So, I wasn't too surprised when Davis suggested that our first family visit would be a one-on-one at his sister Polly's home. Being the primary teacher for our town's children, everyone knew of Miss Polly Bennett. Even though I had never met her, I knew all about this infamously stern but kind woman, whose status as a devout Southern Baptist and spinster was almost as well known as her routine of placing freshly baked sugar cookies into the eager hands of little ones as a reward for good behavior.

The day of the visit arrived, and as Davis and I came to the edge of Polly's perfectly trimmed lawn of stiff Texas grass, there was no hiding my anxiety. My hands were busy pressing down imaginary wrinkles in my starched cotton skirt, only to fly back up to the high-collared neck of my blouse to ensure that the lace had not wilted in the afternoon heat, and was still standing upright to frame my face in the most becoming way. Davis gently reached over and took my arm in his. Such a subtle gesture, but it quieted my nerves so that I could take in the small bungalow standing before us.

The house had a neat and trim exterior with bright-orange marigolds dotting the thin strip of garden that ran the length of the front porch. A bright-white two-seater swing hung from the rafters of the flat porch roof and faced a wooden rocking chair. And right there in the middle of it all, in direct contrast to the formal *Good Housekeeping* image of everything else, stood Polly.

Her simple cotton dress was covered in a pattern of large roses on a white background speckled with tiny violets. But she was no delicate flower. The cloth of her dress was so thin that I could see her practical slip beneath it…and beneath that, the outline of a functional boned corset cinched tightly around her thick frame. The bottom of her dress skimmed the tops of her stockings, which had been rolled down just below the knee. As she stepped forward, the heels of her laced-up shoes clicked on the porch. I noticed that her short hair was cocooned in a hairnet, although I was not quite sure what its purpose was, since the hair plastered beneath it was thin and sparse.

My eyes then went directly to her welcoming smile and all my anxieties melted away. I instantly smiled back into her square, soft face, her eyes twinkling behind the round, wire-rimmed glasses perched atop her broad nose.

"I'm so happy to meet you, ma'am," I said, and I meant every word.

Her smile turned into a grin of tender pride.

"Davis tells me you are his special mother," I continued.

Still grinning, she motioned us to the swing. "Make yourselves comfortable here on my porch." Then, as she disappeared into the dark interior of the house, she called back over her shoulder, "Has Davis told you about my sugar cookies? Boy, I made you a fresh batch this morning!"

We sat on the cozy two-seater, side by side, our arms touching, but not so close as to risk the impropriety of a thigh touch.

Returning with cookies and iced tea, Polly continued as if there had been no break in the conversation. "So, Miss Catherine, I heard your mother has been teaching at the school on my days off. Davis says you are well educated yourself, and I've heard good things from the families whose children you are tutoring. How you manage to get that little Elmer to do anything is a mystery to me."

I was a bit surprised by her knowledge of my life, but it showed she had taken an interest in me, and for some reason that warmed my heart toward her.

"Oh, yes. My father used to teach me in the evenings. He knew five languages, went to Trinity College in Dublin, and even lived in Paris for a time before he married my mother."

Polly situated herself in the rocker across from us and began rocking comfortably.

"Five languages...can you imagine? I feel lucky enough just to teach my schoolchildren how to speak and write English properly. I've read about Ireland, France, and England, their moist air and lushness. What beautiful places they must be..." she trailed off, looking out at her neighborhood in the dry land of Twist Junction. "Leaving must have taken a lot of fortitude. Davis says you too are a woman of fortitude."

"Oh, my mother is the strong one. I was born in New Braunfels and just moved over from East Texas. Not over an ocean, like my parents did."

"Still...you must carry your mother's will in you. It will be my pleasure to meet her one day. Our paths don't cross since she is at the school on my days off."

I was pleased to hear this, but my anxiety crept back as I thought about the vast differences between our families.

As if she had read my mind, Polly said, "Davis has already told me about the different backgrounds of our families, where we differ in our religions and upbringings. This is a small town though, and the arrival of a new Irish Catholic family with three boys and no daddy…and a beautiful young woman…created quite a buzz."

Her tone was light, but I understood the weight of her words.

"It's hard to be different in this town," I said, my hands beginning to worry themselves in my lap.

"Yes, it is. I have seen the pain this can cause reflected in the eyes of some of my students. Why just the other day—I don't know if your mother told you or not—a little group of young boys from our church disrupted your mother's entire school lesson because they kept asking her why the Catholics pray to Mary, and wasn't she afraid of going to Hell?"

I was shocked! Mother had never told me of any prejudices she had been subjected to in town.

Polly went on, her voice much stronger. "Boy, did they get a telling off from me the next day! I even took the paddle to that little Elmer when he back-talked me."

She must have sensed my unease at this new information, and her voice softened. "Oh, I shouldn't be spreading such tales outside of the classroom. It's just, well, the way some people disregard one another hurts my heart. The point is, I am very aware of what you all face in this town…and what you and Davis will face as a couple. And the challenges won't come from just the other townsfolk, but from our family as well, I'm sorry to say. You see, the Bennett family is very rigid. They tend to hang with their own sort, and Twist Junction fits them just right for that."

Her directness left me speechless. I sat as still as a statue, but inside I was waging a huge battle to hold back the tears that were already causing my eyes to sting.

Davis's knee was jiggling fiercely next to mine, threatening to topple the glass of iced tea that sloshed around in his hand.

"Now, Davis Crockett Bennett, you just calm yourself down. No need for gettin' so worked up over some conversation. And you, Miss Catherine, lift your head and show me that beautiful face," Polly instructed.

I surprised myself by doing so without hesitation. This woman had such a commanding but gentle presence. I could see why she was such an effective mistress of the schoolhouse, and why she was so loved by her surrogate son, my own beloved Davis.

"You're a lovely girl, Catherine," she said gently. "Davis is very fortunate to have found you. If he didn't marry you, I'm afraid he'd have a heavy heart for the rest of his days."

My heart soared at these words, and out of the corner of my eye, I caught the blush rushing up Davis's face. All the weighty doubts disappeared from my shoulders, and we grinned at each other and turned back to our newfound ally.

"As a teacher, I've seen lots of different children coming in and out of our little town, and I am not boasting to say that I can quickly spot the cream of the crop. And that, Miss Catherine, is what you are. Mrs. Bennett and the others will warm up to you over time, so don't you fret too much. I will do what I can to hurry them along. Maybe I can have some of them over after church next Sunday. No promises they'll come, though." She gave a hearty laugh and slapped her knee. "Fried chicken and cornbread should bring at least one or two of them out!"

As we walked away from Polly's front porch that afternoon, my heart whispered, *This woman will be a devoted friend for the rest of your life. Her wisdom is something you should aspire to...her open heart is something you should emulate.*

Davis interrupted my thoughts. "You know, she really is a marvel. She can calm our nerves as easily as she can quiet down a classroom full of wild children. I'm sure she could give you some pointers on dealing with those rowdy ones you have to deal with after her school day has finished."

"Yes, I was just thinking that I have so much to learn from her." I didn't add, *even how to be a better wife to you and mother to our future children...* But her words had also been a warning about the challenges I faced in this town, and just as with my tutoring job, there were plenty of little Elmers out there in Twist Junction—no doubt many who were much worse.

Davis must have seen my face set in concentration, because he gave my hand a squeeze and smiled at me. The love in his eyes, and the echo of Polly's statement about Davis's devotion to me, told me that Davis was worth all the work in the world to overcome the challenges and obstacles that life would throw at us.

The days flew by. I kept up the routine of daily chores at my house, making sure the boys were off to school, and then fed before Mother arrived home in the evenings. Then I was off to my never-ending tutoring sessions in some of our town's fanciest houses. In my moments of silence—which were usually right before I fell asleep, with Mother's soft snores coming from the pillow next to mine—I would start to dream and fret about the wedding. That would be a whole job in itself—getting the dress and food ready, finding a date when the priest would be in town, giving Aunt Mary and Aunt Isabel time to plan for the trip over from Channing. Oh yes, and finally meeting Davis's family.

Well, there was no more putting it off. Davis invited me to his church's Sunday social. Most, if not all, of his brothers and sisters still lived in Twist Junction and attended worship almost every Sunday. His mother certainly never missed a sermon. They would all be there.

"Because the weather has been so nice lately," Davis explained, "the preacher made a special announcement that the usual Sunday social will have games for the children to play outside, and he asked especially for all the congregants to try to stay for fellowship and a potluck. My whole family should be there…or as many as I have seen in one room in a long while."

One afternoon, after arriving home from a visit with Polly, I called out to Mother, "I'm home! Mother?"

"I'm here." Mother's head popped up from behind the dining

room table.

"Oh, I didn't see you there. Can I help you with something?"

"No, dear. I just dropped my needle. I'm basting together some linen and lace to see what you might like for your wedding dress."

"How lovely! Thank you..." I reached down and fingered the fine Irish lace, which I recognized as having come from one of my father's many sales trips. I wondered what my mother felt at seeing it. Did it remind her of his absence? Did it make her sad to think he would be missing his only daughter's wedding day? Her face remained impassive and unreadable.

She looked up at me, squinting a bit as she worked on figuring out what was in my head. "What's on your mind, Catherine? Come on, there's lots to do. Out with it! You've got chores waiting."

I knew she would never entertain the questions that filled my head. Instead, I asked, "Can you tell me how to make your special butterbean and ham dish? Davis has invited me to his church social this Sunday, and it's a potluck."

Mother knew exactly what that meant. "So, you're going to be meeting his family? Well, that's a good recipe for impressing folks who will want a good cook for a daughter-in-law."

I blushed.

"Why don't you use my pretty blue-and-white porcelain casserole dish? It always makes a dish look extra yummy."

That Sunday morning, I dashed out of Mass and ran home to grab the dish. Mother had given such excellent and attentive instruction that it was not only heavenly to smell, but also had to be beautifully presented. "So good, it will make a Baptist fall to their knees and thank the Virgin Mary for her blessings," Mother had quipped in her usual dry tone.

When I got halfway to the church, I found Davis running down the sidewalk toward me. "I want us to arrive together," he panted, his tousled blond hair falling over his hazel eyes. He took the heavy dish from my hands and carried it until we got to the church. "Here, you carry it in, so they know that this delicious meal is all due to you," he said, handing the dish back to me.

I hefted the weighty dish in front of myself and stood as tall and straight as I could.

Davis looked down at me with obvious pride. I wished then for my mother's keen sense that made it seem like she could read minds. I caught his stare, the fondness in his eyes, and felt myself blush as he smiled at me. To be honest, had I known his thoughts, I would have shrieked with happiness, dropped the dish, and done a jig right on top of the shattered pieces of porcelain.

Davis opened the door to Fellowship Hall, and the high-volume chatter inside became noticeably quieter. "Go on," Davis whispered to me without moving his lips.

I took the first step forward and felt my confidence grow. I moved across the room to the long table where the food was placed, ready for the hungry hoards snatching greedy glances at it all. I smiled kindly at every group I passed, and they moved aside for me.

Such polite people, I thought. But as I continued to move forward, a little thought started nagging me. *No one is smiling back...* By the time I reached the table, my smile had become a painted mask on my face.

There was an empty spot right in the middle of the long table, but the thought of nestling my beautiful porcelain dish among all the plain Pyrex made me feel like a show-off. Instead, I placed it more subtly to the side. As soon as I set it down, Davis was by my side.

"You always know the right thing to do," he whispered.

He took my arm, and together we walked through the throng of people, any number of which could be his family. Davis guided us over to a small knot of women, and I recognized Polly among the three. "My mother, and my sister, Mary," Davis quickly whispered to me before we were within earshot.

Mrs. Bennett stood between the two women, wearing a thick cotton dress in a dark-gray color that contrasted the spring day this event was meant to celebrate. She was noticeably shorter than her daughters, but there was no mistaking that she was the all-powerful matriarch of their entire clan.

As Davis began to introduce me, a group of men jostled past us on their way to start the food line.

"Bringing the enemy to our peaceful territory, huh?" one of them said.

Davis didn't skip a beat and pretended not to notice the snide comment. I followed his lead and kept my attention firmly on my future mother-in-law, a respectful smile on my lips. Up close, she looked so much like Polly that I expected to find the same smiling eyes greeting me from behind the lenses in her small, wire-rimmed glasses. Instead, I got the simple raise of an eyebrow. Mary, at least, gave a slight smile.

I had no idea how to handle such a reticent response. Luckily, our awkward gathering was interrupted by the preacher calling out, "Everyone, let's bow our heads in prayer."

I followed suit respectfully, lowering my chin to touch my lace-edged, high-collared, crisp white blouse.

When the hearty "Amen!" rang out through the hall, everyone started shuffling toward the buffet.

Davis and I were in line directly behind Mrs. Bennett. I could see everyone ahead of us taking large helpings of a slightly soggy dish made of ground beef.

The preacher called out, "Mrs. Bennett, I'm so glad you brought your beef dish. It's everyone's favorite!"

I saw her lips curl up on the ends at this public compliment. *So...you can smile*, I thought, a bit of anger flaring up inside of me.

Mary passed by, her plate overloaded with food. "Davis, I brought corn pudding. You just have to try it."

Even though her comment was clearly not directed at me, I piped up, "Davis *and I* would love to try your dish. I just may ask you for the recipe, too. After all, every good wife knows a full stomach makes a happy heart."

Out of the corner of my eye, I saw Mrs. Bennett's raised eyebrow again. I was being impertinent, I knew, but the feeling of being invisible among a crowd of people was needling me.

I rushed through the line, not even making it to the end of the table.

Davis followed right behind me and took a seat opposite me at the table near the open doors, where a light breeze flowed in. To my surprise, his mother came over and sat next to him. The mood did not change though, and we began eating in silence. I began to feel guilty for my behavior and remembered that it was my place to win this woman over. She was not completely uninterested in me, I could tell. Her eyes scrutinized every move I made, and I exaggerated my graceful table manners, ever so gently lifting my fork and taking dainty bites. I pictured myself as a princess under the watchful eye of my queen mother. I decided to impress her by making her see how well I could represent their family and her son in social situations.

"Mrs. Bennett," I said after my last bite of her beef casserole, "your seasoning is perfect. It's no wonder this is everyone's favorite. I think it has become my favorite, too."

She gave a slight nod but said nothing. I felt like rolling my eyes, but remembered my plan to be as perfect as a princess. Davis must have seen the internal struggle I was facing and winked at me in solidarity. I calmed down and thought, *At least this time I didn't get the telltale indicator of her displeasure. No raised eyebrow. I may have finally made some headway with this woman.*

Soon enough everyone was standing to leave. The empty dishes lining the buffet were being claimed by their owners, each smiling with pride when they found their dish had been scraped clean. I waited until the hubbub died down before fetching my own dish. There it stood, alone on the empty table, its contents in the same perfect shape they had arrived in, completely untouched. The serving spoon sitting next to it hadn't even been jostled askew from where I had set it so carefully.

Humiliation rose in my chest and threatened to burst from me in tears of indignant outrage. But before I could respond, Davis rushed past me and grabbed the spoon. He scooped up hefty bites and shoveled them into his mouth. I had never seen anyone eat with such ferocity.

He looked up at me in between bites. "I have been dying to try this since I first smelled it on the sidewalk outside. I'm so glad there's some left for me."

"It looks to me like they left *all* of it for you," I mumbled.

"Well, I'm glad. I like this. I like this a lot."

He shoveled an extra-large spoonful into his mouth for emphasis and struggled to chew it all. He took a giant gulp and said, "Everyone sure missed out. I know Polly loves ham...too bad she got distracted at the end of the line talking with some of her students."

My sour mood was not to be so easily placated. I wanted to be practical and face the facts that were right in front of us. "That's not why everyone else in line didn't take any."

"Maybe the dish was just too fancy and it scared them off. We Baptists are a plain-living, simple people."

"I don't think that's it. I think they just didn't want to try anything that came from a Catholic outsider."

Davis stopped trying to make the whole casserole disappear into his mouth.

"Well, Davis," I said, "that's not a problem then, 'cause this is the exact meal everyone is going to get when they come to *my* house for dinner."

Davis was trying so hard, yet the tears welled up in my eyes. He immediately grabbed the dish again and started eating.

"No, don't," I said, reaching out to grab his hand. "You'll make yourself sick. What's worse than no one eating it is someone seeing you throwing it up! I'll just dump it in the bushes so I don't have to explain this disaster to my mother."

"Now, Catherine..."

"No, I'm serious. I will not relive this insult by having to tell every detail to people outside of this hall."

I reached out and grabbed the dish from Davis's hands. The action left him dumbfounded, and when I stomped out to walk home alone, he did not follow.

— 4. 4. 4. —

I didn't know she had it in her, Davis thought, his heart oddly in awe of Catherine's show of will. "Better leave her be," he said, catching the preacher's wide eyes. He had been the sole witness to their little tête-à-tête. "I'll be leavin' now, too. You have a good day, sir."

Davis walked slowly down the street, hands in his pockets, head down. Kicking so hard at a rock that it shot all the way down the street, he gasped out his frustration. "I am so embarrassed!"

Luckily, no one was around to hear him that time. But his insides still rolled and churned. He frantically chanted to himself, *I just can't lose her! I just cannot lose her!* The thought struck him that to secure her as his bride, he had better find them some land and a house, lickety-split. *That will make her see how much I am dedicated to her—to us. That will make her see how proud I am to claim her as my wife.*

He fell asleep that night, his mind filled with more questions than answers. What if Catherine had changed her mind about him? How could he make his mother and siblings know that they could not dismiss the woman he loved? Where was he to find a home that would be worthy of this lovely and proud woman—and the children they would fill it with? *Certainly*, he thought, *we need land. I could secure our future with land…some acreage to farm…maybe even a few head of cattle. I'll talk to Owen tomorrow, see how he got his farm set up after he first married Beulah…*

The next day, Davis met up with his brother.

"Well, look who's here. Our young scamp, Davis. Good morning to you, brother. That was some good eatin' yesterday, huh?" Owen greeted Davis.

"Mmmhmm," Davis responded.

Owen lowered his voice conspiratorially and winked at Davis. "Your little lady is such a looker."

"She's also kind and intelligent. So, why was everyone so rude to her? I'm afraid you all may have scared her off forever."

"Oh, don't you worry about that. That's just the womenfolk establishing the hierarchy. I don't pay much attention to their drama. And I advise you not to, either. It'll keep you sane." Owen elbowed

Davis jovially and chuckled.

"Come on, this is no joking matter. Catherine was really hurt, and I'm so embarrassed. I gotta come up with a way to make this right. What if she decides she doesn't want to marry me and deal with this the rest of her life?"

Owen reached out and put a stop to Davis wringing his hands. "Hey there, brother. I see this is serious. I'm sorry, I was just trying to lighten the mood, but I see that you need practical advice and not some old man's bad sense of humor."

"Well, I've been thinkin' that it will help her see how dedicated I am to her if I get a workable piece of land with a house on it."

"Yup, that's a good idea. Land will give you two a right good start on life. Beulah and I have done really well; no shortage of greens and roots on our table. I can help you figure out what crops will work best. But farming is a hard life, I won't lie to you."

"I'm thinking of doing ranching more than farming. But I gotta get the land first. You know about any tracts that are available, something suitable for running cattle and some plantin'? Catherine's Aunt Isabel, who works up at the main office of the big XIT Ranch in Channing, has passed on some friendly advice that I would do well to secure a homestead for us."

"*Friendly advice*," Owen chuckled. "I know what that means. Well, you will do well to listen to her, then."

Davis's mood lightened as he thought about that blustery old lady. "She may be a spitfire, but she's the accountant for that giant ranch. If they trust her, then I should too."

"You know, Davis, I agree with her. And it's just as well that you get a move on and find you and your young lady a place of your own. You don't want to move her into Mother's place."

"Yeah, we'd have a holy war on our hands," Davis sighed.

"I was thinking that your little bedroom is too close to the kitchen. Mother says your snoring is louder than the sizzle of the eggs fryin'. And trust me, you don't want her to hear anything else!"

The blush burned Davis's face. Owen was nine years older than he was, and had never before talked to him like a man.

"Well, Davis, I can't say I know of any available Twist Junction land off hand. Nothin' comes to mind, but I'll start keepin' an eye out. Hey, did you check with the old-timers at the DeSoto?"

"What old-timers?" Davis asked.

"You know, ol' Mr. Howard, Mr. Pierce, and Mr. Collins."

Davis looked at him with incredulous surprise. "You mean the mayor, the banker who runs the savings and loan, and that supervisor of the railroads, the one they call 'Captain'? Are those the old-timers you want me to go talk to?"

"Well, yeah. They're good fellas and they would sure know what's available."

"I don't think they will talk to someone like me. I'm too young and too green for them."

"Ah, don't sell yourself short. If they see you have motivation and respect, I think you'll do all right with them."

Davis gave this some thought and decided it was worth a try.

A few days later, as he stood under the portal of the DeSoto, Davis couldn't seem to make his feet move. The image of all those tight-knit businessmen and successful ranchers in their workday morning gathering at the hotel's coffee shop petrified him. He imagined all the ways they would rebuff him…yelling at him for his impertinence at disrupting them, laughing uproariously at his audacity until he slunk away in shame, and calling in that burly porter who wore a pistol in plain sight of every visitor. Or, worst of all, simply turning all eyes upon him, then returning their attention back to one another without a word, ignoring him like an annoying gnat.

But his brother's confident words echoed through his head. As long as he showed motivation and respect, he reminded himself, he'd be fine. He pulled open the wide oak door and entered the hotel's main hall. *Motivation and respect…* He repeated the words with every step forward as his heels clicked on the shiny marble.

Motivation… click…*and…* click…*respect…* click.

Motivation… click…*and…* click…*respect…* click.

The cacophony of men's booming voices was his beacon.

Motivation... click *...and...* click *...respect...* click.

He entered the lively room and walked right past the man behind the tall service counter.

Motivation... click *...and...* click *...respect...* click...

He barely heard the "Can I help you, sir?" from behind him. He continued to the group of boisterous men who took up the entire back wall of the coffee shop. Their conversation was in full swing.

"I'm telling you, Bill, those loads of lumber coming from up north are only going to increase. The railroads still have a long way to go till they reach the sunny shores of California. Ain't that right, Captain?"

Mr. Collins merely nodded his head in agreement, keeping his attention focused on getting the tobacco in his pipe to light.

Mr. Pierce pointed his empty mug at the second most well-known Mr. Howard. "You'll do well to tell your brother to make real nice with those big-city folks when they come by our little town next week. A fancy welcome dinner hosted by the mayor's beautiful wife will give us a chance to present ourselves as serious business partners."

"And to make some serious cash," came the deep Texas drawl of the man who presided over them all. Mr. Huntington sat back casually. There was no coffee or tobacco tin in front of him. His right hand was already busy weaving a crisp new one-hundred-dollar bill, sharply folded down its length, between his fingers.

Davis had heard of this parlor trick, something this man was storied to do any time he was making big business deals. It was impressive... and just as intimidating as it was intended to be.

The men noticed Davis and the conversation stopped. Eyes turned to him, but no intrigue was behind them, merely a dull curiosity, as if they were trying to reconcile their need to have their mugs refilled with the fact that Davis's attire did not match that of the wait staff. As the silence became heavy, the waiter's voice rang out pointedly from behind Davis again.

"Sir, *can I help you?*"

Davis nearly lost his nerve completely. It would have been so much easier to turn around and pretend that he was merely lost on his way to order a coffee, and not a hopeful usurper of this powerful group. *Dear Lord, give me strength*, Davis prayed. Tilting his head to the side in acknowledgment, but not taking his eyes off the men in front of him, he said, "No, sir." He focused on the group of men, who continued to stare at him. "I have come to ask whether any of you know about any available land in Twist Junction that may be suitable for some light farming and ranching, preferably with a nice little house on the property."

Mr. Pierce answered him with a dismissive wave. "Make an appointment at the bank, boy."

"Oh, I'm not looking for a loan," Davis quickly explained.

"What are you bothering us for then?" the Captain grumbled. "You want to learn farming and ranching? Hop on the next train out to the XIT. Plenty of jobs…not many women though!" He laughed heartily at his own joke and slapped the table, making mugs jump and spoons jangle.

"Well, I got a lady right here in Twist Junction—"

"That pretty little Catholic girl," interrupted Mr. Huntington.

Davis couldn't hide his surprise. "Yes, sir."

"I know you're a Bennett, but I haven't the faintest idea which one. I'll be damned if I know anyone who could name you all. How many of you are there? Two, three dozen?"

This taunt brought laughter from the group of men. Huntington was peacocking in front of his associates…and Davis. Davis knew that if he backed down now, there would be no chance of ever having the respect of these men.

"I'm Davis, sir. Davis Crockett Bennett. The youngest of fourteen, and I reckon if I work hard and steady like all my siblings before me, and listen to the right people," he paused briefly while he met each man's eye, "I will be able to make something of myself—something that my bride, and Twist Junction, can be proud of."

The men all looked at Davis with interest, probably because they couldn't believe he was still standing there. Mr. Huntington didn't say a word and continued to weave that crisp bill between his fingers, his eyes turned downward. He pursed his lips, seemingly coming to some decision about Davis. With a small nod, he looked up out of the corner of his eye at Davis and grumbled, "So, you think you want to get into this land and cattle business, huh?"

"Yes, sir."

He took a deep breath and turned his full attention to Davis. Even his fingers stopped their undulating and the bill was still. "I know of your family, young Davis. They are good folks. Never heard of any of 'em creating any trouble, and a couple of your brothers bring good crops in."

Mr. Huntington looked over at Mr. Pierce, who gave a nod to confirm some unspoken issue. Davis knew at least four of his brothers had taken out loans from Mr. Pierce's bank and had never missed a payment.

Boy, these men know our town inside and out! That remark about the two-dozen Bennett kids had to have been a strategic taunt to see my reaction. I'm sure they've known my name from the minute I walked in, Davis thought.

"Well, Davis, you come from good stock. So, tell me what you know about ranching."

Oh no, he thought. *I hadn't prepared for a test of my knowledge. Daggum, I just got his interest. I can't lose it now!* "Well, sir, I'm not going to lie to you. I'm green, that's for sure. I know very little about the routines of ranching, but I'm an eager learner and I've always picked up stuff fast."

"Hmm…" Huntington said, lips pursed again.

Davis fell silent and his eyes turned back down. But then Huntington began weaving that bill again and he leaned over, looking at the men at the table. "Anyone know of any land that's available in Twist Junction?"

Heads shaking, it was clear that the men's interest had waned from Davis and was now back to the low levels of liquid in their coffee mugs.

Mr. Huntington sat back with a great sigh. "Nope, guess not."

Davis knew he was dismissed. His polite, "Thank you, gentlemen," didn't get anyone's attention, as they had already pulled into a tight knot and were in a lively discussion about someone who had just bought 900 head of cattle. The Captain's arm shot out toward the man behind the counter. "Jimmy, get a move on. We can't drink this cold swill."

The oak door of the hotel seemed heavier than when Davis had first entered. Pushing it took all the energy he had left after his failed encounter. He plopped down on one of the worn wooden benches that rested against the hotel's portal wall. He had failed, and he had made a fool of himself in front of the most powerful men in town.

He didn't know how long he sat there, legs spread, head hung low, his arms and hands folded with his elbows resting on his knees. Plenty of people went by, and the hotel doors opened and closed to admit visitors that Davis was too weary to look up at and acknowledge.

"Young man, you still here?" bellowed Mr. Huntington.

"Oh! Yes, sir, reckon I am," Davis said, startled.

"What are you so down for? Times are good."

Davis couldn't help but make a derisive snort. "Well, I still need to find a way to be part of those good times, and if there's nothin' available, I'll just be takin' my bride home to wither under my mother's rule."

"You need to look at your situation from another perspective then. Times *are* good in Twist Junction, and that's a fact. But it means that locals are wanting to keep their land, make more profit. There's no need for them to sell right now."

Davis still didn't see how this information was going to do him any good, and Mr. Huntington read his face.

"Think, boy! Maybe someone *out of the area* has a spread. There's lots of land right outside of Twist Junction. Ranchable land."

Davis perked up, and the spark in his eyes spurred Huntington on.

"I was just thinking, after you walked out, about that doctor...what's his name? Well, no matter. That doctor who bought some land east of town many years ago. You would have been just a babe. But I heard recently that he retired and moved farther south. There's a small ranch house on that land. Maybe it's available."

Out there, away from the cloistered group of his peers, Mr. Huntington seemed to be much friendlier. The large bill in his hand was gone, the peacocking session over with. Maybe Davis hadn't made as big a fool of himself as he'd originally thought.

"How could I find out about it, sir?"

"You know, Davis Crockett Bennett, you remind me of myself at one time. Mind you, that was a very, very long time ago. I am also reminded of the people who gave me a break back then, let me move forward one step at a time to pursue my dreams. Of course, it was all up to me whether I would succeed or fail, but the little break helped me along. I want to give you a little break now, and we'll see if you have the spirit to succeed. Leave it to me. I'll see what I can find out about this property and will get back to you."

3
Take Me To The Chapel

"Catherine...Catherine..." Davis's voice wavered as his knocks rattled the screen door. "Are you there? I have news for us."

He was unsure how I would receive him after what had happened at the Sunday potluck, and the unfathomable promise of a house and land made him hesitate before he dared a third knock. I appeared and walked stiffly toward the front door, hurt still written all over my face.

"Yes?" I almost whispered.

"Please forgive me and my family. I know you were madder than a wet hen after the church social. And...well...you're entitled to think that the Bennett clan is a rude bunch. They showed you some real bad manners. Catherine, I'm so embarrassed by them. And I'm so very sorry that I didn't—"

"Davis Bennett!" Mother's clipped voice startled him into silence. "You just going to stand out there and let the world know all your business? Come in here, out of sight of all our nosey neighbors." The door opened and he was ushered inside before he knew it. "That's better. Now, I'll leave you to what you were saying to Catherine." She disappeared into the kitchen as quickly as she had appeared.

Davis carefully positioned himself at the foot of the dining table, standing erect and looking me directly in the eyes. "Catherine, I want you to understand the seriousness of my words."

I didn't say a word, but I also didn't break our eye contact.

"I want to prove my worthiness to you. I think I have found us a home and some land."

My eyes widened at this news.

"I couldn't wait to tell you. I just left a meeting at the DeSoto with the town's bigwigs. Mr. Huntington has become my advocate. All these men now know who I am, and seem to have accepted me as a promising young rancher. But somehow, I especially grabbed Mr. Huntington's attention. Catherine, he is actually willing to help us." Davis's whole body shook with excitement. "He just told me that he's going to contact a landowner he knows, and might be able to persuade the man to consider putting together a deal for us!"

My face broke into a huge grin. "Oh, I'm so proud of you, Davis!"

I let the casserole incident melt into the past. This was it. He had won me back.

Davis reached out and took my hand. "Catherine, I practically ran over here to tell you. I don't have the details yet, but Mr. Huntington will keep me apprised."

"I'm going to make this work, Davis, you just watch me!" My tone seemed to startle him. It was that same powerful indignation from the church social, but this time I was directing it at the people who would dare to stand in our way.

Davis stole a quick look into the kitchen, and seeing Mother's back to us, he pulled me into a huge hug and gave me a strong kiss.

"Well, I have to scoot out," he said loudly. "I want to catch Polly during her lunch hour. She'll be thrilled to hear my good news. Maybe she'll tell Mother Bennett!" He gave me a cheeky wink. "Good day, Mrs. Connelly," he called out to Mother.

I floated back into the kitchen, moving without thought to finish washing the dishes.

Mother and I worked in silence, but just as I was putting away the last plate, she said, "Don't know if you have any interest, but I have the wedding dress pinned and ready to try on."

I felt my cheeks flush and couldn't meet her eye. I nodded a modest yes, and she led me to our bedroom. When she reached into the big black trunk that held her special items and pulled out the dress, I gasped at the unexpected fine beauty that she unfolded in front of me. The white cotton was so soft that it felt almost like silk. Large rose appliqués, expertly folded from fine lace, cut across the bodice.

"Oh, Mother, this looks like Paris couture! You have such talent!"

Mother proceeded to chatter on with pride and enthusiasm. I, on the other hand, went deeper into thoughts about my folks and the man I was sadly missing.

"It was your father who showed me the many details of how to work with lace." She held the dress up to me and set it in place against my shoulders for me to hold. "See this? Inserting these narrow lace strips was your father's favorite idea. He had impeccable taste, you know. His eye for detail was his ace in the hole when selling to all those fine ladies in the Midwest and East Coast cities. He would woo them with unique designs, like this, and they simply couldn't resist..."

My mother's words faded from my ears. I never knew this about my father. I began to imagine him creating masterpieces with cloth and lace.

Her words slowly came back to me. "...now, do you want snug, puffed, or ruffled sleeves? Regardless, I'd like to edge them with that lace over there, the one with a large openwork pattern, right above your elbow. Catherine...are you listening? Catherine?"

As I looked into her eyes, my heart became heavy. "I'm sorry. I just hadn't known about Daddy's talent. I forget sometimes that he wasn't just a salesman, and I was thinking about how much there is about him that I didn't get to know…and never will."

Mother only nodded in her usual stoic way and went on adjusting the placement of a piece of material near my shoulder, her attention focused on a rose that was too close to the seam.

Seeing the stacks of my father's old lace in my mother's chest of treasures made my heart hurt. I fought the lump that welled up in my throat as I wondered who would walk me down the aisle on my wedding day. Every girl wanted her father by her side when her special day came, and there I was, on my own, abandoned, left to make do. My sadness turned into anger, and I found myself yelling at him in my head. *This is two times you have let me down, Daddy! First, I couldn't go to college because you decided to up and die in a drunken stupor in that cursed hotel room, far away from home. And now, I'll be without you on one of the most important days of my life!*

"Catherine..." Mother started, but I didn't want her to see the tears that were starting to sting my eyes. I dropped the dress into her hands and ran out of the room.

"Catherine!" She followed me to the parlor. Her tone changed to one of concern. "What's the matter? Don't you like the dress?"

I couldn't answer. The tears were still too close to coming out. I just stood there.

"Don't you worry, we can change anything you don't like. Do you not like the bustline? It doesn't have to be that way, sweetheart."

I fought to control myself as she guided me to the sofa.

"It's not the dress that's disappointing you, is it, dear?"

"No, it's Daddy. I miss him so much now. And he makes me so mad! He didn't have to drink so much. He didn't have to die."

"We all have our disappointments in life. I'm sure he didn't want to die. He loved you children with his whole heart and soul. He would never have wanted you to experience such deep sadness. I want you to remember that the white of your wedding dress represents innocence, pure love, and a new beginning that will be bonded by the holy sacrament of matrimony. From that day on, Davis will be your partner in all things, good and bad. He will take over your daddy's place as protector, provider, and best friend."

We sat for a moment in silence. I was surprised when Mother spoke again.

"Now, Catherine, I'm going to talk to you woman to woman. Women have to be strong for birthing and disciplining our children, for attending to the needs of our husbands, and for running a household. Discussions of the struggles in our personal lives and feelings are to be done through prayer. Saying the rosary and seeking guidance from our parish priest sees us through the most routine and difficult of life's challenges. You should keep your rosary in your apron pocket or bedside table so that you will always have it handy when troubles enter your head or knock at your door."

I bit my tongue so as not to make an incredulous remark about how pointless I thought it would be to tell an unmarried priest all my woes as a woman, a wife, and mother. How could a priest be objective and answer a married woman's questions, or understand her worries? After all, they weren't married, and in my opinion, were not very qualified to advise on such things. But I knew Mother wouldn't have taken well to this line of reasoning. I was sure she'd found good guidance from her priest when she faced the challenge of a drunken husband, but it seemed to me that the rosary was a much better option.

Mother stood purposefully and went back to the bedroom. I assumed the conversation was over and followed her to resume our work on the dress. I found her bending over the trunk again, rooting around for something. When she straightened up, her hand was balled around something small. "Here is a small rosary that you can tuck away out of sight. This way, Davis and the children you will have won't have to feel the weight of every burden you are carrying. The reason you stick your hand in your apron pocket so many times a day will be between you and God."

Startled, as always, by her insight, I took the thin strand of beads and nodded my understanding of her wisdom. *This will be perfect to tuck under the ribbon tying my flowers together when I walk down the aisle*, I realized.

I didn't object when Mother held the dress back up to my shoulders. I suddenly had a new appreciation for it. *This is something made by both my mother and father, and I will keep it forever. Daddy's Irish lace will always, always be a treasure to me.* I had the sudden idea of its design being reworked into a christening dress for the children that Davis and I were sure to have, and the image of my daddy touching the lives of his grandchildren in this way, even though he was gone, warmed me all over.

The raucous shouts of my brothers returning from school and bursting through the front door stopped our conversation. Choruses of "we're hungry!" and "where's supper?" told us that the day was back to its usual routine. I remembered all the chores that were still waiting to be done, the laundry drying on the line, and the freshly laid eggs tucked in the hay of the chicken coop.

"Catherine, you go get those boys fed and I'll clean up back here," Mother said as she carefully folded the dress.

The boys were already clawing off parts of the leftover bread from breakfast and sticking their fingers into the pot of stew on the stove to taste it.

"Not bad," Liam declared, then turned a mischievous eye to me. "You just might not poison your future husband after all."

"You hush!" I grabbed the dishtowel and snapped it at him playfully. He squealed with delight as he flew out of the kitchen, calling over his shoulder, "I want a big bowl! Lots of meat!"

Just as I stuck the ladle into the pot, Kerrick came dashing through the kitchen, Dennis chasing after him and making barking noises like a rabid dog. The two crashed right into me, and the empty bowl I held flew from my left hand, flipped up through the air, and landed straight on top of my head. The boys roared with laughter.

"Look at Catherine! She's wearing the latest chapeau." Kerrick pointed at my head.

I was not laughing, and my pursed lips caused him to bolt from the room, but Dennis was unfazed and giggled gleefully. "Got you, Catie-watie!"

Their escape was blocked by Mother's solid form. Hands on her hips, stern displeasure written all over her face, she caused the entire house to come to an immediate standstill. Kerrick's moment of glory ceased.

"We were just heading out to get a head start on our chores," he said, grabbing Dennis's hand and pulling him toward the front door.

"Chores! You said we were going to play ball!" Dennis whined, playing his role as the family baby perfectly. "You said Catherine was going to have to do all the work, to practice being someone's wife..." But the look on Kerrick's face shut him up.

I didn't think it possible, but Mother's look grew even sterner. "Liam!" Mother called out over her shoulder, her eyes never leaving Kerrick. "There's work to be done. You boys—*all you boys*—get out there and get busy. There are clothes to be taken down off the line *and* folded. There are eggs to be gathered in the coop. *And* we need all those pickling jars brought in from the shed."

Kerrick opened his mouth to object, but shut it just as quickly.

"The shed!" Dennis whined again. "But it's so dusty in there!"

"Yes, and we don't want dust and dirt in our clean kitchen, so you all will make sure they are sparkling clean before you bring them in."

Even Dennis was smart enough to know that one more peep would just bring more chores. The boys turned without a word, shoulders slumped in defeat, and went outside to get to work. Mother turned and went back to her room, saying, "You've got work too, Catherine, don't just stand there."

As the sun was setting that night, Davis stopped by once again. I was still in the kitchen, making neat stacks of the canning jars the boys had brought in.

"Well, you've been busy," he said.

I peeked around to make sure no one was listening, then told him about the ruckus of the afternoon. He gulped down his hearty chuckles at my description of the bowl sitting atop my head, and said, "Catherine, I wish I had been here with my Kodak. That would have made the perfect engagement photo!"

I was a little surprised. "But I looked like the family clown."

He quickly corrected me. "You looked like the woman I love. After all, if I can love you with a bowl on your head, you know it's real love." His hands encircled my waist and he whispered to me, "You're beautiful, no matter what you are wearing, even crockery. But you're right—your engagement picture should show the world all the beauty that I see." He reached up and twirled one of my dark curls around his finger. "These beautiful curls…"

I blushed. "Davis Bennett, that's enough!"

"No, I mean it, Catherine."

We heard Mother coming down the hall and quickly pulled away to a respectable distance.

"Well," he said a bit loudly, "on the subject of photos, I've scheduled us at Dodge's Studio at 9:00 tomorrow. I've pulled out my wedding suit already, and I'll be wearing it with my best white shirt. And my father agreed to loan all the boys his ruby tie stud when we each got married. I hope I can be half as handsome as you will be beautiful."

I blushed again and swatted away the compliment.

"Can I watch as they take your photo, Catherine?"

"Davis!" I exclaimed. "Do you want a picture of me red as a beet?"

"You would be a beautiful beet," he said. "Well, I'd better sneak out of here before those brothers of yours try to fit me with a colander for a cowboy hat."

We both giggled.

As he turned to leave, I remembered his visit to Polly's that afternoon. "Wait, before you go, tell me, were you able to talk to Polly? What did she say?"

"Oh, yes! I caught her right as the children were let out to play. She was working though, keeping an eye on all the children who were running amok. She spent more time jumping to catch loose balls and sending them back than listening to me. I must have been rambling on, because she cut me off and said, 'Look, Davis, I can't go on chatting about your romantic life just now.' She wasn't being rude," he clarified. "She just had a job to do."

"So, you have a romantic life?" I teased.

It was his turn to blush. "I guess so. You and me...my love life..." He looked reflective for a moment, then snapped back to his story. "Anyway, Polly said she knew I was upset with the family and she was personally sorry—actually, *real* sorry—about the whole situation. I think she resented it too, Catherine. She didn't say so, but I know her pretty well and I can tell. She likes you and I think this has affected her. But when I told her about Mr. Huntington, about the ranch house and land, she stopped dead in her tracks, turned around to me, gave my shoulder a squeeze, and actually said, 'I knew you could do it. I am so proud of you, little brother.' Catherine, she has never said that to me before! I just know things are going to be good for us. So, now we can put extra big smiles on our faces for those photos tomorrow."

"You did tell your lady 9:00, right?" I heard Mary Dodge, the photographer, ask from her perch by the camera box.

I stood at the studio door. Davis rushed over to open it for me before I could grab the handle. The sight of me seemed to make his heart stop. There I stood, outlined against the morning sun. Black tendrils framed my face and my cornflower-blue eyes shone brightly. Pearls trimmed my high-necked blouse, which was embroidered with small, pink roses set in rows between the thinnest pink lines. The blouse made my porcelain skin take on a pink hue. Davis could hardly speak.

When we got inside, I showed him the hand-carved cameo pin at my neck and explained that my father had given it to my mother. He seemed to fall in love with me even more upon seeing the pride in my eyes.

"I want to marry you this very minute," he whispered into my ear.

The photographer's voice rang out behind us, "Let's start with the bride."

I perched gracefully on the wooden stool in front of the camera. Without being asked, my elegant hand gravitated to beneath my chin, grazing my rounded profile ever so lightly. I looked like an angel. I felt so perfect at that moment.

When Davis's turn came, he sat up straight, and with a wink, said he hoped to mirror my elegance. He seemed to be so lost in love, and the camera caught a dazed look. The reason for his small smile would be a secret that he would share when we would lie together on our wedding night...a moment of intimacy that only he and I would know.

Soon after we completed the photos, Polly told us of a date she had picked to have the whole Bennett family over for another attempt at introducing me into Davis's group. Polly had surprised him by quietly adding that she intended to give each of the family members a subtle lesson in congeniality. I didn't complain about the plan and never once brought up the subject of our first disastrous meeting, but Davis knew I wanted to just blink and have it all over with as much as he did.

Davis was surprised yet again when I told him that my mother had agreed to come along with us to the event.

"Why would she want to come to a boring dinner with a bunch of Baptists?" Davis asked.

Don't get me wrong, he was very glad that she was coming. He just never dreamed she would want to. She told me that she needed to be there to assure the Bennett family that I came from a family of non-radical, civilized, reasonable people.

"Oh, boy," I sighed. "So, there's an agenda on both sides. I'm afraid we're going to be standing in the middle of two enemy lines ready to fire on each other." My lips pursed and Davis knew I understood our situation as much as he did. "Why don't we just show up, be polite, and smile?"

— 4 4 4 —

Davis left thinking about the task in front of him. He really needed his brothers, Ernest and Owen, to stand by him at this dinner, and realized some action was needed beforehand. He made a visit to Owen's house.

Leaning on the hood of his tractor, Owen said with a chuckle, "Sure 'nough, you'll need male support when those women get together. Now, I think Catherine's really an okay gal, and I'll stand behind you at this dinner. But don't you expect me to follow you into any Catholic church, okay? God'll send me straight to Hell for praying to those Mary statues, but not before my Beulah would give me such trouble that I'd run there begging to be let in!" He laughed heartily at his joke.

"Enough, Owen," Davis said. "Hey, I've got some questions about crops and raising kids on a ranch."

"Oh boy, Davis! You thinkin' about kids already? You haven't even made it to the altar! Or is there something I need to know? Something I need to help you warn Mother about?"

Davis shook his head vigorously. "No!"

"I'm just teasin' you, brother. But my advice...seriously...it's too early for you to think about this. Better leave that topic alone."

― 🌿 🌿 🌿 ―

The day of the family gathering arrived. At the height of the afternoon's conversations, Polly's yard sounded like a barnyard full of chickens, all clucking at the same time. Davis and I stood silently amidst the hubbub and Polly ran around playing referee, catching and switching topics that became too intense.

Inevitably, someone turned the talk to children. Polly made a beeline for that group, and Davis got a wink from Owen and a strong poke in the ribs from Ernest. Both brothers grinned widely at him, then nodded in the direction of our mothers, who stood together talking. Davis told me that he had silently thanked God that I hadn't insisted on inviting my Aunt Isabel. Otherwise, Polly might not have been able to intervene and the day would have gotten a lot livelier.

Mother Bennett was occupied by my mother, who was telling her all about our ancestry, "a fine Irish family—quite a large one, though not as large as yours." As she launched into her description of my father, the "college-educated man who had provided a lovely home in South Texas before his untimely passing," Davis sighed with relief that the topic of children seemed to die down before she was done.

But Mother Bennett was not one to lose the thread of any conversation, even one that only buzzed around her. She politely nodded at Mother, then launched into her own description about the importance of their church and the expectations for children. Polly sidled up to Mother Bennett and proceeded to interject supportive comments for both sides when needed. Her skill was something to behold, but these two strong-willed women may have been too much for even her. Davis felt me stiffen beside him and knew it was time for him to act.

Stepping up to the group of women, he commented on how the fried chicken was the best we had ever had.

"Why, Davis," said Polly, "you are my best fan ever." Her smile conveyed genuine pride in her cooking, but the quick wink she gave him showed her understanding of his secondary intent. Before we knew it, everyone was unanimously agreeing on the quality of the food and accolades were pouring down on Polly.

A few hours later, the Bennett family gathered their things and said their good-byes to Polly and Davis. Maybe they didn't make a special effort to say good-bye to Mother and me because we were busy thanking Polly for her kindness, and they didn't want to disrupt, but I doubted it. Mother went to gather the dishes we'd brought and I pulled Davis aside.

"Nothing changed, Davis. Polly was sweet, but not one thing changed with any of the others."

"Catherine, some things will have to be what they are for now. That's all. I'll be leaving tomorrow to move that herd I told you about. I won't be back for a while, but I'll have money in my pocket. I'll think of you every day."

"So soon?" We had discussed the cattle drive, how it would be good for his future—*our* future—but my head was so full of thoughts about the wedding and dealing with Davis's family that I guess it had slipped my mind. Knowing I wouldn't see him for a while, I hoped we would be able to sneak a kiss, but Mother was waiting ahead of us and Polly stood on the porch behind us.

Mother and I didn't talk on our walk home. I reflected on Davis's words. I recalled Father Patrick making a similar statement during our last Mass and tried to see the wisdom in it. Mother and I would be meeting with Father Patrick after next week's Mass and I was sure her advice to me would be that if I still had doubts, I could ask him about it.

I hadn't fully resolved my feelings on the subject by the time Mass came, but I had decided on the uselessness of talking to the father about it. After the recessional and the closing song, Mother and I made our way over to the small parish office, where we found Father Patrick already sitting behind his desk making notes.

"Hello, Father. I'm Mrs. Connelly and this is my daughter, Catherine. I believe she contacted you to reserve the church for a wedding. Since the Church does not allow weddings during Easter, she respectfully requested the first Monday after. We realize, though, that you don't usually stay over after the Sunday service."

Father Patrick took a deep breath and gestured for us to sit in the two stiff chairs facing him. "Yes, I did receive the request to reserve the chapel for that Monday. I am glad you came by to talk about it." He set his pencil down and focused his attention solely on Mother. "I am also glad that you understand the responsibilities of a priest to the many parishes to which he is assigned. I am scheduled to officiate Easter Services in Dumas and Channing on that Sunday, so you see, my presence in Twist Junction for a wedding on that Monday will be impossible."

Mother voiced the question that was running through my head. "Could you make a special trip back from the other parishes?"

His answer was a deep sigh, and I feared we were going to get nowhere with our request. He turned his attention to me and asked, "Why don't you young folks consider Amarillo?"

"Father, we would gladly do so," I said, "but both my fiancé and I come from large families. Family is important to us and we wish them to witness our taking of vows. Many of them do not have the means to travel so far. We would like to be surrounded by their support when we promise our lives to each other in front of God."

A look of curiosity crossed the father's face. "Which young man are you marrying? I can't think of any your age in our parish. Wait...you aren't thinking about marrying the widower Carver, are you?"

"Oh no, Father," I exclaimed, blushing at the idea of becoming the bride to the gaunt little man whose wife had died and left him with five children, the oldest girl being my age. "My fiancé does not attend our parish. He and his family attend the First Baptist Church of Twist Junction."

"Your young man is one of those Southern Baptists?" he said indignantly. "What makes you think this marriage is going to work, young lady? What about your devotion? Is he accepting? What about children? He'll have to sign papers, you know, agreeing to raise them as Catholic."

He barely took a breath between each question and his face was flushed red.

"Father," Mother interjected, "we—I mean, Catherine, her young man, and our family—have discussed all these issues at length. My sisters and I shared all of these same concerns and Catherine understands the seriousness of them all, as well. Her young man—his name is Davis Bennett—has expressed his understanding and agrees to all the requirements."

I couldn't help myself, and added, "He would also like to meet with you before the wedding. He wants to assure you of his intentions."

Father Patrick pursed his lips and closed his eyes, then took in a deep breath. To me, it looked like he was saying a silent prayer for guidance…or maybe for patience in the face of two strong-willed women.

Mother took advantage of the silence and spoke as soon as he opened his eyes. "My sisters, Isabel and Mary O'Reilly, have very carefully explained the Catholic Church's rules to Catherine's young man, and they are as confident as we are in his sincerity."

"Isabel and Mary O'Reilly?"

"Yes, sir, my sisters in Channing. They attend your parish there and speak very highly of you."

It looked like Mother had clinched it. Father Patrick sat back in his chair and smiled warmly. "Oh yes, Isabel and Mary. I know them quite well. Lovely Irish ladies. They never miss a Mass."

I felt Mother's foot tap mine and I knew we had gained an advantage for our pleas.

"Father," I implored, "it would mean so much to us to have them at my wedding, but they would not be able to go all the way to Amarillo."

I was delighted when he nodded his head and said, "I understand." But my elation fell flat with his next statement. "Well, I may be able to come back on Easter Monday to perform a joining-of-the-hands service."

"Just a joining of the hands, Father? Not a Mass of matrimony?" Mother asked in surprise.

"I am still not convinced that this mixed marriage is advisable, and it is my duty to keep you within your devotion. Too many people don't stay as devoted to the Church as they were in our homelands, and the Church charges me with the protection of their souls."

When he finished, we sat in silence. My head was bowed, but Mother stayed attentive, as if kindly waiting for him to speak again.

"So, these aunts that spoke to your young man, Catherine, are Isabel and Mary?"

"Yes, Father."

"And these are your sisters, Mrs. Connelly?"

"Yes, Father."

"Are you the sister they have told me about from Carrick, Donegal?"

"Yes, I am."

"Well, why didn't you say so? I'm from Donegal as well."

When I looked up, Father Patrick had a wide grin on his face and looked like a young boy who had just found an old friend.

Mother smiled back at him. "There are very few Irish souls up here in the Panhandle."

He nodded in agreement, thought for a moment, and said with a wink to me, "That's true enough. We Irish folks have to support one another."

I piped up, "Father, we will give you a place to stay and a lovely Easter supper if you agree."

"You are a charming young lady, Miss Catherine Connelly. I am still not completely happy with the situation, but I see that your heart is set on this young man of yours. You realize, though, that everything about this is highly unusual. But I'm a true Donegal boy and we have to stick together."

"I will never forget this favor, Father." I couldn't keep the wild grin off my face, and before I knew it I heard myself say, "I promise here and now to name my first boy after you!"

Father Patrick burst out into laughter while Mother tutted at my outburst and patted my hand. "Now, calm down, Catherine."

"When will I get to meet your young man?"

"Soon, Father Patrick. He's on a cattle drive now. We'll come by as soon as he gets back."

After we left Father Patrick, and while I trudged through my evening chores, my thoughts drifted back to my conversation with Davis about his upcoming job moving cattle. Davis wanted to show his good intentions to my mother and aunts, so by taking on the responsibility of an arduous job like a cattle drive, he hoped to prove himself to my family.

Davis had told me that deep in his cowboy head, he secretly yearned for the open plains, the animals, and the stars over his head each night. He was connected to the land and he loved being caretaker to all the white-faced Herefords.

"Mr. Huntington recommended me, Catherine," he had told me with excitement. "I understand that's quite a compliment since it's very rigorous work, and my only experience was about eight years ago when I helped my brother Owen and some others take about a hundred head of cattle up to slaughter in Dodge City."

I nodded but didn't say a word.

"Now, I won't lie, I could be gone a month or more."

At this, my eyes had widened and my mouth opened to protest, but Davis jumped in. "A hundred dollars in our till would be mighty nice for getting started. That's about five times what I could make here during the same period."

I had pursed my lips at this, and began considering it.

"The weather is a big factor, so they have to leave right away. If they wait, snow and dropping temperatures could endanger the cattle and the cowhands. The canyons might as well be big tunnels, with winds swirling through them and causing dips in the temperature. And if the temperature gets too low, the streams might freeze. We'll need the water running. Water is key for all the horses, our men, and the herd."

"Davis, I don't know much about cattle drives, but it seems to me that this is dangerous. And then there are the Indians, stampedes, rustlers... I have to say, I'm concerned." My shoulders slumped and I reached out for his hand. "And it's so close to our wedding. What if I lost you?"

"I hear you, and I'm a little concerned too. But I've thought about this carefully, and this experience will teach me a lot about how to send off my own herd one day. I need to learn how to choose a trail boss, a cook, cowboys, and at the very least which trail I should be sending those men on. Since I've been on a drive before, and I've heard I'm a little older than the other cowhands, perhaps I won't be subject to being the tail rider. The constant dust and smell can get to you, and I don't want to deal with that day after day—or for that matter, week after week. Looking back, I wish I had paid more attention to what the cowboys were doing when I was younger. I could have learned a lot and not been so green for this ride."

He saw my eyes widen again. I wasn't convinced that this was a good idea at all, and he could tell I was about to protest more strongly.

"You know, in some ways I grew up real fast. I don't want to scare you with some of the stories from my life. I may be green about how to move a herd, but I know a lot more about life and how men behave. Life here in Twist Junction is pretty civilized, and that's all you need to see. But I know about the other parts of this town, of this land, that ladies don't need to know about. I'll be okay, and being out on the range night and day with the animals will do my heart good. It's so quiet out there, you can't imagine. I remember that from the first drive. The quiet at night was my favorite; it gave me time to think. And this time, I'll be lying under those stars dreaming about you, and making plans for us."

My gaze grew tender as I listened to him, and he saw my demeanor become more accepting.

Davis told me that assembling his equipment for the drive brought back memories of the fifteen-mile days of the previous one. Early each morning he would start the herd grazing, then drive them down the trail and end with another grazing, then repeat the pattern. It didn't take long for the animals to understand the routine. He admired the trail boss the most. He was the one who ran the show. He decided who got to be the flank and swing riders. Davis's favorite job was being the point cowboy, leading the head steer. On that first drive, he had impressed the trail boss so much that, even though he was young and new, he gave

Davis the position for the last few days. Riding up in front of the herd, the noise wasn't as loud, and he could talk to the animals. Davis had always been able to create a bond with animals. On that drive, he saw how they came to trust each other after so many days of the same routine. The trail boss even commented to Davis about how well he could get the horses to do his bidding. Davis was so careful with their treatment, always making sure not to wear them out over the roughest parts of the trails and rivers. That memory strengthened his confidence for the upcoming drive.

With a sigh, I looked out the window. Although I still had my reservations, I knew that this was the right thing for Davis—for us—and prayed that he would return to me, unharmed, for our wedding.

— ⊲. ⊲. ⊲. —

When Davis arrived at the Dumas Ranch standing point, he joined the nine other cowboys who were to make up the group of ten. They nodded in acknowledgment of each other. He was surprised to see three black men and two Mexicans in the group, in addition to the four white men Mr. Huntington had mentioned. Mr. Motley, the trail boss, got right to explaining his very strict "no drinking and no gambling" rules. He looked each man in the eye during this lecture, and Davis could tell he was sizing up each of them to determine who would ride which position. Right after he introduced the cook, he rolled into making the assignments. Starting with the positions farthest back, he pointed to one of the Mexicans and the youngest-looking white boy.

"Sanchez, Jimmy, you'll be the tail riders."

Davis heaved a silent sigh of relief as Mr. Motley went on, pointing to each man in turn, barking out their name and position. Davis's heart beat stronger as the next four positions were filled by two of the black men, an older white man, and the other Mexican. That left four places. The two point riders would be among them.

"Men, in addition to the two point riders, I want two men to be ready to float between positions." He then pointed at Davis, and looking him straight in the eye, said, "Bennett, you'll start out with Jeb as the first set of point riders."

Davis turned to look at who his partner was, and saw a black man with a quiet confidence standing slightly apart from the rest of the group.

He leaned over and whispered to the white man standing next to him, "Boy, I'm sure lucky to get that position. I've never ridden with a black man."

The man's face stayed looking forward, but his eyes slid sideways and the toothpick he was chewing stopped its bobbing up and down. "So, you prejudiced or something?" he said in a quiet but stern tone.

Davis gulped. He hadn't intended that. "Oh, no," he whispered back. "I just never have known a black man before."

Oh boy, he thought, *I've really stepped in it.* He hadn't meant to offend anyone, and it was so early on, too.

Mr. Motley's booming voice cut through Davis's silent worries. "Got a problem over there, Bennett? Do I have to change your position?"

"Oh, no sir, I'm honored to be a point man. I look forward to knowing and working with all your men." He nodded pointedly at the man called Jeb.

"That's better. All right men, get to the barn and pick out your horses."

Davis followed the other men in silence. He had learned a lesson right out of the gate. He realized he'd better keep his thoughts to himself.

Mr. Motley led everyone to the stable and trusted each of them to pick their own horse. With his saddle slung over his shoulder, Davis caught sight of a fine chestnut mare. When he approached her, she shook her mane and snorted with apprehension, so he reached out to rub her muzzle. Another horse came up and stood close to her.

"So, you two are buddies?" he asked her in a soft tone.

He looked around to find Jeb, hoping he would take the horse next to the chestnut mare. He didn't want to split the two up and knew they would work well together. He always believed that you needed to start out with teams from the very beginning.

Without Davis's bidding, the sturdy black cowboy came up to him and pointed to the chestnut mare. "That there's Sadie. She's a good choice, Bennett. I think I'll take her friend there. That way they'll work together nicely. By the way," he added, "I'm Jeb. Pleased to meet you."

His handshake was powerful. He looked Davis straight in the eye. Davis's attention was riveted on Jeb. He thought Jeb was going to start up a lecture, like Mr. Motley, but his mouth broke into a wide smile filled with teeth so white they could shine in the moonlight.

"Nice to meet you, Jeb."

As they went about their business of readying their supplies for the trip, Davis got to study Jeb. He could tell they were going to make a good team. Jeb was a thinker and Davis was a feeler. Perfect partners! *That Mr. Motley knew just what he was doing when he joined us together,* Davis thought.

The ride would start at dawn the next morning, so Davis and the others were anxious to settle in for the night. Mr. Motley had them stay in the nearby bunkhouse and made sure they got a good meal before they hit the dusty trail. Davis's stomach was so full of steak, potatoes, beans, biscuits, and apple pie that he thought he would burst, and he quickly fell asleep amidst the deep snores and snorts of the other men.

They were all up before daybreak and nervous energy crackled in the air. Davis was naturally a morning person, always up and waiting to greet the sun with a strong cup of muddy coffee in his hand. As he walked outside, Sadie saw him coming with a treat cupped in his hand. She whinnied, and he took off his hat and bowed to his soon-to-be best horse ever.

Jeb saddled up next to Davis, getting a chuckle out of his antics with Sadie. "You really do love animals, Bennett," he observed.

"Hey there, call me Davis. And yes, I believe if you treat your horse good, she will treat you good too."

"Yeah, but I ain't never saw someone bow to their horse!"

"It's my morning joke," Davis explained, patting Sadie's muzzle gently. "Like bowing to a lady."

"Well, Davis, you sure have a strange sense of humor." His half smile and gentle laughter let Davis know he appreciated it.

"You have to have a sense of humor in life. It makes life easier and go faster if you can laugh once in a while."

Jeb nodded in agreement and hoisted himself up on his horse. Then Jeb and Davis trotted to the front of the herd of 3,000 cattle and began their arduous first day.

As they rode, Davis became aware of Sadie's every nuance, as well as the tendencies of the cattle they were guiding. His horse intuitively seemed to do all the work.

Jeb would look over from time to time and shout out, "Doin' okay, first-timer?"

Davis didn't want to correct Jeb's observation, should more be expected from him if he did. Throughout the ride, the horses would hang together, then do lazy crossovers from side to side. To pass the time, Davis would sing a hymn, low and soft, and Sadie would do a little trot as if keeping time with the rhythm. Her particular favorite, Davis thought, was "When the Saints Go Marching In." When he sang that particular song, he felt Sadie's stride strengthen. She held her head high, taking on the role of a proud steed. Davis was sure Jeb heard him and noticed the spectacle on more than one occasion, but Jeb would just shake his head and chuckle.

Beans had never tasted so good as they did that night when Davis took his first bite of grub. The ground felt like a magnet, and he could barely sit up straight. As soon as he scarfed down his meal, he fell onto his back, feeling pure exhaustion in every limb of his body. He focused his eyes on the canopy of stars above to make himself stay awake and finish his prayers, but he barely got as far as "Dear Lord..." before he fell into a deep sleep.

Day ten had them trading places to a flank position. By that time, their job was becoming more of a challenge as the cattle were starting to fan in and out. Sadie snorted and galloped, and took her job very seriously. Davis was sure she appreciated her times of rest, when the wrangler would give him another horse to ride, but Sadie would always keep her eye on Davis, as if to make sure he was okay with that fresh horse. Tired as they both were, they never wanted to separate because a bond had been established. It was hard to adjust to another horse or another rider.

Many other patterns were established after so many weeks on the drive, like where the men slept, which campfire they sat around, or where their place in line was for the chuck wagon. Davis took all his observations seriously and continued to keep his thoughts to himself, remembering his lesson on that first day at the Dumas Ranch. He was curious though, about why the Mexicans and blacks tended to stay together, apart from the others. His partner was black and Davis wanted to know his story. This racial separation of groups while on the trail seemed a bit odd to him.

Finally, about a month into the drive, Davis decided to see what the separation was all about and walked over to Jeb's campsite. Davis grew somewhat timid as he got closer and saw all the men look up and watch him silently as he approached.

"Mind if I join you tonight, Jeb?"

The other men continued staring at Davis, but Jeb grinned and scooted over, patting a nice soft place next to him, indicating for Davis to sit down. The silence continued. So far, Davis had really only talked to one other man on the drive while resting at day's end. His name was Otto, a loner of a young white guy from Claiborne, Texas. None of the other men around the nightly campfire had shown much interest in talking, but they did huddle around right quick for a rowdy game of cards. Otto was like Davis; he wasn't interested in cards and his conversation held no swearing. His soft-spoken nature had surprised Davis, and when Davis asked about it early on in the trip, Otto told him he reckoned it was from having spent his life under his grandmother's roof.

Otto had indicated that he had no parents, no brothers, no sisters. Growing up, it was just him and his grandmother, who he still referred to as "Mrs. Mars." He said to Davis, "Often, I wonder if Mrs. Mars was even my real grandmother."

Davis had tried to lighten the mood by kidding that he would gladly share his thirteen siblings, but Otto only sighed.

"Davis, you're a lucky man to have a family to share things with."

"Otto, sometimes it's not all it's cracked up to be," Davis found himself admitting. "I had a sister raise me. I didn't call her Mother, just Polly. I didn't know if my Mama and Dad even knew which one I was or what my name was. You don't feel special when you're one of fourteen."

"But you got people around. My granny died a few years back, and now…now it's just me. Just me and the cattle I bring to market. Nobody even knows my birthday or my favorite supper."

"Otto, you're right. That's pretty lonely. I tell you what, come to Twist Junction, meet Polly. I'm sure she'll greet you at the door with a plate of her famous sugar cookies."

Otto's eyes seemed to glass over at the idea of warm sweets fresh from the oven. Davis's stomach ached at the thought too. They'd had another meal of beans and were already growing pretty sick of them.

"No one ever asked me to their house before," Otto muttered, almost embarrassed.

"Well, I'm asking you and I mean it," replied Davis.

"Davis, you're a real nice guy."

"Otto, I'm not anything special."

Now, there Davis was, sitting amidst another group of men he didn't know. Their dark faces were shadowed in the flickering light of the campfire, and they didn't seem to mind Jeb allowing him to join them. Frankly, they looked as if they'd already lost interest in him. Recalling that first conversation with Otto made Davis wonder what he should say to Jeb. He worried that he might say something offensive. After all, he had no idea how to have a friendly conversation with a black man, although Jeb seemed to be at peace with everyone just sitting and watching the embers jumping.

Davis ventured into the conversation cautiously. "So, Jeb…you're quite a rider. How long you been doin' this?"

"My roots are from a plantation in Alabama. My mama stayed on after she was freed, saved a bit and moved on to Louisiana, where I was born."

"Hey, my roots are from Alabama too," Davis said, surprised.

"Well, my brothers used to herd cattle," Jeb continued. "I learned the routines of a drive from their stories, even before I could ride a horse. Guess it just came natural to me. When I was twelve, I went off to live on a ranch. I'd volunteer to be the tail rider for any cattle drives I could. Heck, I knew no one else wanted that smelly position and I needed the work."

"That's downright admirable."

"You know, I didn't mind it so much. I had food in my belly and no one cared if I was black or not."

"Never thought of the color thing. Is that a problem you still get? 'Cause I've never known a black man in Twist Junction."

"That's 'cause not many go there. We're not really welcome. There is a saying in that town, 'If you're black, you'd better get out of town before sunset if you know what's good for ya.'"

Davis shook his head. "Now that's real prejudice. My family is prejudiced, I suppose. They don't even approve of me marrying an Irish Catholic girl."

"No kiddin'?" Jeb asked.

"Yep, Southern Baptists are real rigid."

"Hey, I'm Southern Baptist too!" This time it was Jeb's turn to be surprised. "But us black folk are different. We welcome everybody."

Shaking his head, Davis muttered, "Wish it were that simple for Catherine and me."

"Catherine. Now that's a real pretty Southern name," commented Jeb. "I don't have a girl. Guess I've never had the time or the patience. Always on the move."

"How did you meet the boss, Mr. Motley?"

"When you're on the trail as long as I've been, you tend to run into the real professionals. Mr. Motley noticed me a time or two, and then we started running the cattle drives together about three years ago. He's the best…a real fine and fair man. He treats me right. Davis, he must have seen somethin' in you, too. Puttin' you in lead right off is a major responsibility."

"Yeah..." Davis answered humbly.

The fire was dimming and the other men were readying their blankets. It seemed to Davis that they started snoring the minute they laid themselves down.

"We're not too far off from sunrise," Davis said.

"Staying here?" asked Jeb. "We've got plenty of blankets."

"Why not?" Davis answered.

The next morning, as the sun started to peek over the dusty horizon, Davis heard Jeb rustling nearby.

"Don't move, Mr. Davis," Jeb whispered urgently.

Jeb's words froze Davis in place. Davis slid his eyes to the side to see Jeb grabbing the fire shovel. He jerked the bottom corner of Davis's blanket off of his body. To Davis's horror, a six-foot-long copperhead was curled up beside his right leg. Before Davis could respond, the head of the shovel came whooshing down. *Whomp!* The snake's head rolled off to the side, its body wiggling a bit behind it.

Davis instantly flew up to full standing height. "How did you know?"

"Thought I saw something out of the corner of my eye a minute ago. Guess he'd been cozied up there all night and finally decided to poke his head out to see if it was morning. You make a cozy bedfellow, Davis," Jeb laughed.

The commotion had brought the Mexicans running toward them, and their jibber-jabbering in Spanish was a complete mystery to Davis. He was shaken but didn't want the men to notice. He was also worried because he knew snakes could cause big problems for a drive. It wasn't just snake bites that he feared, but also a snake's potential to scare the cattle and start a stampede.

Jeb was laughing at something one of the Mexicans was saying.

"You speak Spanish?" Davis asked.

"Oh, yeah. You gotta learn it if you're going to work with cattle in these parts."

Davis felt a little embarrassed.

Jeb explained, "Paco here was just telling me a story about finding one in his boots on his last drive."

About midmorning, as Jeb and Davis were in the lead, Davis finally managed to say, "I want to thank you, Jeb. That was a very risky thing you did for me. That snake was looking straight at you and could have gone for you in a split second."

"Nothin' you wouldn't have done for me," Jeb replied. "Let's face it, we're all out here together and have to protect each other when we can."

"Just the same, you're mighty brave, Jeb."

"Don't mention it, my friend."

Jeb calling him "my friend" made Davis smile. As they rode on, Davis played the sincerity of Jeb's words over and over in his head, and wondered, *How can people be prejudiced against one another? Especially out here on the range.*

The ride was nearing its end, and everyone was tired and testy. The same routine, day in and day out, night after night, was trying. Desperation and imagination got the best of a few of the men, and they tried to mix kerosene and corn syrup together to create a powerful drink. The stench permeated the entire campsite and raised the wrath of their boss. They were only three days out from Dodge City—it didn't seem worth it to Davis, but he wasn't a drinker and didn't understand the seduction of liquor.

The next day they rode into a big rain. The terrain turned to mush and they dragged through the slippery trails. The horses and riders were tense with the fear of falling, especially with the exhaustion they felt at the end of a fifty-eight-day ride. Two riders in particular struggled through the day, and everyone else had to come to their rescue at one time or another.

That night, as the campfires were being readied and the cook started to pull out his big pot, the boss came around and commanded everyone's attention. His voice boomed like the crack of a whip. They all stood before him, their aching backs suddenly rigid and their tired eyes fully alert. Davis had easily spotted last night's rabble-rousers during the day's ride. Jeb had whispered to Davis earlier that you didn't have to see their shoddy performance to know who they were; their bloodshot eyes gave it away. But he reckoned the boss didn't want to abandon them in the midst of the morning's storm. Now they all stood in absolute silence as Mr. Motley ticked off the impending punishment on his fingers. Loss of one-half of their salary and a guarantee they would never ride one of his drives again seemed like a stiff sentence to Davis, but Mr. Motley was the boss.

It was a weak mistake on the part of one of the Mexicans, and he was the first one called out. Another of the white buckaroos was squirming in place. It caught everyone's attention, even though no one dared to turn to face him directly. He was busy staring intently at the ground, his feet shuffling and making a little pit in the mud. Mr. Motley sauntered over and stamped down on the toe of the cowboy's boot to stop the man's nervous digging. They were all startled by his actions. The accused winced and almost fell off balance. The others were just plain shaking in their boots. The young man's eyes shot up and his face turned white when he met the stare of his angry, red-faced boss. No words were exchanged between the two, but everyone knew he understood he was going to suffer the consequences of his actions.

"Thank you, God," crossed Davis's nervous lips. He had this irrational fear that he would be wrongly accused of partaking in the Devil's nectar. Jeb stood stiff as a board next to Davis. He seemed to have seen this incident before, and he similarly wanted no part of any punishment.

The next two days were quiet and everything was under perfect control. When they saw Dodge City's stockyards on the horizon, Jeb motioned to Davis and said with a big smile, "That's it. Our final destination."

They rode those last hours in silent concentration. As they ended the drive, Jeb turned to Davis and said the simple cowboy farewell, "See you around someday." He turned his horse and headed west.

Davis stayed to watch the cattle funnel into the corrals and the stockyard's men scattering around them like rolling dice. He made his way over to where Mr. Motley was handing out the well-earned pay. Davis felt a surge of pride when Mr. Motley added, "Good job, Bennett," and shook his hand. "Noticed you have a real affinity for Sadie. She's worked long and hard for me. I'd like you to have her."

Absolutely shocked, Davis answered, "It would be my honor to keep her, sir. I'll take real good care of her, too. Thank you, sir."

With a nod of understanding, Mr. Motley tipped his hat and left.

Davis had heard that the local Baptist church provided overnight accommodations for "pass-through" cowboys. "Hey, Otto!" Davis called out. "I'm going to check on the rooms run by the Baptists here. Want to bunk up?"

"Thanks, Davis. Those downtown women aren't how I'd like to part with all the money I just earned." He looked over at some of the men who were already hitching their horses outside a rowdy saloon. "No carousing for me."

The bed was simple, but felt like it was fit for a king. The rooster's morning crow startled Davis, but it wasn't long before he could smell fresh eggs, bacon, and real coffee. All through breakfast, thoughts of getting home beckoned him. Rations in tow, he jumped on Sadie and headed her south. He had only gotten a few buildings down the road when he heard the clomps of a sturdy horse coming up fast behind him.

"Hey, Davis, wait up!" came Otto's voice. "Can I come too?"

"Sure thing," Davis said.

Otto let out a loud "Yahoo!" and they were off.

With Davis's baptism-by-fire cattle drive over, he spent the whole trip home imagining his up-and-coming ranch, his wedding, and, almost giggling, the Davis Bennett brand for the cattle he and Catherine would have on their ranch.

Mr. Huntington caught sight of the two bedraggled and dirty cowboys coming down Main Street. Leaning against the DeSoto portal, he called out, "Thought you'd never come back, young man. Been looking for you to share some good news! Come on in and let's have a cup of coffee."

"Ah, Mr. Huntington, I'm so dirty," Davis protested.

"Call me CH. Don't worry about the dirt. I've seen worse."

"All right then. Otto, can you take a rest and find a room? I've got to go take care of some business with Mr. Huntington here."

"No problem, Davis. Good luck."

Davis had shared with Otto his future plans and the many kindnesses of Mr. Huntington, so he knew the business Davis was talking about. Brushing inches of dust off his pants, Davis followed Mr. Huntington into the coffee shop.

"Think I got ya a real deal, Davis. You know the doctor I mentioned a while back? We've been talking. He isn't interested in coming back to his land. He doesn't want to sell it right now, but he said he would consider you and Catherine leasing the land and the ranch house, and eventually buying it from him. I explained you wanted to raise some livestock and do a bit of farming out there. And he said he's interested in making a deal to share in your profit of those things as payment. Now, how's that sound to you?"

"Gee, Mr. Huntington, it sounds great! I can't thank you enough."

"Leave the details to me then. See you here Monday morning, 6:00 a.m. sharp. I'll take you out to see the spread."

Davis could hardly contain his excitement. "Thank you, God," he said under his breath.

Forgetting his friend Otto, he ran down the street until he reached Catherine's front door. Out of breath, he knocked ferociously, yelling out, "I'm home…I'm home, Catherine!"

– 4 4 4 –

I heard Davis's voice and dashed for the door. When I answered, Davis couldn't contain himself. "Guess what? We got it…the deal went through on the ranch!"

I didn't have time to react before Davis picked me up and twirled me around and around. He was covered with dust and grime, but I didn't care. I was so happy to see him.

"Davis, how did you do it? When did you get home? How was the drive? Oh, I missed you so very much!"

Every thought came pouring out of his mouth at once. We sat on the porch, going over every detail of our days apart, until he blurted out, "Oh shucks, I forgot my man!"

I looked utterly confused.

He kissed my cheek and said, "Be right back!"

"Davis Bennett, whatever are you talking about?"

He had already jumped up and was pulling me up with him. "Oh Catherine, I'm so sorry. I've found us a cowhand. His name is Otto, and he'll help us on the new land. I met him on the drive. He's a real nice and honest guy who needs a family and needs work."

"Davis, you are too kindhearted. We need all our money," I said with a grimace.

"Don't you worry just yet. It'll all work out. Why don't you come with me and meet him? Then you'll see for yourself."

"Why don't we clean up a bit first?" I suggested, looking down at the dirt stains all over my yellow dress from where he had hugged me.

"Okay," he agreed sheepishly. "I'll come get you in an hour."

"Davis, why don't I fix dinner, and you and Otto can come back here together to join Mother, the boys, and me."

"Catherine, you are amazing! Thanks," Davis said, and dashed down the porch steps.

Otto fit right in with our little family, joking with my brothers and using his best manners whenever he conversed with Mother and me. I could tell immediately that this man was more grateful than we could imagine at becoming a part of our home.

"Otto," Davis said, "I think my brother Owen has an extra bunk. I'll ask him if you can stay there until we get moved out to the ranch next week. I have to go see the ranch this Sunday. Mr. Huntington said everything was empty and cleaned out, and ready for us to move in."

"Davis, that sounds mighty fine. And I'll work the room and board off, I promise. Every single cent."

And with that, Otto became a permanent part of our family.

Before I knew it, my wedding day had arrived. "Catherine," I said to myself that morning, "everything is happening so fast!" I had never felt such excitement. I don't even remember getting dressed or making our way to the chapel. I do remember seeing Father Patrick at the altar, grinning widely. He seemed confident that ours would be a good, solid marriage. I knew it was Davis's cooperation, respectfulness, and openness that impressed him most and caused him to put the seal of approval on our union.

When the organ music started playing "Here Comes the Bride," my brother Kerrick, the oldest of the three, looking so grown-up in his dark suit, took my arm.

"Well, here goes Daddy's Bonnie Lass," he whispered to me.

I choked with emotion but managed to make my trembling lips curl into a smile. Up at the altar, I saw Davis take a deep breath before he held his hand out toward me. The ceremony was a blur of prayers, vows, and a kiss, all of which happened in rapid succession. When I opened my eyes, I saw a loving husband, serious smiling faces in the pews, and tears of joy flowing from Aunt Isabel and Aunt Mary. Mother stood stoically as the boys gathered her up to walk her back down the aisle.

I hardly noticed the absence of Davis's family. Looking over at him though, I detected disappointment on his face. Even though no one had promised to come—no one but Polly, that is—I could not blame him for feeling let down. I was ever so grateful for the presence of Otto and Polly. Davis knew now that they would be his strongest supporters from that day on.

Davis cleared his throat and said softly, "My mother missed seeing the most beautiful girl in the world today."

I bubbled with pride. I felt beautiful and I felt loved.

At the reception table, Mother bustled around passing out chicken and cucumber sandwiches. Her eyes lit up as she headed straight toward me.

"Catherine, did you know that Mrs. Steel, the woman whose son you tutor, sent the lovely bouquet of daffodils? And Beulah, Davis's sister-in-law, made the wedding cake." She lowered her voice. "She might not have come to the church, but she wanted to wish you both well." She smiled at me and added, "Everybody adores you, Catherine."

I responded with a smile big enough to fit the whole cake into my mouth in one bite. Out of the corner of my eye, I saw little fingers swiping at the buttercream frosting on the cake. Dennis and Liam caught my eye and ran away, squealing with glee and sucking at their sugarcoated fingers.

"You little devils! It's my wedding day! Behave now," I blurted out.

Everyone turned to watch the commotion and the room filled with laughter.

Davis beckoned me to the door. "Otto says he has some kind of surprise for us out here, but I don't see him anywhere," he said.

"Outside?" I asked. "What could it—"

But the sight of Otto pulling up in a white carriage stunned me into silence.

"I've arrived, sir and madam, to drive you out to the first night in your new house," he exclaimed with the mock air of a fine gentleman.

With fanfare and well wishes from friends and family, Davis and I boarded the carriage.

The wind was gentle as we pulled up to the white clapboard farmhouse. It was modest, with a front porch stretching the width of the exterior. Excited, I envisioned us sitting in two sturdy rockers, each of us with a baby on our knee, with flower pots on the steps and a dog at our feet.

"I love it!" I exclaimed.

"Look at the view of the land and the sky," Davis said. "As far as you can see."

"Davis, I am so happy." I looked around in awe. "Look!" I said, pointing to a big cottonwood tree in the front yard. "A place for a swing...and there's room for a garden."

Otto helped me out of the carriage. Then, as if by magic, he disappeared, horse, buggy, and all, leaving us to our new home and our new life together.

That night, I melted into Davis's arms as we stood in the yard looking at our home and looking into each other's eyes. Somehow, without any consciousness on Davis's part, he allowed me to take his hand and we began to sway in the moonlight.

"Mr. and Mrs. Davis Bennett," he breathed into my ear.

I blushed at his words, and he blushed as he realized what this moment symbolized. I, without shame at my trickery, threw my head back with a hearty laugh, for Baptists don't dance and we had naturally fallen, so innocently, into a rhythm with the sound of the rustling leaves. From that time forward, Davis was mine and I was his.

4
Cattle, Barbed Wire, And Babies

I just want to jump and yell to the prairie dogs, "I am Catherine Bennett!" After you marry, you can become a whole new person! I no longer have to be an Irish immigrant's daughter if I don't want to be. I am no longer Catherine Connelly...at least, not on the surface.

Thoughts like these always grabbed me when the sewing machine motor was humming away. And in those early days of my marriage, my thoughts often retreated to the man that Davis was supposed to be replacing—my daddy. I'd even find myself talking to him.

"Daddy, do you remember how you used to sing to me? I loved 'When Irish Eyes Are Smiling' and 'Danny Boy.' When I was curled up at your feet, your Irish brogue made me feel like a cozy kitten. I will always be your wee lassie." Tears would come then, as I remembered why I couldn't sit on his lap. There wasn't enough room for me and the big beer mug that was always balanced on his knee. But he would stroke my long, black hair with his free hand and tell me stories about living in Paris and Dublin. I yearned to go there, to study many languages, to read the newest literature and see the latest art. "Please promise to take me someday, Daddy," I would plead.

Sometimes he would talk of his hometown of Kilcar, Ireland, where the young girls would spend their days sitting at large, carnival-sized looms weaving wool yarn into beautiful plaid patterns. "Clack, clack, clack. All day long," he would say.

"Daddy, I wish I could learn how to weave or knit the laces with the Irish patterns of roses and trailing vines," I'd say.

"I will show you one day," he would promise, adding, "Go get my Donegal wool vest off the bedpost."

And we would sit with our heads bent close together while he showed me the weave of the soft fabric that made it so fine. I would press it to my cheek, catching the wool's natural scent. That scent was still with me, even in the present, when the memory was from so many years ago.

As I sat at his feet, story after story would tumble off of his lips, until his empty mug would begin to tilt and his words would slow to soft, deep breaths. I never wanted my Irish lessons to end, or my learning about other parts of the world, for that matter. But my dream of going to Ireland was never to be. God had much more for me to learn right here in Texas.

As a new wife, sitting in the quiet house that Davis and I shared, those thoughts of my father and his beloved Ireland could easily overtake me, and my mornings would slip away into Irish dreamland. I would dream of how, someday, Davis and I would have a finer house with a large verandah where I could paint and read. Davis would arrive home in his three-piece business suit and Stetson hat, our dogs barking gleefully at his arrival and our children running and squealing to meet him in the driveway. It was always a struggle not to let my thoughts wander so much that I would almost miss my noontime dinner preparation.

On this particular day, I was jolted out of my reverie by noises outside. I heard horses clomping through the gate and saw dust flying, then a yelp coming from Davis. I barely had time to get the stew on the table before the men came in.

Davis grabbed me up in a big hug. "I'm so happy to be home with my little Cate. The calves were so frisky today, wouldn't you say, Otto?"

"Yes, sir. We've still got a dozen or more yet to brand this afternoon."

"Maybe they'll get sleepy with the afternoon sun and won't put up so much of a fight," Davis said. He looked at me and winked. "And maybe my roping will improve with some of this hearty stew." He threw his head back and said in a mock whisper to Otto, "You know, Cate has a special ingredient she throws into it. L.O.V.E."

The two men laughed and I joined in. "Oh, Davis! You will make me blush."

The men chewed ferociously, but I couldn't find much interest in the tender beef.

"What's the matter, Cate? Don't you like the cook's work today?"

"Oh no, it's fine. It's just that nothing seems to taste good to me today."

"Well, you're missing out. This is pretty darn good, right?" Davis nodded to Otto and the lanky cowhand grinned his approval.

An hour passed before Davis and Otto prepared to ride off. I kissed my husband's cheek and gave him a tap on the top of his straw hat—enough affection to last the whole afternoon.

— 4. 4. 4. —

As Davis and Otto returned to the pasture that afternoon, Davis was deep in thought. His lighthearted tone from lunchtime had turned to something more reflective. As he looked out at his small plot of land, he thought that there was nothing better than this life. It was darn hard work, but he loved being out there with his white-faced Herefords. He could almost identify each one with his eyes closed. He was mighty proud of his "open four" brand as he burned the symbol into each calf's hide.

Davis reached over to pat one heifer and spoke to it as if talking to a child. "You are mine. My babies to birth, feed, and tend to if you ever get hurt or lost. Otto, I sure wish this herd would stop rubbing up against all those new fence posts. You just watch, these posts will give way before too long and then we'll have to pick those confused, disoriented animals out of Mr. Reynolds's herd." He laughed at the thought. "They can sure test a man's patience! Good thing I'm a hard, steadfast worker, wouldn't you say, Otto?"

"You know, Mr. Davis, I've been around a long time and worked with many types of cowboys, and I can say that I've not seen many with your ethics and optimism."

"Now, now, you don't have to go so far to flatter me. I know that being steadfast means a steady income, and I owe that to Cate."

"Mr. Davis, I've also seen the animals act differently around you. I think they sense your tender caretaking. Too many men are too rough and the heifers become obstinate." Otto suddenly cried out and pointed. "Sure enough, Mr. Davis! Look over there! Do you see what I see? Those doggone calves followed one of the heifers through that weak spot in the fence."

"What a mess! Get going, Otto. We've got to get all those calves back before dusk. Looks like they're the ones we haven't branded, too. Daggum it! I'll ride over to Charlie's spread. We're going to need help real fast. I can't afford to lose any of those calves."

— 4. 4. 4. —

The afternoons were always a bit lonely after Davis and Otto headed back out to the pasture. I busied myself by tidying up the kitchen. I still wasn't feeling good, but worried about bothering Davis with such silliness when he came home that night, so I decided to call Mother and talk to her about it when she and the boys got home from school.

"Mother," I said, after cranking up the wall phone. "I have a little question to ask you. My stew was tasteless this noon and I got dizzy when I smelled it. And all this afternoon—well...all the past weekend, actually—I've felt like I'm dragging a barrel behind me."

"Catherine, is that all? I get tired like that too."

"But Mother, this feels different. I don't usually want to sleep all day."

"You'll be okay. Now go back to your chores." She hung up without saying good-bye, as she always did.

"Oh, Mother," I said under my breath, and hung the earpiece back on its hook.

I jumped when the bell immediately let out its shrill ring.

"Hello?"

"Catherine, this is your mother..."

I waited and waited. Mother's last words to me raced through my mind. The sun was setting and still no Davis or Otto. I was so mixed up, one minute weepy and the next anxious. I alternated from sitting slumped over with my head in my hands to pacing the floor and wringing my hands.

Looking out the kitchen door into the darkening night, I asked aloud, "Where are you, Davis?"

To my relief, my eyes made out the outline of two horses coming into the yard. The men dismounted and Otto led their horses to the stable.

"Davis, you look beat," I blurted out. I took his hat and smoothed his hair as he sat quietly at the kitchen table. Somehow, I had managed to prepare a sandwich, and I set it and some cold well water before him.

"Cate, I got me some naughty calves in that bunch. They wandered off, but I got 'em."

"That's my man! I know you're tired. I'm just happy you're okay. How about telling me all about it in the morning?"

I started to return to my little nest in bed, but as I started to leave, I was so overtaken with exhaustion that I had to lean against the doorframe to keep from falling over. Hanging on for dear life, I didn't want Davis to see me shake. I tried to sound casual. "I'm pretty sure I got some good news today too..."

Total contentment and joy cuddled me as I slept soundly in Davis's arms that night. When the sun peeked through the lace curtains the next morning, I felt a rush of excitement and jumped out of bed. I hurried to dress and rushed into the kitchen with the intention of making a big celebration breakfast. But that was just wishful thinking. Everything, especially cooking, was a much harder task than I had anticipated. My stomach sent big, lumpy rushes up into my throat every few minutes.

Two strong hands slipped around my waist and a tender kiss landed on my forehead just beneath my curls.

"Good morning, beautiful. You're up mighty early."

I grinned and handed Davis his coffee. "Now, tell me all about that crisis with the calves yesterday..."

Davis took a seat at the kitchen table. As he spoke, his words faded from my ears. I could hardly hold back my news. As the story came to its end, he took a breath and immediately started telling me about his upcoming day.

"Cate, my day is not going to be so rigorous as yesterday. Can Otto and I help you around the yard? I know you aren't feeling good. Don't deny it. I can tell. And besides, I think we should lie low before we get out there with this crazy herd again."

"Well, that is just what I was about to get to. You noticed I didn't eat much yesterday..."

"As a matter of fact, you have been picking at your meals most of the past week."

I was surprised that he had noticed so much. It warmed me inside that he was so attentive. I wondered what else he might have noticed. "I seem to have more of a tummy too…"

His eyes got bigger and a special twinkle came to them as I told him the good news. He leaped out of his chair and squeezed me almost in half. Before I knew it, he had dashed out the kitchen door and was yelling Otto's name.

"Otto, Otto! We're going to have a baby! Got to make sure this fence is close enough together so little ones can't climb through. We need a swing in the old cottonwood tree. All kids need swings. And a crib, yes...we need to start cutting up the fallen pine for a baby crib. We've got lots to do, young man. Don't just sit there!"

I stood at the door, watching those two run from one side of the yard to the other, shouting about each project's materials. I laughed. It was like watching a comedy act. Calmly, I proceeded with morning chores and tried to keep the lump in my throat from shooting straight out of my mouth.

By noon, they had three piles of wood neatly organized. Davis sent Otto off to tighten the fences.

"Cate, I want to be the one to make my first child's crib. I might let Otto carve the heart at the head, but I want my love to go into it."

I knew Davis was probably no woodworker, but the sweetness in his voice convinced me that it would be, with God's help, the most beautiful crib ever.

"The cattle will continue to keep me busy, but I promise you will have your baby bed finished by November. I'm thinking I'll take the young calves off the upper section and put in some winter wheat, mixing crops and cattle for success and assured money after the baby comes."

"Davis, did you question the old-timers at the DeSoto? Do they mix their crops and cattle?" I queried.

Fall was rushing by. I looked out the window and saw some early winter snowflakes. *Yes,* I thought. *The fences are done...the swing is battling the blowing wind...and the last shavings are scattered around the rockers on the crib. I have the last ruffle to sew around the pillow's edge. I hope Mother brings the knitted wool blanket. I wonder what color she made it?*

That afternoon, Mother, Aunt Isabel, and the boys arrived.

"How's my little mama-to-be? We thought we'd surprise you, Catherine dear," chimed Aunt Isabel.

"Look, sis, I carved a toy car, in case you have a boy," shouted Kerrick, holding it up as he tumbled out of the buggy. My other two brothers had already spotted the swing and were off to test it.

I put my china cups out and brewed some tea. Mother's tied cloth satchel was bulging. I gave her a curious look as she pulled out the palest cream, hand-knitted throw.

"Mother, I hope you teach me those fancy stitches someday. I will treasure this always," I said.

"But dear, you haven't seen anything yet. Isabel, open your surprise."

"I hope you like it, sweet girl," Aunt Isabel said. "I made it from apron scraps I got from your mother, Mary, and Davis's sisters. See? This blue one is from Polly. I love to quilt and this has been a special task for me."

Patting it, I said, "I can feel the love of my whole family in this quilt. I remember all of these aprons...the one you used to wear for Thanksgiving, Aunt Isabel. Oh, this will be handed down forever. I don't know what to say…"

With that, the boys came bursting in. "Got any hot chocolate, Cate?"

I nodded, so full of emotion it was hard to speak. As I stood to make the boys their hot chocolate, I managed to say, "You all have surprised me with your kindness. I really wasn't expecting anything... and now a toy, a quilt, and a blanket!"

"Well, my dear, Aunt Mary wasn't feeling up to the trip today. I had XIT business in town, so I brought this for her. "

In the satchel pocketbook my Aunt Isabel always carried was a stuffed doll with a stitched face, and an apron matching one of the quilt sections. She pulled it out and handed it to me. My lips quivered a bit as I held it up to my protruding tummy.

Liam giggled. "You're getting kind of fat there. Won't be long now till I'm an uncle. Imagine that! Wish I was going to be around, but we'll be going to Dallas in the next few years. There's opportunity for us boys in Dallas."

I adored my family. I felt particularly sad to see them leave that day. I whispered, "I love you" as the buggy disappeared down the dirt driveway. I knew my life would be changing soon. I was a woman alone, and I was soon to be a mother. I would be known as Mama.

After baby Elizabeth was born in late November, part of Davis's herd had been sent off to slaughter. Little Elizabeth loved her routine of sleeping and nursing, which allowed me extra time for my special project. Timidly, I pulled my wedding dress out from its box under my bed. There it was, neatly folded between layers of linen. I touched every seam. I studied the different Irish laces. My gift of love from my mother stared back at me. Could I do it? Could I actually put scissors to it, even though I would cut it with caution? What if I saved it for Elizabeth's wedding? Mother had already commented that this baby was twice as big as I was at her age, so I assumed that my tiny wedding dress would probably not fit my sweet Elizabeth when she grew up. Nevertheless, I called to ask Mother's permission.

"Would you be upset if I cut up my wedding dress for Elizabeth's baptism gown? I love it more than anything, Mother, and I don't want you to think I'm being ungrateful or disrespectful."

"Dear, your decision to use the laces and fabrics in such a loving way would deeply please me. I'm certain you were thinking a boy or girl could use it, one or the other. Do you need help with your sizing or design?"

"Could you? I'll bring it to town when I come on Sunday."

That weekend, as I stood beside Mother, I teared up with restrained emotion with every cut. Mother laid out the linen with precision. She cut out the lace embellishments with care and placed each piece strategically on the long baby dress. Once again, another beautiful creation appeared as the result of my mother's hands.

"Mother, what happened to our christening dress?"

"I had to leave it behind. I couldn't take everything. The parish church kept it for a child who didn't have an appropriate dress. They gave us the lovely gravesite for your sister, Bridget, and I gave them the dress. Your father was gone and I wasn't having more children. Yes...you had a beautiful big sister. She was named after my sister, who we lost on the ship coming over. Dysentery caused so many of the children to die back then."

"You have suffered so much, Mother," I whispered.

Our beautiful afternoon reverted to sad memories for Mother. She didn't blink an eye, but kept sewing. Stoic and strong, she kept sewing.

That night, after our visit, Davis, baby Elizabeth, and I had a late dinner with Mrs. Bennett. I was lost in thought during the drive home. I gloated that this reserved woman, Davis's mother, had actually asked to hold little Elizabeth. Davis caught my shocked expression, and he turned his head as he chuckled silently. She was changing. Finally, changing.

"Davis," I blurted out, making the baby jerk out of her peacefulness. "I forgot," I said almost breathlessly. "We need godparents for the baptism. I can ask one of my brothers, but who can the godmother be? I don't know many Catholic girls and certainly no one very close...oh dear..." I fretted.

"Ask Liam to be the godfather, Cate. He seems to be lighthearted and is a serious Catholic. Kerrick might be shipped out on Navy assignment and Dennis doesn't seem to really like children."

"Yes, good choice, I agree. One down and one to go, so to speak."

"What about Aunt Isabel?"

"Too old."

"Aunt Mary?"

"Even older."

"Margarita Gonzales? I know she's Catholic. She walks down the street praying with her rosary every day."

"Davis, I don't think you understand. A godmother would have to take her in and promise to raise her in the Catholic Church. I'm not sure you want your daughter being raised as a Mexican, speaking Spanish and never leaving Twist Junction, going to college, or…"

"Okay, okay, I'll let it be up to you, Cate. How about Polly?"

"No, Davis, she has to be a Catholic—unless she wants to convert real fast."

"Wouldn't that curl our mothers' hair?" Davis said.

The joking had taken a turn for the worse.

"This is no laughing matter, Mr. Bennett," I complained. My temper was about to pop.

Father Patrick seemed content with a stand-in altar woman, giving all rights and responsibilities to Liam. Liam glowed with his new godchild in his arms. A trickle of water dripped down the baby's nose, and she wriggled it. Liam leaned down and patted her forehead with the fine linen altar cloth, which made everyone smile.

Davis said in a light voice, "Is that it?"

I responded, "That's it. We can give her to Liam if she turns out bad." I winked at Davis. "I'm joking…"

"We have to scoot home. Do you have much to do before the family comes?"

"The casseroles are made, the table is set, and my mother said she'd bring a luscious chocolate cake. I'm not sure I have enough chairs for everyone...our mothers and aunts will take five. Do you think Liam needs a seat of honor with the baby? And Davis...do you think your brothers and their wives will come too? I made enough food for an army going to battle."

Davis shrugged as we headed for home.

My mind reverted back to the celebration we had just witnessed. "Baptism is a sweet ceremony, don't you think?" I was nervous that we had delayed our responsibilities for five months. The winter months made travel dangerous on the dirt roads. Babies were usually baptized within the first month, but Father Patrick seemed less concerned. He was pleased we had kept our promise of a Catholic upbringing for our children.

"Just thought it would amount to more singing or something, I guess. You Catholics have more rituals and we have more songs."

"Yes, the old Latin prayers are often hard to follow, but I think it gives a feeling of the ancient traditions."

"Guess I wanted to sing something along with your priest. I didn't feel like I was much a part of anything."

"Hmm...hadn't thought about it that way. I guess we have always had the priest in charge. You're right, it wasn't very inclusive for the rest of us. Little Elizabeth seemed to realize she was special and Liam was very proud to be her godfather."

"Well, here we are, home," Davis said as he pulled up the dusty road. "It's time for a party, girls!" He smiled at me and the baby. "I'm going over to the bunkhouse to get Otto. Isabel and Mary will enjoy meeting him and hearing of his life as a cowboy. Bet he's never been to a christening party before."

"And you, Mr. Bennett? You'd better get used to them." I reached for his hand and had it pat my tummy. He blushed, then rushed out the door to find Otto. I could hear the men talking as I carried Elizabeth into the house.

"Want to come to the party, Otto ol' boy? We just got back from church and Elizabeth's christening. Just heard we're going to have another christening next year, too."

"Davis, you're quite the man. Pretty soon you'll have so many kids you'll have to share them with me." He licked his hand, smoothed down his hair, and came hobbling back to the house behind Davis.

"You need your rest today, I can tell, but I didn't want the rest of the family to miss meeting my sidekick," Davis said, and slipped his arm around his loyal buddy's shoulder.

I gloated as the ham and lima bean casserole was licked clean. I was determined to have everybody at least try it, even though I served a chicken dish too. Unconsciously, Mrs. Bennett helped herself to a large spoonful. Aunt Polly winked at me when she recognized the infamous church social supper dish. Father Patrick sang praises of my dish being a sight for sore eyes.

Davis seemed ecstatic to have Father Patrick in our home so that the father could see how well he was providing for us. "You look like you have four-leaf clovers growing in your yard," the father grinned with approval.

"All we need around here is a little leprechaun help for Catherine," Davis joked.

Convivial, the afternoon slipped by. The family bonding over our little angel Elizabeth caused our hearts to pound with pride and joy.

Davis stood and announced, "Afternoon, everybody. We have an announcement. Elizabeth will have a brother or sister this year."

The room rocked with clapping and cheers.

Glancing over to the kitchen, Davis looked at me. I motioned for him to join me.

"Next time," I whispered, "I think I should ask your Southern Baptist preacher and his wife to join us for the christening party. Today's gathering is going better than I ever could have imagined."

"That's because you're the perfect hostess."

The last of the Connellys and the last "thank yous" left Otto standing off to the side behind us and baby Elizabeth innocently sleeping in the crib that her daddy had made. Otto shuffled some extra dishes from the parlor to the kitchen.

"Many thanks, my friend," Davis said. "Hope you enjoyed yourself.

Sunrise is going to come early for us, I'm afraid. Tomorrow maybe we can decide which pasture will be best for the new herd, and where to start plowing for crops."

A little whimper and then a little bird tweet, sounds of the morning, made my ears perk up, but my body seemed to be stuck in bed. With a one-eyed peek I could see Davis leaning against the porch post watching his favorite thing—the morning sunrise. By the time he came back inside, I had Elizabeth on my hip and was flipping buttermilk pancakes.

"Are you ready for another wonderful day, my honeybees?" Davis greeted us.

"Did you bring that sunshine into my kitchen, Davis?"

"I tried my best." Leaning over, Davis gave me a kiss and then, leaning way over, he grabbed his smiling baby girl. He set his coffee cup next to his plate so that he could use both hands to raise Elizabeth above his head. He said, "I don't know who's cuter, you or my new calf, Dottie."

"Oh, Davis, behave. We know that answer."

He couldn't let go, so he ate his pancakes with one hand and jiggled Elizabeth on his knee.

"You're spoiling her! I'll have a crying baby on my hands when you leave."

"Gotta go...barbed wire and fence posts await me. I'll be home with the noonday sun. Otto beat me. He's got the horses saddled already."

With that, Davis downed the last of his coffee, handed me the baby, and left for the day.

— 🐄 🐄 🐄 —

"Let's get a move on, slowpoke," Otto jabbed.

Davis said, "This place is getting mighty nice thanks to your help, Otto. I think my feeling about crops together with the cattle could guarantee me some nice money...if it works."

"Just need some high grass and plenty of room between them, boss."

"Reckon you're right. I'm going to the DeSoto to see what the old guys say. But first, let's see what we've got to work with..."

Spurring the horses gently, they passed the new calves and a few leaning fence posts. Davis nodded in recognition of tomorrow's work. They slowed and could see rich brown dirt before them for miles.

"If I get real lucky, I could make a good payment toward buying this land. And how about a raise for you, cowboy? The cattle could graze over there." Davis tipped his hat, pointing to the grove of cottonwoods and a small stream. "What pleasant shade. Since there is water, we could hook up a windmill for a water tank, too."

"Lots of plans, Mr. Bennett."

During the ride back, the sun seemed to be getting hotter. "Going to be a scorcher this summer if we're getting the heat this early. Better get the crops in soon. I don't want them to burn up before harvest time," Davis commented.

"I'll rub down the horses and look at fixing the front gate…seems it's leaning after one of the boys backed into it yesterday after the party."

"That's not a lean," Davis laughed. "It's almost out of the ground. I'd hate to count all the gates I've hit in my day."

The DeSoto was lively that morning. There were conversations happening around every table of the coffee shop. Twist Junction was bursting at the seams. There was talk of a new post office, banks, a livery and feed store, grocery stores, and even an opera and playhouse. And all of this because of the coming of the railroads, and good farming and cattle-raising practices.

The insiders maintained their spot at the back, and cigar smoke hung over the table of the notables. Davis was flattered to be welcomed by the group.

"How's it going, young man?" Mr. Huntington greeted.

"Heard you got a baby and another on the way! You've been busy…" Mr. Pierce added.

And they bellowed with laughter.

"Davis, make any money on that first herd?" questioned Mr.

Huntington.

"Oh yes, sir, and I sent Dr. Dawson his check too."

"Now that's keeping a promise."

"I need some technical advice this morning," Davis said as the conversation paused.

Mr. Pierce looked over at him. "Want to buy into a bank or livestock stable?"

"Not yet, sir, but maybe someday," Davis almost boasted. He leaned back in his chair and presented his idea of the pasture-and-crops concept.

"Pretty risky venture, young man," Mr. Huntington piped up immediately. "You got to have double sturdy fencing and enough grass to keep your animals well fed. They could get real curious if you had some nice crop growing under their noses."

"My land configuration is a real flat piece with rich soil. I thought I'd put in a narrow pick-up road between it and another piece that does a slight roll down to a cluster of cottonwoods and a small stream for the cattle. I got myself a helper, too."

Mr. Huntington frowned as he listened. "If there is anyone who can give this a shot, it might be you. Wish I still had your energy and enthusiasm, Davis," he chuckled.

Mr. Pierce added, "Maybe you'll teach us all something."

Davis left the meeting feeling encouraged to a point, but then his excitement turned to doubt and a little fear. *Can't tell Cate the fear part. She's such a good saver. She'll be excited to think how much she could stow after our bills and debts. That's counting on $25 a head and $3 a bushel. Now me, I'd like to buy my children something special. Real special! Having a Shetland pony to ride surely could make them learn about animals and the outdoors. Yep, have to give that some serious thought! I like being ahead of the game.* His thoughts raced through his mind as he drove his Model-T pick-up back to the ranch, navigating around the many ruts in the old dirt road.

Not wanting to rip his good suit, Davis slithered off of the pick-up's seat. Immediately, he started calling to Otto, who was cleaning in the barn.

"Think we should double our order of fence posts so the cattle can't knock them down. Can't be too secure, especially with this feisty bunch. Need to get some of that super heavy barbed wire, 12.5 gauge, for the new pasture. Perhaps we can hold off on the water tank and windmill until we see how much the creek supplies us. I'll put in an order for the wheat to plant."

"You plannin' on planting with a horse and plow?" mentioned Otto casually.

"Daggum it! I always forget something…looks like I'd better price a tractor as an option. Owen has an old one I might talk him out of. Always somethin'! We're in for some hard work, real fast, Otto. Looking down the road, it would be mighty good to have a couple more boys to help out with getting these calves rounded up and branded. Do you have room in your quarters for one or two guys?"

"You planning on leprechauns?" Otto joked. "It would be real tight. Are you saving any of the lumber out there in the stable? I could build me a lean-to and give up my old space for a while."

Leaning up against the bunkhouse porch post, Davis began to think. *Wonder where Jeb is? He'd never leave Mr. Motley, but maybe we could grab him between drives. He's worth three men. He's a Cracker Jack cowboy all right. Sure do miss that guy. He held my feet to the ground through a tough cattle drive.*

After finishing his thought about needing more help, he sauntered back to the house.

— 4. 4. 4. —

A few weeks later, the heat was beginning to subside and we were enjoying occasional rain storms.

"Glad the weather is cooling down with all this rain. Got that wheat in just in time. Otto will be working the last half mile of fence. You'd think we were building ourselves a little Twist Junction. Too many projects too fast." Davis paused as he glanced out the window at the front gate. "Well, lo and behold. Look who's coming through our gate."

I looked out to see a chestnut horse with a black rider. Davis jumped up and slammed open the kitchen door. The bunkhouse door echoed at the same time. Davis's grin was so broad, it looked like his cheeks almost hurt. Otto grabbed the bridle as Jeb slipped off of old Rusty.

"Mighty good to see you boys again!" Jeb yelled as his boots hit the ground.

Sadie, who was in the stable, called to her old friend Rusty. The energy of lost friendship shot across the yard.

"Cate, look who's here!" Davis called out to me. "It's my cattle-drive partner, Jeb!"

Otto and Jeb almost squeezed the air out of each other as Davis dashed up the porch steps and pulled me out of the house to the shade of the cottonwood. Elizabeth wobbled behind me, calling, "Mama, Mama."

That night, as we sat over a table of fresh vegetables, homemade biscuits, and steak, the men celebrated their reunion. When dusk came, Davis squirmed.

"Hey, don't worry, Davis," Jeb said. "I skirted town when I came over from Dumas. Only the jackrabbits know I'm here."

"How did you know where we were, Jeb?" Davis asked.

"Mr. Motley keeps track of all his favorite cowboys, so we agreed I should pay you and the missus a visit. Otto was the surprise."

"No, *you* were the surprise."

They all agreed. I smiled from the kitchen. It was nice to see their camaraderie.

"Looks like God has blessed us all." Davis glanced at me, Elizabeth, and then Otto and Jeb. "Can you stay a bit?" he smiled. "Otto is building a lean-to and he will have plenty of room."

"Hey man," Otto piped in. "You a cook?"

"Nothin' ol' Jeb can't do," said our black guest quietly. "I'll happily help you out till mid-June, when Mr. Motley has me for our next drive. Promise I'll keep a low profile and stay out here. How's that sound?"

Davis said, "Yes, good idea, Jeb. Some people out here go crazy with the old rule of 'no blacks in town after sunset.' Not me. I can't go along with that prejudice. I must be a real renegade." He laughed. "An Irish wife and a black friend and helper. Yep, that's me…a real renegade. Or, I prefer to be a man called 'Even Steven'—open and accepting."

"Davis, there ain't anybody more fair than you," Jeb spoke up.

Otto nodded his agreement.

"Well, let's get to it first thing in the morning!" Davis enthused.

— ⊰ ⊰ ⊰ —

With Jeb's help, the barbed-wire fencing seemed to go up overnight. With the use of Owen's old tractor, Otto plowed and planted the first crop. Jeb cooked up the grub. Together, the two men finished the lean-to at the bunkhouse.

When Davis checked out their progress, he was impressed. "Good job, Otto and Jeb. That went lickety-split. I'm going to bring Cate out so she can see what all this flurry of work has been about. Then she'll be more confident that she will have something to put in her teapot," he chuckled.

Otto stared at him, and Davis assumed he was thinking, *Teapot?*

"Jeb, are the new calves coming tomorrow?" Davis asked.

"Yes, sir. I'm going to meet Mr. Motley and his boys five miles from here, and I'll bring them to our pasture around 4:00."

"Otto and I can meet you at the lower gate. Right, Otto?"

The sweat poured off of them over the next few weeks after the cattle arrived. They became a production line, cutting them out of the herd, roping them in seconds, tying them, then branding them.

"Jeb, I've never seen you rope and tie," Davis said. "You're so fast you ought to be in the rodeo."

"Don't think I haven't given it some thought. Not sure being out in the public is good for me, being black, you know. Might tie me down too much to follow the circuit. I like being on the open range and workin' for Mr. Motley and folks like you."

"Guess we all must agree, or we wouldn't be out here staring at each other," Davis chuckled.

— 4 4 4 —

Later, I met the men in the yard, waving my dish towel feverishly to get their attention.

Otto noticed and shouted, "Gotta be something going on!" and pointed Davis in my direction.

"Davis!" I shouted. "I just got a call from Owen. He says some men in town are raising a stink. Heard you had a black man out here. You'd better get in here fast and talk to your brother."

"Daggum it, why don't people mind their own business?" Davis muttered as he stopped what he was doing and headed for the kitchen. The kitchen door slammed behind him. "If any of them were half the man Jeb is, we'd have a better world. Think we've got some jealousy here, too." He grabbed the phone and listened for a few moments, then said, "Okay, okay, Owen, I hear you. I don't want trouble for anybody. I'll take care of it." With that, he slammed down the phone and stomped out the door.

As soon as Davis returned to where the men were working, Jeb spoke up. "Guess I better hightail it out of here, Mr. Davis." He seemed to read Davis's facial expression with clarity.

"Get your stuff. And hurry," Davis anxiously instructed.

"Wait, Jeb, I've got food for you," I shouted from the house. I hurried to pack a basket for him.

Just as mysteriously as he had arrived weeks before, Jeb was off, headed back to Dumas.

I stood at the gate with Davis and Otto. We were speechless. Proud, accomplished moments had twisted into a flurry of fear. "We didn't even get to say thank you or good-bye," I said sadly.

"Your fine food was a good enough thank you, sweetheart."

"Davis, did you pay him?"

"No, but I'll get it to him over in Dumas. He knows I'm good for it."

Later, meatloaf and mashed potatoes, usually Davis's favorite, sat on his dinner plate untouched. Finally, he said, "Life isn't fair. God blessed me with Jeb's friendship. He took a risk coming here, and now he's riding like heck to get out of town, away from our prejudiced neighbors. I should have ridden with him. Now he needs my friendship and help. I'm very nervous for him, Cate."

Davis, Otto, and I exchanged worried glances.

The rumble of a car motor and the sound of the front gate flying open set the scene that Davis was dreading.

"Let me handle this one," I said to Davis in a determined tone.

Davis shook his head as I headed out the door. He knew I meant business. Otto's eyes got bigger. He didn't say a word.

"Okay, gentlemen," I said as I approached the car. "What's all the commotion? I've got a sleeping baby in there, and if you wake her I'll be madder than a wet hen. Got that?"

"Howdy, ma'am. Is your husband here?" asked Mr. Pierce, one of Davis's advisors.

"Why Mr. Pierce, Mr. Finch, Mr. Howard," I said. "Thank you for coming all the way out here to pay us a visit. Mighty pretty day."

"Is Davis in?" Mr. Pierce repeated.

"May I invite you into the parlor? I'll get you boys something cold to drink."

"We've come to see Davis," Mr. Howard said.

"Yes, yes, let's get out of the sun," I babbled.

Directing them around to the front door and parlor, I was determined to detain them as long as possible. I knew they were gentlemen and would not be rude to a lady. Once they were seated, I excused myself and went into the kitchen. After taking another minute or two, I came back into the living room with a tray of cold drinks and shortbread.

"Now, Mrs. Bennett, you know why we are here. We just want to talk with your husband," huffed Mr. Finch.

"Oh yes, of course. He has been out on his new spread all morning. Guess he didn't have time to come to town to have his coffee today. I have to take care of my man. He is just finishing up his noonday dinner."

Minutes passed as we smiled at each other and made small talk.

"We are very busy men and we need to talk to your husband right away," Mr. Pierce finally grumbled.

"Why didn't you speak up, Mr. Pierce? I'll see if I can get him for you."

"Davis, Davis..." I called dramatically, going back into the kitchen, where Davis was waiting and listening.

"I tried, but I can't keep them busy any longer," I whispered. "Do you think Jeb is far enough away by now?"

Davis scooted the kitchen chair, rubbing the floorboards loudly. He cleared his throat, then stood and walked to the parlor with an air of pride and respect.

"So sorry I didn't get to the DeSoto today, gentlemen. I could have gladly saved you the trip, but time is of the essence for getting my crops and cattle ready for the upcoming summer. I'm sure you understand."

Davis noticed that Mr. Huntington was missing, but the outspoken others were rigidly perched on the edges of their seats.

"Now, how may I help you?" Davis said, his face turning serious.

Three of the men began to talk at the same time. They spotted me stationed at the kitchen door. I was there to temper the discussion if need be. There wasn't to be cussing or rudeness in my home.

"Davis, you know very well the town rules...the ones referring to men of color," one of the men expounded.

"Gentlemen, with all due respect," I piped up. "Davis and I did not intentionally break any town rules. After all, we live twenty miles outside of town and you are on private property."

The men were taken aback. First, at hearing from this feisty woman; and second, what I said was true, even though they didn't want to admit it.

"Thank you, Mrs. Bennett, we will take the opinion of you and your husband under consideration," said Mr. Pierce.

One of the men popped up out of his seat. It seemed that he just wanted to get out of there. One cleared his throat again. One said in a gentlemanly fashion, "Thank you for your time."

And last, Mr. Pierce turned to Davis. "We'll speak more about this over coffee, young man," he said gruffly.

They left the house and got into their car, and the car rumbled down the driveway.

"The nerve," I huffed, clanging my glasses and plates into my tray.

"I haven't heard the last of this, Cate. I'm afraid I've fallen out of favor with the town fathers. Big mistake. Think I need to put my 'conservative' hat back on. You have given me such added confidence. Guess I got carried away."

He reached all the way around my "showing" tummy, pulling me toward him with a show of unity.

"Oh Davis, you're a good man. Don't let those old fogies get to you. Send them to church to learn godliness."

"You are amazing, Cate. I've never seen such determination for the good of things."

"You just have to stand up for what is right," I blurted out in my fired-up, Irish fashion.

The next morning, we got word that Jeb had arrived at Mr. Motley's ranch safely. We were relieved. And to our surprise, the tempers of the DeSoto men soon cooled and they slowly accepted Davis as an up-and-comer again. They realized that I had a point about being twenty miles out of town and the private property issue, and that they had no leg to stand on. Besides, Mr. Huntington was never in favor of the whole incident being an issue. Davis was his "golden boy."

A few months later, our second daughter, Sybil, arrived, giving Elizabeth a curly-headed playmate. Davis, now the proud father of two, wanted to surprise us all with a cocoa-colored Shetland pony named Punky. Jumping up and down with excitement, Elizabeth tried and tried to climb on Punky's back. Davis showed her how to hold on to the pony's mane. He led the pony slowly, one armed stretched to Elizabeth's back for support.

I shook my head as I watched them. *Wish I had the money spent on that pony for my secret savings in my china teapot*, I thought. The joy on their faces was worth all the money in the world. But a pony?

The thought of denying Davis and the children the joy of their Punky made me feel bad. However, being the big saver and planner, I had to be looking down the road. I could tell I had another surprise for Davis—yes, another baby!—and knew we would be needing a car for our growing family soon.

"Davis, how's your new herd coming? And the corn crop?" I asked later, when we were back inside and the children were napping.

"If I can bring in the money I did last time, we'll be riding high. I was so happy to be able to pay Jeb, give the doctor some profit, and buy a little more land too. Cate, I gave Otto a raise. When I did, you would have thought I'd given him the moon. Don't know what that man does with his money, but it sure makes him happy when he gets it. Meant to tell you, I had to pull in another cowhand for the branding. Nobody will ever be able to replace Jeb though. The only good thing is, I don't have to pay him quite so much."

"We need to be able to buy a car," I said. "I didn't realize we would be having more expenses."

"A car?" Davis repeated, eyebrows raised. "Why do we need that now?"

"Our family is still growing."

"Oh Cate, another baby?"

"I'm afraid so...you don't have to be so good at everything!" I teased.

He snuggled into my neck and kissed me tenderly.

"Okay, I'll pick out a car. You want to see it? I can go up to the dealer later this fall after the crops come in."

"Davis, I'd love to, but after you buy it, why don't you drive over, get your mother, and give her the first ride? Bring her out to see Elizabeth, and Sybil, her newest grandbaby, and I'll cook supper."

"Are you sure, sweetheart? What a generous invitation! Cate... you're *really* sure?"

"Davis, it's so much easier to corral these children if I stay put. And I have to cook anyway."

"Having ham and lima bean casserole?" Davis blurted.

I shot him a withering look.

"Just kidding," he added.

"Davis, go away. No jokes for now."

With the spring and summer crops finished, fall upon us, and Christmas coming, the girls grew to become more precious to us. I did not serve the casserole. I did have the two girls in their starched dresses, with bows in their hair, as Grandmother Bennett drove up with their daddy. The big event called for fried chicken and apple pie.

"Hello, Mother Bennett," I said, holding my newest curly-headed, blue-eyed girl. "How did you like the ride in Davis's fancy Buick? A seven-seater, I hear!"

"Oh Catherine, you make such pretty babies," she said without a breath or any comment regarding the car.

"Hello, ma'am," said Elizabeth as she curtsied.

Sybil giggled and squirmed.

"Hello, girls," was the extent of her conversation with the children.

I just rolled my eyes as I turned away. My conversation broke her clipped greetings to the children. "Davis, the car is lovely. Are you proud of it? I can't wait to sit in it and feel that leather upholstery. The dark-green color is so handsome."

"Yes, it turned a few faces as I drove it off the car lot. Polly gave me a wave as I picked up my mother. I think she stood there for an extra long time looking it over. She had a pretty proud look, if you know what I mean."

After dinner, as Mother Bennett rocked on the porch, Davis told her stories of all his successes. She would rock, nod, and *almost* smile...rock, nod, and *almost* smile. Things seemed to be thawing in our relationship. *Thank you, God,* I said to myself.

"Good-bye, my dear," Mrs. Bennett said abruptly, pulling herself from the rocker. "Davis, it's gotten to be a long day for me. Can you drive me into town now?"

"Mind if I dust off the car before we leave? Want it to look its best when we pull up."

"Certainly, dear. I know that this first car is your pride and joy."

Mrs. Bennett sat patiently as she watched her youngest son wipe the loose dirt from the car's body. I sat quietly as I observed her hidden pride. Elizabeth and I waved as Davis pulled the Buick from the yard and through the gate. I had plenty to do, dishes to wash, and children to put to bed, so I said good night and went inside.

Always appreciating being part of our family, sharing our meals and special times, Otto offered to help with the kitchen clean-up. His thoughtful generosity of always helping endeared him to us through the years.

Davis arrived back home a little after sunset. We always treasured our evenings, to be able to snuggle and talk about the many topics on our minds. Many months later, on one of those evenings, long after baby #3, Daphne, was born, Davis and I broached the religion and church subject.

"Davis, I've been thinking. I think it's time to start taking the girls to church. Elizabeth will behave fine, I'm sure, but it will be hard to control Sybil."

"I know getting back to church would be good for you, Catherine. It soothes your soul." He paused. "I sure do miss singing my songs at the Baptist church, too."

"We agreed this is what we would do with raising the girls, but I suppose I didn't realize how hard it would be. I'm not complaining, but it's just hard, isn't it?"

"Why don't you give it a try next Sunday?"

"We'll have to get up extra early for me to starch their dresses and put bows in their hair."

That very next Sunday, I took a big gulp as Davis dropped us off at the little Catholic church. I grabbed Sybil's hand, tugging and pulling, and Elizabeth took Daphne. We managed to find an empty pew near the front.

Oh dear, I thought.

Sybil looked over her shoulder and peered between the people in front of her. With almost a full voice she blurted, "Why is everybody jumping up and down when they come to the benches?"

I whispered, "Dear, the benches are called pews."

"Mama, I thought that meant something was stinky."

"I'll explain later, Sybil."

"But Mama, why do they touch the ground with their knees?"

"They are honoring God."

"I don't see Him. Where is He?"

I was beginning to think this was a very bad idea. I hadn't prepared the girls for what would happen here. They were too young for Sunday school yet. With a look from the corner of my eye, I saw a white-haired woman in a gray felt hat slide into the pew on the other side of Daphne.

"Oh, Mother, am I glad to see you," I whispered, feeling relieved.

She gave me a controlled smile without letting her eyes stray from the altar. Her left gloved hand slid over to Daphne's right knee. The wriggling stopped and I noticed Daphne did a little jump as Mother tightened her grip. That took care of that!

I prayed. I prayed hard. "God, please give me the patience and compassion to raise these girls in your holy ways. Amen."

Davis picked us up after Mass. He hummed all the way home. I didn't want to ask him too much for fear of being jealous of his less-stressful and more meaningful church service. Satisfied that God would hear my prayers, I tucked my children into bed that Sunday night. Monday would be a new week of challenges.

Three years passed. I moved around in the kitchen with yet another big tummy, not as nimble as usual. Daphne and Sybil were late for the school bus. They whipped around the kitchen table at breakneck speed. Sybil darted out the back door with Daphne on her heels, just as I was taking a pot of boiling water off the stove. They crashed into me, sending the water sloshing onto Daphne's long curls. Daphne screamed hysterically. Her heavy school clothes held the water to her skin, scalding her shoulders. Sybil turned back with a huge gasp.

"Elizabeth!" I screamed.

She and I worked frantically to pull off the hot clothes and cut away the hair next to Daphne's face and neck. The chaos brought Otto and Davis running to the door. Davis grabbed Daphne and ran to his truck, with Elizabeth close behind. He drove his weeping girl and her sister to the doctor's office in town, twenty miles away, Elizabeth holding on to her sister as the truck kicked up the dust on the country road. I stood at the gate. I could only wring my hands with worry as Sybil clung to my shirt. Outwardly, I appeared calm, but with my rosary in hand, my worry penetrated my core being. I was glad to have Elizabeth, my responsible nine-year-old, riding with Davis and calming Daphne.

The skin healed, but scars of that day's chaos remained long after. In some respects, life's challenges were only starting. My stern lecture to Sybil and Daphne shook them. I had never been one to raise my voice or reprimand them in such a way. As Davis sat by my side, I knew that his "serious look" probably was what made the girls cry. They never wanted to disappoint their beloved father. I was always the one who had to say "never do that again," and so on, but his look was the memory that lasted, I'm sure.

5
Dancing With Grasshoppers

I felt like a spinning top as I went from day to day, child to child, crisis to crisis. Daphne's accident had me blaming myself for my careless actions, and the what-ifs of the event tormented me. Had I failed as a responsible mother? The days ran together in an unending blur.

By 1926, three more girls were added to our family. We were now eight. Sweet, petite, black-haired Margaret followed Daphne in 1921. She seemed to be the tireless companion of her dimpled and timid sister, Nancy, who was born in 1923. Nancy, like her sister Daphne, resembled their father. While all the time hoping for a boy, another Davis lookalike, Charlotte, arrived in 1926. My poor, dear husband lost all hope when Charlotte was born. His hopes had been so high that he had a boy's name already chosen, but John Howard was not to be. I was too overwhelmed to think about raising any more little ones. At that point, the "tagalong" Charlotte became almost like an only child, flourishing on her own. Otto and Punky the pony became her best friends during those days on the ranch.

In the 1930s, our weather patterns changed dramatically. Violent winds seemed to blow endlessly. Dust constantly swirled, and the banging swing created a continual, dull thud against the cottonwood tree. My screen doors flapped. The windows rattled, and it seemed that the wind itself had a terrifying voice of its own.

One day I turned around and saw Margaret, carrot in hand, leading Punky into the living room. *Clump, clump, clump...* went the pony's hooves on my wood floors.

"Margaret, there will be no horse in my parlor! Animals are for outdoors."

"Mama, Punky can't see. The wind is blowing too much dust. And all the grasshoppers are taking horseback rides on her." She leaned into the pony's muzzle. "Poor little Punky," she cooed.

"Margaret, I don't think you heard me. No animals inside my house! Daddy bought you girls a Shetland pony to ride in the yard." My calm was being tested, but Margaret never did much to arouse any anger in me. How would I handle this impropriety? Out the animal went, stubborn hooves dragging on my wood floor, but I couldn't help but think that Davis would have thought the incident to be sweet and quite funny. *I can't wait to tell him tonight,* I thought. Our evenings were constantly filled with children's stories of good and bad, happy and sad.

Davis only thought of what would make the girls happy and didn't consider the consequences of adding another animal-child to my already rambunctious six. I didn't want to take on conversations with a horse like I did with my daughters, but I oftentimes found myself doing just that. I certainly was going to make it clear to that animal that I was boss and my flowers were off limits. More than once I pulled Punky's mane, looked her in the eye, and said, "Leave my flowers alone, understand?"

Verbal reminders of wearing bonnets or wool stockings outside so the girls wouldn't look like farmhands were far more important to me. "Girls, driving on these rutted dirt roads and swimming in the algae-filled water tanks makes it difficult to remember that you are ladies, but some things are what they are," I would say to them.

"Mama, Sybil sneaks out to the pasture and rides Daddy's horse," tattled Daphne. "I thought you told us horseback riding on anything other than a side saddle wasn't ladylike."

"I did not!" Sybil shouted from outside, trying to cover up her off-limits adventures.

"Daphne, I can't control you all. I told you the rules, did I not? What you do beyond that is up to you. You obey or live with your own guilt, and that's all there is to it. Perfection is my expectation of you girls. I believe you know that ever so well."

Sybil sheepishly meandered into the kitchen. "Sometimes I just go out to pet the animals."

"Then why do they have saddles and bridles on? Caught you this time!" refuted Daphne, then headed for the bedroom with Sybil on her heels.

"Oh, okay, enough," I sighed with exasperation. "I've told you girls...no bickering."

And then Margaret decided she had to tell me her story.

"Nancy won't leave me alone. Sometimes she even follows me into the outhouse, too."

"Maggie, I want you and Nancy to sit on the sofa, one at each end. No touching, no talking, no giggling...do you hear?" I said, fed up with the whole bunch.

With a quick step, Elizabeth came into the kitchen's tattletale scene, holding Charlotte in her arms. She whispered, "The clouds and sky are getting dark, Mama." With more voice, she said, "Is Sybil back from riding?"

"Oh yes, she's in the bedroom with Daphne, but Daddy still seems to be in the stable."

Suddenly, Sybil came out of the bedroom when she heard that her daddy was still outside, and anxiously spoke up. "Should I get him to come in, Mama?"

"No, he'll come back when he sees the sky's color," I said.

Elizabeth blurted, "The sky is greenish black. Do you want me to stuff papers? It looks like a whopper of a dust storm. They're so scary. It will be inside, all over everything at any minute. I just know it!"

The windows began to rattle and we could hear the powdery dust hitting the panes. Elizabeth handed off Charlotte to Sybil like a football. She dashed to the bedrooms. I madly stuffed the kitchen and living room windows with paper, but it was too late. The black dust had already put a line across the lace curtains.

Sniffling came from Nancy on the sofa. "Mama, I can't see Maggie," she whined as the room darkened.

The front screen door banged against the house, causing the little ones to jump with fear.

Knowing my babies were scared but safe, I kept working. Margaret looked like a stone figure and didn't move an inch as she sat on the opposite end of the couch. Within seconds the dust had penetrated every inch of the house and clouded the air.

Elizabeth grabbed Daphne and they felt their way to the front screen door to latch it. They ran from room to room, covering the beds with dust sheets.

Sybil was bouncing a crying Charlotte in her arms while looking for Davis to make his way across the yard. Spotting his figure as he weaved through the wind, she put Charlotte down and ran to the kitchen door, leaving little Charlotte sobbing for attention. In her excitement, she opened the door too soon. The screen flew off its top hinge and slammed against the house in the wind.

"Oh no!" I yelled. The dirt funneled into the kitchen on top of the pie, in the soup, and all over the neatly set plates. My checkered tablecloth caught the wind, flapping like a flag at the start of a race. It was a race all right—a race between nature and man.

I gasped as I saw my precious husband being whipped around on the porch. Davis grabbed the back doorknob and slipped through the door, then slammed it with giant-like strength.

"Daddy, Daddy," Sybil squealed as she flung herself against the dirt-caked man. She grabbed the kitchen towel and rubbed two clean spots on his black face, enabling him to squint past the remaining sediment. Lovingly, she said, "Daddy, you look like a barn owl with two blinking eyes."

I took a look as Davis turned around. My shriek brought Nancy and Margaret from the sofa, Elizabeth and Daphne from the bedrooms, and Charlotte into the kitchen. We cried and hugged each other.

The cottonwood tree cracked and popped. We gathered together even tighter. I could feel the children shaking as the dust swirled around us, stinging our skin. A big limb from the tree combed the side of the house, its branches scraping like fingernails on a chalkboard. Another strong gust blew, and another. Then, just as quickly as it started, the wind stopped and there was silence. It left us all barely breathing with fright.

I tried to move, to take charge of my practically decimated kitchen. Frozen, my feet felt like lead, immobile, stuck to the floor. My eyes were closed. I opened them to meet my husband's dazed stare. We both teared up.

Davis said, "It's okay, I'm here."

The children didn't let out a peep and stood in silence, almost in shock.

Davis's soft but comforting voice broke the silence. "Elizabeth, can you take your sisters into the bedroom while I help your mother with the kitchen clean-up?"

"Yes, Daddy," she whispered.

Twelve little hands clasped together, then filed into the bedroom behind their sister. They sat quietly on their beds, tears rolling down their faces. Only sniffling could be heard.

"Davis, do you want to check on Otto and the horses? I can handle the kitchen for the moment," I said.

Davis silently kissed my forehead, then tugged on the back door. It squeaked and offered him a reluctant exit. He kicked away the six inches of dust that had wedged itself against the door frame.

Otto met him halfway in the yard. "Everyone okay, Mr. B?" I heard him say to Davis.

"Yes, Otto, very shaken but okay. You?"

"Okay too, but noticed the horses got pretty darn scared. Sadie kicked down her stall door, but I found her back in there when it was all over...I'll get to it in the morning. Tonight I'll make sure the barn door is secured real tight."

"Got some grub, Otto?"

"Sure enough. I had just finished my beans and hog jowls before the big blow."

"Okay, rest well then."

"You and the family too. Good night."

Later, grasshoppers joined us for a gritty supper. They hopped across the kitchen floor, then danced on the spreads as we all climbed into gritty beds. I shook my patchwork quilt, sending the irritating insects flying across the room to resume their "Mexican hat dance" moves. Disgusted, I pulled my flannel nightie tighter around me. Davis and I were lying side by side, rigid, as though we were in coffins. I knew we both had our eyes wide open in the dark. Davis, still damp from washing down his dirt-caked body, settled heavily beside me.

"Davis, what shall we do?" I whispered.

He didn't respond right away. Then, holding my hand gently, he said, "First, Cate, I want to make my children feel calm and loved." He squeezed my hand as he slowly got up to go into the girls' bedroom. I followed, and stood in the doorway to watch my husband and our girls.

He appeared at the bottom of their beds and gently played "piggy went to market" on all their toes. Heads smothered in down pillows created a reverberating, laughing hum and a feeling of love and calmness. I smiled as their laughter reached my ears.

"Oh, Daddy," Elizabeth said when it was her turn. She pulled her legs up to avoid the childlike game.

Slowly pulling them back, Davis whispered, "Everyone needs to laugh and be loved, no matter how old you are. Give me those princess toes."

Once the girls seemed to be settled, we returned to our room.

Davis whispered, "Cate, I think I even calmed the most responsible of our children."

"Good night, my children's best father," I mumbled.

He leaned over to stroke my loose, flowing hair.

I awoke with a chilly back. Davis had gotten up with the sunrise. I dressed, then scooted off toward the kitchen, trying to avoid seeing every particle of dust. My heart was heavy. My body ached.

As I reached the kitchen door, I prayed, *God, thank you for keeping my family safe, but I wish you would send in the angels to help me clean up today. Maybe it will be easier once the children are out the door and off to school.*

I entered the kitchen to find my husband already at the table.

"Davis Bennett, you are remarkable...you made your own breakfast and coffee! My tablecloth is already on the line, too." I put my arms around his stiff, broad shoulders. Leaning my head on his, I said, "I can feel that you're deep in thought, sir. What is it?"

Davis answered, "I'm going to ride up to the upper forty this morning and see how dry the land has become. That blow was mighty big last night. The dirt could be in Pennsylvania by now."

I had to drop my arms around him as he eased up from his chair. He set his coffee cup in the sink and headed out, only to turn and give me a wink. "Might not make noonday dinner today. I'll bet the DeSoto guys will have a lot of stories this morning."

Creak went the screen, still hanging by one hinge, as he left. "I'll get that door later, Cate," he called over his shoulder, and he was off.

I watched him as he got into Georgie Bell, his 1928 Model A Ford pick-up. His back was rigid as he sat behind the wheel.

— ⊲⊦ ⊲⊦ ⊲⊦ —

The narrow tires slipping over the slick ground made driving difficult and slow. Davis noticed that tumbleweeds had plastered themselves against crooked fence posts, and corn and wheat had bent down to the gray-brown, dusty land.

Cate, you just wouldn't believe this sight, Davis thought.

He opened the truck door and slid off the leather seat, dropping down to the hard earth with a jolt. "Ouch."

It was worse than he thought—parched land as far as he could see. He bent over to feel the ground. Rising back up, his eyes fell upon a pair of legs and boots. Out of nowhere, an old Mexican gentleman had appeared next to him. He had a kind face and knowing eyes, and wore a straw hat with a striped band over his gray-streaked hair. Surprised, Davis took a step back. The gentleman smiled, then told Davis things he didn't want to hear.

"Things are going to get worse, señor. Things are comin' we never seen before. The sun tells us stories I never heard before."

Before Davis could say anything, the sun shifted and the Mexican was gone. Blinking, Davis looked around, perplexed. *Am I dreaming? What just happened? Are you going crazy, Davis Bennett?* He shook his head and adjusted his hat, trying to make sense of this bizarre happening. "Did you see that, Georgie Bell?" he said, talking to his trusty Model A. Again shaking his head, he got behind the wheel and headed straight to town where coffee and "man talk" were waiting for him at the DeSoto. He pulled up in front of the impressive, cream-colored stucco hotel and stumbled as he got out of the truck, still a bit shaken by the morning's encounter.

Davis found his way to the morning coffee group, where he heard the men deep in animated conversation. He looked. He listened. Some raised concerns about the lack of rain along with the unusual dust storms, which were increasing in frequency. He joined in meekly, "My screen door blew off, along with a major limb off the cottonwood tree. My Catherine can't seem to keep the dust out, even though we stuff paper in all our windows. And if that wasn't enough, I think I have a grasshopper infestation in my ranch house."

"Saw some people nail plastic to the windows, but it is daggum expensive and hard to come by," Mr. Howard muttered.

"Gentlemen, let's talk about the big picture…rain. We've had bad runs before, but not like this," Mr. Huntington confessed.

"We can't be pessimistic. Rain will come soon," Mr. Howard said.

"Can't be naïve either, Mr. Howard."

The tension was rising. Throats were being cleared right and left.

"Mr. Huntington, some of us don't have the money to gamble, like you."

Another man joined in, "I'm down to my last draw at the bank."

"Don't you worry about the bank. We'll stick by our farmers, as we always have in the past. Why would the future be any different?" Mr. Pierce interjected.

Davis was confused. He was young. Experience was the best teacher in these parts, and Davis didn't have much. As the conversation became quieter, he reluctantly asked, "On the north side of town, has anyone seen an old Mexican with a striped hatband? He may be somebody's temporary helper."

The others shook their heads. Davis didn't want to relate his story and no one asked anything further. Davis decided to tuck the whole incident away in the back of his mind. He had to think on it. He didn't want to tell Cate, either. He didn't want to worry his wife about something unless it was something they both could take care of.

"Good day, sirs," Davis said, and stood up to leave. "Guess I'd better get back to my house, fix that screen, and cut up my cottonwood limb."

Mr. Huntington glanced out the café window and caught sight of Davis going to the general store. "Mighty fine young man, that Davis Bennett." He motioned to Sam at the front desk. "Call over to the general store and tell Bill when Mr. Davis Bennett comes in, put whatever he needs on my account."

"Right away, Mr. Huntington."

"You really do like that boy," quipped Mr. Steel. "If I need a new tractor, will you take care of me too?"

"Okay, let's settle down. A hinge or a nail is a different kettle of fish than a John Deere."

Davis pulled together a modest collection of repair items. "Bill, how much is an ax blade?" he asked the elderly store clerk.

"I gotta look it up, just a minute."

"What about just a flint stone to sharpen my old blade?"

"Always thinkin', Mr. Bennett. Not much difference though," Bill said with a smile.

"I got me a pretty good sized cottonwood branch to cut up."

"I'd go with the new blade. You need somethin' really sharp. They're tough goin'."

"May I pay you over time?"

"Just so happens that a Mr. Huntington called over and said for you to get what you need and I'm to put it on his account. What did you do to get that treatment, young man? He sure must like you."

"But...but Bill, I can't do that..." Davis sputtered.

"Look, there aren't many times in your life when you get favors. Accept them. You'll get to pay it back or do something for a young person yourself someday. Times aren't easy now. We all must swallow our pride. You should accept this goodwill if you know what's good for you."

"Yes sir, guess you're right."

Sheepishly, Davis crossed the street, guilt weighing his every step. As he climbed into his pick-up, he looked at the DeSoto's café window. Mr. Huntington stood there, nodded, and smiled. Davis nodded back with unspoken appreciation.

The truck seemed to drive itself home. Davis was dazed by the thought that a tough old bird like Mr. Huntington could have such a tender heart. *I feel like I'm becoming his adopted son. I definitely need all the help I can get. And who was that in the field with me today? Secrets I think I'll hold on to...Cate would be embarrassed if she knew I was accepting handouts from Mr. Huntington.* He saw Cate outside at the clothesline. *There's my girl, hanging clothes,* he thought with a smile.

— ⊲ ⊲ ⊲ —

I had one clothespin in my mouth and one on the line as I waved at Davis, who was coming up the driveway. I crossed my fingers that no more storms would stir up today, so that our laundry could find its way into the house before any dirt could get to it. Punky poked at my backside, then saw Davis drive up. As Davis unloaded his truck, Punky hoped for a carrot or an apple, but was disappointed when she saw only tools. Shaking her head and mane, she pawed at the ground with her hoof to show off and hopefully get a treat.

Otto appeared. "Yes, yes, you're a pretty girl," he said to the pony, and led her to the stable before he and Davis began working on the tree.

Davis said, "Cate, I'm going to fix the screen door. Any changes if I get to painting it?"

"You know, now that you mention it, I'd love a perky yellow door. Wouldn't that be welcoming? But realistically, we don't need a bill for new paint. Just use whatever you can find in your shed." As I turned and went back inside to my ironing, I thought, *Davis is such a thoughtful man. I'm so very lucky.* With that, I put extra starch in his Sunday shirt and put extra care into the hot iron's movement over the fine cotton as I listened to the men going about hammering and sawing outside.

"Otto, want to get to the tree chopping before dusk? I got us a new blade when I was in town. Look at this! Don't think I've seen a blade as sharp as this in years." He walked over to Otto and handed it to him. "You take what you can get when you first start out." He ran his hand over the dull edge of the old blade. "Not much of an edge. No wonder Owen gave me this old thing. Do you need help prying the old one off the handle?"

"No sir, just stick to your door. I'll give you a yell if I need any help."

After supper, I glanced over to see that Maggie had climbed into the rocker with Davis, and was snuggled on his lap with her big brown eyes looking up at him, studying his sunburned face. "Daddy," she started with her puzzled, little-girl look, "why is the wheat looking like it's taking a nap? And the corn tassels don't look like Goldilocks's hair anymore, either."

"You're right, sweetheart. We sure need this wind to stop blowing day after day. Rain is what we have to pray for tonight. Can you do that for me when you say your prayers before bed?"

"Sure, Daddy, I'll do anything for you."

"One more thing," Davis added. "I'm thinking about selling Punky."

All of a sudden he had *all* the girls' attention.

"Do we have to? I'll take care of her every day, I promise," said Elizabeth.

Silence.

"Well, maybe Daddy's right. Punky likes little children and needs grass," Daphne commented.

Thinking long and hard, Maggie piped in, "My legs touch the ground now…we're just too big except for maybe Nancy or Charlotte."

"I'm big too," Nancy repeated.

"Mr. Crockett still has young girls who aren't all in school yet, Daddy," suggested Elizabeth.

"Yes, Elizabeth. Don't you babysit for them from time to time? I'll stop over and offer Punky to them. They have a little money and are a nice family."

That night, Maggie's evening prayers included, "...and my daddy says we need the rain really bad. One more thing, God...please find a nice home for my Punky. Amen."

Later that week, I met Davis at the newly fixed kitchen door when he arrived home after tending the cattle. "Davis, Mr. Crockett came by. He says he'll take Punky. He offered twenty dollars and I said twenty-five, and we'll throw in the saddle and bridle. He agreed. Would you mind if I kept the five dollars in my teapot savings?"

"Now that's my little businesswoman! Gather the girls. I'll see Mr. Crockett in town tomorrow after the DeSoto, and will tell him to come before suppertime."

I rounded up our daughters at our modest kitchen table. "Girls, we are all going to say good-bye to Punky on Thursday after school. You can choose her good-bye gifts. I'll have my wooden bowl filled with carrots and apples."

Nods acknowledged my announcement, but when Thursday afternoon arrived I perceived a less-than-enthusiastic reception to Punky's going-away party. Elizabeth and Daphne picked apples reluctantly. Punky pawed her hoof with excitement as she was handed the treats.

Sybil wanted to lead her around the yard and talk to her longtime friend. "We're going to miss how you met us at the fence when we got off the school bus. I know you just wanted a treat, but I pretended you were my stallion, waiting to take me off to faraway places. Remember when I told you we were going to the most beautiful mountains with freshwater streams? You could drink the cold water and I would lie in the flowery meadows. Remember? Oh, Punky, you be good for those Crockett girls. Miss you..."

Looking about, I noticed that I was missing one of my little ones. "Charlotte, why are you hiding behind the tree?" I saw that she was crying. "Don't worry, you can meet Mr. Crockett and see what a nice man he is. Maybe he'll bring one of his children and you can meet them.

You'll see...Punky will be very happy with little children around her again."

"Will they braid her mane? Can I go see her sometime? May I give her a carrot now?"

"Sure, sweetheart. The bowl is on the kitchen table."

I spotted four legs under the waving laundry. "Nancy and Maggie, Mr. Crockett will be here soon."

"Mama, can you put some carrots in a bag for Punky? She'll be hungry later," Maggie called out.

"Don't you want to come say good-bye?"

"We're not ready yet. Can Daddy take us over to say good-bye? We want to sing Punky a good-bye song."

"Here I come," Davis called. "What do you think we should sing, girls?"

"'In the Sweet Bye and Bye' would be good, Daddy," offered Maggie.

Nancy nodded shyly and the good-bye song began with intermittent sniffling.

A truck rolled up. We bunched into a small group, and after meeting Mr. Crockett, he loaded Punky into the truck and headed off to Punky's new home. We waved good-bye at the gate. Davis's eyes were teary, as were mine, and each and every girl's, as well. We didn't expect so much emotion. Otto, who had been standing by the stable door, came out and closed the gate. I could detect a lump in his throat, too. He had one of those large Adam's apples, and when he was stressed it would visibly move up and down in his throat. Now was one of those times.

Davis pulled the twenty-five dollars out of his pocket and handed me five dollars. I barely smiled over my negotiated deal as I realized that getting money for something we loved wasn't necessarily going to make us happy.

Supper was solemn that night, not that I expected much chitter-chatter. "I'm proud of you girls," I finally remarked. "That was a very hard thing you did today. You all behaved like perfect ladies."

Pent-up crying flooded the silent atmosphere. Sybil, Nancy, and Charlotte scattered to the bedroom and slammed the door behind them. Instinctively, I started to rise from my chair.

"Leave them be, Cate," Davis said and patted my hand. "Sometimes we have to do what we have to do. Next week I plan to drive the last of my herd to Kansas before the dust wraps itself around everything. That will be *my* week of great remorse."

When Sunday morning came around, I cheerily spoke up, "Davis, I think we need to take a drive down to Aunt Isabel's and Aunt Mary's. Twenty miles isn't so far and it might do us all a world of good."

Davis nodded, then went outside and pulled the car around. "Climb in, everyone. We're going on an adventure."

"Oh Mama, I love going places. This will be such fun," enthused Daphne.

"You're right, Daphne. You climb in after Maggie, and Elizabeth, you take the middle seat. Sybil, you get in on the right side."

"I'm so glad to be going. I've been wanting to talk to Aunt Isabel about a creative project. I'm bored and she mentioned painting porcelain," Sybil said.

"You can't paint. You're a pretender, Sybil," Daphne chided.

"Daphne, enough," I scolded.

"Mama, do I have to sit next to her? She's Miss Know-it-All," Margaret complained.

"Margaret, it's only for a few miles."

Nancy spoke up, "I'll sit next to Daphne. She doesn't bother me. That is, if you sit on the other side next to me and hold my hand, Margaret."

"Young ladies—and that means you, Nancy—you settle it. I'll be in the front holding Charlotte."

Davis said nothing. He was listening to the motor and focusing on the road.

The bumpy drive gave lots of opportunities for the girls to give exaggerated "jump-ups" in their seats. Laughter ensued, making the trip feel shorter.

"I see it. I see the white picket fence!" shouted Nancy as we approached the house.

"Me too," said Charlotte.

Daphne rolled her eyes.

"Oh Davis, look at those roses. Our winds are too harsh. At least Punky won't be chewing on them any longer. My pink ones give only a little show to my garden."

The two spinsters stood at the garden gate, grinning as they welcomed their precious nieces. As the girls filed into the house, Aunt Isabel said, "Easy girls, I just swept the parlor."

Aunt Mary chimed in, "Can I get anyone some iced tea and shortbread?"

The tiny white Victorian home fascinated the girls. It was like a mini-museum of finery. Daphne stood by the collection of colored glasses that framed the window, turning each glass to admire its design. Sybil had scooted into the next room with Aunt Isabel to examine the painted porcelain plates.

"Sybil, you would be a perfect candidate for painting. I could buy you a plate or two and you could use my paints," Aunt Isabel offered.

"How long does it take? What happens if I make a mistake?"

"Now child, that is part of the learning process. I know you will be wonderful. You are already talented. The thing that takes time is the shipping of the plates off to be fired, which is a process done in high-temperature ovens."

"Like in our kitchen?"

"No, dear. Much hotter than that."

I walked in to see what was keeping Isabel and Sybil. Both were smiling big grins. The sight of seeing Sybil so happy was a joy.

Sybil always enjoyed her horseback riding, much to my dismay. I never did encourage things that didn't reflect ladylike actions. I didn't want my daughters to grow up to be ranch hands. Art and painting were acceptable pastimes, but I'm afraid I never had much time to encourage even that. Aunt Isabel was perfect for this role. Sybil's creativity needed to be directed in a positive channel, rather than being a scary, goblin tease to all her sisters. School bored her, and aside from the boys, it wasn't the happiest of her experiences. The porcelain painting project was uniquely Sybil's.

"What are you two up to?" I said.

"Catherine, I think I've found someone to paint porcelain with me! Right, Sybil?"

As she looked out the bay window, Sybil couldn't help but say, "Daphne is smelling your roses and hiding the broken ones behind the bushes so she doesn't get in trouble."

"I'll take care of it, dear. Go sit with your father, Sybil," Aunt Isabel said.

Davis became restless in his seat. The grass was still as he glanced outside. Leaning over in the stiff Victorian chair, he whispered, "Elizabeth, gather your sisters, quick. I think we're in for a big one. Look yonder. The big greenish-black clouds are forming in the distance."

"What is going on?" I asked.

Davis nodded in the storm's direction.

I looked outside and my heart fell. "Guess we're going."

Elizabeth herded her sisters into the front room to say good-bye to their great-aunts, and with that, the girls ran to the car, followed by Davis.

I hugged my nervous aunts as I raced to join my family, and within minutes, we were off.

The winds picked up anything that was loose. Tumbleweeds bounced off the windshield and car hood. Davis struggled to see the road in the thickening dust as the wind roared past us.

"I want Elizabeth on my left running board, and Margaret on my right—the road is disappearing in front of my eyes!" Davis yelled. "Girls, I need you to keep me in the middle."

I realized that if we ran off the road, the tires could get buried in a ditch and we'd be stuck. We stopped and Elizabeth and Margaret got out and stood on their respective running boards, holding on to the windows with one hand and shielding their eyes with the other. Their skirts swished around their legs and the dust stung their skin. As Davis drove, they shouted out, "Stay left!" "Stay right!" every few feet. The tires hugged the almost invisible road.

Davis bellowed, "Girls, you're doing a perfect job! Keep me steady!"

Within an hour, we rounded the fence and rumbled through our gate. Elizabeth and Margaret jumped off the running boards immediately. Coughing and wheezing, they ran inside for a drink of water.

"Oh, children," I groaned as the dirt whipped through the air. "I left my bedroom window open. My yeast bread is on the stove and the laundry is flapping on the line." I jumped out of the car, ran to the clothesline, and began to gather the dirt-plastered clothes, which were still damp and now caked with sticky black dirt. "Shut our bedroom windows and shake the sand off the spread, Sybil!" I yelled through the wind as everyone tumbled out of the car.

As usual, Elizabeth flew into action. "I'll get the paper and stuff the windows!"

I counted heads as everyone ran for the house. We were all accounted for. It was all I could do to drag the laundry toward the kitchen, but Davis helped me, and soon we were sitting around the kitchen table. We managed to eat our vegetable soup and gritty bread.

At bedtime, I heard the little ones whimper as they lay in sandpaper-like sheets. The older girls admitted to not being so grown up.

Sybil said, "Were you scared riding on that running board, Elizabeth? I mean, *really* scared?"

"I thought I might die," Elizabeth admitted.

The fear fell asleep with each of us. The memory remained forever.

The next morning, I had to prod the girls off to school. Elizabeth had already gone to the bus stop, but Daphne and Sybil were late. I could hear their conversation as they walked out the door.

"Elizabeth, last night's memories are too fresh. After all, it could all happen again at a moment's notice today, while we're in school," remarked a serious Daphne.

"What would happen without Mama and Daddy?" asked Maggie as she listened to the older girls' comments. "I'm bringing my prayer book and my rosary, just in case."

"Oh Maggie, if it's time for us to go, we'll be taken," Daphne chided.

"Daphne, you don't know."

"Go? Where are we going? I don't want to go anywhere," poor little Nancy whispered.

I sat almost numb at the kitchen table as Davis looked at me blankly. Otto banged on the door. "Morning, Catherine. You folks okay? How can I help today? Mr. Bennett, I know you probably don't really want to know what damage that storm did yesterday."

Davis kept staring at me as he replied, "Reckon you're right, Otto, but let's get going."

He got up and went outside. I followed him to the back door.

"Cate, don't look for us at the noon meal today," he called over his shoulder. He stopped and returned to me at the door. "Don't worry," he said softly as he held my face in his hands. "I'll figure out something."

I nodded, giving him my complete trust. Then he kissed me gently.

— ⊲. ⊲. ⊲. —

Davis, Otto, and the horses lumbered out the gate. Davis's eyes scanned the raped landscape. They came across clusters of ravaged cattle, piled in small mounds. He and Otto dismounted and started pulling apart the tangled masses. He found a surviving calf or two, only to have them look up at him and drop dead in his lap. His chest heaved. Immobile, he sat while Otto started digging a pit in which to bury the poor animals. Later, he did rescue some of the livestock that had roamed over buried or broken fences.

"Otto, I spot about ten near that brush. Come on, quick! I'll ride over to the water tank and make sure I can get water for them. Corral them when I give you the signal." These were the lucky ones. The others were buried. An accounting at the end of the day left Davis estimating that half his herd had succumbed to that storm of 1931.

– 4. 4. 4. –

Daphne came home from school. "Mama, Mama! Phyllis's family lost their outhouse and J.C.'s truck turned over in that terrible storm. I can't believe all the stories we heard in our classroom. The teacher had to change the subject because some of the kids started to cry. Then she played dance music…" Her words trailed off as she went into the bedroom.

"Mama, may I talk to you?" Elizabeth said.

"Of course, Elizabeth."

Quietly and seriously, she began, "This Dust Bowl of ours is filling my head with doom and gloom. All I can think of is, will we die covered in black or red sand, to be found fifty years from now as skeletons holding hands with each other? I'm afraid all our breath will be taken away by pneumonia. I'm ready to get an education and go to college. I don't want what happened to you to happen to me. You had to take care of brothers. While I love my sisters, I don't want to be stuck taking care of them the rest of my life. I want more. Do you hear me, Mama? I don't want my sisters to die and be lined up in white starched dresses in pine caskets, either."

"Elizabeth, I think you're way too worked up today. Your daddy would never, *ever* let that happen to you or your sisters. We're thinking of a plan and everything will turn around, you'll see."

It seemed that Davis and I couldn't act fast enough. The grass became dryer and the threat of fire became a reality.

A few days later, Davis had just come in from the day's work when an afternoon storm began raging in the direction of our planted field. "Cate, did you hear that lightning crack?" he said to me, then yelled out the door to Otto, "Saddle up! We have some riding to do through this storm. We can't lose this crop."

Davis was concerned that our money was dwindling fast. "Just give me a sign, God. We need your help—fast," I heard him mutter under his breath.

I nervously looked out the window as Davis and Otto headed out.

The winds blew on and off for the next four hours. I saw a red, glowing thread stretching across the horizon. A fire! I called to the girls, "Children, bedtime."

"I have to go to the bathroom," winced Nancy.

"We'll have to use the chamber pot tonight. It's too dangerous out there."

The vision of the fire stayed with me the entire night as I lay in bed with eyes wide, staring at the ceiling beams.

Sybil came into the kitchen with the dawn's light. "Mama, I have to go find Daddy and Otto."

"Sybil, we don't know where they are."

Speaking in a determined tone, she said, "I'll follow the smoke. I promise I'll stay on the road till I see them."

With that, she grabbed Davis's extra hat and proceeded outside, across the sand, and to the gate. "I wish I had Punky," I heard her mumble to herself. "She wasn't fast, but I could save some walking."

I shook my head. There was no way I could ever change Sybil's mind.

I managed to feed the other girls the oatmeal I had cooked. I peered out the window so many times that the cereal came close to being a total loss. No way to start my day, for sure.

The school bus driver gave me a report. "Pretty bad fire down the way, Mrs. Bennett. Saw Mr. Davis and a few others coming a mile back. Someone was riding double. Hope a horse wasn't lost too."

"Thank you, Ruby, I'm so relieved. Sybil must have doubled up with her dad. She went out at dawn looking for him."

The girls had lined up in the bus aisle to hear the news. Smiling when they heard the report of their father, they continued to their seats. Maggie leaned over to the boy next to her. "My daddy was out there last night," she said with an air of importance.

"Liar, liar, pants on fire. Nobody could live through that fire."

Maggie's eyes teared up. She became silent at the thought that someone would not believe such a story, especially coming from Margaret Bennett.

When I saw Davis, Otto, and Sybil coming through the gate, a sigh of relief poured out of me. "Davis, you're a sight...honey, black dirt is dripping off you from your perspiration," I said, and glanced over to see Sybil leading her father's horse, behind Otto, to the stable.

"Cate, we were mighty lucky. The fire stopped just fifty yards short of our wheat crop. I think most of it will survive. I know you probably don't want to hear this, but Sybil worked like a man, handing bucket after bucket down the water line. She sure helped save our grain."

Sybil stood in the doorway, just as black as Davis. She grinned when she heard her father's words. "I told you I'd find Daddy, Mama. I did a good job, too."

As the two of them walked to the bedrooms, I called out, "Give me those smoke-filled clothes. I'll get to washing them this morning."

Clean as a whistle, Davis returned to the kitchen. "Cate, I think I still have time to meet the men at the DeSoto. I have to hear if there was any more damage last night."

— ⊲. ⊲. ⊲. —

As Davis walked into the hotel, an unusual hush prevailed over the lobby.

"Did you hear?" Sam, the desk clerk, asked. "One of last night's hotel guests committed suicide. The coroner is upstairs now. Times are real tough, Davis. The stock market took a bad turn, too. Banks are closing. Someone just north said a fire raged for fourteen hours, completely frying three hundred acres of planted wheat." He cleared his throat after the dissertation of all the news.

"Yes, Sam, I was helping with the fire all night. It came mighty close to my land, too. We were blessed." Davis glanced into the café. The men had dispersed early. No wonder. Checking on the banks, no doubt.

"Hey Davis, I poured you some coffee," the waitress called.

"Don't think it will taste right today."

"You're not turning sissy on us, are you?"

Stepping away, Davis gave a weak smile and pulled three

grasshoppers off his hat. He passed a small crowd. Deep in thought, he clenched his teeth tighter and tighter. Davis knew he and Cate had a big decision to make. He hoped that California was the right place for their family. His brother Wyatt had encouraged him that it seemed to be a safe idea. At last, Davis was convinced. It was 1932. Time to go.

6
Daddy's Gone, But California Loves Me

The coffee pot lid did a *clink*. I was dreading this day; the day I would leave my home and my husband. Feeding us all a hearty chicken soup the night before didn't seem to help any of us sleep a wink. Full tummies didn't outweigh our racing minds.

The back door opened and closed, opened and closed, as Davis and Otto loaded the luggage into the car's trunk. The sounds of oatmeal bowls being stacked in the kitchen sink echoed in the otherwise quiet room. I could see eyes full of emotion, and sadness and fear building behind the children's innocent faces. Davis could feel my body trembling as I kissed him good-bye.

"Believe me, Cate, I'll be there before you have time to miss me. You'll be so—"

I pressed my finger up to his lips in midsentence. My strength was waning. There I was, taking myself and our children away from my dear Davis. I had to rush off to stand by the car. My heart would break if I saw each child say good-bye. Standing there, my gaze was distracted by the childlike ghost twisting and turning on the swing. Within minutes the life of this close-knit family would be fractured as three-fourths of us left for California.

I was grateful for Otto's offer to drive me and the girls. It gave me the added support I needed to make this arduous journey. The tears dried after a few days, but the slightest mention of "Daddy" sent ripples of tears inching slowly down the girls' faces—especially Sybil and Charlotte.

Surprisingly, the dust followed us almost the entire first day, but somehow, the moisture generated by all our sadness seemed to hold the dryness at bay. Otto's pursed lips and steel-like grip on the huge Buick's wheel reminded me that with fortitude, you could do anything.

I leaned over to say, "Otto, thank you for helping out. Thank you for driving us all this way."

"You and Mr. B have been so welcoming and kind to me, I'd do anything you would ever ask."

I sat back and remembered the sight of Davis's contagious smile and how his strong arms waved good-bye to us as we started our journey to California. Between Otto and Davis, I had a real, deep-down belief that everything was going to be okay. It was as though I could feel Davis's energy sitting next to me, providing me comfort for the long journey to California.

Otto took charge when he sensed I needed help with the squirming, rambunctious girls. Just clearing his throat seemed to color the situation and threw out an air of "I mean business."

Calmness took over as the days rolled by. Skies became clearer, and the rays of the sun were like little shawls around our shoulders. The warmth encouraged us in a nurturing fashion. As we left the tumbleweeds and cottonwoods of Texas, I asked the girls if they could see the roads change from dirt into flat-iron asphalt. Several days later, Glendale, California, welcomed us with its beauty.

"Look! We're seeing a whole new world...green pines and palms... rose bushes and bougainvillea..." I pointed out.

The girls' faces lit up as if they were seeing a fresh new watercolor painting evolve right before their eyes.

Otto spoke up, "Catherine, I think I will get out at the rooming house Wyatt recommended. You girls can drive on and find Wyatt and your new house. You might need some private time between you."

"Otto, you're our family too," I said.

"No, Miss Catherine, this is going to be a big adjustment for everyone. I'll be just around the corner if you need me."

We pulled up to the rooming house and Otto got out with a wave and a smile.

"Elizabeth dear, would you like to drive?" I said. "It's only a few blocks. Look at all the pink, red, and purple bougainvillea covering the gates...and oh...on the side of that peach-colored house. I don't think I've ever seen such beauty. You certainly don't need your wool stockings or coats here!"

Elizabeth took over behind the wheel and we pulled back out into the street.

Little Charlotte asked, "Mama, where are we? Are we still in America?"

The forever Miss Know-it-all Daphne chimed in, "Of course we are! We're in sunny California, home of movie stars and Hollywood. Daddy was right. We'll be just fine here."

"He said he would come out between plantings, and I want to show him all around," Sybil interrupted.

With Wyatt's directions in my hand, I directed Elizabeth straight to Wyatt's driveway. I barely said, "Here we are," before the front door swung open and half the girls were out of the car and running into their uncle's arms. With broad smiles and hugs so strong, the gathering was almost overwhelming.

"It was a long, long trip but I'm proud of my girls," I remarked to Wyatt and his wife, Maude. As I approached the door, I added, "I'm impressed, Maude. You must have had the table set for days in anticipation of our arrival."

It seemed that within minutes a magic wand had produced a ham, fried chicken, greens, mashed potatoes, and lots and lots of fruits we had never seen, let alone trusted. Pies from the backyard peach tree stood at attention on the buffet.

"Mama, Aunt Maude, can we take a piece of this good peach pie to Otto?" Nancy thoughtfully asked.

"Yes, yes! He did such a good job driving for us," joined in the always polite and obedient Maggie.

"I wanna go, too!" Charlotte jumped up to join them.

"Wyatt, is it safe for them to go around the corner to the rooming house?" I asked.

"Sure, we're like a small town in this neighborhood. California is big, but we have small-town pockets."

The girls scampered out, pie in hand, as I called behind them, "Got the piece of paper with the house number on it?"

"Oh, yes ma'am," Maggie answered back.

"Hurry back, we need to get to our new house..."

"Hold my hand, Maggie," shy and timid Nancy gestured.

"Charlotte too," I added as they hurried down the sidewalk.

— ♩ ♩ ♩ —

"So many flowers...so much green grass. Look at all those children playing!" Nancy almost shouted, coming out of her shell.

A little blond girl came over to them. "Where ya going? Where ya from?"

"We have a very important family friend at the rooming house over there," Margaret responded with kind authority.

Charlotte said, "We're from Texas."

"Oh, there are so many people coming from Texas."

"Daddy's still there, but he's coming soon, " Nancy added.

"Well, see you around. Maybe at school. It starts next week. What grade are you?" the girl asked, looking back at Maggie.

Charlotte decided she wanted to brag. "I'll be in first grade this year!"

Winking at Maggie, the girl responded, "Okay, bye!"

The girls approached the rooming house and knocked on the door.

"Is Mr. Otto here?" chimed the three girls when a large, kind-looking woman answered.

"Sure enough," she answered. "What you got there?"

"Peach pie. Our Aunt Maude made it this morning."

"He must be a very lucky man to have three girls bring him such a present! Let me get him a fork and call him to come down for you."

Slightly dazed from sleep, Otto appeared in his stocking feet. "Girls, did you get lost?"

"No, Otto, we've got a surprise for you." Maggie presented the warm peach pie.

"I think I'm going to cry! I'm going to miss y'all so much." He sat himself down at Mrs. Young's dining table, hardly taking a breath between bites. "Yep, mighty good! You going to learn how to bake like this when you get older, Charlotte?"

She nodded proudly at her best ranch friend. The girls said goodbye to Otto, and Charlotte skipped ahead of Nancy and Maggie all the way back to Uncle Wyatt's, where Maude was waiting for them.

"Oh, there you girls are! Your uncle took your mama and your sisters over to your very own new house. Come on, I'll show you. It's only one street over, on Oakdale."

On the walk over, Charlotte kept skipping and Maggie walked ladylike, holding hands with Nancy behind Maude.

— 4 4 4 —

"Mama," Nancy called out as the girls arrived with Aunt Maude. "This house has a front porch! Look, I can hide behind the big columns when Sybil and Daphne try to tease me."

I was thrilled. "Wyatt, this living room is big enough for all my family...and the dining room has so much light for homework and sewing. I'm sure we'll have papers covering the whole table. You know, Elizabeth is now in college, Daphne and Sybil are in high school, and the others in grade school. I have to get over to register them first thing tomorrow," I said as I looked around.

"Oh gee, Catherine, I wanted to take them to see the zoo and to stick their toes in the ocean at Coronado Beach. I have only a few days off before I go back to my next train run. So how about if I take them and you and Maude can find the schools?"

"Uncle Wyatt, you have the best ideas," called Daphne from the bedroom. "I want the single bed," she added.

"Gladly, my dear," Sybil teased as she hung her clothes in the closet next to Elizabeth. "You are such a twister and turner, you take it!" She turned to Elizabeth. "You, Elizabeth, are like a rock. I'll sleep with you any day."

"Where do I sleep?" whined Nancy.

Margaret called down from a loft with two beds and a pull-down. "Up here! It's peachy keen!"

"Everything all right, girls?" I called up.

"Oh, I love it!" Elizabeth responded.

"Well, I love this kitchen," I added. "Maude, isn't this black-and-white floor the cat's meow? And the six-burner stove, inside water, and a corner for my sewing machine. Wyatt, thank you for finding such a homey house for us. I can't wait for Davis to see this."

Silently, I wandered into my bedroom in the back. I turned around quickly, and my rosary beads fell from my pocket. Wyatt noticed with a smile and picked them up for me. "God helped me find this place. Guess from the sound of it, your prayers were answered too."

"Thank you and Maude so much. You are simply the *best* in-laws!" I reached out and squeezed their hands.

"Need us anymore, dear?" Maude responded warmly.

"No, we're fine, thank you again," I said as Wyatt and Maude departed.

"Everybody settle in. Uncle Wyatt will be here at 9:00 a.m. He said to be sure to bring a towel for the beach."

After closets were filled and beds made, it was off to bed for my girls.

"Good night, girls," I called out.

"Night, Mama," echoed their voices from the bedrooms.

I was too tired to start a letter to Davis that night, so I mentally said a few words to him. *We made it, dear! Your energy next to me in the car helped me so much. Thank you. Thank you, God. We're going to be just fine, just like you said, Davis.* Then I dozed heavily into the night.

The next day, with the girls off with their Uncle Wyatt and after touring the schools with Maude, I began my letter to Davis.

Dearest Davis,

The schools are so impressive, dear. Open, sprawling classrooms and a very organized curriculum. I can see Elizabeth, Daphne,

Margaret, and Charlotte thriving. Well, who knows—Sybil and Nancy might get stimulated if the teacher is engaging.

Wyatt took the girls to the ocean at Coronado and the big San Diego Zoo. Here they come now, jabber, jabber. I'll tell you what they said later. I'll take a break from writing now, so I can hear about their day.

I picked up again after the girls and Wyatt had regaled me with their stories.

Wyatt almost couldn't stop laughing as he told me stories of Sybil and Nancy making faces at the monkeys and apes. Nancy threw a banana at one ape and he immediately came over, flirting and fluttering his eyes at her. Sybil had their attention and showed them back flips right there outside the cage. Daphne teased Sybil unmercifully, calling her names and saying how she knew Sybil was off her rocker. Guess you have to have a sense of humor to communicate with those creatures. Sybil certainly does.

Oh, Davis, Daphne said she went into the ocean up to her knees. She ran back in and took Charlotte and Margaret by the hand out into the surf too. Can you imagine the surf crashing and the loud giggles of the girls? Nancy didn't want to get wet. Never mind. Some things don't change. Elizabeth sat with Wyatt on the beach, enjoying the fresh air, and Sybil had her sketchbook, so she showed me some charming sketches of the children, waves, and rocks. The drawings are quite good.

Wyatt said they did some picture taking and he used a whole roll on just the girls. I'm excited to see the pictures and to have them for you when you come…the house, the yard, the town…so much to show you.

Wyatt says he has a special surprise for us all next week. He told me the battleship USS Texas is coming into port. Getting an invitation for a tour is quite difficult, but he's giving it his best shot. Wouldn't that be exciting if it happens? Nothing is too much for him to do for us. You have an extremely kind brother. He's a lot of fun too!

Thank you, dear Davis, for the opportunity for us to come to California. You are so selfless.
I love you with all my heart.
Your adoring wife,
Cate

When Maggie and Nancy saw that I was writing to their daddy, they insisted on writing too.

Dear Daddy,
I picked some flowers for you today. Wish you were here. I love my feather pillow and my own soft bed.
Love,
Maggie

Me too.
Love,
Nancy

The horn of the *USS Texas* bellowed from its immense smokestacks as it pulled into San Diego Harbor. The most impressive ship of the U.S. fleet caught everyone's attention. All conversations centered around her. Wyatt's letter requesting a private VIP tour had worked somehow. Wyatt Bennett of Dallam County, Twist Junction, Texas, sounded so official that we were mistaken for one of the Texas visiting senators and his family. I wrote Davis on the day of the tour.

Dear Davis,
Wyatt's shiny big Oldsmobile was escorted onto the base with all flags at attention. You should have seen the men lined up on the decks, stiff as boards, in full dress whites. Impressed beyond belief, we filed past the captain, officers, and crew. Elizabeth, Sybil, and Daphne got giggly as they surveyed the handsome lineup. I think I even detected a wink or two from Sybil. Winking back were thousands of sets of eyes as they followed the fine, handsome "senator" and the girls. You

would have enjoyed laughing at Wyatt. He was the perfect senator! The girls were perfect in their draped sheath dresses, large-brimmed hats, and tapered high heels. Now, don't get jealous, but even my new crimped hairdo and baby blues still seemed to catch a look or two. What a day in our memory book!

Our life has not been one of great wealth or notoriety, but Mr. Bennett, we've done a darn good job raising our family to be well mannered and beautiful enough to turn any man's eye. This was certainly one day when my teaching of perfection paid off. Hoots and whistles followed us down the gangplank. I noticed that being in the public eye didn't seem to daunt even Nancy.

I can almost see you grinning from ear to ear as you read this.

Lovingly,
Cate

During the second week, I wrote another letter to Davis.

Dearest Davis,

Otto has been most helpful. I hate to see him go tomorrow. I've been practicing how to drive, how to have the old Buick filled with gas, and all the things you men know so well. He has been a great teacher and chauffeur. He showed the girls where their schools are. I think everyone is comfortable as to which way to walk. And I found the Catholic church on one of my driving outings.

Things seem to be coming together, but I can clearly see it takes two to raise all these girls. We all miss your love and support. I think Otto would agree that it's pretty tough around here. He even said, "Miss Catherine, I'll raise calves any day over trying to keep up with your girls!" I laughed, but he was right. When do you think you can come?

I have an idea, honey. When you come, do you think you could bring Mother Connelly? I have a little savings still in my teapot and I think that might cover her train ticket.

I'm going to miss Otto. His support has meant the world to me. But I know he misses you and the open range. California is no place for him.

Other news... Wyatt took the girls and me on another adventure. He let Daphne and Sybil practice driving on the highway, but I still don't want Daphne backing out of the driveway. She almost took out the largest palm tree in our yard today. Otto promises to fix the tire marks in the yard. God bless him. Wyatt just shut his eyes!

Oh, Davis...another thing...you should see the forest of Big Sur. More Kodaking. While walking among the redwoods I caught Sybil pretending to be Billy Goat Gruff, jumping out to scare Nancy, Margaret, and Charlotte. Frightened, Nancy cried, but recovered and pretended to be Snow White with her cape and basket. I had to tell her, "Nancy, you have the most imagination of us all."

The fresh air is doing us a world of good, with no hay fever symptoms for Margaret and the older girls. I'm pleased that we can avoid the cost of summer camp in Colorado this year. Little blessings I thank God for each day.

As always, sending my love,
Cate
PS: The girls want to say hello without me seeing their notes.

Dear Daddy,
California is my kind of place. So much glamour here. I don't miss the dust one bit! I have missed you very much. My jokes and games aren't nearly as funny without you. I'm drawing a lot and I'm happy.

Love,
Sybil

Dear Daddy,
Can you come soon? I have three new friends at school. It is pretty. There are pink and yellow flowers outside.
Nancy

Daddy,
Otto leaves tomorrow. I will miss him. Come to see me. Can you bring the dog?
Charlotte

A few weeks later, Wyatt and I picked up Davis and my mother at the train station. People were so busy bustling around the open-air platform that we practically walked right past my tiny little mother.

"Mrs. Connelly. Howdy! Did you drop Davis out the window somewhere along the way?" Wyatt said when he recognized her.

"I had him get the luggage so I would have a minute with my daughter. Once he appears, I'll be invisible to Catherine," she winked.

"Oh, Mother!" I said.

And then, sure enough, there came Davis, looking like a porter, bags under his arms and two in his hands. I ran to him and he dropped everything, picked me up, and twirled me around in the middle of the multitudes. Wyatt quickly grabbed a couple of bags and escorted Mother down the long, concrete platform while we became completely absorbed in each other's arms.

When we arrived at the house, it was pandemonium. Daddy was home! After chatting Davis's ears off and hugging him unmercifully, each girl went over to Grandmother Connelly. Less exuberantly, she got a kiss on the cheek or a squeeze of her hand. She smiled, understanding full well who was top dog.

Charlotte enthusiastically showed her upstairs to their "secret" double bed. "Look, Grandmother. We have a bed in the wall. I'll take the inside. Is that okay?"

"Oh, yes dear. I get up sometimes in the night and can help your mother early in the mornings without disturbing you. Thank you for sharing. You are such a sweet girl."

"You can put your bag on my chair, too."

"Maybe you would like to be the first to see what I brought you…a corncob doll from your daddy's crop. Your Aunt Polly gave me the checkered fabric for the skirt and scarf. She got some new kitchen curtains and thought of you."

"Did she send any cookies?

"I think your daddy has those."

"Really?" With that, Charlotte, the youngest and the smallest, was down the steps and out the door to the front porch, where the other adults sipped their iced teas.

"Daddy, Daddy! Grandmother Connelly said you have some cookies from Aunt Polly!" With that, like bees to honey, the others formed a tight circle around his rough leather satchel.

Charlotte, almost getting elbowed out, had Davis's support. "Charlotte was first; she found out about the sugar cookies," he said.

I blinked as half the box was emptied in seconds, almost before I could offer Wyatt his sister Polly's favorite family treat.

Davis spoke in a somber tone. "Wyatt, it's amazing that Polly still does this baking. She doesn't have much money for the sugar. Times are tough. She's going to take on another job at the post office. School is only a half day now. Everyone needs the children to help out either in the fields or with odd jobs around town. The granary is full with no one to buy. The land values have plunged. Mr. Dawson's rangeland of 160 acres I believe was originally worth about $2,500; now it has been appraised at $125. Mine is at least working land. Hey, do you have any money in the First National Bank of Twist Junction? Owen had a small amount in it. The bank closed its doors. It shocked everybody—$350,000, gone! Wyatt, you're lucky you settled out here. Doggone lucky. I'm okay, not great, but okay. Catherine has helped manage our money. Just when I think things are really bad, she pops out her secret 'teapot fund.' That's how we brought Mother Connelly out. She's amazing, that wife of mine."

Shaking his head with every comment, Wyatt said, "How long you staying, Davis?"

"Just long enough so Cate will be sad to see me go. In a few weeks, I'll head back. I can't stay away too long. Every day something changes. Storms are still really bad. Otto is there alone, caring for our two horses. We have to keep them in the stable most of the time so that daggum dust doesn't cake in their eyes and ears. It would break your heart to see the poor animals. I'd stay here but I don't want to lose everything. And I have an obligation to Otto. We're a team. You have to keep things going as best you can. We've worked too hard and all our money is tied up in our little ranch. If I'm lucky, I'll squeeze a small crop in and get some money if I sell it locally for feed. Owen and I are working so hard. He doesn't say anything, but I think he has more at stake. The land lingers with more unplantable sections. The only one doing fine seems to be Miss Scarlett's on the other side of town. Men are so down, that's the only place they can raise their spirits. When I was with my DeSoto Hotel men's group, I saw pearls drop out of Mr. Howard's pocket. A few days later, I saw Miss Scarlett strutting down the street wearing those very pearls. I think I was the only one to see them. Mr. Howard clearly started to bend over, coughing to cover it up. No one caught on, I'm sure. It's doggone tough. The opera house has boarded up its doors too. Shelves are empty at Swearingen Grocery."

Wyatt shook his head. "Hmm. I had no idea. Think Twist Junction can hang on?"

"Well, people have invested so much into the train's crossroads, it will be the savior I think. The town fathers keep meeting and try to stay upbeat, but they worry. They're always dashing off to take care of one crisis or another. I think they leave the conversations when a subject gets too tender, if you know what I mean. I'm young and I don't have as much to lose, so I observe the nervous tapping of fingers on the table. Even Mr. Huntington doesn't flash his hundred-dollar bills around anymore. Different times..."

After settling the girls into evening homework and activities, I returned to the men's grim conversation. I finally spoke up. "Are many people leaving?"

"Oh, Cate, the newspaper predicts the population could drop to 500. It's the biggest mass exodus ever recorded in this part of the country. Oklahoma has it worse, but I'm glad you're here, little lady. The storms are so frequent, you can hardly breathe from one to the next...lots of dust pneumonia. But Otto and I are extremely careful. We stay in the big house mostly, with rags in the windows all the time."

"Who cooks?"

"Now that's where you are truly missed. We dabble, but it's only one step up from the cattle drive. But my cornbread is mighty good."

"How are we ever going to go back home? I can't see you, Davis Bennett, staying in California. You're not your brother Wyatt."

Wyatt chuckled. "Think it's time for me to go."

"Okay, Mister City Man. Thanks for the pick-up," Davis teased.

Mother had prepared a light supper from refrigerator leftovers. Being so glad to see Davis, no one even noticed what we were eating. After our last bites, Davis had a girl on each knee and the rest hovering around his sides and shoulders. Practically everyone talked at once, and there was a tiff or two as to who would be next to talk Daddy's ear off. I smiled at the sight of my family being together once again.

Mother cleaned up the dishes with Elizabeth's help. This gave me the support in the background that I looked forward to for the next few months…a body quietly there, day after day. Mother was never one to chat about the girls or situations like Davis, but I knew she could stir a pot, sew a button, and count noses at the dinner table.

My confidant was my love, my six-foot-tall Davis, calm, gentle, and wise. He was my balance to my quest for perfection and my heart's meter for my underlying Irish fire. The weeks in California became a respite for us and a stable comfort to the girls. Seeing the nearby ocean and floral vegetation gave Davis an understanding of the girls' stories and their adventures with Uncle Wyatt. Otherwise, a quiet calm prevailed as we sat on the front porch amidst the girls coming and going.

One day, after coming home after school, Margaret said, "Hi, Daddy."

"Hi, Maggie," Davis answered, calling her by her nickname.

She pointed to three girls who were walking past the house. "Those are my new friends. They have lived here forever, but they know another family here from Twist Junction. Lots of Texans are coming. They like to roller skate and sing at church, too. Want me to play you something on the piano?"

With perfection, she played "Onward Christian Soldiers."

"I learned that just for you. Let me get something." She ran to her room and grabbed the prayer book and her doll from home. "I read every night and I think of you. Then I talk to Dolly, and pretend you are talking to me."

"You are a sweet child, Maggie," Davis said and ruffled her hair.

Her friends reappeared and shouted her name. "Coming!" she called back, and dashed down the verandah steps to join them.

"Nancy, what do we have here?" Davis said, turning his attention to his other daughter.

"This is my reading book from school. Reading is hard…the words jumble together, and Dick and Jane are the most boring kids ever! Fairy tales are magical, but ugly pictures of two children and their dog make me want to go to the bathroom. I wiggle so much that the teacher asks if I have to be excused. I usually jump up and then skip down the hall to the girl's room at the end of the building. One of the other girls comes to get me, but this way I don't have to follow the reader with my pointer finger and read the words aloud. Why can't the stories talk about Jane's pretty skirt or the flowers in the yard? All I want to do is draw pictures of flowers on the page. Daddy, one day I drew polka dots on Jane's skirt. That made me like looking at that page. I even colored Spot the Dog's tongue red."

Charlotte was standing by, listening to Nancy talk to Davis. She piped up, "I sit still and follow the rules. Numbers are like building blocks and I can count fast. I love calling out the words from my *Dick and Jane* book. They are easy to me. I like the teacher. School is fun. I like the other children and all the other teachers, too. There's always something to do at school."

We heard laughing. It was Sybil and Daphne, coming down the block in their friend George's car. George had become Sybil's best friend. He was polite, handsome, and gregarious. Maybe a little *too* polished, from our point of view. I nudged Davis as they drove up, holding back my opinion until later. George opened the car door and the girls jumped out.

Hmm...polite but... I thought.

Davis cleared his throat when George bounced up the porch steps and introduced himself.

"How ya doing, sir?" said George. "Pleased to meet ya!"

"Daddy, this is my very best friend, George," said Sybil.

"I should say," mimicked Daphne.

Pages of beautiful drawings dropped from Sybil's notebook.

"Oh, I see you had art class today," Davis said.

"No, that's tomorrow, but I draw every day."

"Do you study English or math?"

"Oh, sometimes, Daddy, but..."

George could see the conversation was going downhill. "She's really okay in math. I sit next to her. If you make English like lines in a play, she's really good as a character actress. She can woo anybody, Mr. Bennett."

Davis rolled his eyes. Sybil giggled.

"I help her sometimes too, Daddy," said Daphne.

"Well, I help Daphne too," Sybil said. "I help her flirt with boys and dress and walk girly."

By this time, Davis was exhausted, between all the back and forth and the side-splitting antics of it all. What each girl held important at this stage of life both fascinated and concerned us.

The group of teenagers continued to chat on the steps, sipping Cokes and talking classroom gossip.

"Hey, here comes the queen," George glibly exuded.

Elizabeth glided past everyone, ignoring his tacky remark.

"Come sit with me," Davis motioned to her. "How do you like your California college, my sweet pea?"

"Oh, thank you so much, Daddy. You were so generous and thoughtful sending us here. I mean, what isn't beautiful and wonderful here? I get to sit under a big flowering magnolia tree during literature class. We read poetry and comment on the writings of all the greats. Some of the girls bike to class, then head to the soda fountain for lunch break. I do bring my own sandwich, but I get a soda when I have a little extra money."

Davis stuck his hand in his pocket and pulled out fifteen cents. "How's this for those extras, princess?"

Elizabeth, not known for being effusive, jumped up and gave him a great big kiss on his tanned, square jaw.

"Now that's my girl!"

Davis relished his time with his harem…mostly laughing with Sybil and watching the little ones play dress-up, paper dolls, or hopscotch on the sidewalk. But it was time for him to return to Twist Junction.

"I don't want tomorrow to come, dear," I said. "The girls will return to their mischievous ways again. Do you know that Sybil and Daphne have scary villain characters that they use to frighten Margaret, Nancy, and Charlotte? In the middle of the night, they appear with pillow cases or stockings over their faces, making evil sounds, then they grab them and lock them in the closet."

Davis turned red with laughter. "Where do they get all this imagination? I never had this much fun when I was young."

"Davis, I'm serious, this is scary to the little ones."

"Catherine, it's just play! Life has to have fun in it. God knows we don't have much back in Twist Junction."

"Humph," I huffed.

The next morning, Davis and I woke up early and talked in bed as we relished our morning snuggling time.

"Davis, you take care of yourself, and Otto too," I said. "Things have got to get better. We'll be home soon."

"I'm not so sure Sybil or Daphne will want to go back home. How about I try to look for a house in town? They can have friends and fun, like they do here," Davis responded.

"That might help some. We need to be thinking about their education, which isn't the best in Twist Junction. Elizabeth could go to that nice girls' Catholic college in Denver. Something…Heights. Sybil and Daphne just have a little high school left. Davis, lots of changes can happen in the next few years. I'd like to do something interesting, too. I'd like to be downtown with all the hustle and bustle. I want to be able to fill my teapot again." I flashed him my elfish grin. Davis shook his head and held my hand.

— ◁ ◁ ◁ —

It was hard for Davis to leave. The train, joggling his body inside and out, seemed to break off little parts of his heart, as if he were leaving a piece behind for each girl. Facing the horrific days on the dust-ridden plains and trying to keep a meager income coming in made him weary with thought.

When he arrived back in Twist Junction, the town looked tired as he exited onto the barren train platform. There was no hustle and bustle. Only a passenger or two passed him as he meandered down the dust-blown, almost empty Main Street. Even the DeSoto had only three or four lights on in its normal, carnival-like façade. Otto picked Davis up by horse and wagon in front of the hotel.

"Otto, what's going on?" Davis asked with raised eyebrows. "Something happen to the pick-up?"

"No, boss. Just saving on gas. Getting to be an extra I save for to go out to the upper forty. How was the trip? And the girls and Catherine? Did you ever get Mrs. Connelly to talk all that way?" he chuckled.

Davis nodded with each question but said little. He needed to rest in his own bed, lonely as it was. He needed his thinking time. Finally, Davis asked Otto, "Any rain?"

"Well, we did have some yesterday. Looked like it was up yonder near the cottonwood creek section."

"Maybe I'll ride up and try planting some winter wheat. Maybe it won't dry up with the heat and dust. The winds seem to die down a bit in winter. I'll have to drive Owen's old tractor up there. I hope it will make it."

Davis realized his voice was rather lifeless when Otto said, "Are you okay, Mr. Davis? You're not acting like yourself."

"Sorry. It was hard leaving my family. I wish I could do more for them. I wish God would make all this go away. Where did our good life go? We didn't have much, but now we have almost nothing. Hey, you been eating okay? Do we need to stop for supplies?"

"Don't worry none. It's going to be okay. You're back and you're going to make everything good again."

The quietness of the plains seemed to take over the noise of the horse's hooves and the wagon wheels on the rutted road. When they finally crossed through the gate, Davis muttered, "Wish everything was easier, Otto. I try, but I think it's gotten the best of me right now. Good night."

"Don't you want some vittles? I'll make you something lickety-split."

Shaking his head, Davis went into the house and disappeared into the bedroom.

Davis let the next day pass. He sat and did his thinking. Otto busied himself, nails in his mouth and hammer in hand. Davis rarely looked up to see what Otto was fixing. Somehow food appeared, but they ate in silence. A little bit of rain came that night. Davis prayed, thanking God.

Determined, Davis went out the next day to ready the soil. As he drove the old truck to the upper forty, his intuition said everything was exactly right, but he had to get the crop in if there was going to be any hope. He passed the pasture. The cattle were gone. As he began to plow that day, he was calm, but the sun did go in and out enough to make his eyes unsure of the tractor's direction. The earth beneath him was different; hard and soft, hard and soft.

As he turned to put in an alternate row, he felt something slip. He began to slide off the bucket seat and the tractor began to lean to one side. He hit the ground hard enough that he didn't recall what happened next. The tractor toppled onto its side, and his leg was pinned under the weight of the machine. The softness of the dirt cradled it, but not enough. He knew from the pain that it was broken. Davis tried to push the machine's weight off his leg, but passed out.

In a daze, Davis came to just as the dust was about to blow again. The old Mexican man he had seen years before now knelt beside him. "You're hurt, señor," he said with his soft accent, shading Davis's face with his straw hat.

Somehow, the tractor let go and released his mangled leg. It was his left leg, so Davis figured he could drive back to town using his right one. He grabbed something to help him stand. The pain shot through him with a throbbing intensity and he blacked out again. He awoke for a brief moment, and found that he wasn't driving—somehow, he was on the flatbed of someone else's Ford pick-up, and someone else was driving. He blacked out again. When he came to again, he was lying in the hospital with Mother Bennett and Polly at his side.

"What happened to you, Davis?" they chimed.

"What were you doing out there alone? How did you get here?" Polly added.

Davis couldn't answer a thing, partially embarrassed by his poor decision to plant, and partially because he didn't have the rest of the answers.

"Machinery is not as safe as a horse and plow," Mother Bennett said. "Don't you remember that your father was killed when Owen turned the car over rounding the Main Street corner? Davis, these inventions are just not safe."

Davis lay there with a minor concussion and his painful leg throbbing. He was sore. He was mad. His pride cloaked him with embarrassment. Polly sat with him for three days, taking time off from her teaching and post office jobs. She brought in pen and paper so that she could write to Catherine to inform her of the accident.

> *My dear Catherine,*
>
> *Your beloved Davis had an accident while planting. His tractor overturned on his leg. Your husband will be okay and the leg will mend over time. I am taking good care of him and will be taking him home to my house for recuperation. He will not be driving out to see you and the girls as planned this spring, but I will make every effort that he will be as good as new when you return.*
>
> *Respectfully,*
> *Polly Bennett*

He was grateful for his sister Polly, but Davis would have given the world to be with Cate when she read the letter. As reassuring as the letter was, Davis knew Cate would be inside out with worry.

A letter from Cate arrived on the heels of Polly's note.

Dearest Davis,

I do not like someone else caring for my husband, but if it has to be someone, Polly is my choice. However, I have concern that Polly is a teacher and not a nurse. A thought has crossed my mind. I have to come back. Wyatt and Mother Connelly can manage here with the girls. I will be there soon.

My love to you, my beloved,
Cate

Davis recuperated in Polly's guest room, looking out the window at the cottonwoods lining Main Street. The rare sounds of the humming car engines, clip-clopping of the horses' hooves, and the chickens in the yard pecking at the corn Polly would toss to them each morning, made him doze off. When Polly came home from school, she would help Davis sit in the white rocker on her front porch. There he could see Twist Junction, lazy with small-town activity, and he patiently listened to Polly's stories of who had gotten a whack with the ruler that day.

More often than not, Davis would try to recall the vision of the old Mexican, and what had happened on the west forty track. Who was he? Where had he gone? Bits of memories came back to him. Davis could almost hear the old Mexican tell him, "Now push it hard, Señor Davis, push!" as Davis tried to push the tractor off his leg. He had saved Davis's life. This was only the second time Davis had seen him, but somehow Davis knew it wouldn't be the last. It bothered him that he couldn't tell the men at the DeSoto about the stranger, and maybe not even Cate. *Someday, when the eucalyptus trees rustle in the evening breeze, Cate and I will be sitting quietly on our own front porch and maybe I can tell her the story,* Davis thought.

Thoughts of moving into town from the ranch played in Davis's mind. He knew that living in town would be better for the girls. Thoughts of the mysterious Mexican soon faded, but not the limp that stayed with him.

— ⚜ ⚜ ⚜ —

"Davis, I'm here!"

Taking the train couldn't make my anxiety dissipate fast enough. I wasn't the type to outwardly show my affection. After my father's death, I had separated myself from feelings of sadness, but Davis made me lift off the floor when I saw him. He was so handsome and looked so vulnerable as I observed tears sliding over his square cheekbones.

"I don't know if I could go on without you, Davis Bennett. The girls send their love, and Wyatt says I can stay as long as you need me." Then I gently touched his leg. My shoulders rose and fell as I heaved a sigh of relief.

Polly made us dinner and we all talked until the stars came out. Polly asked so many questions that night, like firecrackers exploding out of her mouth. Davis just sat and smiled.

"How's the school for the girls? Are they getting along with math and reading? Must be better teachers out there. Wyatt says he's been taking you sightseeing everywhere. Did the different animals at the zoo excite Charlotte? Did the water at Coronado Beach thrill Daphne? Did she swim?" She leaned back in her rocker. "Oh," she said, her eyes closed. "Catherine, the flowers, the weather, the parks…they all must be just wonderful."

If anyone deserved to be in California, it was Polly—a devoted mother figure to Davis and the best teacher to all the children of Twist Junction.

In the morning, I quizzed Davis as we sat on the front porch. "How are you feeling? What do you think we should do next?" I said.

"Oh, Cate, doin' fine. I should be up in a couple of weeks. I know I have to take it easy and start bending the knee, but I don't know if I can come out to California."

"You're my brave man. I know you want to be with us. The girls really do miss you. Every day they say Daddy this and Daddy that. You know, I feel invisible sometimes. The house is quiet without your singing..." I thought for a moment and paused. "Margaret still plays the piano. But there is nobody to make them laugh and giggle like you. You are magic with the girls. They even squabble more when you're not there."

We sat in silence for a moment before Davis said, "Oh Cate, where is God's plan? We've had some rain, but not much. With Mr. Steele's help, I did manage to get the crop in. People have been so kind, but I miss my coffee with the men. I can hear the train come through, but I don't get to see the people come and go like I used to. I can be patient, you know, but I just don't know how to make decisions without hearing the gossip. What do you think about permanently moving into town? Have you given that further thought?"

I liked that idea. "Life would be so much easier in town. We really love being on Orange Grove Avenue. Elizabeth, Sybil, and Daphne have many more friends in town, so many more parties and activities. It's really good for them. They're really growing up to be social butterflies. The schools will be closer. We can have indoor plumbing, with a washtub and a toilet. We could have more trees. Davis, I could even get a job! Charlotte is in school now. I always wanted to work and save some money. What do you think of that? We could even rent something for a while."

"I know it wouldn't be possible to sell the land or the ranch right now. I'm not going to give it away. I know things are going to get better. I miss my cattle, the land. The land and the animals are my life. We'll think about how to make it work. Cate..." He sat in silence for a moment. "I think it's all right if you want a job. You're smart. I think you'd be really happy."

"Oh, Davis! Are you sure? I do promise, with the help of the girls, I could make it doing a job with numbers. What do you think? The older girls will be off soon. It won't be so hard. I want to see them go to college, learn some skills, and get jobs too. I hear Loretto Heights College in Denver is good."

"My, little lady, you do think big!"

"Why not? Life is short. I want those girls to be the best that they can be. Pretty is as pretty does, or pretty is as pretty knows, as far as education goes. If you're doing well next week, I'll go back to California. We'll finish off the school year and if everything comes together, and you think it is safe, we'll come back... What about trying to walk a little bit tomorrow? I'll help. You can lean on me and I'll try to find you a cane."

"Don't know if I can chase you around the bed yet, but I'll try." His grin was as infectious as ever.

My tenderness helped heal my husband as I worked Davis's leg that week. We hadn't been alone for many years. Thoughts of one more baby came to mind. "Davis, you think we should try for John Howard before we quit?"

"No, no, no. You were just thinking of a job and having all your children in school."

"I know, but you always wanted that boy."

"God thinks I do better with girls, I guess. Cate, you're a great caretaker...sure you want to work with numbers?"

"It must be the patient I like caring for."

We sat alone on the porch that evening. Davis turned to me, and almost in a whisper said, "Cate, there is something I have to share with you. Before you and the girls left for California, I was observing the upper forty, and a stranger appeared out of nowhere...a small Mexican man with an oversized sombrero. He spoke to me of the future...the coming dust storms..." He paused. "He came again and saved my life when the tractor gave me a roll and pinned me under it. Do you know it was he who lifted that tractor and drove me to the hospital? I alone am not so brave or as strong as you thought. This puzzles me. I've never experienced anything like this before."

"Davis, what a remarkable story! I believe you have a very special guardian...a guardian angel, if you will. All I can say is, you are an extremely lucky man. God does provide, doesn't He?" I reached for his hand. "Thank you for telling me."

"You will keep my secret, just between you and me?"
"You know I will, sweet man."

Bad news came over the weekend. Davis's sister, Jennie Ruth, died after an eye operation gone awry at the Mayo Clinic. She lived up the street from Polly on Main Street, and her husband had died the year before. They had no children. The family gathering would span days.

"I know you hate to leave me now, Cate, but I'll be okay since everyone will be arriving soon. And I'll tell everyone how very sorry you are about Jennie Ruth."

"I hate to go. I was really fond of her and would like to show it."

"We don't know when the body will be shipped back from Mayo. It will probably come by train. The girls need you."

"Okay, I'll leave on the 9:05 on Wednesday. That way I'll be home when the girls come home from school on Friday afternoon."

More walking each day had Davis getting stronger. I, on the other hand, felt the weight of the next few weeks without his support and our daily conversations.

— ◁ ◁ ◁ —

Davis's heart was heavy as Catherine left on the train. So many thoughts and questions raced through his head. He wondered how he was going to make the dream of the house become real. He was determined. He knew his family needed to be settled. The Dust Bowl, which they were experiencing, had to end.

As Davis napped, he dreamed of his old Mexican man. He was picking Davis up in the same flatbed truck, but this time didn't take Davis to the hospital. He drove him down a beautiful, tree-lined street and paused at a brick bungalow with brick piers, a gable roof with eave brackets, and large 6/1 windows. A pretty stone wall surrounded the front yard. It was a blurry vision, but it looked familiar somehow.

"What do you think, Señor Davis?" Before Davis could answer, he said, "You need a new house in town, right?" He winked. Then the moment was gone, and so was the vision.

Davis squirmed. His dreams weren't usually that vivid, praying for something, then having a realistic picture appear. Slumber became deeper. Davis could hardly move after his strenuous walking and the emotion of saying good-bye to his Cate. Again, he wanted to share his vision with Cate, which made him miss her even more.

— ⊲. ⊲. ⊲. —

Days passed. I sent Davis a short letter with photos of the girls from the *USS Texas* tour. He could see our beautiful girls flanked by handsome naval officers. I knew he would feel a sense of pride, but also sadness, as he knew they had grown up so fast without him.

Jennie Ruth's funeral and the family gathering happened. Although I was back in California and couldn't attend the funeral, I experienced a repeat of the sadness I'd felt many years ago, when my father had passed. Shock shrouded everyone's emotions, as Jennie Ruth's death was so unexpected.

— ⊲. ⊲. ⊲. —

One afternoon, shortly after the funeral, Davis hobbled to the door to answer a determined knock. A solicitor stood on the porch, carrying his valise and staring at Davis. He introduced himself as Mr. Findlay.

"Mr. Bennett, we have had considerable difficulty trying to locate you. Our notices at your ranch house have gone unanswered. Due to the confidentiality of the matter, we hesitated to contact your family members. May I come in?"

"Yes sir, by all means." Davis motioned to Polly's cozy living room sitting area. "Mr. Findlay, if you will."

"I have the Last Will and Testament of Mrs. Jennie Ruth Starnes, which I would like to read to you."

Davis nodded as they both took a seat on the squishy couch. Mr. Findlay began reading the will.

"I, Jennie Ruth Starnes, being of sound mind, hereby bequeath my home at 619 Main Street and the contents within, upon my death, to

Davis Crockett Bennett and his wife, Catherine Connelly Bennett. Dated this 28th day of September, 1931."

Davis's silence filled the parlor. You could hear a pin drop. He cleared his throat. Unsure what the proper response was, he stuttered and said, "I...I...I accept."

"Sign right here, Mr. Bennett. I have another envelope here with the keys, title, and list of the contents of your late sister's house."

Davis stared at the paper before him, still in shock.

"Sign here, sir," Mr. Findlay repeated. "Sign here, at the bottom of the typed page." After a brief moment, he continued, "Would you like me to escort you over to your new home?"

"That would be much appreciated, since I'm recovering from a leg injury."

Davis hobbled after Mr. Findlay to Mr. Findlay's car.

"Jump right in, Mr. Bennett," Findlay called as he opened the door to the dark-green Model T.

Davis hadn't been in Jennie Ruth's house since his father died in 1913. Now it was 1934, and it was his. Davis was grateful to God and to Jennie Ruth. Disbelief rushed over him as he stepped over the threshold of the beautiful home.

"Thank you, Mr. Findlay. I think I need to sit in quiet for a while."

"I understand. Good luck, young man," Mr. Findlay replied, then he was gone.

Davis sat alone for an hour, wondering what Cate would say when he told her of Jennie Ruth's great gift. He knew she would have tears of happiness.

With the help of his cane, he pulled himself up proudly. With one step in front of another, he managed to walk across the uneven road and down the concrete sidewalk over to Polly's. With each step, he wondered how he was going to tell Cate. He wondered whether he should tell Polly, but then decided he wouldn't tell her until Cate knew. With great thought, he asked Polly, "Are you using that small Sears box that your stockings came in?"

Surely, she was puzzled as to why Davis needed a box, but Polly was restrained and never asked too many questions. She'd save that inquiry for another day.

One of Davis's brothers drove him to the post office to mail the mystery box to Cate. Davis had included a letter, taped on the outside, regarding the surprise, explaining the contents of the box, and asked that she surprise the girls. He marked on the letter: *Open me before you open the box!* Davis thought he hadn't been this excited and nervous since he had asked Cate to marry him.

— ⊲⊦ ⊲⊦ ⊲⊦ —

My mother and I had gone out and had not yet returned when Elizabeth arrived home after her morning classes. Junior College stimulated her much more than her Twist Junction High School days. Elizabeth would tell me that there was nothing better than open classrooms. Dreams of romantic interludes were so easy for her to conjure up in this land of filmmaking.

When we arrived home, we met Elizabeth in the kitchen with bags of special dinner treats.

"What's up, Mother?" Elizabeth asked.

I didn't answer, but asked her to finish bringing in the groceries from the car. Elizabeth watched me pull out the corn pudding pan. She watched as I made the biscuit dough ball. Next, she noticed I was taking out the roast pan and the chocolate cake pans, which we generally used only for birthdays.

Elizabeth whispered to her grandmother, "Are we having a party?"

Mother Connelly winked at Elizabeth, and before I knew it, my other children were home from school, tossing book bags and sweaters, purses and shoes, everywhere.

"Set the table and get out the Sunday china," I called out.

Elizabeth was busy stringing and snapping beans while I, with a great whack and the weight of the meat cleaver, prepared the roast. Margaret played the piano as we all worked. Everybody wondered what was going on. Was Daddy coming? Were we having a new baby? Did Daphne or Sybil have a special boyfriend?

Wyatt and Maude joined us for dinner. I kept secrets very well, but this time I could tell my excitement was evident to my family, and we could barely eat. Finally, as the chocolate cake was being cut, I pulled out a small box. Elizabeth peeked over my shoulder, and I was certain she saw Davis's writing and his return post office address. I opened the box slowly and displayed a photograph for all to see, along with a piece of paper with the outline of a key drawn on it. Below the outline of the key was written *619 Main Street*.

Wyatt knew immediately whose house this was, but grinning, he kept quiet as the girls tried to figure out the puzzle. They shouted out guesses, talking over each other in their excitement.

I covered my mouth and gave Daphne a nudge and a hint. "J.R.," I said.

Her eyes lit up. "Oh Mother, Aunt Jennie Ruth is letting us stay in her house?" Daphne replied.

None of us could believe it, and shocked expressions circled the room. My voice was muddled with excitement as I told the story of the solicitor and Jennie Ruth's will, and how the house now permanently belonged to Daddy and me.

The children immediately wanted to run to their rooms, pack their bags, and squeeze into the car to drive to our new home in Twist Junction. Charlotte did a little twirling dance while the others chattered about which of their friends they would see first upon their return.

As the dishes clanked while being washed that night, you could barely hear the sound through all the nonstop conversations. Wyatt and Maude slipped out almost unnoticed. As they paused at the front door, Wyatt turned back and said, "Catherine, you and Davis *really* deserve a break. The family will be real happy for ya."

– ⊲̣ ⊲̣ ⊲̣ –

With all the good news, Sybil felt a certain remorse. Her days in California were about to end. She would miss her friends, the advanced education she was receiving, the flowers and the fun. Life was fickle…the good and the bad of changing places.

Imagine, Cowboy Daddy living in town! He would do anything for us. He could have sold Aunt Jennie's house and put the money into cattle or crops, Sybil thought. But she knew her daddy and how he loved the open spaces, his land, and his animals. Sybil thought he would now be like an apple in a basket of peas...out of place. He would be happy for everyone, but out of place.

Sybil did miss her daddy. What she didn't miss was Twist Junction. She thought Twist Junction was a podunk town filled with redneck boys. She thought she belonged in California, with all the breaking news. She ran down the street to see her friend George.

"I stopped by to see if you wanted to sit on the beach and talk." She hesitated, then said, "We're going back to Texas. We now have a lovely new house to go back to." She shared the inheritance story and surprise, then said, "California is more exciting, and you and the rest of the boys are more exciting. I know we're just friends, but do you think we could come up with a way that I might stay here? We could pretend we got married or something. Does your father know anyone who needs an extra down on the movie lot? I can't sing, but I could strut across the camera. I'm a good artist. I could draw all the movie stars. What do you think they would pay me for one of my sketches?"

"Sybil, you're some kind of a doll," George said fondly. "Many men would want you, but you might fall into a bad crowd. Too many things could happen to a kid like you. I like you too much. You'd better go on home to Twist Junction, where you'll meet a handsome cowboy. I'm just a singer and dancer. I only know the pretend world."

Sybil's conversation with George kept nagging her mind. She was desperate to think of another plan. Determined, she thought, *Just watch me. I've got plans for my life and they don't include Twist Junction.*

Daphne knew that Sybil didn't want to go back to Twist Junction. She wasn't sure she wanted to, either. Thinking that she could share a one-bedroom apartment with Sybil, Daphne hoped they could get jobs and meet all the glamorous studio men. Their classmates were already trying out for movie parts. They might become famous one day, and Daphne and Sybil would be right there with them. Daphne envisioned she and Sybil, arm in arm with their escorts, as they attended all the right parties. She knew Sybil would get the dates, and the leftovers would be hers. She thought she wasn't as pretty as Sybil, but knew she was smart and could dance the night away.

Daphne knew for sure she didn't want to end up in Twist Junction. It might be her home, but she knew that the world was big and interesting, and she wanted to see it all. She knew California might not be a place for a top-notch typist or a mediocre actress, and then thought, *My legs are too fat, too. I'm refined, yes, but not swishy enough to be in the 'sexy, buxom-blond world.' I'm a somebody, but I'm not sure who that somebody is yet!*

So, giving the California experience one last try, Sybil and Daphne borrowed backless, fringed party dresses from one of the high school's "fast lane" blonds. George knew guys with fancy cars and contacts and agreed to take the girls to one of the hot clubs where they could see "the buzz" first hand. George felt responsible for their adventure, and he tried to stay two steps behind them at all times. Then, there they were, at Club Z. The unmarked door flew open and smoke and raucous music poured out from inside. The girls had the outfits, bobbed hairdos, and the fancy make-up. George was sporting a red jacket with a canary-yellow tie and handkerchief. His hair was slicked back and he looked the part of a notable gangster.

Though their mother had never taught the girls how to slink, slither, and schmooze, Sybil was intuitively smooth. Daphne followed suit and George held his own, saying, "Hiya, foxy" or "What'cha doin', babe?" Once in the door, George set the girls up with their dates, who immediately vanished with them to the nearest bar. Sybil and Daphne hadn't figured on that part of the "wild girl scene." Before Daphne could flutter her lashes at the newest prospect, a tall pink drink arrived.

Sybil leaned into Daphne and whispered, "*Sip* it...slowly."

Daphne wondered how Sybil knew to tell her that...something Daphne would discuss with Sybil at a later date. Both girls were thinking, *Thank God we told Mother we were spending the night with some girlfriends.* They both began to realize that this was going to be a night of firsts.

Bobbing heads and twirling boas filled the dance floor. Daphne was dying to get out there. The pink potion had gotten to her head, but she didn't want to toss it down. With a bump and a shove, half of it was on the floor. She took one sip before a guy grabbed her half-empty glass and lined it up with others on a round, silver cocktail table. He took her hand in his and off she went with Mr. Nameless to the vibrating dance floor.

Daphne could see Sybil being tossed up and slid along the floor between George's lanky legs. Yes, he was a dancer. The evening alternated between pink party drinks and more Charleston dancing, which Daphne had never done. Daphne didn't realize that George and Sybil had vanished, as her pink drink had clouded the situation. She was experiencing hugs, tugs, and roving hands at every turn. She wondered, *Where do these guys come from who think I'm a piece of meat?* The kisses on her neck were the last straw. She tried to focus, then saw a door where people wandered in and out. She exited and found herself on an outside patio.

The evening air felt good to her, but she soon experienced other raucous behavior. This time, under the moonlight in the corner, a group of cute guys stood laughing at a tall girl with dirty-blond hair. It was Sybil. Daphne knew Sybil could capture a man from a mile away. She could see Sybil's arms flailing, making comic gestures with one hand, holding a cigarette in the other, and balancing the pink potion, her sparkling hazel eyes dancing as she entertained. Seeing Sybil seductively leaning against the wall, Daphne realized her sister was quite the woman—a woman ready for almost anything life tossed her way.

Joining the group as "little sister," Daphne managed to squeeze between the party-goers. She looked for George. She could feel herself fading. Then, a giggle came from a redhead not too far away. She was twirling a yellow tie. Daphne's head was twirling too, but she tried to focus and squinted her eyes to get a better look. The tie was George's.

There was a thing called fun, and then there was *too much* fun. The little redhead wasn't happy when Daphne sauntered over to George. Taking one look at Daphne, he excused himself, then gathered Sybil and their boys.

"Party at my house!" he said.

George's parents were gone for the weekend, so his house gave them a place to party. But Daphne didn't remember whether there was a party or not. Her own bed was her only thought. She knew that she and Sybil were in no condition to go home. Shortly after arriving, Daphne fell asleep on George's bed, slinky dress and all. After searching the whole house, Sybil finally eyed her sister, sound asleep in George's room.

The next morning, Sybil stumbled in, coffee in hand. "Oh no, another first! I've just stayed up all night partying," she mumbled. She sure knew about parties and how to recover. Last night's events would later be shared and discussed in private once they got back home.

Daphne told Sybil she wasn't really sure whether they were behaving as Mother's perfect girls. But looking back, Sybil certainly had been the perfect entertainer.

— ◁ ◁ ◁ —

I raised an eyebrow slightly as Sybil and Daphne, ever so slowly, came up the walkway. "Girl's, did you have fun? The house was pretty quiet without you. I have some leftover blueberry pie and milk in the refrigerator."

Daphne hesitated. "In a bit, Mother...thanks..."

Sybil ignored the question. She headed straight for her room and immediately flopped on her bed.

Margaret ran into the room and jumped on the corner of the mattress.

"Can't you see I have a headache?" groaned Sybil.

Walking toward the girls, I said, "Now, now, girls, you know I can't abide squabbling."

"But Mother, I just wanted to hear the stories about Sue Ellen's overnight party," Maggie protested.

Meanwhile, Daphne seemed to think there were too many girls in the house and there was no room for privacy. I think she realized now, as she got older, that time to oneself should be treasured. She needed time to think. To plan. To dream. Going out to the backyard was her only "alone" place. She sat on the swing for a while, lifting her face to the breeze. She rubbed her stomach, then her temples, then went to find a hidden Coca-Cola in the fridge. She came into the kitchen and reluctantly sliced herself a small piece of pie.

I noticed every move she made out of the corner of my eye, and I know Daphne knew it. She knew my sharp intuition could detect when things weren't quite right with my children. Daphne hated it when she disappointed me. She probably knew that eventually she would get a lecture, and waiting for it was the worst part. I'm sure she was glad her daddy wasn't there. She could probably hear my lecture in her head. It always started out, "You know, pretty is as pretty does. Isn't that right, girls?" Then it would fade into words of rules and perfection. Daphne knew that she and Sybil were too old for the switch, but losing privileges would be worse. No stops after school, no parties, no overnights, no boy visitors.

Though I knew Daphne could see it coming, it didn't seem to bother Sybil. I saw her in the bedroom on her bed, grinning, probably thinking of last night and all the boys and fun she'd had. Nobody was going to take away Sybil's great moments…not me or God! Sybil did what she did, and she was glad.

Daphne seemed to be so ridden with guilt that she could hardly eat supper. I knew that she wanted her daddy and me to think she was a better girl than Sybil. I watched as she sat on the swing that evening, and wondered what she was thinking. I knew my daughter. She was probably recounting whether the good time she'd had was worth the upcoming consequences. It wasn't worth it to her to have me mad at her, and the guilt had a way of gnawing at her. Daphne knew if I was really mad it could be really bad, and I think she had a feeling this was one of those times.

Maggie went outside to the swing.

I could hear Daphne say, "Oh, no..." as Maggie headed toward her to try to push the swing. I guessed that Daphne's head was already spinning, and she probably didn't need more motion. Knowing Maggie, she was just being nosey. I'm sure she hoped she would hear some exciting stories about her older sisters' night out.

Then I heard Daphne again. "Don't you have somewhere else to go, Margaret?" she said, shoving Maggie away.

Maggie grumbled and walked away.

After their party evening, I surmised that Daphne could tell that the California way of life and wild boys were clearly not for her. Even though she liked to make her own decisions, the California life didn't seem to have roots. "The moment" was all there was. No history, no upbringing with rules or traditions. Church was an afterthought. Somehow, I knew Daphne realized that her upbringing was different. Twist Junction had a solidness to it. I had no way of knowing, but I would have been proud of my girl had I been privy to her thoughts.

— ⊲ ⊲ ⊲ —

Daphne finally realized that California wasn't all it was cracked up to be. *Maybe I won't stay in Twist Junction for the rest of my life, but it will always be home...and my family will always be important to me. I was raised knowing what's the right way and the wrong way of doing things. God will take care of me. I'd say He did a pretty good job last night. I could have gotten into real trouble. The smoking and sex were all around me. Thank you, God. I didn't want "it" to happen with some stranger in an unremarkable place.*

Sybil sauntered out to the garden. She spoke quietly. "Wow, that was some party, Daphy. I could have laughed and danced till the sun came up. This is my kind of place. I like it here. Life is full here. The boys are exactly like what we see in the movies. Everything and everyone is crazy. *Romantic*...yes, that's it! It makes me feel free and romantic. You know what I mean? If it weren't for Daddy, I'd stay...I've been thinking a *lot* about staying here."

"Me too," piped up Daphne, "but I've changed my mind. It isn't real here, Sybil. I don't think I could ever know whether someone was serious or pretending. Somehow, I know there must be more to life than parties and fun, fun, fun."

"You're a stick in the mud. You sound like Mama. Fun is good for you. And beautiful men make me swoon! It's like I can't get enough."

"Yes, that's the point. There's too much of *everything*. I want to be somewhere where something really matters. I want to go to college."

"You're too much for me. You're stuck in conservative ways. Now we'll see, missy miss, whose life is going to be better."

Maggie had hidden behind the bushes, listening, trying not to breathe lest she'd be discovered by her older sisters. *Wow,* she thought. *My sisters are really different. I don't know who is thinking right. I don't know who I want to be like, but I love a party, the boys, and staying up late at night. Mother always said we'd do well if we could type and take good dictation. I do know I want to be able to do that... My leg is falling asleep and I'm getting hungry... Mother, don't come looking for me... I can't let them know I've been listening all this time. They'd kill me, make my life miserable, and tease me till Sunday. Oh dear, I don't have a getaway plan!*

Sybil stretched. "I'm going over to George's house. Maybe he needs someone to help with the clean-up. You just stay there stuck in that darn swing."

"That's not fair! I can have my own opinions," snapped Daphne.

Daphne walked to the back door as Sybil left for George's house.

Maggie slithered out of the bushes, brushing the mulch and dirt from her clothes.

— ⊲. ⊲. ⊲. —

Only five more days in California. The thought took my breath away. That morning, Daphne, Sybil, Elizabeth, and I took Mother Connelly to the train station, where she would board the *Silver Zephyr,* nonstop to Phoenix. Amidst the crowds around the train, I could hear Sybil trying to convince her grandmother that she would be safer if someone came with her. Her helpfulness was in direct proportion to her desire to leave early. Sybil helped carry my father's scuffed brown leather valise that my mother had inherited. Mother boarded the train and I waved to her. Then, right before my eyes, Sybil jumped on the train, squeezing past the porter and conductor. Even Mother was unaware of her granddaughter's escapade. Sybil waved a fistful of money in one hand and a small travel bag in the other. Opening the Pullman car's window, she waved at me and called out, "Don't worry, Mama, I'll be fine."

My frantic answer of, "Where are you going?" became muffled by the thundering engines and the shrill whistle. I reached into my pocket, flipping my rosary beads madly between my fingers. *What is that girl going to do next?* ticker-taped through my thoughts. *And where did she get that money?* I turned to Daphne. "Daphne, did you know about this?"

"No, Mama, but I did see her sneaking into the closet and dresser late last night after she got home from seeing George, probably saying good-bye to him."

"Is that where she got the money?"

"Don't know…don't really know anything except she wasn't keen on going back to Twist Junction. That I do know."

"Daphne, can you ask George what he knows? I'm just concerned. I won't be able to change her mind, but I'll at least have peace of mind knowing where she might be off to."

I turned abruptly on my heels as the train chugged down the tracks and out of sight. Elizabeth and Daphne followed me out of the station without a sound. Gravel flew as I pulled the old Buick out of the station's parking area and headed back to Wyatt and Maude's, who were watching the young ones play hopscotch with their neighborhood friends.

Wyatt piped up, "Did your mother get off easily? How about some tea, Catherine? You look like you could use a rest here on the porch."

I nodded to all his questions while the girls shook their heads in contrast. Wyatt changed the subject quickly after sensing the awkward situation. Shifting his questions to Elizabeth and Daphne, he asked, "What special place do you girls want to see before you leave in a few days?"

Responding simultaneously, one said, "Hollywood," as the other said, "The coast."

"Oh, I see. That may be a challenge for me," Wyatt responded.

"Oh, Wyatt, you've done enough for us," I interrupted.

"Calm down, Miss Catherine. I can spoil my nieces if I want to."

A moment of silence passed.

"Don't know when I'll see them again. I've loved having my family around me. Your girls make me proud." Looking around, he counted heads. "Where is Sybil?"

With that, Elizabeth, who always knew the right thing to do, jumped up. "I think it's time to go. Mama, let me help you get supper started." She grabbed my arm and towed me out of the house.

We left Wyatt with his mouth open, shaking his head.

"Something wrong?" He glanced over at Daphne.

"Uncle Wyatt, I don't know exactly, at least right now."

The evening light lasted until past eight o'clock. I convinced Daphne to go to George's and return before dark. "Don't dilly dally, girl," I said as she scurried down the sidewalk. I had a feeling Daphne was just as curious as I was. What was Sybil up to?

"I want every detail of her plans," I called after her. "Do you hear? Thank you, dear."

— ⊲. ⊲. ⊲. —

Daphne practically ran up the curved driveway to George's huge family home. Knocking madly on the door, she realized they had a fancy brass doorbell. Embarrassed, she cleared her throat of her anxiety as the door opened. A maid in a starched uniform answered.

"Is George home?" Daphne said in her most low-key, feminine voice.

George pushed his way past the maid. "I've been waiting for you to come. What took you so long, sleepyhead?"

"Let's not joke at a time like this. Where can we talk?"

"Let's go out to the verandah. It's a making-whoopee kind of night."

"No, not now, George. This is a serious visit."

"Maria, can you get Miss Daphne and me a Coke, please?" George called to the maid.

Daphne almost burst as they walked to the verandah. "Okay, what's going on?"

George grinned. "You don't want me to spill the beans before my best friend gets herself set up, do ya?"

"Okay, but Mama is sick with worry."

The maid appeared with two Cokes.

"Thank you, Maria," George said, and took a sip. "This tastes super."

Daphne was almost shaking at George's coyness. "Don't play with my emotions!" she almost shouted.

"Boy, you got that Irish in you, don't ya?"

"George," Daphne said, now infuriated, almost staring a hole right through him. "Did you give Sybil the money?"

"Yes, yes, I did. But Daphne, I got her to leave this town. This is a no-good place for a girl like Sybil. I had to do some quick thinking or she was going to do something stupid, and then I wouldn't know where she was or how to protect her."

Daphne pondered this for a moment. "George, I do believe you love Sybil."

He hesitated. "You Texas girls are different…beautiful…beguiling, if you will. I'm no one special. Your sister needs a strong man. I'm a showman, an entertainer, a Dr. Jekyll and Mr. Hyde. Yes, I care. I care a lot, but I'm not going to tell you where she is. I promised Sybil. She did write her daddy. I mailed the letter for her today."

"You're a good guy, George," Daphne said.

"Let's just say I'd go to Hell and back for her if she needed me to."

Daphne stared out at the pristine yard. It looked like a movie set. Almost whispering, she said, "I hope someday I have a man as devoted to me as you are to Sybil."

"I'll always be her friend and this is what friends are for. Tell your mother I'm taking very good care of her. I'll tell her everything before you all head back to Texas. Sybil just had to get that wild streak out. She'll be fine."

Tears started to come, so Daphne got up with her back turned to George. "Thanks a bunch, George," she said as she started walking around the house to the driveway, where she had come in.

George ran to give her a hug. "Tell your mother everything will be okay. I promise."

— ⊲⃒ ⊲⃒ ⊲⃒ —

When Daphne got home, I was waiting anxiously. "What's the matter, Daphne?" I asked, noticing her tears.

"She's okay, Mama. George is a real peach. What a friend. He'll come tell us everything before we leave." She sniffed back her tears. "A *really good* friend!"

For the moment, even though I was still worried, I felt relieved.

— ⊲⃒ ⊲⃒ ⊲⃒ —

Sybil helped her grandmother change trains in Phoenix so that Mother Connelly could head to Twist Junction. Otto, who was headed to California to drive Catherine and the girls home, happened to be there at the same time and spotted them. He held back, watching as Mother Connelly and Sybil went their separate ways on different trains. He had known Sybil for a long time, and he figured she was up to going out on her own, wherever that was. Mrs. Connelly looked fragile but seemed well settled on the eastbound *Silver Zephyr*, now headed back to a less hectic schedule. However, she too was concerned about her independent granddaughter, Sybil. Her observation of the situation was all she had, since she and Catherine had not discussed Sybil's plans. Deep inside, Mother Connelly knew this girl could do anything she set her mind to, with or without her mama's consent. Not feeling that Sybil had that consent, she assured herself that Davis and Catherine would know what to do.

Otto strained his neck to see where Sybil was headed, but she escaped his line of vision. He stared at the backs of people's heads and the blurred landscape, remembering the day Davis had told him that

#2 baby Sybil was on the way. Otto had so many memories of that girl...the day she helped with the fire and the times she would ride the horses when her parents weren't looking. She was always the one who played jokes on everyone, but this running away didn't seem like a joke. What was she up to?

— ◁ ◁ ◁ —

George came by on our last day in California. He and I spoke quietly in the back yard. He told me about all the plans he had arranged for Sybil. He told me how special she was to him, told me not to worry, and to contact him any time. Only somewhat content with his explanation, I decided the entire event would have to be discussed with Davis, and not soon enough. All the girls, except for Daphne, seemed satisfied with my excuse that their sister had taken a little trip to see friends. But Daphne was determined, whether by hook or crook, to find out the truth.

Finally, Otto arrived. He was a welcome sight for my sore eyes. Although he was exhausted, he pitched in, helping us close up the rented house and pack the car. Soon we were in the Buick and headed back to Texas. I guessed that Daphne's thoughts were preoccupied with her sister's whereabouts, and the trip back to Texas was relatively quiet. Three years in California had passed with record speed, and now Davis and a new house were waiting for us. I looked forward to this new chapter in our lives.

7
Rollers & Bobby Pins

The rumblings of war echoed from Europe. In an effort to keep men working during the bad times, bricks replaced dirt and now lined the entire length of Main Street. The fancy paving beckoned us home, right to the front door of our new house. The girls were so excited, their words tumbled from their mouths.

"Otto, you are a genius, getting us back on Saturday," I enthused. "And Davis should be around too! Girls, your chatter is deafening. Daddy will hear us coming all the way through downtown."

"Mama, look at all the people!" Daphne said. "The train must have just come through. I don't remember all the trees around the courthouse. Is that Fannie coming out of the drug store? Let's stop. I want to say hi. Where did she get all those boys following her?"

Daphne jabbered on and on. I snapped my head around to see who wasn't listening to me.

"Enough, Daphne. You're not stopping anywhere. Your daddy will be anxious to see us and to show you your new house. Besides, I think you might want to freshen up before you go gallivanting around. You know how first impressions are. You want to put your best foot forward."

"Oh, Mother..." her voice trailed down to a mumble.

I spotted Davis as we slowly drove down Main Street. "There he is, walking on the sidewalk with a brown bag. He's coming from Aunt Polly's house," I observed.

"Yum! Bet I know what he has in that bag!" Nancy exclaimed with authority.

Davis glanced up as Otto turned the big green Buick into the driveway. Girls squeaking and piling out of the car, he almost dropped the bag, which held a plate of Polly's cookies. I rushed to catch it before it crashed to the ground. His hazel eyes watered with a joy and happiness I hadn't seen since each of our daughters came into the world.

"How's my handsome cowboy?" I said, but my words were drowned out by the jumping, giggling, and hugging of his adoring daughters. Nancy and Maggie had already run up the front steps to open the screen door to the house.

"Oooh, Mama...wow! Look at this beautiful fireplace," Maggie exclaimed with enthusiasm.

Charlotte took Elizabeth's hand as they climbed the porch steps. I took Davis's hand.

Daphne stood on the porch, looking out on the lawn and Main Street as the cars drove by. I figured she didn't want to miss any more friends. She turned, fluffed her hair, and looked at all the party space on the generous brick-columned porch, and the stone wall where people could sit as well. I knew my daughter. She was probably thinking that this was going to be the best gathering spot in town. Then her thoughts seemed to shift, and a shadow fell across her face. I guessed that she was missing her sister.

"Daphne, come see the bedroom! We all have our own beds!" echoed Nancy from the back of the house.

Davis squeezed my hand. I winked proudly.

"We did it, Cate. Life is good now."

Otto had managed all the suitcases and lined them up on the porch. "Mr. Davis, I'll be going now. Glad we have Sunday to rest up."

"Otto, thank you, my man," Davis said warmly. "You brought my family home safe and sound. Here's a little something so you can get yourself some vittles." He reached out and gave Otto a manly hug around his shoulders, then placed some money in Otto's palm.

I joined them at the door. "Otto, do you want to join us for a family Sunday supper tomorrow? You can see the house and we can all be together, like in the old days."

"I'd like that," Otto grinned. "I'll bring some chickens off the ranch and clean 'em up for you."

"Otto, I can't thank you enough. You're always thinking how you can help."

"Take the Buick," Davis said. "We won't need it tonight. I'll take you back to the ranch Sunday evening."

"Thank you, Mr. B."

I walked slowly through the house to my very own kitchen. It was so big. Chuckling, I commented to Davis, "We could waltz in here! A kitchen table with a built-in banquette—how very charming! Oh, and a lilac bush right outside the double window above the sink. Just perfect!"

"Oh, Cate," Davis breathed. "I can't take my eyes off of you. You're just like my kerosene lantern. All lit up and glowing." He pecked my forehead with a tender, light kiss.

Smiling warmly, I turned to hide a tear and called to the girls, "Anyone for lemonade and cookies?"

The girls had found their beds and were happily testing their pillows. One by one, they showed up for Aunt Polly's treats.

I looked at Davis. "It's been a long trip. Want to sit on the front porch? We have some talking to do about Sybil."

"Cate dear, she can wait. I just want to sit and hold your sweet little hand in my old rough one," Davis chuckled.

How could I resist? I treasured our quiet times…our Davis and Catherine time.

— ⊲. ⊲. ⊲. —

Sunday morning felt good. We could walk to our respective churches. I put a pot of green beans on the stove to boil down while I was at Mass. I chuckled to myself as I got ready. Seeing Father Patrick again was definitely going to shock him. He hadn't seen the girls so grown-up, and I was quite certain he missed Margaret's beautiful voice during the hymns. *I hope Mother, Dennis, and Liam will sit with us,* I thought. I felt comforted being with my family again, in my own church in my own town of Twist Junction.

Slipping my rosary beads into my Sunday dress pocket, I followed Davis and the girls down the sidewalk. Davis went left to get his sister Polly on the way to the Baptist church, and we went right, down the block to the tiny white Catholic chapel.

I spied my mother and brothers sitting in the second pew from the altar. I filed the girls, each in a neatly ironed Sunday dress, into the second pew from the altar, hoping we could sit next to them. Seeing them immediately brought me comfort. I felt supported by just being in their presence. Father Patrick entered the church with his eyes cast down and immediately started Mass. When he said the gospel from the pulpit, his eyes glanced our way and an immediate grin covered his face. His dear family friends had returned; the little family he had almost refused to marry. His voice lifted with excitement when it came time for the announcements.

"I want to take time today to welcome home the Davis Bennett family from three years in California." With that, he stepped down to shake my hand. He then shook each girl's hand, calling them hesitantly by name. Many of the Irish railroad workers sat up straight, trying to catch sight of the lovely girls. Other school friends gave low, timid waves from their laps.

Father Patrick certainly made us feel special, and I wanted to thank him with a Sunday supper invitation. He waited at the front door as we all exited, but I was disappointed to learn that he had a previous baptism commitment in Hartley. "Maybe next Sunday, Father?"

"You can count on that, Miss Catherine," he said and gave me a hug.

Mother and the boys resumed the welcome-home celebration, and agreed to come for Sunday supper. Mother exited the church in a frenzy so she could hurry home and make her potato and cheese casserole.

A few hours later, I glanced over at Mother as we stirred the last of the beans. "What do you hear from Kerrick?"

"He's good, Catherine. He's in Galveston training on one of the docked warships. They will go to sea at a moment's notice, but for now, he's commissioned to ship out in April of next year. Liam and Dennis miss him terribly, but they love hearing the port stories of the rough sailors' fist fights over a bottle of beer and that sort of thing. Kerrick says he's taking some language and law classes when he's off duty. He's clever, you know, and will manage to get an education somehow."

"Looks like he will get some travel in, as well. Hope if we have a war it doesn't amount to much, or at least not with major skirmishes at sea."

"All war can be brutal and senseless," Mother continued. "I would be lying if I said I wasn't worried."

"We all have our worries," I replied, almost in a whisper.

"The paper and movie news show terrible fighting in Europe. You're lucky, Catherine. You have no boys to send off."

With almost a harsh tone, I said once again, "We all have our worries."

Davis appeared at the kitchen door. "Can I help? I had an inkling you might be having a problem in here."

"Sorry, chicken's ready. I was just waiting for the biscuits to brown up a bit," I answered as I slid the pan of hot biscuits out of the oven. "Comin' right out in just a minute." I turned to my mother. "Sorry to be short with you today. I'm worried...very worried about Sybil."

"Whatever do you mean? She told me she was off to see a friend when we parted at the Phoenix train station. I had an inkling that something wasn't right with Sybil's unexplained, last-minute trip, but wanted to make light of the situation to lessen the weight of the conversation. Is something wrong?" Mother pressed.

"I don't know. That's the problem. I just don't know."

"Let's get this food on the table, dear. We'll talk about this later."

"There's nothing more to say." My voice, chipped with frustration, startled Mother. She stared at me with raised eyebrows.

Before I knew it, I had eleven smiling people at my Sunday supper table, the first of many Sunday gatherings we'd have in the years to come. Only Mother and I knew about the tense conversation we'd just had in the kitchen.

I was tired that night. My nerves were frayed from worrying about Sybil. Davis and I talked about where she was off to and what she was doing. Davis shared the letter Sybil had written to him before she left, and after reading it, I felt a little better. She apologized for her actions, but said she wanted to follow her dream, that she would be careful, and that George and his friends were watching out for her. Davis said he thought she needed to get this out of her system, and felt she'd be home soon. I hoped he was right.

Davis took Otto back out to the ranch, and I tucked the girls into bed. Charlotte had insisted on driving with her daddy and Otto. She had her own little-girl agenda, and Davis said she talked the entire trip about how much she missed Otto, the wide-open spaces, and her dog and pony. She wanted to know if the winds still blew hard out there, and wondered where the flowers were. She noticed that her swing was broken, the house was gray, and that it looked so sad. She wanted to stay out there with Otto, but of course, Davis wouldn't let her.

Charlotte verbalized our sadness in her own words, but she didn't understand what we had been doing or what we had been through over the last few years. While she had returned with excitement and sunshine in her heart, we were barely optimistic. Toast and a ten-cent cup of coffee at the DeSoto had become a treat. The men there had changed. Conversations shifted many times from the loss of a herd or a crop to a neighbor, a fortune, a home, or a son. The challenges of life had been severe. But we had to keep our chins up high for these children now. Day after day we had to welcome numerous strangers as they got off the trains, hoping that Twist Junction had more to offer.

— ◁ ◁ ◁ —

Davis, Otto, and Charlotte pulled up to the ranch gate.

"Davis, see you in the morning," Otto said, and got out of the Buick.

"Me too, Otto," said Charlotte, and started to get out of the car.

"Don't think your mother wants you livin' out here any longer," Otto said.

"I can if Daddy says I can. Right, Daddy?"

"Not much water and food out here any longer, pumpkin," Davis explained dryly.

"I don't eat much. Otto will take care of me."

"We'll see, Charlotte." Davis put his arm around her, holding her in the car. "Night, Otto."

Davis drove home deep in thought. Charlotte had talked herself into an exhausted state. Slumped over in the front seat, her straight bangs wiggled like fringe as the car hit the ruts in the road.

Davis thought, *My sweet little girl...I promise to take good care of you, but I'm not clear how best to do it.*

— ⊲. ⊲. ⊲. —

When they arrived home, Davis scooped Charlotte's limp frame into his arms and carried her into our bedroom, where a single bed was pushed into the corner. Charlotte's eyes fluttered open for a second as she said, "Good night, Daddy."

Those words Davis always loved hearing seemed to weigh on his heart that night. He joined me in bed. I was curled in a possum-like ball. Even though Davis was heavy with thought, he fell into a deep, sound sleep.

The next morning, embedded in the soft down bed, Davis didn't detect any of my movements as I stole out from under the covers and started my day.

When he finally awoke, he shuffled into the kitchen and said, "Gracious, lady, you are an early bird."

"I have to make my plans, Davis, before the girls turn my day into theirs."

"I can smell something cookin' in the pot. What's up?"

"I'm still working on it. We've got a lot to talk about tonight... schools, activities, missing children, money, jobs...the usual." I smiled. "I'm here to help. I've got BIG PLANS."

Shaking his head, Davis downed a cup of coffee and the plate of eggs I had prepared for him.

"Don't know what we're going to find today on the ranch, but wish me luck."

"Dinner at noon?" I asked.

"Far as I know. Love you, Cate."

After Davis left, Elizabeth joined me in the kitchen. She grabbed a cup of coffee and noticed the extensive list I was scribbling out. Sliding into the padded banquette, she motioned to my list. "What's that, Mama?"

"Getting organized, dear. That's all."

"Am I on that list?"

"Of course, darling."

"Hmm. I've been thinking. I like it here. Twist Junction people tip their hats and smile when you walk down the street. It was good, Mama, to hear 'howdy' as we came into town. I felt like I was home. I've been thinking about the town boys. Many of my friends are married now. I liked my years at college, but maybe I should stay home now...where I can meet a boy."

"Elizabeth, I know what's best. You can't be too prepared in life. You need to expand your horizons, dear. Finish your schooling and you will be ready for whatever life throws your way. You're only 20 years old..."

"But all the boys will be gone."

"The best will be the last, and you will get him. Look around the church. There's a good Catholic boy just waiting for you. In the meantime, you and Sybil can go to the nice girl's college outside Denver. It's run by the nuns who just started our new hospital here in town." With hardly a breath, I rambled on. "The train takes you practically to the door of Loretto Heights. Can you imagine? You can be the first Bennett girl to graduate from college! I'll be so proud. Now watch…"

"Mama...Mama!" Elizabeth tried to interrupt.

"You'll be the perfect potential wife, Elizabeth," I continued.

"Mama," Elizabeth said sharply.

"I know you can do it, and it will make you proud, too."

"Mama, you're not even sure where Sybil is!"

"How do you know that?"

"I just do. Daphne says she's run off."

"Nonsense," I lied.

"Mama, I might not want to leave again, college or no college."

"Elizabeth, you know I know what's best. What happened to my obedient girl?"

"California! That's what happened. I want to tell you what *I* want for once."

"Just think about it, dear," I prodded.

Daphne appeared in the kitchen and chimed in. "So, what's she supposed to think about, anyway?"

"And where are you going, all dressed up so early this morning?" I inquired.

"Elizabeth, can I help you think?" Daphne added.

"It's college," Elizabeth snapped. "You wouldn't know a thing about that."

"You're right. But I do know this; it will be wonderful. And you can just bet I'm going. A girl who has gone to college is smarter and looked up to. She can make a lot of money, too."

"She's right, Elizabeth. Just think about it," I added.

Elizabeth went to sit in the living room as I quizzed Daphne. "How do you know about college?"

"I read."

"So...what else do you know?"

"I'm hungry. Got any toast and jam?"

"Daphne, you know what I mean."

"Got juice?" she asked with arrogance, opening the icebox.

I sat quietly, waiting for her to become civil. *A piece of toast should do it*, I thought.

Daphne opened up. "Well, Sybil didn't want a life here in Twist Junction, so she had to leave on that train. She wanted a big-city life, or at the very least, excitement. She's clever, Mama. The men love her. She's beautiful."

"Yes, Daphne, I know all this, but she has no real education or training. She could be anything. Did she make it to Denver?"

"Don't know just yet. I'm sure she'll drop me a postcard. Pretty neat job George got her, don't you think? He told me all about it after he told you. What a guy! Just think, modeling and showcasing all those beautiful clothes! Pretty smart business plan of Montaldo's, to preview like this in Denver. They want to open a premier Western store there. Sybil will show all those ladies how glamorous they can look. Just you wait. She'll be a big hit."

"All right, but she should have told me."

"Mama, you never would have said yes, and then you both would have gotten Irish mad. George is watching over things. She'll be fine."

"What makes you so self-assured?"

"I have to be. I'm #3. I have to take care of me. Aren't I right?"

"Not really. I take care of you and I love you all."

"Loving me has nothing to do with it. I'm talking about being paid attention to," Daphne said with almost a shake in her voice.

"Don't worry, dear. I pay attention and I have some wonderful plans for you."

"College?" Daphne asked anxiously as she got up and opened the screen door to sit on the front porch.

I let her be. She seemed to be deep in thought, making her own plans. Pretty soon the rockers were filled with giggling neighborhood girls discussing the newest hairdos, lipsticks, and fashions.

"Mama, Daphne's friends woke us up," Maggie said. She and Nancy stood in the hall doorway, rubbing their eyes and smoothing down their scarecrow hairdos.

"Come on, girls, Mama has some nice eggs for you this morning," I said.

The girls took their places at the table, then Maggie piped up, "Hey, this paper says my name. Yours too, Nancy."

I scooted the list off the table as I put down the plates of eggs. "So, what are you girls up to today?"

"Maybe I'll walk down to Phoebe's."

"I'm going to play paper dolls, Mama," answered Nancy. "Don't go to Phoebe's house, Maggie. Play with me."

"That's not a big-girl game for me anymore."

"But I'm still your sister and I like it."

"Ask Charlotte. I'm getting my friends so we can skate over at the gas station later."

"Margaret's mean!" Nancy stomped out of the kitchen, leaving eggs on her plate.

The music blared and the screen door opened and closed a thousand times that morning. I peeked out to see Daphne gathering several girlfriends on the front porch. Boys, spotting a party-like atmosphere, casually flocked to the front yard, where they hopelessly flirted with Twist Junction's beauties. Our Bennett porch became the go-to meeting place.

Calling Daphne from the kitchen, I said, "Time for everyone to go home for their noonday dinner."

"Oh, Mama," she protested, "the cutest boys have just arrived. We want to make our movie plans for later."

"Where are you all getting your money?"

"We loan each other from time to time, or maybe one of the boys takes us."

"Very well, but I need you to set the table. We can discuss plans, short-term and long-term, later, after dishes. Now, shoo! Everyone out before your daddy arrives. He'll want some quiet and his favorite rocker."

I could tell this idea did not suit my social daughter.

"I worked so hard to get everyone together this morning," Daphne pouted. "This isn't fair."

"They'll come back, no doubt... Dishes, placemats with the flowers, and here is the silverware, dear."

Daphne sent her friends away and came into the kitchen with a big sigh.

Elizabeth snapped her head around as she sliced the tomatoes. "Daphne, we're all working here and all you want to do is think about yourself."

"You're all wet. I'm only trying to put some life into this small-town social life. I'm doing everyone a favor."

The pick-up pulled up with dust and dirt billowing off the tires.

"Daddy's home!" shouted Maggie midway through her potato-mashing job.

"Think I've come to the right house," blurted Davis as he came inside. "Something sure smells good."

"Mama made blueberry pie and I helped roll the dough. Look at the wavy edges," Nancy said, pulling Davis to the stove to examine the gold-tinted crust.

As we finished the last of the preparations, I found Charlotte back in the bedroom, rocking and talking to her favorite doll, Molly.

"Okay, little mama, Daddy's home and we're almost ready to eat. Come and get it," I said.

Off in her own little world, Charlotte, in an almost dream state, slowly pulled herself from the chair. "Take a rest, dear," she told her doll. "I'll be right back. I'm going to the store to buy some milk and bread."

I waited by the bedroom and put my arm around Charlotte as we returned to the kitchen madness. Davis had slipped out to the porch, where Daphne had grabbed his sympathetic ear.

"Mama made all my friends go home just when I had worked so hard to have everyone meet here. Oh, Daddy, I've got to show these Joes some California fun."

"If anyone can do it, you can, Daphne."

"Thanks, Daddy. That means a lot to me."

"Davis, dinner's ready. You hungry?" I said, motioning him to the table.

"Well girls, I can see some real changes in you since you all lived in California," Davis remarked, taking his first bite of mashed potatoes and gravy.

"Yes, I learned to play hopscotch," Nancy responded with pride.

"I borrowed Sarah's bike, and we rode piggyback to the park. That was fun too," Maggie added.

"I learned the newest styles. Some of those girls were real gold diggers, trying to attract anything in pants," Elizabeth spoke up as she rolled her eyes.

"Elizabeth, that doesn't sound like ladylike talk," I protested.

"Mama, it's true. They were just looking for a man without caring two hoots about the literature we were studying."

"Who are you kidding? You were looking, too," Daphne said as she took over the conversation. "Daddy, they had the biggest wingdings I've ever seen, and they would try to slip you a mickey in your drink."

Davis's eyebrows shot up. I was quite certain he had no idea what she was saying.

"Daphne, that's enough... Davis, we'll discuss California lingo later." He coughed. "Guess I asked for it and opened this can of worms."

"Eww…a can of worms! Whoever heard of that?" Charlotte shook her head, bangs flying on her forehead.

"How was your morning? Any crops coming up?" I asked my weary husband.

"It's daggum spotty, but hopeful. I went to the tract nearest the house and Otto took my pick-up to the upper section. We both came up with the same perspective."

"What's a perspective?" Nancy groaned.

"Don't interrupt, Nancy, Daddy's talking," I scolded.

"It sounds like a mean man, Mama."

"No, no, the word means an opinion or thought," I said.

My comment put Nancy into silence as she tried to sort out my explanation. Elizabeth and Daphne rolled their eyes and giggled.

"Girls," I frowned, "we all have to learn." I nodded at Davis to continue.

"Conditions are subsiding and we agreed we should try for a small herd and some wheat in the fall. I'm hoping the bank will agree to a small loan. We do have a fine reputation, but they've been stiffed by a con man or two in the past. The dust storms took what other drifters didn't."

"Don't get us too deep in debt now, dear. You're the most positive and optimistic man I know, but we can't be risky these days. We have girls to send off to school."

"Off to school!" Elizabeth's chair screeched away from the table as she started to clear the dishes.

Maggie and Nancy joined in the clearing. Charlotte and Daphne had dishwashing duty. Content to put off her task as long as possible, Daphne offered her father more iced tea and another slice of pie. She wanted to hear my plans as I revealed what activities were cooking in my head.

"Remember the job conversation we were having when you were laid up with your broken leg?"

"Uh-huh," Davis replied.

"I think I need to research that possibility again." I turned to Daphne, who was hovering around the table, trying to look busy while she was eavesdropping. "Daphne, don't dawdle. Dishes are waiting."

"Yes Mama, but can I listen? I like to understand family things."

"You'll hear about it all soon enough. I have many details to work out. The city offices, the DeSoto...they all need competent help. I'm sure—"

Davis cut me off. "Yes, the DeSoto needs a cute little barmaid!"

"Good golly, Davis Crockett Bennett, you are not taking me seriously."

"Come on, Cate, where's your sense of humor?"

"Well, if *you* had all these wild girls on your mind, and were worried about what *you* needed to do with them, *you'd* be in a much more serious frame of mind. You should have been around this morning. I've got fillies growing up to be mares and they need to be trained if they're going to amount to anything. Good schools are what we need—education—for them all."

"Oh no, here we go again," Elizabeth echoed, walking out the front door and letting it slam especially hard.

"What is going on, Cate?" Davis said, looking in her direction.

"California had its good and bad effects on these girls. Elizabeth is afraid all the boys will be taken if she goes off to college."

"And she might have a point in this small town."

"Now, now, that thinking will never do. She'll be worth so much more to someone if she is skilled. They will flock to her then."

"You're always right, Catherine dear. I must get back to other business. I'm meeting with the bank and hearing about the possible

TVA project rumor. Let's talk about all the ideas tonight. I'm staying in town this afternoon. Be home early. Now, I have to clean up to meet the muckety-mucks of this here town. Daphne," he called into the kitchen. "Don't use too much hot water on those dishes. I have to take a shower to meet the president."

"Oh, Daddy!"

"Okay, Nancy and Charlotte," I said. "If you lie down for a rest, I'll let you visit Aunt Polly later and get some of her sugar cookies."

Not a peep and the two of them were down. The others scattered to friends' houses and I found myself resuming my planning list.

Schools
Elizabeth to Loretto Heights College
Sybil to Loretto Heights College
Daphne: skip one more year as a junior at Twist Junction High School and go into the Senior Class
Margaret: Kansas Girls' Boarding School
Nancy: Twist Junction grade school or possibly Kansas
Charlotte: Twist Junction grade school or possibly Dallas

Jobs
Davis: ranch and possibly TVA
Catherine: downtown office job
Elizabeth: cashier, drug store
Sybil: ...
Daphne: babysit
Margaret: teach piano
Nancy: babysit
Charlotte: ...

Activities
Elizabeth: ...
Sybil: learn porcelain painting
Daphne: dance class, violin lessons

Margaret: singing and piano lessons
Nancy: dance class
Charlotte: religion classes at church, singing

With my Irish persistence, I could arrange a schedule and suggest jobs and lessons. I would share all my research with Davis. Suddenly, I realized I had a summer job ahead of me before I could even begin to think of my own new career. All I could think of at this point was Davis's old saying, "I'd much rather keep track of a whole herd of cattle over managing our six girls."

My eyes closed gently as my pen slipped out of my hand and my head bobbed in the heat of the afternoon. An hour must have passed before a knock came at the front door.

"Afternoon, ma'am."

A questionable-looking young cowboy stood at my door. His friend, who stood shadow-like behind him, remained silent, but tipped his cowboy hat shyly. The hard-boiled-looking, younger man, spoke up.

"Is Mr. Bennett in? We heard a rumor that he might be in need of some cowpokes."

I acknowledged him with a not-so-friendly expression. "He's in town. Can I have your names? I'll tell him of your interest."

"Why, yes. My name is Nicky Lambert and this here is my cousin, Leroy Roberts. Thank you kindly...Mrs. Bennett, I assume."

They left with sloppy swaggers.

I sensed something wasn't right with those two. I wasn't even sure I would pass their names on to Davis. Rethinking that, I concluded that Davis was able to choose his own men. Otto and Jeb were the finest men I knew, so Davis could decide on these two strangers as well. Times were tough. Everyone was desperate for a job. Everyone deserved their fair chance. We were Christian people and believed in generosity and trust. But I suspected that Davis might have his hands full with these two.

I noticed Elizabeth sauntering past the overhang of the locust and oak trees that lined Main Street. The two cowboys paused as she passed them on the sidewalk. They were taking a little too much interest in her, I thought, but Elizabeth seemed to be in her own world and paid them no never mind. They looked back as they saw her change direction and head into our front yard. She hesitated, and I could see she was debating whether she wanted to sit on the low wall that framed our property, or come on up to the front porch where I had relocated with my afternoon glass of iced tea.

"Did you have a nice walk, dear?" was my nonconfrontational greeting.

She paused. "That iced tea looks like it might loosen my parched throat. I can't even swallow today. Be right back." Elizabeth returned with a tray holding her glass, an ice bucket, and the hob-nail, clear iced tea pitcher. "Thought you could use a little more, Mama."

I smiled, appreciating my thoughtful, efficient girl.

"Mama," she slowly began to speak. "I'm sorry...I'm grateful that you want the best for me and you will sacrifice things for yourself so I can get an education. I realized you were right just as I started down Second Street, seeing all the poor women sweeping the rich peoples' front porches or hanging out their laundry. I don't want to work as a domestic or be stuck in a ramshackle farmhouse with no lights or water for the rest of my life." Sniffling, she looked up at me. "Will you forgive my arrogance this morning? Please don't tell Daddy. He would be disappointed thinking I could be so rude to you, Mama."

"Elizabeth dear, we all have those moments of being renegades. That's called becoming an adult and thinking for yourself. Sybil has her way, too. At least you don't worry me like she does."

"Mama, you must be worried sick, but I think Daphne got a postcard yesterday from Sybil. Don't know where she hid it but I'll look real quick." With that, she set down her glass and scurried into the house.

Maggie, who was sitting on the sofa reading, looked up as Elizabeth tiptoed past her to the bedroom. "Whatcha doin'?"

"Looking for something that Daphne is hiding."

"You mean the postcard from Sybil?"

"Oh, Maggie. You know everything," Elizabeth whispered.

Maggie got up and joined her sister in the bedroom. "Here it is, between her favorite scarves," Maggie said, reaching for the postcard.

"How did you know?"

"I see what everybody does around here," she grinned with impish certainty. "What are you doing with it?"

"Mama wants to read it."

"What if Daphne comes home? I'll get in trouble."

"No, no. I'll stand up for you."

Elizabeth eased the door open and came out onto the porch where I rocked. Anxious, I squirmed as she handed me the postcard. My hand shook. It was Sybil's writing, all right. And it had a Denver postmark.

Daph,

Things are peachy keen. Denver would blow your wig. Making lots of money. Twenty-five dollars per month to just walk through the Brown Tea Room in pretty clothes every day. Miss you and Mama and Daddy. Send me a note. The Brown front desk will make sure I get it. They are all my friends.

Love,
Sybil
PS: I heard from George. He has been checking on me.

Sighing, I handed the card back to Elizabeth. "Can you put that back where it belongs, dear? I feel better now. Thank you. We're much too close a family to have her run off like that. If I'm not careful, Daphne will repeat Sybil's outing on the train. Remember when she was five? Do you remember her leaving to go to Channing? I think you, Daddy, and I were the only ones upset that day. You girls didn't even know she was gone. I was surprised the train conductor let her on without a ticket or someone with her. Daphne has a self-assurance so strong that you wouldn't question what she was up to. It gave many people a laugh and many others a struggle. I don't think she will ever want to get her Aunt Isabel that upset again. She called me when she saw Daphne. I remember thinking I didn't know who she was most mad at…Daphne, us, or the train conductor! Daphne was sure proud of herself. I guess Sybil is proud of herself now. It's hard to let go of you girls, Elizabeth. You'll see as your children come."

"Guess that was the point when I got mad this morning. Will I ever meet a man, marry, and have children? I'm getting old, Mama. I got scared. I'd like a family. I don't want to be an old maid like Aunt Isabel or Aunt Mary."

"I understand."

Maggie, Nancy, and Charlotte, lined up like stair steps, came out to join the discussion.

"Understand what?" Maggie said. "Is it cookie time at Aunt Polly's?"

Getting permission to go to Polly's house became more important as they became less interested in my conversation with Elizabeth. I sent them on their way. Glancing over Elizabeth's head, I saw three little heads bobbing down the brick street to Aunt Polly's.

I turned to Elizabeth. "You'll be fine, Elizabeth, and glad for the added education in the long run. Do some life-path thinking. What else besides being a wife or mother do you want to accomplish?"

"I suppose I hadn't thought of it that way. Thank you, Mama. Shall I take the tray and iced tea inside?"

"Yes, that would be nice."

My eyes closed again as the eucalyptus trees rustled a breeze across the porch.

Out of nowhere, the serenity was shattered by the sound of tires screeching to a stop and the newest Big Band sounds blaring on the radio. Opening one eye, I saw Daphne and three other girls jump out of a Ford. I could hear them chattering.

"Do you think the Pouting Pink is the best lipstick for my coloring?" Daphne was saying.

"How about the Apple Red?"

"Come on, let's go try them on in my bedroom," Daphne instructed her friends. "Let's try the new hairdos from one of our latest magazines.

I've got the new rollers and rats. You'll be the cat's meow." As they trampled up onto the porch, Daphne noticed me. "Oh, I didn't see you there. Sorry, Mama! We were just going inside."

They ran to the bedroom, and I resumed my rocking on the porch.

– ♩ ♩ ♩ –

Bags, wrappers, Kleenex, brushes, combs, and various sizes of bobby pins were spread all over the bed.

"I'll get a chair and a towel, just like Marvel's Beauty Shoppe," Daphne said.

"Got a mirror too, Daphy?" said one of the girls.

"Want some nail polish? I just found it in the bottom of my purse," said another.

Grabbing some of the little girls' coloring paper, a sign was created and hung over the door.

DEDE'S DARING DOS, ETC.
(Appointments Only)

After skipping up the sidewalk, Nancy stopped dead in her tracks after she entered the house. "There she goes again, taking over the bedroom," she pouted.

Maggie began playing the piano without bothering to push the "soft" pedal. She'd show those loud, giggling girlfriends of Daphne's!

"Does she only know church music?" complained Phoebe. "How about a little jazz out there? Get with it, Maggie!"

Maggie called back to Phoebe, "That's all you girls think about… party, party, party."

"No, that's not all. We think about boys too."

Laughter filled the make-believe beauty parlor. Maggie, curious to see what transformations the girls were making, left the piano and peeked around the door.

One of the girls shouted, "Do you have an appointment, miss?"

Their teasing was unrelenting. Maggie blushed and pretended she was stopping to tie her shoe.

— 4 4 4 —

"Mama, what are you doing?" Maggie asked me. She spoke with a sweet interest, hoping she wouldn't be run off like Daphne's friends had just done.

"Margaret, I'm trying to get you girls organized with activities this summer and good schools next year."

"Hmm. That sounds swell."

"How would you like to teach first-level piano? Maybe take voice and advanced piano lessons, too?"

"Mama, I'd be happy as a clam."

"We could throw the money in the teapot."

"Teapot?" Maggie questioned.

"That's where I keep my extra for important activities. Margaret, I've been dreaming. If I can get you in and if we can afford it, I've been thinking about Mt. St. Scholastica School for Girls in Kansas as the perfect place for you to get a fine lady's education. You could learn typing and stenography and have a good basis for making your own way."

"Mama, do you really think I could do that?"

"Sure, honey. Anything is possible."

"I'd miss you and Daddy."

"Sure you would, but you'd be home for holidays and summers. Margaret, you could meet girls from Kansas City, St. Louis, and perhaps Chicago."

"Where would I live?"

"Right at the school. The nuns have lovely rooms for the boarders, home-cooked meals, and the classrooms are all right there. You'd have your very own room, or maybe share with one girl. You'd wear uniforms and go to Mass every morning. Doesn't that sound wonderful?"

"I think I'd like it, except for missing you."

"Well, let's see what I can do before we worry about that little thought."

"Going away to school...that sounds pretty grown-up to me."

"Now, don't go talking about it till I have all my ducks in a row."

"Okay, Mama," she mumbled. "I may be going to boarding school, boarding school, boarding school..."

Well, that's one happy one, I thought. *I've got a lot of work to do to get the other plans to fall into place.*

A few hours later, Davis came home for the day.

"You're home nice and early," I said. "Some unsavory-looking young men came looking for you this afternoon. Said they heard you needed some cowpokes this fall. I wrote their names down somewhere here."

"Hmm...they came by the house? That's pretty aggressive, I'd say, but maybe that's good. Maybe they'd be hard workers, and not too laid back."

"All that is your area, Mr. Bennett. I just have to say I didn't like them much…a little too interested in Elizabeth... Got some energy left to have a long talk tonight? I have so many ideas and thoughts for the girls. Soup will be ready in a minute."

Sighing, Davis responded, "I'll be sittin' on the porch."

— ⊲ ⊲ ⊲ —

As he passed through the living room and headed for the porch, Davis could hear cackling girls in the bedroom. His head did a spin as he caught sight of the sign over the door. He noticed Nancy, sitting like a doorstop on the floor, her chin on her knees, observing all the beauty practices happening within.

"Hiya, Daddy. I'm going to be a haircutter someday. Looks like fun, doesn't it? Daddy's home, Daddy's home!" Nancy shouted.

"Hurry up, brush me out! I can't be seen with pink rollers on Main Street," Cherise declared.

Davis chuckled and settled into his rocker.

One by one, the girls swished by, fluttering their eyes at Davis.

"Night, Mr. Bennett," they echoed as they sashayed off the porch and down the front walkway.

"We had quite a shop going, Daddy," Daphne bragged.

"And I'm going to be a haircutter when I get older," Nancy said again with conviction as she climbed onto her daddy's lap.

"Nancy, you don't know anything," Daphne huffed.

Nancy blinked sadly as Davis held her in his lap. She was a little too big, and her legs dangled off the rocker's arm.

"Girls, looks like you had a busy day," Davis observed. "Daphne, did you make any money in that beauty shop of yours?"

Daphne grinned. "Yup, enough to pay for the supplies and a Coke at the drug store."

"I think the dining chair has to come back to the table," Elizabeth proclaimed.

Quickly, Daphne retreated back into the bedroom, and within moments a sign that read "Closed" appeared over the bedroom door. She carried the chair back to the dining room.

— 4 4 4 —

We chose our bedroom, with a closed door, for our evening chat. Davis could tell he didn't want distractions as he looked at my three-page list of plans. He mostly nodded and smiled as I spouted off job after job, lesson after lesson, and school after school for the girls.

"Sounds like a lot to bite off all at once, Cate. You're so good at making them all feel important. How do you know their interests so well? You're amazing... Do you think I can get us enough money to pay for all this?"

"You can do it, honey. Can you get the calves soon and start the crops in August, instead of September?"

"Depends on these daggum winds and the heat. You'd better do some Irish praying for some rain, too."

"Davis, I've figured we can save a little with the girls and their jobs, so they can help pay as well. Next week I'll start looking for my job, but I promise not to take on anything till everyone is off to school this fall."

"You're a hard one to disagree with. Are you sure you haven't been taking lessons from Mr. Huntington? This plan sounds like one of his presentations. I'll do what I do with his ideas...nod and smile."

"Oh Davis, you don't have to flatter me...I really hope you agree. I need your support and all this isn't going to be easy...but it doesn't do any good to dream and not try. I have my parents' determination. I'll make it work."

"Wonder what Mother Bennett would think of you now?" Davis grinned, giving me a squeeze and a kiss.

"Guess her eyebrow would raise up, as usual," I retorted. I hung my apron on the doorknob, giving Davis the hint that I needed my privacy for undressing.

My dreams came with a fury that night. Plans became schedules, and then Sybil would appear, go away, and appear once again. Troubled, I tried to sort out the meaning of all of this. The rooster next door broke the dream, and before I knew it, I had my apron back on and my fingers diving into its pocket, rosary in hand. I began praying for my runaway daughter again. Summer was flying by. My school ideas for the girls were finalized, but Loretto Heights did not know that my #2 daughter was missing.

Praise be to God, let her come home, I mentally prayed.

"Let's see what we can put in the teapot girls," I said that morning as we all gathered around the kitchen table.

"Mama, I made $10 this week tutoring my piano students," Maggie bragged.

"Elizabeth?"

"I made $12.50 babysitting."

"Daphne?"

"You just won't believe it. When we were practicing for our Dancing Darlings Review that's coming up at the opera house, the manager asked if any of us would like to usher for Saturday night's opening. I said yes and got $3. Phoebe bought my brown cardigan and gave me $2. I have $5 total," she said, slapping the money on the kitchen table.

Nancy ran to the bedroom to pull out her little brown leather purse. "Mrs. Nutley gave me this to watch little Joey after school last

Wednesday."

"One more dollar!" I said. "What a nest egg for the week! Daddy will be so proud of all of you."

I wished that I could start a job and contribute too. At least Davis had taken on the TVA job, a payrolled position, two days a week. The Tennessee Valley Authority was started by President Roosevelt to create jobs across the country, which helped boost the economy. Twist Junction was lucky enough to be one of those areas to receive help.

"Pennies make nickels," I repeated to myself.

Davis studied his cattle and crop costs. "I'm feeling comfortable putting in my orders tomorrow, Cate. Between the girls and my added TVA salary, I think we can make a go of it. Wonder where those cowpokes ended up? I'll be needing them to help with the herd. Otto can switch back and forth with me between the crops and the calves, but I'll need some extra hands to do the branding and to move them up to market. Those fellas haven't shown up again, have they?" He paused and chuckled. "We sure have a lot on our minds, don't we honey?"

Thinking briefly about those two scallywags, I dismissed questioning their integrity. Davis felt enough pressure about getting his operation back in gear.

"Tomorrow I'll check on their whereabouts," he said.

I didn't respond as I hung my apron on the doorknob. My rosary dropped like a handful of corn onto the floor.

"Cate, that rosary is working mighty hard these days." Davis walked over the skinny floorboards and picked up the shining cross and my precious beads. He handed them to me, then pulled my head to him and nuzzled his nose in my hair. "I love you, Mrs. Davis Bennett," he said, pride pouring over his words.

— ⊲⊦ ⊲⊦ ⊲⊦ —

The next morning, going straight to the DeSoto in search of potential help, Davis noticed a heated conversation as he entered the coffee shop.

"Yes," Joe was saying to one of the waitresses. "There were two of them and they just got up after finishing the Hungry Man's Special breakfast and left while I was pouring Mr. Pierce's second cup of coffee. Didn't wait for the check or nothing," he finished, raising his voice. He waved his receipt book in the air. "Said their names were Lambert and Roberts, that they were looking for work. Lowlifes, I'd call 'em."

"Where do you think they went?" Davis piped up, recognizing the names.

"Straight out of town if they know what's good for their hides!"

"Now, Joe, there must have been some mistake. They'll be back to settle up, just you watch," Davis said.

Having said that, Davis headed to the back booth to join his men's group, who had ignored the ruckus and were deep in a banking conversation.

"Things are loosening up. Five farmers have come in for loans this week alone. I haven't seen such confidence that we've turned the corner in over six years. I was happy to take the risk with them," Mr. Pierce bragged.

"I was coming to see you later, Mr. Pierce," Davis said. "Can you carry one more loan this quarter? Otto and I are ready to work hard and I'm hiring one or two more hands."

"Well, well, Davis. I'm glad to hear your optimism and willingness to work through these times. Guess your six beautiful girls require a man to work in his sleep."

Everyone laughed. The coffee cups hit the table as Joe scurried to refill all five.

"Someone said they saw Sybil in Denver. What's she doing there?"

Before Davis could put his thoughts or words together, Joe yelled, "There they are!"

Davis jumped up and ran outside. He approached the infamous boys to question them, catching up to them as they suspiciously sauntered past the hotel.

"Mr. Lambert, Mr. Roberts, I'm Davis Bennett. My wife said you boys were looking for some cattle work."

Visibly shaken, Nicky spoke up. "Oh, yes sir. We've been out at the

Morris Ranch these past few weeks."

"Don't they pay you out there?"

They shuffled the dirt under their boots.

"Oh, yes sir, why do you ask?" Nicky said.

"I heard a story about an unpaid bill by two guys right here at the coffee shop." He motioned to the café window. "If I went into the saloon, would I find another one there?"

"Oh, no sir. We paid that one."

"Hmm, I see. I was getting ready to offer you jobs, but I can't support vagrants."

"We were just going down the block to collect some money we won at the gambling table last night, then we were going to make good on our breakfast bill."

Mr. Pierce passed Davis and the two young men as they stood under the portal. His clipped gate told Davis that Mr. Pierce had business to attend to, and Davis wanted to be in line to get his loan.

Clearing his throat, he wanted to leave the questionable scene. "I will catch up to you boys later."

"Thank you, Mr. Bennett," they said sheepishly.

As Davis tried to catch up to Mr. Pierce, the boys' disturbing stories clouded his mind. Putting the morning's trauma behind him, Davis straightened his tie and opened the bronze bank doors. Mr. Pierce's office was to the left and Davis glanced to see if he was meeting with anyone as yet. Davis's pace had been "two people" slow. Mr. Pierce was pounding his desk as he gave a forceful, "No!" to some poor merchant. As the merchant exited Mr. Pierce's office, Davis noticed the frown on his face. Davis's heart was pounding as he thought about the weight of his interests.

Smiling sweetly, Mr. Pierce's secretary came over to Davis. "Mr. Pierce has one more customer before you. Would you like some coffee, or would you like to come back at a later time?"

Davis's hands were shaking a bit, so he rejected the coffee offer and decided he needed to get this request over as soon as possible. "Thank you, Miss Ginny. I'll be glad to wait for him."

Davis's brain felt like it was swimming with thoughts. By the time he walked into Mr. Pierce's office, he could barely get his words out. Mr. Pierce felt Davis was confident in his plan; however, Davis was not feeling like it was a good day.

"Davis, you doin' okay, boy?" Mr. Pierce raised his voice with fatherly concern.

"Oh, yes sir. I witnessed an unfortunate incident with Joe at the café. He had someone walk out on their bill, and I come to find out they were the ones I was going to hire to help with the new herd."

"Can't be too careful with strangers around here. Trust your instincts. You'll do the right thing. Your business plan sounds well thought out and sound. Now," he hesitated in midsentence, "just get some good workers. If you don't, a good plan can turn awry." He stood up, towering over his oak double-pedestal desk, and stretched out his hand. "Congratulations. I'll get the paperwork ready for you to sign this afternoon."

"Many thanks, Mr. Pierce. I guarantee a home run."

"I know you will, boy."

Davis was relieved he had gotten his loan. Consciously looking down the street, he hoped not to confront his dubious possible employees. His old limp slowed him a bit, but he managed to return home in record time.

— ◁ ◁ ◁ —

"Supper won't be ready for a few minutes. Can I bring you something, honey?" I asked Davis as I looked down at him. He sat in the kitchen banquette. "Are you feeling done in?"

"Guess you could say that. Just anxious."

"Did everything go all right?"

"Somewhat, but don't fret, we got our money."

"That's my man. Pork chops comin' up."

Slightly dazed, Davis got up and went to the front window. He caught sight of two girls walking on the other side of Main Street. One had a suitcase flapping against her leg. He pushed his glasses up so he could rub his cloudy eyes. By gum, it *was* her! Daphne was walking with Sybil.

"Catherine!" Davis yelled as he ran out the front door.

Davis had tears rolling down his face by the time he reached the sidewalk. The girls had crossed the street, and Sybil flew into her father's arms, sobbing.

"Oh Daddy, I guess I'm not such a big, grown-up girl after all. Pretty faces aren't enough in this world!"

As Sybil cried more intensely, Daphne placed a calm hand on her sister's arm. Davis gave her his most compassionate hug.

"What is going on?" I shouted as I dashed out onto the porch. The words, "Oh my God in Heaven," seemed to fly off my lips. "I thought somebody died when I heard all that crying."

"Oh Mama, the only one who died was your *bad* girl, but I'm the *good* girl now, and I'm home," Sybil sniffled.

Rolling my rosary beads between my fingers in my pocket, I prayed, *Thank you, God, thank you, God!* as I leaped down the stairs to hug my daughter.

Davis lifted up the suitcase. "Let's all go inside and get into your mama's pork chops and scalloped apples."

Daphne grabbed another dining room chair and set a place for Sybil at the table. Elizabeth and the others squealed with joy when they saw their sister.

"Well, how's my wayward sister?" Elizabeth winked, half smiling. "I was getting used to the bed by the window. Guess I'll have to give it up to our celebrity, Sybil, Famous Denver Model."

Questions came right and left as Sybil ate slowly. The questions continued after dinner, in the bedroom, where she flopped appreciatively on her very own bed.

"Let's leave her be. I think this has been quite a traumatic adventure, don't you agree?" I said to Davis. I promised myself I'd wait a week before I shared my plans for her to go off to Loretto Heights College. Crossing my fingers, I hoped the last piece would fall into my family puzzle.

Within days, Davis's seed and cattle would arrive, and the girls would be wrapping up jobs and days of lessons. I noticed that Davis seemed to be distracted, which to me was quite unusual. His plans were coming together and his family was intact. Normally, these were the very things that gave him joy. As Tuesday evening rolled around, I had to prod him to sing at choir practice. His humming seemed less energetic, his steps slower.

"Are you going to tell me?" I blurted out as his last footstep hit the porch on his way home from practice.

"I can't hide a thing from you, Catherine Bennett. So...you've seen my worry written all over my face. I did something that is bothering my gut. You know those two cowboys that came looking for a job?"

"Yes, the ones I didn't like?"

"Yes, well, I caught them in some dishonest activity. They skipped out on their bill at the DeSoto café. They 'fessed up and settled their unsavory actions. Thought I'd give them another chance. I just need them for two weeks. What harm can they do in two weeks? Otto and I will be with them all the time. Otto will be in charge at the bunkhouse. But something is gnawing at me...and I don't have time to change plans now."

"Davis, it can only be so bad. Don't worry. I've never seen you not handle a tough situation. I'll help if you need me to check on things. We're a team. You, me, and Otto."

I had become distracted with the daily chores of the house, getting everyone ready to go off to school, and looking into my upcoming job opportunities. "Our worlds are revolving so fast," I said to Mother one day. "I don't even know if my own husband is fine. How does this happen?"

Mother, a woman of few words, would only say, "That's life, my dear."

Mother's curt answer left me less than satisfied. Davis continued to be preoccupied. I continued to be preoccupied.

The cattle were branded. The fields planted.

Davis's new cowboys stopped by, thinking they should be paid since the job had been completed the day before. I became nervous. I could see the surly men blocking Margaret and harassing her as she tried to come up the front steps. That did it. I ran to my bedroom and slid the shotgun out from under the bed. I hurried to the front door and managed to hoist the heavy gun onto my shoulder.

"If you good-for-nothings don't leave my daughter alone, I'll have your brains for dinner. Get off my property—and you'd better get out of town while you're at it."

Startled, they did a quick about-face and ran down the street. Davis intercepted them on the sidewalk, pay in hand. They grabbed their money, then kept going, out of sight, I'm sure never doubting that I would have used my intimidating weapon.

Maggie was frozen in her tracks. Davis came running at the sight of me holding a gun on the front porch.

"Mama!"

"Cate!"

My name came rolling out of their mouths in unison. "I'll show them," I exclaimed as I turned on my heels and headed back into the house.

"That was just like in the movies, Daddy," Maggie enthused.

"I think a little more realistic, honey," Davis chuckled nervously.

8
Trains, Trains, And More Trains

I felt a sense of pride as the buzz over school began to rev up. My plans were falling into place. Sybil was even on board. She had come to me soon after arriving back home.

"Mama, I see what you've been trying to tell me. We need more skills to be able to survive in the adult world. I really liked my experiences modeling, but that was all I was good for. It was hard to get along. My paycheck barely covered the rooming house rent. Mama, George was so good to me. He set up the job contact and the nice place to live."

"Have you thanked him and told him you're back?"

"You bet I did. He's my forever friend. He laughed when I told him I had to come home. You know what he had the audacity to say? 'The grass isn't always greener in the other pasture'... The nerve!"

Smiling, I almost giggled as Sybil paced, regaling me with her Denver antics. Finally, I interrupted her and asked, "So, dear, what is it you want to do now?"

"Well...I was thinking...maybe I should go with Elizabeth to Loretto Heights and try out college. I'd meet nice boys and learn some of those skills you talk about. Mama, do they have art classes?"

"Of course they do. I talked to Sister Mary Patricia. She says you can paint outside on nice days. Can you imagine, breathing in that fresh air while you do something you love?"

"I think I'm going to be happy... Can I go into town from time to time? I want to visit some of my favorite shops. Elizabeth will love it too. Imagine, me showing my big sister the ropes!"

As her enthusiasm built, I knew I could count on Sybil to get on that train to Denver.

Elizabeth and Sybil were the first to leave. The Fort Worth and Denver City Railway would take them to within a mile of the college. College representatives met each new student at the train station with a welcome packet and a beanie. I knew Sybil would be horrified by the beanie, but I figured she could handle that trauma by herself.

Davis and I drove the girls to the train station after their morning good-byes with their sisters. The little ones hugged and kissed Elisabeth and Sybil, while Daphne stood to the side, green with envy.

I whispered to her, "It will be your turn soon. Do you want to come with us to the station and see how to get a ticket and check which car to board?"

"I've taken the train before."

She huffed off before I could say another word, muttering, "You don't even remember when I was five and ran off and took the train to Channing all by myself..."

As we walked the girls to their Pullman car, Davis leaned over and whispered, "I didn't expect to be so sad."

Funny, I felt the same way.

Davis and I stood in silence on the platform, watching our two eldest girls go off to college. I felt my heart's memory of my very own dreams from long ago...my dream of going to college. I was happy to see my beautiful girls fulfilling my goals.

— ◁ ◁ ◁ —

The girls chattered with excitement as they boarded the train.

"Did you see him?" whispered Elizabeth.

"Who?"

"The tall, lanky cowboy with the hat, standing on the platform."

"I'm much too busy looking at my own male choices here on the train," Sybil remarked curtly. "I have to fluff my hair; it got windblown on the way down the platform." Looking in the silver compact she had purchased while modeling in Denver, she added, "There, I think my lipstick is the perfect shade. Don't you like it?"

"Look! I think he's looking at me. He just tipped his hat and smiled. Who is he?"

"How should I know?" Sybil said, rolling her eyes. She glanced up, then smiled with recognition. "Well, well...I *do* know him...Bruce Pearson. His family owns everything...the funeral parlor, the furniture store, and a new mattress company, I understand. They own everything that Mr. Huntington doesn't. He'd be a pretty good catch if you're interested."

"Are *you* interested?"

"Heavenly days, no! I don't want any of these hometown boys! But you'd better watch out for Daphne."

Elizabeth retorted, "I don't worry about her...she wants to go to college."

— ⊲. ⊲. ⊲. —

As we got back into the car, Davis reminisced. "We have to let them go sometime, Cate. Isn't that what you want?"

"Yes, that was my plan, but it's hard when you come right down to it."

"Look girlie, you can't have your cake and eat it too. You've got other chicks to tend to now."

I hated it when he was so right. I knew the house would be much quieter now. My responsible and oldest daughter was gone, and Davis's clown and giggling companion was gone once again.

Davis dropped me back at home, then went to work. I poured some iced tea as I passed through the kitchen from the back door. I heard Margaret playing the piano, and saw Daphne flopped on a living room chair.

"Are the witches gone?" envious Daphne snapped.

"That is not Christian or ladylike talk," I scolded.

"I want to go."

"Soon enough, I told you."

"Well, at least I'm the oldest and can be the boss now."

The conversation did not make me happy, and as I proceeded to the porch, I knew that Davis wouldn't have liked Daphne's tone, either. If she had been younger, he would have had the black strap out. Discipline was more difficult as the girls matured.

I did call back, "I thought you wanted to go to the moving picture show with your friends tonight."

"*Yessssss,*" came her sarcastic reply.

"Well then, change that attitude, miss."

A few days later, I decided to venture out for a day to myself.

"I'm walking into town for an hour, girls. Daphne, you're in charge," I said, then questioned my wisdom in giving Daphne authority.

The day was crisp and the bustle of Twist Junction's slowly resuming economic boom gave me confidence that there must be a job out there for me somewhere. Noticing which office or store looked to be the busiest helped me make my choices. Yes, the DeSoto Hotel was one of the top establishments. And the local grocery and Swearingen Dry Goods had their constant stream of clientele.

City offices...now that's a possibility. They always need help, in good times and bad.

"Cate!" Davis called out, pulling open the DeSoto's massive door and waving at me. "You look lost. What's up?"

I hurried over to greet him. "Doing some looking and thinking, that's all. Almost time for me to get my job. Got any ideas?"

"Let's see...the newspaper, the school, the hospital?"

"Well, I didn't consider writing, children, or sick people."

"No, I guess they're not your cup of tea—at least the children, because you have enough of your own; or the sick people, unless you wanted to sit by them and pray."

"Oh, Davis. I'm leaning in the direction of the DeSoto. Bookkeeping...or maybe work for the city."

"What about the bank?"

"I don't want to know too much about all the people's money."

"Hmm."

"Let's walk home together. Did you see the men for coffee today? Getting hungry?"

Davis quietly nodded to my queries as we strolled home.

Later, as I heated up beef patties and gravy, I realized that Davis wasn't as keen about me working as he said. I couldn't open up that conversation or I might have to back down. I had to become an office girl and not just a housewife. Buttoning my lip, I pretended not to notice his unusual silence, and began thinking.

Monday I'll put on my Sunday dress, hat, and gloves and go job shopping. Getting Daphne, Nancy, and Charlotte out the door, fed, and dressed for school will be the test. Margaret doesn't go away to her school until Saturday, so maybe she can go with her father for the morning.

I heard the train whistle blow and wondered how Elizabeth and Sybil were doing at Loretto Heights. A quick note from Sybil answered me. She was thrilled with her new single room and large window with a mountain view.

> *Imagine, Mama, a room all to myself! I think I have died and gone to Heaven. Thank you. Hope I like my art classes as much as my private quarters...*
> *Love,*
> *Sybil*

I shook my head. *This time next week we'll be walking away from the train platform once again, to send Margaret on the Chicago-Rock Island to Mt. St. Scholastica School for Girls in Kansas.* I had promised Margaret that the nuns would be there to meet her and that the train conductor would check on her from time to time. Satisfied with my explanations, Margaret was excited to have her own special adventure.

One week felt like a minute, and before I knew it, we were at the train station and Margaret had boarded amidst Nancy's and Charlotte's sobbing. Davis and I held our anxiety close to the vest, since we had witnessed quite enough family emotion already.

I was ready. I had gotten an interview at the DeSoto and it had gone well, resulting in the offer of a fine accounting position. Downplaying my excitement, I decided not to mention my enthusiasm to Davis just yet; instead, I concentrated on the girls getting situated in their schools. Davis's less-than-pleased attitude had to be handled carefully. I did feel that once the added income began to fill the teapot, he would change his demeanor. My new bookkeeping job at the DeSoto was about to begin! I would get my feet wet, then maybe pursue a city job in a few years.

Time was flying and it was soon Monday morning. My chores were done and the children were off to school. I stood before my favorite gold-leaf mirror. "Good luck, Catherine," I said to my reflection in an official tone of voice. "You look very professional in your hat. Pull your hair out on the left side, so it comes over your brow."

Before I could walk out of the house, the phone rang.

"Good morning," I answered assertively.

"This is Sister Agnes at Mt. St. Scholastica School for Girls. I want to report on your daughter, Margaret. Is this Mrs. Bennett?"

"Oh yes, how is she?"

"She arrived safely, and I'd say it feels like she has been here forever. She is fitting in so beautifully. The other girls are very fond of her, and the teachers have told me how thrilled she is to start all of her classes. I'm sure you'll be hearing from her soon. We require the girls to write home every week, you know."

"Oh, thank you, Sister."

"Let me know if you have any concerns, Mrs. Bennett. I will try to always be available for you."

"Have a lovely day. I appreciate the call," I answered politely.

Uplifted by the good report, I snapped open the screen door and was halfway down the block before I realized I was practically running. I, too, was thrilled. I was starting my first job.

The girls must have felt like this on their first day of school, I thought, knowing that my dream was coming true. *I can't be late...I can't be late... First impressions are the most important,* I was now saying to myself, and not the children, for a change.

I arrived at the DeSoto, took a deep breath, and opened the heavy door. Mr. Meyers, my new boss, was waiting to greet me.

"Good morning, Mrs. Bennett," he said, looking at his pocket watch. "Nine o'clock on the dot. Very good."

"I'm pleased to be here, Mr. Meyers."

He motioned for me to follow him to the accounting department at the end of the hall.

"Thought you might like the desk by the window. It's easy to see the comings and goings that way."

I pulled out a utilitarian oak chair on casters, sat down, and scooted it up to the desk, only to find that my chin practically rested on the edge of the desk.

"Oh, we'll have to adjust that," Mr. Meyers said.

I got up and he cranked the chair up as high as it would go, then scratched his head. "Just one minute," he said. He then placed two thick books on the seat.

I sat down again, but it still wasn't quite the right height.

Mr. Meyers picked up the phone and dialed an in-house extension. "Housekeeping, this is Mr. Meyers in accounting. Do you have an extra pillow?"

A few moments later, Rozana, the maid, arrived in the office to see me sitting low in my chair.

"The pillow?" Mr. Meyers said, reaching out his hand.

"*Sí, sí,* Mr. Meyers," she answered, as I stood and she placed the fluffy mound on my chair.

I sat down again. "Much better now, thank you," I said politely.

"Can we go to work now, Mrs. Bennett?"

I nodded as his monotone voice began to reel off detailed instructions.

Oh dear, I thought. *Can he just slow down...or at least explain what is most important?*

His fuddy-duddy voice drove me practically insane. Eventually, I learned to tune him out and look out the window from time to time. Yep, this was a "job" all right, and I had to learn coping skills in order to survive my boss and my beige-walled office at the end of the hall.

One day, I asked if I could retrieve one of the surplus pictures I had spotted stacked under the back stairs. Mr. Meyers nodded his permission. Enthusiastically, I got a hammer and nailed up a painting of a pueblo scene with an arched stucco wall, hollyhocks, and a bent tree in the background. The sky, a vibrant blue, added some color to my drab surroundings.

"What do you think, Mr. Meyers?"

Dryly, he answered, "Hmm, yes, very nice, Mrs. Bennett."

Those were the only words I could get him to say that entire day.

Pretty soon I had devised a reason to collect all the money from the tills, except for the till in the saloon—a place in which no respectable woman would set foot. On occasion, I would catch sight of Davis and the men in the coffee shop. He always made me proud, sitting with the town fathers. On my coffee breaks, I walked over to the post office to check our glass-front mailbox, hoping to find letters from the girls.

Luckily, my tedious days were only three days a week, but the paycheck excited me the most, and soon I got another teapot in which to stash my savings.

Finally, one night I said to Davis, "Can you imagine me working in a beige office with dull oak chairs and desks, and not one picture on the wall? At first, I thought I'd go crazy."

"Well, looks like you didn't."

"Of course not. I found a picture to hang. I even have to sit on books and a pillow."

"So, this job isn't all it's cracked up to be, huh?"

"It's okay, but here's what I really wanted to show you."

I pulled out $50 in cash. Davis raised his eyebrows with surprise.

"And that's not all. I've already sent off money to the girls for Loretto Heights College for next semester, and to Margaret's school as well."

"Cate!" Davis enthused. "You're my treasure! Wish I'd let you work before."

The fall and Thanksgiving disappeared like a dream, and as December showed itself on my large wall calendar, I remarked, "If it's okay, I'd like to go out Christmas shopping for something small for each girl. We had a nice Thanksgiving, and now I'd like to do something special that they won't be expecting."

"I love you, Cate. Always planning ahead. Always creating memories for us."

On my days off or after work, I'd go to the drug store or dry goods store, where soaps, lotions, ribbons, and the newest make-up were collected, purchased, and wrapped. One evening, Davis surveyed the purchases and laughed.

"This looks like Santa's workshop, dear. Hope you remember your loving husband. We're going to have a wild week. Otto and I are rounding up the cattle to take them up to Dumas for the winter. Mr. Motely and Jeb will fatten them in corrals till next spring, and move them to Kansas City with other herds. Should be back the end of the week."

"Take that extra heavy jacket, your gloves, and blankets," I said. "Will Otto cover the rest?"

"Yes, yes. We'll be fine, but I did get Owen and his grandson to help us with the drive. He offered and I took him up on his suggestion."

— ⊲. ⊲. ⊲. —

In town, Owen met Davis and called out, "Hang in there. I just saw Otto getting supplies. My grandson, Donel Dean, and I will be ready lickety-split. You'll need a trail boy and another flank rider. We're mighty lucky Donel Dean is up here for a visit. This will be a growing-up experience for him."

Davis grinned. "Okay. Many thanks. I'll tell you my story as we ride."

Owen hurried to get his grandson and a few supplies, and joined Davis.

"Let's get going." He eyed his brother. "Davis Bennett, I know you're brave and are a hard worker, but it doesn't sound like you and Otto had this one covered. That doesn't sound like you."

"My plans fell apart. A couple of guys walked out on me." As they drove to the ranch, Davis told his brother about the two good-for-nothing ranch hands that had deserted him. "I wasn't sure they'd show up for more work, even though it was offered. But that was before Cate chased them off from the house with the rifle, so I guess I don't blame them." He chuckled as he recalled the vivid scene.

"That's water under the bridge," Owen said. "I'm glad they're gone. You're right, Davis, good-for-nothings, that's all they were."

Once everyone had gathered at the ranch, they mounted their horses and prepared to drive the cattle. Otto had already loaded their supplies.

"Are we ready, men? Let's move 'em!" Davis called out.

"We got a lazy bunch, Mr. B!" Otto shouted as the cattle slowly began to move.

"Hey there, young man, nudge them along," Davis yelled to Donel Dean.

"Looks like they know they're going somewhere and don't want to leave you, Mr. B," Otto grinned.

"Going to miss singing them my lullabies," Davis joked. "Maybe I'll sing a good-night song tonight."

The joking made the arduous day pass. It continued into twilight at the campfire, as Davis bellowed his ballad to the herd.

"You boys can sure cut up," said Owen. Leaning over to Donel Dean, he added, "See boy, we cowboys know how to have some fun from time to time."

Young Donel Dean smiled a buck-toothed smile.

At daybreak, the men heard a car rumbling down the nearby road. Owen's wife, Beulah, appeared with scrapple and hot biscuits in her basket.

"Figured you couldn't have gotten but so far yesterday. Glad I could find you. Wouldn't want my grandson to go starving on his first cattle drive."

Owen boasted, "I've got a honey for a wife, but she sure likes to spoil Donel Dean here. Beulah, how can I raise him to be a man if you follow him around like his shadow?"

Belly laughs erupted from the others.

"Never mind. You'll wish I was there tomorrow morning when you're cold and hungry." She smiled, and with a wink, she was off.

"I'd say we were a bunch of softies," Davis said. "If we don't get a move on, Jeb will think we're not coming. We'll lose our main man!"

The second day of the drive the cattle seemed to understand that they weren't just changing pastures. The pace picked up to Davis's satisfaction, and the bedrolls were welcomed to cradle the men's weary bones at the end of the day.

Davis observed his men sleeping, then blew out a deep sigh and looked up at the stars. He listened to the low moans from his cattle and the far-off coyote barks. Sounds of the plains filled him with a "home sweet home" feeling. Yes, his true passion was being with his animals, out under the open sky. The ground was hard, but it melted him into God's earth and he felt at one with the land. His ears picked up a slight movement as a young head poked up.

"Need the necessary?"

"Yes, sir."

"I'll keep watch for you."

Donel Dean scrambled out into the brush, then returned like a house on fire.

"Well, how do you like your first cattle drive? The latrine facilities are a little rustic," Davis teased.

Without directly answering his great-uncle, Donel looked up at the sky. "Sure is quiet out here. There aren't this many stars in Amarillo, either."

"You know, Donel Dean, you have quite a grandfather. He's well known in Twist Junction as being one of the best ranchers around. You should be mighty proud."

"Yes, sir."

"Your grandfather must be proud of you. He says you make good grades in school. I always wanted a son. Do you know that I have six girls?"

"Six? Jiminy Christmas!"

"I even had a name for my boy…John Howard. Can you imagine naming a baby you don't even have?" Davis laughed quietly. Looking up at the stars, almost praying, Davis said, "Maybe my girls will bring me some boys. Maybe I can bring them out here or on a cattle drive someday. Maybe they'll want to be a rancher cowboy..." Davis looked over at Donel Dean again. "Life is full of maybes, young man." The words seemed to tumble out of his mouth. "Sorry, Donel Dean, you need to get some shuteye, son."

The cows' mooing sounds were like a symphony of cellos. The horses' tails slapped off the irritating flies. Davis caught himself catnapping during his nightly watch, but who was going to reprimand him?

He awoke with a start to see a figure coming toward them, about five miles out. He could just make out a rider leading two extra horses, kicking up dust in the distance. "Daggum, I think it's Jeb!" Davis shouted. His enthusiastic outburst awoke the others and they jumped up.

After downing a fast cup of coffee and Beulah's biscuits, the men packed their bedrolls, readied their horses, and began rounding up the herd. They headed the cattle in Jeb's direction. The shuffling of hooves echoed as the wind shifted around them.

"Mornin', boys!" Jeb greeted. "I thought I was going to get stiff waiting for you all. You need a real cattle driver around here!"

"Jeb, you can say that again. It isn't the same without you," Otto remarked, reaching out to shake Jeb's hand.

"Yahoo! Let's get these young ones to do some high-stepping." Jeb's voice reverberated across the grasslands and gave everyone a new burst of energy.

Owen shot a look at Davis, Otto, and Donel Dean. Each man nodded that they were ready, and they were off for the last day of their drive.

Jeb called out to Davis, "Mr. Motley will meet us just outside the cattle yard. You can almost smell it from here! He can see us coming across. Hang in there, boys...you've got it licked now. We should have them in their corrals before noon tomorrow."

Jeb's presence renewed their confidence. Davis appreciated his good friend's help even more as they settled in that night.

Jeb pulled out his bedroll with his hidden treasure rolled up inside—his guitar. "Look what I got," he grinned, and, plopping down beside the crackling campfire, he began to strum.

As the others began singing old cowboy tunes, Davis and Owen joined in, humming along. They grinned at each other.

"This is a real cowboy sing-along," Donel Dean said, his eyes wide as he took it all in. He leaned over and whispered into his grandfather's ear, "I think I know the song 'Granddaddy.' I think I can sing it with Jeb."

As Davis looked at the stars and his friends around the campfire, and listened to the jovial singing, he hated to think that this might be his last night on the plains for a long time...if not forever. Times were changing and the trains would soon take over the job of the iconic cattle drive. Melancholy, Davis fell asleep with this memory of Owen, Donel Dean, Otto, and Jeb out on the wide-open plains.

$$- \triangleleft \; \triangleleft \; \triangleleft -$$

On Saturday morning, I returned home after a quick walk to the post office. "Nancy, Mama's home! I had to get the mail before we head our separate ways today. Finish your cereal. We won't be eating for a while. It's a long way to Channing... Daphne!" I called.

"She's at Phoebe Ann's," Nancy said between bites.

"Already? It's only 9:00."

"They're making pancakes for Phoebe Ann's brother, Ray. It's his birthday."

"Oh, how dear! We didn't even get to say good-bye!"

Nancy moped. "I wanted to go, but she said it was his *private* party. So instead, I get *cold* cereal."

"And a whole day *alone* with your mother. Lucky girl!" I retorted. "Charlotte, are you ready to go to Aunt Polly's? She says there is going to be a Christmas Fair at the Baptist church."

"Ready, Mama."

"This is going to be a wonderful day. I haven't seen my aunts in *soooo* long. Did you know that they've raised a Christmas turkey for us? We can take a look to see how big he is." I ushered the girls outside to the car. "Climb in, girls."

The old Buick rolled out of the driveway and we drove to Polly's house.

"Howdy, my little missus." Polly glowed as she hugged Nancy, then reached for Charlotte and slipped her hand around her tiny waist. "Have a nice drive, Catherine, and send your aunts my best."

In the rearview mirror, I could see Charlotte skipping down the walkway with her loving Aunt Polly. Nancy sat humming in the front seat, settling in and smoothing her skirt. Out of habit, I consciously looked up at the clouds. It was a beautiful, sky-blue, late-fall day. *Hope you're coming home soon, Davis darling*, I thought as I turned onto Channing Road.

"Nancy, do you know that Aunt Isabel and Aunt Mary are Grandmother Connelly's sisters? She had four sisters. Almost as many as you."

"Where?"

"They grew up in Ireland."

"Where?"

"Across the ocean..." I looked at the trees. "Pretty soon all the leaves will be gone." I paused. "Winter is coming..." I looked over at Nancy and saw that my little girl's eyes were closed.

After a lovely drive, I pulled up to the white picket fence that surrounded my aunts' home. I marveled at how Mary and Isabel were always at the window waiting, just like two doves on a wire. Putting my fingers up to my lips and pointing at my sleeping beauty, I quietly opened the car door and got out.

They opened the Victorian front door gently as I walked up the sidewalk to greet them.

"Catherine, you look beautiful. That job must agree with you," Aunt Isabel remarked.

"Oh, let's be honest, it's the money," I said as I stepped inside.

"What a shame. I always loved my job, but there was no one quite like Mr. Goodnight and the XIT Ranch. It was *so* interesting. Do you know he couldn't read? I had to read everything to him and write his letters. Those were the days!" Aunt Isabel laughed.

"Oh, Aunt Isabel, you've led such an exciting life!"

Reminiscing, she said, "Someday, Catherine, would you take my beautiful sidesaddle for safekeeping? Mr. Goodnight had it hand carved for me. I want you or one of the girls to have it."

Aunt Mary spoke up. "Enough of the past. How is that fine husband of yours?"

"Moving some cattle to Dumas this week. Otto, Owen, and Owen's grandson, little Donel Dean, are helping, and that nice black man, Jeb, was meeting them outside of town."

"Always did want to meet that Jeb fella," Aunt Isabel said. "He sounds like a real interesting character. What a shame there's such prejudice against black people in these parts. What's the matter with people? It sure wasn't easy being Irish Catholic in the early days, either. Kind of amazing that Mr. Goodnight put such trust in a woman, who was Irish Catholic to boot..."

"He just trusted those honest, china-blue eyes and your no-nonsense behavior," I chuckled.

"Now, now..."

"I'm sincere. I wouldn't want to cross you in a business deal, Isabel O'Reilly."

With a *creak*, the front door opened slowly and a sleepy Nancy came inside. She ran to Aunt Mary first, and then Aunt Isabel, with big hugs for each.

"How would our girl like some hot chocolate today? Tea, Catherine?" Aunt Mary said.

I nodded gratefully.

We settled into our warm drinks and tea sandwiches. Before I could tell all the stories of the girls' successes, it was 3:00 and we hadn't even looked at the Christmas turkey yet. Aunt Mary took Nancy's hand.

"Let's see if it's big enough to eat," she said as they went outside.

Nancy called from the fenced back yard, "Come see, Mama!"

"Another week and a half and he'll be perfect," Aunt Isabel said proudly.

Reluctantly, the ladies returned to the parlor. They all knew that was where they would have to say their good-byes. Visits were rare and treasured.

"Thank you, my wonderful aunts," I said, looking at my watch. "It's time for us to be going. I don't know when I've had such a relaxing afternoon."

We hugged and placed small pecks on each other's cheeks. Nancy did a curtsey. We laughed out loud.

"Don't know where she got that!" I said.

"Dancing school, Mama."

"You're really raising them to be perfect little ladies," Mary said.

I smiled as Nancy sauntered out the door, through the gate, and climbed into the car.

As we drove home, Nancy said, "Do you think Charlotte is home yet, Mama? She said she'd bring me a treat from the fair."

"We'll see. We'll be home soon."

And so we were. Nancy scooted out of the car and into the house.

As I turned off the car motor, I heard a bloodcurdling scream. I bolted out of the car and ran inside so fast, I didn't remember going up the back steps. Nancy was shaking. I was shaking. I looked around my house. A splintered gun shaft lay across the threshold. My house, my house! Shards of dishes were scattered all over the kitchen floor. My glasses were broken in the sink. My pans were gone, and my savings teapot! Who could have done such a thing?

I grabbed Nancy's hand and we walked slowly through the dining room into the living room. No sofa, no tables, no chairs, no piano, no buffet... My prized Irish linens were gone. Aunt Isabel's gold-leaf mirror had been lifted off the wall, as had my favorite oil painting, which I had painted before Elizabeth was born. I leaned against the old oak dining room table, which was still there, probably because it was too heavy to move.

Daphne and Phoebe Ann came in the front door. "We saw the car and knew you were—"

Daphne gasped. Phoebe Ann screamed.

"*Oh, Mama!*" Daphne ran to me and Nancy. "What...what happened?" Her voice shook. She ran into the bedrooms, then walked into the music room. "No Christmas tree, Mama! Our beds are gone, the dresser and our clothes, and the closet is almost empty. Oh golly, how did they miss my favorite black dress hanging in the back of the closet? Guess it was too dark for them to see...must have been in a real hurry, but lucky for me."

"Can you look in my room please..." I held on to the table to support my knees, which were rapidly weakening beneath me.

Daphne and Phoebe Ann circled back around through the kitchen, tiptoeing gingerly over broken plates. They went into our bedroom. I heard closet doors open and close, footsteps, and muffled conversation. Then they came back to the living room and sat on the floor with their backs against the fireplace surround.

Shaking her head, Phoebe Ann said, "Mrs. Bennett, I am *so* sorry."

Daphne had her head buried in her hands.

"Is it that bad, honey?" I whispered, hardly able to speak.

Daphne nodded. Tears rolled down her face. "The..." she sobbed, "...the Victorian bed and dresser are gone. Daddy's rocking chair, where he used to hold us at night, is gone. I couldn't find your pearls..."

"I always hide them on the window ledge behind the curtain."

Daphne jumped to her feet and flew into the bedroom. "They're here! I've got them!" she shouted triumphantly.

"Look on the doorknob. Is my apron there?"

"Yes, yes!"

"Bring it to me, dear."

205

Daphne walked back to me as if in shock. She handed me my favorite items and I pulled my rosary beads out of the apron pocket. Then I sobbed right in front of my children. Phoebe Ann sat silently as she watched Daphne, Nancy, and I hugging and crying uncontrollably.

I walked into the kitchen and picked up the phone to call Aunt Polly. At least the phone was still there and worked.

"Polly dear, can Charlotte and Nancy spend the night? Yes, everything will be fine. I'll tell you about it later."

Phoebe Ann piped up, "Daphne can stay with me, Mrs. B."

"That's lovely, thank you, dear."

Daphne opened the front door. The rockers were still there on the porch.

"Come on, Phoebe. Help me bring these in," said Daphne as she wiped the fall dew off the arms, backs, and seats.

The girls set up the chairs in the living room. Daphne took my hand and led me over to the lineup of white, slat-backed porch chairs.

"You feeling sturdy, Mama?"

"I haven't felt like this since I spilled the kettle of hot water on you, Daphne," I whispered.

"Oh, Mama." Daphne bent down, crying again. She hugged me.

I couldn't move. I couldn't muster the energy to call the sheriff. I just wanted Davis. "I must be in shock..." I looked down at little Nancy and realized she hadn't spoken during all the trauma. "Are you all right, sweet girl?"

She began to tremble slightly, but was still quiet. I squeezed her hand.

"Do you want me to drive you over to Aunt Polly's?" Daphne spoke up in her take-charge manner.

"No dear, you backing the Buick out of the driveway would do me in."

We all laughed, recalling how backing up a car was not Daphne's forte.

"I think walking over to Polly's would be good for all of us," I added. I slipped the apron over my arm and touched my rosary beads, which I had slipped into my dress pocket. "Daphne, grab my pocketbook out of the car. I'm afraid I left it there in all the commotion," I added as we left the house.

When we got to the corner, Phoebe Ann said, "Daphne, come over when you can. Would you like me to go back and get your black dress for you? In the meantime, you can borrow whatever I have."

"You're such a pal," Daphne said, and hugged her friend with gratitude.

"Thank you for being such a good friend for Daphne," I added.

"It's nothing, Mrs. Bennett. She would do the same and more if this had happened to me."

Daphne took my one arm and Nancy's hand and walked us cautiously across the street.

Polly came out onto the porch. "It's a party!"

"Well, not exactly," I responded with hesitation.

Polly noticed how shaken Nancy was, and my pallor. Without hesitation, she ushered us inside.

Charlotte came out from the kitchen, where she had helped Polly take out a fresh batch of cookies.

"Honey, can you help me for one more minute?" Polly said, not taking her eyes off Nancy and me. "Can you put them on the cookie rack to cool? I need to talk to your mother." As Charlotte returned to the kitchen, Polly said, "Catherine, *what happened?*"

"Daphne dear, can you tell Polly the story?"

Polly's worried eyes darted between us, looking at our forlorn faces.

Daphne began, "It's *awful*, Aunt Polly," she said, her voice not as strong as usual.

"*What?*" Polly could hardly hold back.

"*Everything* is gone. Our home is empty. Robbed! They must have pulled up into the alley so none of the neighbors could see them over the high fence. They hauled everything away!"

Everyone sat in silence, the only sound the scraping of the cookies off the baking sheet in the kitchen.

Polly took my hand in hers. "Where is Davis?"

"On a cattle drive with Owen, up near Dumas."

"What can I do? I know, I'll call Ernest. No, no, I'll call Owen's son, Donel Dean's father, in Amarillo."

Up in a flash, she rushed to the kitchen. "Good, good job, Charlotte. The cookies will be ready to eat in five minutes. Go tell Mama, Daphne, and Nancy about your day at the fair." She picked up the phone. "Operator, give me the number for Davis Crockett Bennett II, in Amarillo."

"Mama, we threw bean bags for prizes and…"

Charlotte's voice was overshadowed in my head as I tried to hear Polly's conversation.

"This is your Aunt Polly... Yes, they should be finishing up at the cattle station in Dumas. Can you ride over and try to find your Uncle Davis? Catherine needs him back in Twist Junction very quickly. No, no, no one is hurt or has died, but it *is* important. We want you to drive him to my house as soon as you possibly can. Thank you, sir."

She hung up the phone and brought a tray of cookies and cold water to where I sat. No one spoke. The water tasted just right, but we could barely touch our favorite cookies.

"Catherine, I did the best I can do for now. How about lying down for a rest while I fix dinner? Come on, Daphne, grab me some chickens out in the yard. Catherine, why don't you take Nancy to bed with you?"

Like a command sergeant, Polly had Daphne and Charlotte helping with dinner and me and Nancy resting. Still in shock, I nestled next to Nancy and fell into a fitful sleep.

I felt a soft hand shaking my shoulder.

"Are you feeling better, Catherine?" I heard Polly whisper.

I cracked open my eyes.

"I've gotten you something to eat. You'll feel stronger after you eat."

I crept out of bed so as not to disturb Nancy, who was sleeping soundly. "I think I'm going to let Nancy sleep. She really had quite a shock. Wish my Davis was here, Polly. I always feel better when he's with me. He gives me strength, you know." I rambled on, still in shock, as we made our way to the kitchen.

Polly finally stopped me, sat me in a chair at the table, and said, "Here, you need to eat."

The girls and Polly joined me. Our forks scraped the plates, but still, no one spoke.

Daphne and Charlotte cleaned up the kitchen as Polly sat with me in the living room. It was dark and cold. "Where is Davis?" I mumbled as Polly sat there patiently.

"Coming soon, coming soon..." she said over and over.

Daphne motioned to Polly from the kitchen. Polly patted my hand, then got up and went to Daphne.

"I'm worried about Mama... Should I stay here tonight? Where's Daddy?"

"I'll take care of everything. They're looking for your father. Dumas isn't that big. He'll be here soon. You can go now."

"I'll be at Phoebe Ann's. Good night, Aunt Polly. I'll be back first thing in the morning."

"Night."

Daphne leaned down, kissed me, and whispered, "I'm so sad for us, Mama. I love you. Good night."

— ⊲⋅ ⊲⋅ ⊲⋅ —

Daphne walked up to the corner, staring at the house as she passed by. It shook her to see the house like that...no lights, nothing. It seemed so cold, so unfriendly. It frightened her. She didn't expect that reaction and ran the rest of the way to her friend's house.

Phoebe Ann answered her door. "Are you okay?"

Daphne nodded.

"Did anyone call the sheriff?"

"No, I guess not."

"I'll ask my daddy to help. We'll help your family deal with it tomorrow. Come on, let's hit the hay."

With mixed emotions, Daphne lay there for a while, grateful for her friend and mostly grateful that nothing really, really bad had happened to her family. What if they had been home when the robbers came?

What if something had happened to her sisters, or Mama? It could have been so much worse. Her emotions raw, she prayed, "Sleep, help me to stop worrying. God, help my family..."

— ⚜ ⚜ ⚜ —

Polly kept vigil for her brother and Owen's son well past midnight and into the early hours of the morning. She had sent Catherine, Nancy, and Charlotte to bed. Her thoughts raced from compassion to anger. Poor Catherine and sweet Nancy. She was afraid they would suffer from shock and fear for a while. Polly thought that if she ever found out who had done this to her family, she might get out her rifle and point it straight in their ugly faces. She was so worked up, she was almost shaking when she heard the coupe pull up. Polly tripped on her untied shoelaces as she raced outside and grabbed the car door, her glasses cockeywable and her dress twisted around her body.

Davis jumped out of the car.

"Davis, I'm so glad you're here. Our world is upside down. Catherine and Nancy walked into your house yesterday afternoon to a broken shotgun across the door and all your furnishings gone. Davis, *everything* is gone!"

"Where's Cate? Where are the girls?" Davis asked, his face lined with worry.

"Here, Davis. Here sleeping."

He glanced into the guest room and his body gave a visible sigh. "Let them sleep for now. I'll be right back. I want to see the house."

"There are no lights. The lamps are gone too. We'll be able to see in another hour or so when the sun comes up. I'll get you some coffee. Come on in."

"Uncle Davis, do you need me any longer?" Davis's nephew asked from the door.

"No, son, many thanks."

"I'll be at my grandmother's if you change your mind. Call Beulah if you need anything."

"Yes, yes, okay. Say hello to Beulah for me."

Polly guided Davis into the kitchen and sat him in a chair, then poured him a cup of coffee.

"Here, honey. Here's your coffee. Now stop looking at your watch every minute. You can't make the time go any faster."

"Don't know what I'd do without you, Polly," Davis muttered. "Anybody call the sheriff?"

"No, we were waiting for you to come."

"Well, Cate was right. I can guess who did this. Those two scallywags I hired were no good. I'd bet the ranch they were the ones that pulled off the robbery."

"You don't know," Polly said and waved her finger at the ceiling.

"No, you're right. But I think I'll get the sheriff just the same, to get some fingerprints and check if they have a record. It would settle my mind." He sighed and spun his cup on the saucer. "Polly, I didn't pay attention to my gut. I had a bad feeling about them, but I was in such a hurry to hire help and get to work. I didn't pay attention to Cate, either. Daggum it. This is a pretty hard lesson to learn."

"Don't you go getting mad. What's done is done, and your family is upset enough."

Davis patted Polly's hand. "You're right, as usual. Can't just sit here. I'm going to walk off all this steam and see if Sheriff Rodgers is in yet. When Cate wakes up, you know where I'll be—at the sheriff's, then the house. Are you teaching today?"

"Lordy, no, I've got some hand holding to do."

Davis found Sheriff Rodgers at home, still in bed. They met at the house a little while later.

"Thank you, Sheriff, I appreciate you coming by so early today."

"No problem, Davis. I'll get right on the case. You know, we have a lot of vagrants coming through these days. They aren't always the most forthright kind of people. I'm just afraid we may not be able to track 'em. Sorry this had to happen to you, young man. We'll get some fingerprints, I hope."

"Thank you, sir."

"Can you make a list of the stolen items for me, Davis?"

The words just echoed in Davis's brain. Nothing was adding up. He couldn't make sense of anything. It seemed like he sat for hours on the porch rocker that was now their living room furniture. He couldn't move. He didn't want to touch anything. Finally, his frustration boiled over. "Those good-for-nothing bastards!" he yelled, shaking his fists in the air.

"Davis Bennett, I've never heard you use a swear word in my entire life!"

Ernest stood with Mr. Huntington in the doorway.

"Oooh," he added as he looked around. "Now I see why you're a little hot under the collar."

"This looks intentional…calculated…planned," Mr. Huntington said. "No one from around here would ever do a thing like this. Mighty glad Catherine and the girls aren't here now. Davis, I hate to tell you, but news of this robbery is all over town this morning. I know you folks are private, but people have to know that we may be harboring thieves in town."

The men walked slowly through the house, inspecting each room.

"A real shame, and right before Christmas, too. Let me know what you need, son," Mr. Huntington said, giving Davis's shoulder a supportive squeeze. "I'll tell the men at coffee the terrible news. Don't worry, you and Catherine have lots of friends in this town."

Davis nodded and smiled gratefully.

— ⊰ ⊰ ⊰ —

Daphne stopped by Polly's to get me. Immediately, I told Polly, "I'll be back in an hour," and headed for the door. But before I could finish my sentence, Nancy was hanging on my skirt. "Nancy, Aunt Polly will fix you a nice breakfast and you and Charlotte can play for a while and wait for me."

Pools of tears formed in her eyes.

"Don't worry, honey, I'll be right back. I need to go find Daddy." I loosened her cemented grip and gave her hand to Polly. "Be good for me, now."

Still silent, she nodded her head sadly. As Daphne and I walked down the block, I looked back and saw Nancy's face smooshed against Polly's front door pane.

Daphne took my arm, steadying my step.

"I do *not* want to go back there," I said through gritted teeth.

"Daddy's waiting for you, Mama."

We stood in front of the house for a moment, then I pulled myself up straight, wanting to appear strong for Davis. The latch clicked like it had unlocked a jail lock. The hollowness echoed in the empty room.

"Cate! My poor, sweet Cate," came tumbling out of Davis's mouth as he ran over to hug me. He ruffled Daphne's hair. "Daphne, I hear you have really taken charge. I'm so very proud of you. Good job." He guided me to a chair. "Let's sit a minute and gather ourselves," he said, patting my hand.

We heard a noise on the front porch.

"Now who's at our door?" Davis blurted.

"Don't worry," Daphne said with authority. "I'll get it and tell them to come back later. I'll take care of everything."

"Good girl, Daphne."

"Jiminy Crickets!" Daphne squealed. "It's George!"

I leaned back in my chair and saw her hug him. She grabbed his hand.

"Drop your bag. Let's walk to the DeSoto coffee shop," she said. "Be back soon, Mama and Daddy!"

— ⊲⊦ ⊲⊦ ⊲⊦ —

George laughed as Daphne dragged him down the block.

"What's the hurry, doll? Guess this wasn't the best time for a surprise, huh?"

"Actually, don't know when I've been so glad to see you." With that, the horror story of the past twenty-four hours tumbled out of her mouth. Before they got to the massive door of the DeSoto, Daphne had rambled on enough to give George the whole picture.

They entered the DeSoto. Daphne whispered to George, "Glad I could tell you everything before all the coffee shop ears heard all my grim robbery details."

"Come on, hon," George said, guiding them to a table. "Wish we had some vodka to pour into our orange juice! Let's order ourselves a real Texas breakfast."

"George, you never change. Always the party man."

They settled into a booth, and after ordering, George continued.

"Let me give you the real scoop. Friends of Dad's are filming a new musical and want me, the hometown boy, to be there for tryouts. This is an over-the-top opportunity, filming on location in New York City. Can you imagine? I've heard that Frank Sinatra and Gene Kelly might be the headliners." He laughed. "Here I am, telling you everything, and I was saving my surprise for Sybil. Where is she, anyway?"

"Don't think you'll believe this one," Daphne chuckled. "Mama talked her into going to college in Denver."

"Now I get it…that's why I haven't heard from her. She must have been embarrassed, no doubt! She swore she would never be caught dead in college, especially a Catholic girls' college." He began to laugh out of control and slammed his hand on the Formica table.

The whole café crowd looked at them. Daphne wanted to hide under the table.

"Oh, Wildman, you've got to be more restrained in our small town. People are pretty shook up this morning, what with the robbery and all. It will be some time before they overlook strangers."

"Sorry, I forgot for a minute," George said sheepishly. "When is Sybil coming back?"

"I *think* next week, but who knows? Mama will tell her and Elizabeth about the robbery. We don't have any beds to sleep in, don't forget, or chairs for the dining room table. You didn't see inside, but it's a war zone. There's nothing there really. All our clothes and everything—it's all gone." Tears began to well in her eyes.

George reached over with his muscular arms and hugged her. He leaned his head into hers sympathetically.

"Well, I planned to visit with your folks today, but let's get to work and see what I can do. Hold on a minute." He jumped up from the table and vanished. A few minutes later, he returned from the front desk. "I'm set with a room, and I ordered dinner here for your family tonight."

The waitress brought their plates.

"Let's eat and get back. Think it's okay if I go see your parents? I want to offer my help and tell them about dinner."

Daphne nodded.

George handed her a fork. "Get a move on, girlie!"

After breakfast, as they walked back out onto Main Street, George looked up and down the block. "Daphy, got a furniture store here, doll?"

"Pearson's is right over there. I've heard they carry the finest outside Denver and Amarillo. One of the new factories here is a mattress company, which they own too."

"Good information…we make a swell team."

When they arrived at the house, Daphne hesitated for a moment on the sidewalk. "I'll walk in first, if you don't mind, George."

"Sure, I understand," he said.

– ⊲. ⊲. ⊲. –

"Mama, Daddy, where are you?" I heard Daphne call from the front room.

"Back in the kitchen, Daphne," I called back.

"Sorry, this isn't the best time, but guess who's here to help? George Worthington, from Hollywood. You know, Sybil's friend."

"My, my, it's George!" I came out, wiping my hands on my apron. "Wish this was a better visiting time. I've never had a visitor I couldn't offer tea and shortbread to. I'm so embarrassed."

Davis walked into the room.

"This is my husband, Davis Bennett," I introduced.

"How do you do, sir. Sybil spoke of you as the nicest and funniest man on earth. Something about singing to your calves...am I right?"

"Well, guess I've done that in my day," Davis almost blushed. "We're in a bit of a topsy-turvy state around here. Sorry we can't be more hospitable."

"Never mind...got a broom? And Mrs. Bennett, the hotel is cooking dinner for the whole family tonight as my gift to you and your family."

I was so grateful, I couldn't speak.

George began sweeping feverishly, doing his crazy soft shoe every now and then. Daphne held the dustpan. I wiped out the cupboards. Pretty soon Davis began humming.

"Beginning to look like a spotless stage set," George observed with his hands on his hips. "Think I'll be right back, if you don't mind. Daphy, give me my bag. I'll walk to the hotel."

And with that, he left, headed with purpose down Main Street.

— ◁. ◁. ◁. —

In front of the DeSoto portal, George signaled to Joe, the bellman. "Hey, bellman!" he called out. "Can you take this to my room? Mr. George Worthington." He popped a five out of his pocket and handed it to Joe.

"Yes, sir! Right away, sir!" Joe said.

"So, how far is the furniture store?"

"Next block on the other side. It is at the end, Mr. Worthington."

"Gotcha," George called back, halfway down the block already.

He found the furniture store and went inside.

"Afternoon," his voice bellowed, as if talking to an audience of chairs. "Anybody...hellooo..."

A young woman came out of the back room to greet him.

"Miss, got a decorator here?"

"Mr. Pearson's son, Bruce, is the best one around these parts. Very clever, they say."

"Okay."

They stood looking blankly at each other.

"And..." George said impatiently. "Is he here?"

"Well, I think so. Would you like to try out our bestselling lounge chair while you wait?"

"Don't have that much time, doll."

"Oh…yes, sir. I'll go get Bruce."

A few moments later, Bruce Pearson sauntered out from the back.

"Howdy," he said, offering his hand to George.

Turning around, George said, "Well if you aren't a tall drink of water. You look more like a cowboy than a decorator."

"I stay in disguise so I don't scare off the country folk," he laughed.

"I like that. Very clever."

They both laughed again.

"Want a drink later?" George offered.

"Might do that! What can I help you with in the meantime?"

"Well, some friends lost all their belongings yesterday. A robbery. I want to buy some furniture for them. Say, you got mattresses?"

"As a matter of fact, we do. All hand stuffed. Best you can buy."

"Yep, that's what I want. Four doubles would be good. Now, they have only one fancy oak dining table, so we'll need chairs—10…no, let's make it 12. Always good for a growing family. I want a tufted Greta Garbo sofa and chairs to go with it. Make one a wing chair. Colors, fabrics, something nice…very nice. Got to have you select everything to go with it. Good china and kitchenware, too." He looked at Mr. Pearson, who was frantically writing everything down on a small notepad. "Can you handle this size of an order?"

"No problem for me, but it's going to be expensive."

"Well, I'm George Worthington from Hollywood and I'm good for it. Here's a blank check. You can send me the receipt later."

"You got it, Mr. Worthington."

"Hey, if you want that drink, I'm going to be at the DeSoto saloon at about 7:00. Heard they have a fine bar."

"I'll see what I can do. I've got a pretty big order to work on," Bruce grinned and winked.

"You'd better get the lead out of your feet. Hey, when can you deliver this order?"

"I think I can get right on it."

"Can it be before the train comes in from Denver next Friday?"

"If you don't mind me asking, why that train, that day?"

"Some special girls will be coming home then."

Bruce smiled. "You mean the Bennett girls?"

"How do you know them?" George's voice had a small tinge of worry. "Guess we'd better have that drink, all right."

"See you later!"

— ◁. ◁. ◁. —

"Daddy, you got any clothes?" Daphne asked. "They missed my favorite black dress in the bedroom closet. Now that was luck! Don't think George realized we didn't have clothes when he asked us for dinner."

"We will manage," I piped up. "Since when do you have to dress like you're going to a wedding when you go to the hotel coffee shop?"

Later that evening, we arrived at the DeSoto. George waited in the lobby for his guests, clinging to a bouquet of flowers in his hand.

"Evening!" he said cheerfully.

I blushed as George caught me by genuine surprise, handing me the thoughtful bouquet.

"Now...*who* is this young man, Cate?" Davis whispered. He was still in a semi-shocked state.

"One of the Hollywood bon vivants—a friend of Sybil's and Daphne's. He's the one who arranged for Sybil's job in Denver."

I could see Davis smile and shake his head in disbelief. "Oh, yes, I forgot..."

Aunt Polly joined us while George chattered on.

Daphne interrupted, "This is our wonderful Aunt Polly, Daddy's sister, one of fourteen children."

"Oooh, my pleasure." George bowed and shook her hand. Clearing his throat, he continued, "Mrs. B, I hate for Sybil to miss my party tonight. The fact that I've been missing her is an understatement. I'll have to try to go through Denver on my way back." He paused as though a thought had crossed his mind. "Hey, would you mind if I took her to New York for New Year's Eve?"

This time, I could really see Davis's eyes roll, almost completely to the back of his head.

"You're a pretty presumptuous young man, Mr. Worthington," I decided to answer, lest Davis's sheer disbelief of the whole scene got the best of him.

George could see the wink out of the corner of my eye. I was secretly thrilled to think that Sybil could be standing in Times Square as the classic New Year's Eve ball dropped.

"You're right, Mrs. B. I have no idea what I'll be doing New Year's Eve. I've been asked to try out for a movie. Might be working with no time off. She could see me dance if I get selected. Pretty darn exciting times." George oozed with enthusiasm. "Order up. I'm sure you must be starving. What's good, anyway?"

"The chicken fried steak is supposed to be one of the DeSoto's specials," I answered.

"That's my favorite," Nancy said, finally finding her voice. "Do you remember *me*, George?"

"Sure I do…you're the one always playing paper dolls or hopscotch," he said.

Nancy grinned and nodded her head.

"Nancy, if you say their chicken fried steak is the best in Twist Junction, guess I'll just have to give it a try."

"Cate, what will you have?" Davis's voice was full of exhaustion.

"Dear, I think it would only be polite to follow my host, but I bet you want their Blue Plate Special, the meatloaf, right Davis?" I added, "Everybody know what they want? Joe can't stand here all night while we discuss the whole menu."

Aunt Polly grinned as she ordered the fried chicken. "I want to see if I do chicken better than the famous DeSoto," she teased.

The solemn mood changed dramatically over the next hour. George joked around with the younger girls, and he and Daphne chatted about the newest songs, dances, and romances in Glendale. Leaning over to Daphne, George said, "Sure do miss you Bennett girls. Everyone says so. You all were a breath of fresh air in our glam-glam scene."

Davis tried to cut off the bill as it was being delivered to George, but George had distracted everyone with chocolate sundaes with cherries on top. He slipped out and paid the bill at the front desk. When he came back, he pulled up a chair next to my husband, and said, "This must be a very demoralizing time for you, sir. It was my pleasure to buy you folks dinner. Believe me, I had plenty of meals at your house in Glendale. Mrs. B was really nice to me. She let me join your family. My mother and father were *always* gone to social affairs. It was mighty lonely, and she'd say, 'What ya doing for dinner, George? Here's your place at the table!' It isn't often you get to repay people for simple kindnesses. I can't do much, but I do have money. I realize it must be hard to lose everything. And I guess I'm presumptuous. I had to give back to you and your family. Mr. Bennett, sir, I walked into the furniture store…Paulson's…"

"Pearson's," Daphne interrupted.

"Oh yes…anyway," he continued, "I talked to their cowboy decorator. Don't be upset, but I ordered a sofa, chairs, beds, everything taken from your home. It will all be here before the girls get home for Christmas. I wanted to do this for your wonderful family, for all you've done for me."

I looked over at the one-sided conversation. I saw Davis's eyes get big and he began to grit his teeth. I'd recognize that clenched jaw a mile away. I jumped up from my seat at the end of the table to intervene.

"George," I said. "What party are you planning now?"

"Well, actually, a decorating party," he said.

"What?"

My mouth dropped in shock. I gripped Davis's hand, which had a minor shake at this point. His mouth hung open in disbelief.

"That lanky fella, Bruce Pearson, at the home furnishing shop, is coming next week and is setting everything up for you, Mrs. B!" George said.

"George, we can't have you doing that," Davis responded emphatically.

"But sir, your family is my family. Who else has been so kind to me?"

Davis looked over at me, questioning George's words.

"I've never had folks be so kind and not want *anything* in return," George continued. "You know, in Hollywood, people always want something from you. They *always* have an angle! It's hard to find genuine kindness."

I motioned to Daphne and Polly to walk the girls home. I was still digesting this young man's proposal as I took one of the empty chairs and sat down. Looking over at Davis, I could see how humble this whole incident had made him feel.

"George..." Davis cleared his throat. "May I call you George?"

"I'm honored, sir."

"Can I tell you something, young man? There have been many fine townspeople who have taken Catherine and me under their wing. God has blessed us. Guardian angels have protected us when we were in danger. I felt *completely* forgotten this time—like God was busy with so many other people who were in despair. I lost only furniture—*not* my family, *not* my house, *not* my land. I still have what is most important. You know what I'm saying? We get tied up in material things; things that feed our importance. But I still felt that God had not protected me. My belly began to shake. Then here you come, son...some highfalutin moneyman from California, and I realize God's plan was bigger... better than I could have ever hoped for. George, this act of yours has made me humble. This time of questioning how I was going to provide all these things for my wife and family has made me an even stronger believer in God. Son, God has sent you at the perfect time. That train dropped you off in the perfect town. I am very grateful for your kind heart."

My eyes watered as Davis's humble words of wisdom pierced this youngster's heart.

"*Thank you* for accepting my gift, Mr. Bennett. But more than that, thank you for talking to me about the importance of things. My parents have never taken time to talk to me as you have tonight. These words will stay with me always. Thank you."

We all sat in silence. Our hearts touched each other. George would always be a bead on my rosary from that day forward.

George slowly pushed his chair from the table. "I'd better get some sleep. Trains come early around here. Tell my girlfriend Sybil a big hi from her ol' boyfriend George!"

He extended his hand to shake Davis's hand, and then to me, gentlemanlike, as he helped me up from the table.

"Good night, my Twist Junction family," he said, escorting us down the wide, paneled hall and out the hotel's heavy oak doors.

"Stop here *any time*, son," Davis said.

Davis's head shook all the way back to Polly's house. "Our life is so blessed, Cate."

George had one more piece of work to take care of before he left Twist Junction. Glancing at his shiny gold watch, which he had strategically hidden under his starched shirt cuff and v-neck sweater, he motioned to the time—6:50. He wondered if the lanky cowboy decorator would show up.

When he opened the saloon doors, broke and painted women greeted George. Eyeing the long oak bar at the far end of the room, he headed past the riffraff of men playing poker and pool. Immediately behind him, Bruce Pearson entered, nodding to all his constituents as he passed.

"Well, right on time, Mr. Decorator," George remarked. "Pull up a stool right here."

George had chosen to sit on the far left end of the bar, hoping to be less conspicuous to the nosey "townies."

"What'll you have, my friend?"

"Think a gin straight up will do."

"You're my kind of drinker...make it two, bartender. Sooo, tell me about those Bennett girls. How do you know them?" He nodded at the bartender as he set down their drinks.

"Oh, *everybody* knows the Bennett girls...the most beautiful Texas girls in these parts. They've been to California, as you know, and now Elizabeth and Sybil are off to college in Denver. Rumor has it that they're coming home for Christmas next week..." He looked at his empty glass. "Boy, either you or this drink has me talking up a storm.

How do *you* know them?"

"I knew them when they were in Glendale."

"Oh, yes, your check said you were from Hollywood. That adds up. I heard about the robbery, but why did you buy them all that furniture?"

"They were very kind to me when they lived in California. Sybil is my best friend. She's gorgeous, don't you think?" George was fishing for Bruce's interest in her or Elizabeth.

"Oh, yes, Sybil is a kick in the pants, but I'm keen on Elizabeth. She is so elegant and smart, and responsible too...you know, the *real* marrying kind. I've been waiting a long time to find someone special."

"Another round, bartender," George said, pointing to their empty glasses. "Yes, Elizabeth was a pretty serious student. She was always reading poetry and stuff...never really wanted to party with the rest of us. I did see her with other guys from time to time, but I wasn't her type. No, Sybil was my babe! She could be the life of the party and woo any guy!"

"Glad to hear more about Elizabeth. I guess I knew who she really was, but ya wonder when she's in California, the party place."

"Who knows...we could be brothers-in-law someday!" George laughed.

"Well, wouldn't that be a kick? We could reminisce about our night at the DeSoto bar!" Bruce added.

Laughing, they toasted the thought with half-filled glasses.

"Hey, buddy, I got a big job to start working on tomorrow," Bruce said. "Wish me luck. Stop back by Twist Junction and see if you like my work. See ya sometime."

"Drinks are on me," George insisted. "Pleasure to meet you. And good luck with Elizabeth."

9
Riding On Moonbeams

The Ft. Worth-Denver train pulled into the station a few minutes early. Bruce could hear the release of the steam and the brakes. Grabbing the store's best ecru silk shade, and admiring the last lamp he would take to complete the Bennetts' living room, Bruce yelled to the store manager, "Be right back!" Then he whisked his treasures into his arms and headed for 619 Main Street.

"Good morning..." he called into the empty house as he poked his head through the front door. What with work and school, everyone was gone. Bruce was deep in thought as he began putting his final touches on the décor. He angled a chair just so, then set an ashtray on the end table. He had just plugged in the lamp behind the sofa when the front door opened and there stood Elizabeth, suitcase in hand. Startled, Bruce jumped up. She screamed. He laughed.

"My oh my," said Elizabeth. "You almost gave me a heart attack."

"I'm Bruce Pearson, from the furniture store," he said as his long legs straddled the tufted velvet, Greta Garbo sofa. "Sorry, I wanted it to be perfect when you girls arrived. Just making the last adjustments. Guess I didn't disguise myself as the latest décor statue!"

Almost giddy, Elizabeth responded, "I'm Elizabeth Bennett." Eyes wide, she looked around. "It's a magazine cover...a beautiful magazine cover." She twirled to see the entire redesigned room. "Yes, beautiful. That's what it is!" Shaking her head, she added, "Sybil will faint when she sees this. That's what she gets for running off with some looker this morning. There's *nothing* she loves more than beautiful things, except maybe a handsome man."

"Well, she's quite a beauty herself," Bruce blurted out. "I think it was her rich Hollywood boyfriend who bought you all this stuff."

"What? You don't mean George, do you? How? How did he? I'm confused."

"Better talk to your parents about that. All I know is he came in with a blank check and told me to make tracks."

Elizabeth wandered into the music room. "A piano! A decorated Christmas tree!" Then she walked to the bedroom. "Oh, the bedspreads!" A thin layer of delicate netting was draped over Celadon silk. She flopped onto her bed by the window. "Bruce Pearson, I feel like I'm on a cloud…"

"Let me see!" Bruce teased and came to the bedroom door. He could be brazen, but thought better of it as Elizabeth blushed and popped up off the bed.

"*Two* big dressers! I'd better grab my drawer before the clothes horse takes over! Someday, I want things just as elegant of my own..." she mumbled in a dreamy state.

She turned around and found herself uncomfortably close to Bruce. He wanted to grab her right then and there, but instead, he looked deep into her dark, mysterious eyes. Who was this tall, elegant creature named Elizabeth Bennett?

Bruce thought, *You'd better come back from Denver right into my arms. I've got to woo you now—not tomorrow, now!*

The kitchen door came unlatched with a big thump and within seconds Daphne stood in the bedroom doorway. "Well, well...Elizabeth is having a bedroom soirée! Bruce Pearson, you really have moved in."

"Don't go telling tales on us," Bruce said, a bit nervous. He didn't want Catherine and Davis to get the wrong impression, especially since he had worked so hard to make them happy with the house. Clearing his throat, he defended himself. "I brought the last lamp today. Did you see it?"

Daphne heard him but ignored him. She was immersed in the situation.

Elizabeth was impressed with Bruce, and slightly intrigued. *Hmm,* she thought. *Something's happening here...am I falling for this guy?*

They all headed back to the living room, and Bruce flicked his finger, knocking a bell on the Christmas tree as they passed. Its delicate *tinkle, tinkle, tinkle* filled the air.

"Did you get to show off to my other sisters?" Daphne queried.

"Sybil is downtown with some guy she met on the train," Elizabeth said. "Don't know if Maggie is back home yet. What time was her train?" All of a sudden she straightened her posture and took on her Miss Organization role. "Better get our noon meal started…oh yes, and I want to unpack before all the dresser drawers are gone." She looked at Bruce and smiled. "Nice to see you, Bruce. Why don't you come back later today? I'm sure Mama would like to give you a tip for making everything so lovely."

"No need, but you can bet I'll stop by…just to check on things… customer service, you know," Bruce fumbled.

After he was sufficiently out of sight, Daphne flopped onto the new living room chair. "I do believe I see some stars in your eyes, Lizzy! You haven't budged an inch since Bruce left. Stuck. Yes, stuck on him! What a pushover you are!"

"Daphne, it just happened. I've only seen him once before…at the train station last fall." Talking in her hazy voice, she repeated how they had scared each other when she got home. "The house is beautiful… He really is talented. I guess he swept me away. I didn't meet anyone in California like him." Her normal "take-charge" mode was melting into daydreams personified.

"Lizzy's been bitten by the love bug," Daphne chanted, teasing her sister.

"Let's keep this between us. I would hate to have Bruce hear that I care about him, and you know how Maggie and Nancy can blab gossip all over town," Elizabeth said.

"Gotcha," Daphne winked. "We'd better get the lead out. Mama will be home from work and will expect a steak dinner on the table." She eyed her sister. "Okay, come down out of the clouds, Lizzy!"

— 4, 4, 4, —

Margaret, bag in hand, burst through the door, followed by Davis, Nancy, Charlotte, and me, like a trail of cattle headed for the feeding trough. Gratefully sliding into our new chairs, we enjoyed every bite of the dinner Daphne and Elizabeth had prepared for us. And then, in walked Sybil, followed by Joe from the DeSoto. He balanced a cherry pie in one hand and a jam-packed suitcase in the other.

With arms flailing, she announced, "And here is dessert, straight from the hotel oven!"

Everyone squealed with delight, including me. I was so happy. My family was together once again.

Sybil ran to Davis and gave him a squeeze, then directed poor Joe to put the luggage in the bedroom and the pie on the table. She grabbed a quarter out of her purse, handed it to him, and thanked him.

"You're a real dear! I couldn't have done it without you, honey!" Sybil expounded in her princess-like fashion as she showed Joe to the door. "Can you believe I got everybody's favorite?" she said, spinning to face us. She cut the pie and began passing around the plates. Then she stopped with a squeal as she noticed the new dishes and the new furniture. "What's this? The house looks like a movie set. Mama, Daddy, it is drop dead!" She left the pie cutter dangling off the edge of the pie dish and ran from room to room, shrieking, "Wow!" and "Holy moly!"

Maggie jumped up to follow her sister. "This is just gorgeous."

"Margaret, Sybil, come eat with your family!" I called. "I took the afternoon off. We have lots of stories to tell."

"Wish I could stay while you tell her who paid for all of this," Davis smiled. "Quite a young man, huh, Cate?" he almost whispered. He rose from the table. "I gotta tend to my other babies. Just have a small herd of heifers...took the others to Dumas to fatten this winter. Jeb is babysitting those. See ya for supper, girlie girls."

The girls waved as Davis left.

"Nancy, I want you, Charlotte, and Daphne to do the dishes and make me, Elizabeth, Sybil, and Margaret some tea," I instructed. "Come on girls, let's sit in our new living room."

Sybil sat down and looked at me expectantly.

"Well, the house story," I said, eyeing each of them. "Do you want the long version or the short version?"

"Tell me the whole thing," Sybil immediately responded.

"We hired on some rough-looking cowhands to help Daddy with the new herd. You sometimes get a gut feeling that something isn't right about someone, but Daddy needed the help. One afternoon they came to collect their money. They harassed Margaret right in the walkway—this was before she left for school—and I was so mad I got the shotgun. Apparently, they didn't like this treatment by a woman."

"Oh, Mama," Sybil breathed. "How scary...you with your gun!"

"A few weeks later, your father was on a cattle drive to Dumas. Nancy and I came home one afternoon and found the house ransacked. Poor Nancy went into shock. Oh, Sybil, we were all stunned. Your Aunt Polly helped so much. The sheriff is conducting an all-out search. They have been knocking on every door. Then George showed up and took charge. He took us all to dinner at the DeSoto because we had no food, no dishes, no chairs—nothing! And then he wrote a blank check to the Pearson furniture store. *Can you imagine?* Soon Bruce and the furniture started to arrive."

The younger girls brought our iced tea.

"George?" Sybil said, her eyes wide as I passed her a glass. "*My George?*" She teared up as she softly sputtered out his name. "His heart is made out of gold. How did I deserve such a friend?"

"The nicest part of all was when George told your father how much it meant to him to be included in our family, eating with us from time to time when we were in California. We never know what small acts of kindness mean to people." I sipped my tea in silence to emphasize the depth of the story.

"Mama, I'm so sorry that I missed seeing him."

"You haven't heard the end of him...don't worry."

"And Mama, what about the cowboys?" Sybil asked.

"Do you know for sure they were the ones who did it?" Maggie asked nervously. "I'll never forget how rude they were to me on the sidewalk that day."

"They have found a record for each of them. They work as a pretty slick team. The sheriff did trace some records up to Guymon, Oklahoma, but it takes longer to get information from out of state. Your daddy has some pull with your uncle up that way. Everybody is horrified and wants to help us. We have been quite humbled by all this and have done a lot of praying."

"Where's that rosary?" Maggie asked.

I pulled out my dulled beads. "This bead is for your friend, George, Sybil," I smiled. "God saw that they didn't get my apron with the rosary, or my favorite pearls."

Elizabeth interjected, "And the teapot?"

"It's gone, but I had taken out the money for all of your tuition and a few Christmas treats. My job salary wasn't in there. Losing that would have been like going to the bottom and back. I'm so grateful it was spared."

Thoughts of my missing Irish linens surfaced enough that the girls could tell the raw reality was pushing my stoic threshold. I was never as good at hiding my emotions as my mother, but my pain was not as raw as her Irish memories of starvation, poverty, and leaving her beloved home.

Sybil continued, "Mama, I'm grateful that none of you were hurt. They sound like they're real ornery thugs. What a *horrible* experience for everyone. Especially for Nancy, being so young."

I lowered my voice. "Yes, I'm a bit worried about her... Margaret, your daddy and I think she should go back with you to your school. Getting away from here would be a good thing. Her nightmares are beginning to worry us."

Maggie piped up anxiously, "I understand, Mama, but I don't like her hanging around me all the time."

"She will be in a different grade…a different room and different friends. Isn't that the way it works, Elizabeth and Sybil?"

"Last I saw of you," Sybil said to Elizabeth, "you were on the train, when we arrived at Loretto Heights…" She paused and grinned. "Just kidding, but I *never* see you... You'd have to smoke and play bridge to find me! *Oops!*" She clamped her hand over her mouth, realizing that she had just admitted, in my presence, her deepest, darkest secret—smoking.

I raised my voice. "Sybil, you aren't..."

Sybil's eyes turned downward in guilt. "Guess I can't say Twist Junction is a boring town anymore," she chattered on, obviously hoping I wouldn't pursue the smoking subject further. "Not Denver in a glamorous sense, but we *do* have action. I'm so, so sorry to have missed George. He sure was able to turn lemons into lemonade..."

"You girls can pick some mighty nice young men, but George really tested your father for a while. His persistence to help us made Daddy uncomfortable. The entire ordeal humbled us all."

With that, the phone rang.

"I'll get it," Maggie said, and dashed into the kitchen.

I heard her say, "Yes sir, I got it...a special delivery letter and package from New York City. I'll tell my mother." She hung up the phone and came into the living room. "Mama, can I go to the post office for you? There's some package and a special letter," Maggie repeated.

There was a knock on the door before I could nod a yes to Margaret.

"What now?" I said. "This place is becoming the action center of Twist Junction! I'll get it."

I opened the door to find Bruce standing there.

"Well, Bruce Pearson, nice to see you. Won't you join us for some iced tea and shortbread?"

Catching Elizabeth's eye, he grinned at her and spoke to me. "Just checking to see if you're happy with everything, Mrs. Bennett. I brought the last of the lamps over this morning."

"Oh, I'm so very sorry, Mr. Pearson. I hadn't had a minute to notice." I pointed. "Sybil just came home and there has been a bit of excitement, to say the least."

Bruce smiled at Sybil and walked over to one of the lamps, tilting the shade straight. "Nice color, don't you think? I picked the handmade silk shade especially for you, Mrs. Bennett."

"Come, sit down," I offered, and went to the kitchen to get him a glass of tea. I could hear immediate small talk as I put the ice in his glass. At this point, I thought Bruce might be the perfect match for Elizabeth, and I was more than willing to secure his interest in her. Realizing I was not the only one with this idea, I had to clear my throat before either one saw me extending the icy drink.

Maggie changed the atmosphere with her anxious plea to go to the post office.

"I'll come, too," said Sybil.

"Yes, yes, run along, girls... Please excuse me. I have something to get you, Mr. Pearson. I surely will tell everyone about your furniture store's excellent service." With that, I turned toward the kitchen to see how my clean-up girls were doing.

— ⊲⊦ ⊲⊦ ⊲⊦ —

Horns honked and the local boys waved as Margaret and Sybil walked past the courthouse to the post office. The postmaster welcomed the girls with the day's mail and the mysterious box.

"Look, here's my last postcard to Daphne," Sybil said, shuffling through the mail. "'For your eyes…coming home. Sybil.' Didn't think I'd be on the same train as the mail!"

"Sybil, look at this box from Berg…uh, Bergdorf Good…man. Bergdorf Goodman. That's a funny name! New York City, New York. Who is he?"

"That's a *store*, silly, but who could be sending something? I do have a new beau from the East Coast. But this is also addressed to 'The Bennett Girls.' Hmm. George said he was going to New York..."

"Cool!"

"Christmas presents!" Sybil shouted, and the girls hurried back to the house.

— ⊲⊦ ⊲⊦ ⊲⊦ —

The big box held shiny boxes wrapped in red paper, with gold ribbons and each girl's name on cream vellum envelopes tied to the appropriate package.

Bruce and Elizabeth jumped up to see what George had sent.

"Well, those are the cat's meow," Bruce exclaimed. "That guy is certainly not your average Joe. I liked him. We had a nice drink at the DeSoto. He can be a real kick." Laughing, Bruce added, "Once he explained he was Sybil's friend and not yours, Elizabeth, I liked him a lot better." He leaned back in his chair and winked at her.

"What's the letter say?" Maggie asked.

"That's addressed to *me*, and I'm going to my room to read this one." Sybil grabbed it and pranced off into the bedroom.

"Okay, Miss Priss. I'll put the presents under the tree," Maggie said, rolling her eyes.

Bruce looked at his watch. "Daggum, I'm gonna get fired!" He jumped up and shot for the door.

"Hold your horses, young man." I scooted over to my worn leather purse and pulled out five dollars. "Thank you for all your help. The house is lovely. Stop by any time. Our table always has an extra chair. Next Sunday, after church perhaps? We go to the Catholic church."

"Oh, that sounds nice. Maybe I'll see you then, Elizabeth."

We all sat staring at each other, except for Elizabeth. She was in the clouds. None of us dared say a word.

After Bruce left, Elizabeth said, "Mama, don't you think that dinner invitation was rather forward?"

"Well, *I* said it, not *you*. Thought you would like to have him come. You must remember, *he's* the one who stopped by here, my dear."

She nodded.

Daphne started to sing, "Elizabeth has a boyfriend" until daggers came from Elizabeth's eyes.

"Oops." Daphne backed down.

"You girls wear me out. I'm going in for a nap," I confessed.

I turned my head back to Daphne. "Can you take Charlotte to the movies with your friends tonight? She isn't socializing like she should...

too much time at the ranch with Daddy and Otto."

Sighing, Daphne mumbled, "Okay, Mama."

That night, at about 11:00, I was just settling in when I heard the window in the girls' room creak open, and Maggie whisper, "Where are you going?"

"Shush. Go back to sleep," Sybil answered.

I heard the sound of her climbing out the narrow window, and *crunch*, she landed on the bush below, kicking the brittle leaves. Her footsteps told me she was making her way past my window to the alley. I knew Sybil was up to no good again. My heart sank and I grabbed for my apron pocket and my rosary beads. Lying there awake, I finally heard another set of crunches at about 4:00 a.m. *At least she's home*, I thought. *What next?*

— 4. 4. 4. —

Sybil's long legs almost didn't make it. Her plan to sneak out of the house was one thing, but climbing up the bushes to sneak back in was quite another feat. She thought she might have to get a step stool if she planned to sneak out every night. And Sybil did sneak out every night for the next week. She thought if she didn't, she might never see her new dreamboat again.

She'd first met him on the train. He was two seats ahead of her, and his blond, wavy hair crept down his neck and his long eyelashes caught the sun when he looked out the window. She would elbow Elizabeth whenever he moved, but Elizabeth dismissed him for her favorite murder mystery novel. Sybil, on the other hand, would saunter up the aisle, slowly passing him as she went to freshen up in the water closet, or to the club car to get a Coke.

Two stops before Twist Junction, he joined Sybil in the club car.

"Don't believe we've met. I'm Tanner Mercer II, from points east. And you? Where are you from?"

"I'm Sybil Bennett from Denver and Twist Junction."

"Were you in Denver for business?"

Hesitating, she said, "I worked in Denver last year, but I decided to go back to school to study art. I'm studying painting primarily." Her brain, pumping ideas, was trying to sound intelligent and interesting. "My sister and I go to Loretto Heights College."

"Oh yes, the all-girls Catholic school. Where all the mackerel snappers go!"

"Excuse me?" she said indignantly, and turned away to sip her Coke. Little did he know that she could see his reflection and his mischievous expression in the train's window. She thought he was drop-dead gorgeous, even when he was being rude. Trying to rectify the situation, he said something that she ignored, and again she snapped her head back around to catch him in a desperate "I'm sorry to have offended you, it was just a little joke" look.

They were both aware of the immediate attraction they felt for each other. Starting once again, he regaled her with his family history and business. He spoke of steel, gas, and oil…money, money, money was written all over his face. Sybil thought she had a real catch.

"Twist Junction stop, commmming up!" shouted the conductor.

Sybil jumped off the train. She heard running behind her and turned, nonchalantly, to see Mr. Mercer II.

"Thought you were going to Dumas, Mr. Mercer II?"

"A man can change his mind, can't he?" Tanner said coyly. "I'll be at the DeSoto. Maybe I can see you later?"

She caught sight of Daphne running down the train platform, and almost forgot her suitor. Her wave was immediately welcomed.

"So sorry to be late, Sybil, but all the girls were meeting at the soda fountain. We're planning a wingding of a Christmas party and I almost forgot you! Who is that handsome shadow you have following you?"

"Well, I'm dying to tell you—"

"Hey, where's Elizabeth?"

"She ran off ahead. I think she was looking for that Bruce guy." A big grin came across Sybil's face.

Whispering, Daphne continued, "Sooo, do tell. Who is that blond hunk?"

"Just met him on the train…you never know who might be sitting two seats away. Cute, huh? I kinda like him. He got off here so he could see me again. He's staying at the hotel." She babbled on and on.

"I'm curious how you're going to get Mama's approval on this one!"

"Just wait until she meets him. Hey, let's stop at the hotel. I need some help with my bag and I'd like to get a pie for dessert."

"Okay, but I'll run ahead home. I have a sneaky feeling you're going to be doing some room number research or something equally clever." Daphne's voice trailed her sister down the street.

— ◁. ◁. ◁. —

And so it began, the days of having Sybil home again. Somehow I had to let her just "be," and worry about praying on my rosary beads.

About midweek, Sybil approached me. "Mama, I met a lovely Kansas City and Dumas man on the train the other day, and I wondered if he could come to Sunday supper. Elizabeth says you invited Bruce. It would be the cat's meow to have a table full of elegant men."

"I would like to meet him first, dear. I'm sure your father would agree, especially after the George episode. Daddy recovered well, but these out-of-town boys take some getting used to."

"I'll ask him to stop by today or tomorrow, if that's all right."

I nodded my agreement.

"Thanks a bunch, Mama!"

Sybil ran to change into her soft floral dress and primped in the bathroom until I thought she had taken a nap in there.

Finally, she came out and headed for the door. "I'm off to find Tanner."

The door slammed behind her. Nancy and Charlotte climbed on the back of the sofa to look out the picture window as their sister did her best swishy walk down the sidewalk.

"I can do that too, just watch me!" Charlotte jumped down, put her hands on her hips, and performed her exaggerated imitation of Sybil swinging her hips. "See?"

"Okay, enough, Charlotte," I giggled under my breath.

− 4 4 4 −

Davis was in his VIP men's meeting as Sybil peeked in the coffee shop door. Tanner sat with his back to everyone as he slowly consumed his breakfast of chipped beef on toast. Davis shot Sybil a glance but pretended to ignore what was about to transpire.

Sybil came up behind Tanner and stopped. She tapped her toe, cleared her throat, and finally asked Joe to bring her a coffee in the lobby. Davis's head turned and Tanner's head turned—Davis's toward the men's conversation, and Tanner's toward the sound of Sybil's familiar voice. He jumped up, slapped $10 on the counter, and called to the new waitress, "Keep the change, honey. Buy yourself some stockings!"

"Yes, sir, thank you!" she exclaimed.

The men turned around to check on the exuberant waitress and the out-of-town show-off. Eyebrows raised as Tanner then boomed, "Whatcha doing here, honey?" to Sybil.

Everyone shot a look at a squirming Davis, who by this time was blushing as red as the stripe on the coffee cups.

The conversation had been focused on the upcoming XIT rodeo and reunion. Davis kept the topic on target. "Yes, I'd be honored to be a part of it this year. I feel certain I can provide enough brisket for the free cookout."

"You know, Davis, you will be reimbursed for your meat. It will come from the Chamber of Commerce funds," Mr. Huntington clarified.

"No, I wasn't aware of that, but I'm glad to get some repayment, gentlemen. It's killing me to keep up with all my girls." He tilted his head in Sybil's direction.

By this time everyone could see the casual friendship between Sybil and Mr. Out of Town.

"We'd better be off to check on the world," said Mr. Pierce.

The men scattered, glancing over at the beautiful Sybil as they made their way out of the coffee shop.

Davis decided to check on Sybil and her admirer. "Sybil, what's going on here?" he asked as he approached the pair.

"Hiya, Daddy. I'd like you to meet my good friend, Tanner Mercer." She had decided not to say, *Tanner Mercer II*, which she was sure would *not* impress her daddy.

"Well, young man, you belong to a big club."

"I beg your pardon, sir?" Tanner said in a perplexed tone.

"Why, Sybil has quite a fan club from coast to coast," Davis said emphatically.

"Daddy!" exclaimed Sybil.

"Well, it's nice to meet you, Mr. Bennett, and I'm happy to be part of the club. I'd like to be president, if no one has called it yet."

Blushing, Sybil wanted the banter to stop. "I'm here to invite Tanner to come by and meet you and Mama, but I guess half of that has been taken care of."

"Don't mean to embarrass you, young man. You're welcome to my house of girls. I'd welcome another male companion. Did Sybil tell you she has five sisters?"

"Really?" Tanner's eyes danced at the thought of all those girls.

"See you this afternoon then, Tanner?" Sybil said without hesitation. "Our address is 619 Main Street."

— ⊰ ⊰ ⊰ —

At the noon dinner table, Davis gloated as he told me he had some news. "Mr. Huntington has contracted me to provide this year's XIT cookout beef. Do you know what this means? I won't send all my herd off to slaughter, and I've presold fifty or more head! That will fill your teapot, huh? I'm so honored and grateful, to be sure... Do you know about Sybil and this character named Tanner?"

"Yes, I asked her to bring him by so we could officially meet him. Thought we would have him to supper when Bruce comes on Sunday," I said.

"Well, I met him already. Just a pretty face, if you ask me."

"Now, Davis," I admonished.

"All these men of hers make me nervous."

"That's what happens when you have a houseful of beautiful girls," I said, shrugging my shoulders. "Let's not be hasty judging this poor boy. I'm anxious to hear his story."

"He may be coming by this afternoon," Davis warned me.

Later that day, Sybil entered the house with exuberance. "Mama, Daddy, we're here!" I heard her call.

"Who's *we?*" Maggie said as she came out of the music room.

Nancy came from the kitchen table, and Daphne from the bedroom after freshening her lipstick.

"Where's Mama?" Sybil asked.

"Resting, I suppose, but I'll get her," Maggie continued, her inquisitive eyes on Tanner.

Davis and I appeared together in the dining room as Tanner stepped forward with a warm handshake and an engaging smile. "I'm Tanner Mercer II, from Dumas and Kansas City. I'm the lucky man who met Sybil on the train from Denver the other day. Yes, a lucky day for me. We were in the same passenger car." Looking around, he added, "Looks like you have a houseful of lovely women." He cleverly started by looking at me, then looked at the circle of girls assembled on the living room sofa and chair arms.

"Come, have a seat, Tanner. Can we get you an iced tea or sarsaparilla?" I asked.

"A sarsaparilla would be very nice, thanks."

Margaret helped serve so she could get a real close look at the movie-star-looking man.

Sybil piped up, "Don't you girls have something else to do? Mama and Daddy…"

"No, not really," answered Nancy.

Clearing her throat, Sybil repeated, "Mama, Daddy, and I have some visiting we want to do with Mr. Mercer II."

Nancy seemed oblivious, but the other girls exited for parts unknown.

"So, you have kin in Kansas City? That's where I drive our herds from time to time," Davis said, starting off the conversation.

"Yes, sir."

"Will you be going there for the holidays?" I interjected.

"Yes, I was on my way to Dumas when I met Sybil. We decided we both had a few days before the holiday to get to know each other."

"Wasn't your family expecting you?" I prodded.

"They know I often make unexpected stops, especially when I sniff out a business deal. I was thinking this looks like a town that could use a Conoco gas station. Things look pretty prosperous in Twist Junction. Am I right?"

"We're just coming out of the dust storms. They call this the Dust Bowl. Have you heard that term before?" Davis said.

"Everybody knows about those bad times, sir."

Davis continued, "Now we've got the war breathing down our necks. We're lucky we don't have any boys to send off."

"So I see," Tanner commented, leaning back to peek down the hallway between the music room and the bedroom.

"Our churches are having Christmas carol singing on Sunday, and we will be having supper here after the Baptist and Catholic church services. Sybil's sister, Elizabeth, and her boyfriend will be joining us. Would you like to come as well?" I reached out to him.

"Golly, that's mighty nice, Mrs. Bennett. I'd like that very much. Meanwhile, I hope you don't mind if I keep seeing Sybil. We thought we'd go to the movies tonight."

"Movies are the most popular activity here in Twist Junction," I interjected. "Young ladies don't frequent the DeSoto bar. I hope you understand it doesn't bring the most refined sort there. It isn't like going to the Brown Palace in Denver."

"I understand, Mrs. Bennett." Tanner got up. "See you later, Sybil. And Mr. and Mrs. Bennett, very nice to meet you and I certainly look forward to the Sunday supper." He shook Davis's hand, headed for the door, and let himself out with Sybil close on his heels.

Sunday morning was a flurry of girls taking on and off their special outfits and shoes, clothes flying through the air, hair rollers lying everywhere, make-up on every surface, and constant chitter-chatter. I had most of my supper preparation done before we left for Mass. Charlotte had set the table for the family and our two guests, who were strategically placed next to Elizabeth and Sybil. Margaret made sure her place was across from the lovebirds, where she could do her spying more easily.

At the very last minute, I noticed Sybil slipping away to go to the Baptist church. She wanted to join Davis and hear his wonderful singing. She had always been tied very close to her father, so I wasn't surprised and decided not to call out to her. Today, inspired by the Christmas season and our special guests, was to be a day of great importance.

After wonderful holiday church services at both of our respective churches, the family was together again at home.

"Margaret, please start playing the Christmas music when you hear the doorbell," I said. "Daphne, if you can get your father to come cut the roast when I take it out of the oven... These potatoes are just perfect!"

"I'm so excited about the Waldorf salad. It's so festive, Mama," Elizabeth said. "And I will pour the eggnog when they first arrive."

"Oh, I'll do that," Sybil piped up.

"Okay, I'll be in charge of the dessert then," Elizabeth agreed.

I welcomed the nattily dressed men, who arrived laden with gifts galore. The younger girls giggled as they observed the small treasures from Bruce. Tanner carried tins of candy and fruit, as well as a wreath that he had slid through his arm. I looked over at Sybil and Elizabeth as they appeared nonchalantly from the bedroom. Catching a special twinkle in Elizabeth's eyes, and a mischievous grin on Sybil's face, I knew it was going to be quite a supper. That I could predict!

"Bruce, how lovely of you to bring gifts," Elizabeth commented, looking at the Pearson Store holiday bag. "That was *too* kind."

"I thought you all would get a kick out of the newest holiday ornaments. We have many more choices if these don't suit you." He gleefully engaged the younger girls. "Who would like to be the unwrapper? Who would like to be the decorator?"

Maggie jumped right in. "May Charlotte and I unwrap?"

"I'd like to decorate," said Nancy.

"Well, that didn't take long, but I'd like Elizabeth to put this somewhere," he said, handing her the largest box, which was wrapped in red tissue.

Almost blushing, Elizabeth stood next to Bruce. She reached for the box, but hesitated to open it.

"Oh *come on*, it won't bite!" Bruce teased.

"I know, but it is so thoughtful and I want to savor it," Elizabeth responded. The next minute the tissue hit the floor and the box was opened to reveal a gold star.

"Oh, Bruce! It will light up this whole room! I know, let's stick it in the table centerpiece...or we could put it in the wreath Tanner just brought...or how about we put it on top of the tree?"

I saw Bruce grin at each creative suggestion. Their creativity and excitement with each other was a joy to watch. I knew this boy was for my Elizabeth. How could I have ever questioned her choice? Remembering what I had said early on, "Where did you find him? In a Cracker Jack box?" embarrassed me now.

Wrappers and ornaments in hand, the girls ran from tree to table to mantle, placing each decoration just so. I put the food on the table with the help of Daphne, Sybil, and Tanner.

"Daddy, can you lift me up so I can put the shiny angels on the mantel?" Charlotte said as she tugged on Davis's hand.

"Supper is on the table," I called.

Everyone sat down.

Davis spoke in his church-like tone. "I'd like to give a small prayer to God, thanking Him for this meal, and a prayer for our friends and our family."

His words were mellow and strong; his heart open and giving. His tears sat on the rims of his eyes as he looked at each beautiful face around our dining table.

We all chimed in with an appreciative chorus of, "Amen!"

The chatter began...something my girls were especially good at. Throughout dinner, Bruce's jokes entertained us all, and Tanner's business knowledge engaged Davis. Margaret entertained herself, pretending to drop her napkin or tie her shoe, enthralled with the hand holding going on between the couples under the table. Frustrated, with no beau in sight, she announced, "How about some Christmas carols as we get dessert on the table?"

She bounced up to go to the piano. Elizabeth had to let go of Bruce's hand to get the fresh coconut cake from the kitchen.

"May I bring out your lovely candy and fruits, too, Tanner?" Elizabeth asked.

"Absolutely."

"We would like that, Tanner," I added. "This is a treat we don't have often. The hard Christmas candies are my husband's favorite."

Davis, embarrassed a bit, popped over to join Margaret at the piano, where his baritone voice began bellowing out Christmas carols.

A knock interrupted the festivities. I opened the front door to find the sheriff standing there, waving a handful of papers. The singing stopped and, startled, everyone was motionless.

"Won't you come in and join us, Sheriff?" I offered.

"Sorry to interrupt, Mrs. Bennett, but this news couldn't wait." He grinned. "We caught 'em! We found your antique bedroom furniture in Guymon. The robbers, your former cowhands, were taking the furniture to the local pawn shop. Davis, they were wanted for theft, horse and cattle rustling, and actually shot a man in Amarillo a while back."

"Scoundrels, that's what they are," said Davis.

The room filled with oohs and ahhhs.

Shifting the intensity, I insisted, "Come have dessert with us, Sheriff."

"Oh, no ma'am, I've got to fill out the rest of the paperwork and make a report to *The Texan*."

"Are we sure they were the two boys I hired?" Davis eagerly blurted out.

"Oh, yes sir, indeed they were."

"Cate, if you had blown them to pieces that day it could have saved the law a lot of trouble!" Davis chuckled.

"Just imagine *The Texan* headline: *Gunslinging housewife captures outlaws on Main Street!*" I said.

Everyone laughed. Tanner had to be filled in later; however, he did like the newspaper headline.

The sheriff loved bringing the good news and the satisfying relief to our family.

"Merry Christmas, folks," he said as the front door closed behind him.

"Well girls, the moral of that story is, trust your gut!" I said. "If you think someone is no good…trust your instincts. I'm glad I didn't shoot the gun, though."

"Mama, you're not so tough after all," Sybil joked.

Davis gave me a hug. "Glad that chapter can be closed." He toasted with his eggnog, "Merry Christmas, everyone!"

As we closed our bedroom door that night, I said, "This Christmas certainly brought us lots of unexpected happiness. Guess I didn't believe that God would provide. My faith was shaken, but we received much more than I could have imagined…a whole houseful of furniture, new friendships with two potential sons-in-law, the possibility of Nancy in a new school, and the presold cattle for the XIT."

"Catherine, think of those two cowboys, who were so desperate they had to steal to survive… Wish I'd had more opportunity to try to show them honest ways. When we do the right thing and work hard, good things do come, don't they? I'm so grateful that I've sold my cattle. The XIT reunion is so prestigious. It will give us money, but also a real name for me as an important Twist Junction rancher."

A few days later, Davis told me that during their breakfast meeting at the DeSoto, Mr. Huntington had explained the establishment of the three million acres of XIT land in the 1880s by one of the Farwell brothers. They had driven hundreds of thousands of cattle through those acres. It was the largest ranch in the United States. Huntington even said, "Catherine's Aunt Isabel saw some real history when she worked for Colonel Goodnight at the Channing headquarters."

Davis recounted his conversation with Mr. Huntington, and added, "It's an honor to be part of the XIT reunion activities. Bruce mentioned that he's involved in the parade this year. Did you know that he asked me if the girls would be allowed to participate? I didn't give him an answer because I thought I'd ask you to think about it. Cate, if we ever allow it, this would be the year. Bruce will take good care of them. They might do something to honor your Aunt Isabel."

"I have to give that some thought, Davis. I have worked hard to make the girls ladies, so they would have to depict themselves as such," I said.

A short while later, when the holidays were over and the girls were all back at school, I cornered my husband.

"Davis, it was hard for Nancy to go off to school with Margaret, but I'm feeling good about it. Would you write a note for her at the bottom of my letter? I'm sure she misses you. I'm a little worried about Elizabeth and Sybil...hope they stay in school. I know that's not where their hearts are, but if I could get one more semester in them, it will be better for their lives later. Just think, Daphne will be at Loretto Heights next year...one more in college! I've been thinking about Charlotte. She would do better being out of Twist Junction for high school. What about Dallas, with my mother and brother?"

"Cate, don't push them all out of the nest so fast. They'll be gone soon enough...life will go fast enough. When you think about it, your children are away from you longer than they are with you. That makes me sad."

"I just want them to have exciting lives. The world is in turmoil and we must live each day, one day at a time. Who knows? Soon we could be in another world war or something. The newsreels at the cinema are showing a lot of disruption in Europe. They're our allies and we're going to have to give them support... Do you remember dear George?

Sybil heard from him. He made it into the movie as a dancer, but he was called up as a military standby should the war escalate. He's sitting on pins and needles, poor boy. We're fortunate we don't have sons. We pray for the young draftees every Sunday at church...but I'm afraid we'll have to do more than pray if things escalate."

"All I know is I'll have to get more crops in and more cattle to feed everyone... Oh, Cate, we go from one thing to another...a war with the wind and now maybe a war with the world."

"We need our girls to be prepared, Davis, and save our money beyond that."

Time flew by and soon it was summertime, 1936.

"I did it! I'm graduating high school in three years instead of four!" Daphne shouted as she saw Grandmother Bennett, Davis, and I enter the school's gym.

Elizabeth and Sybil had just returned from Loretto Heights, and they proudly filed into the Bennett aisle to celebrate Daphne's graduation. Bruce Pearson came too. He and Elizabeth held hands as they joined us. Nancy and Maggie came running into the auditorium directly from the train. Their Uncle Owen, having picked them up at the station, whisked them to the graduation without a moment to spare.

Daphne spoke with pride on behalf of her class. She reviewed the Dust Bowl days, the short years of recovery, and wished her classmates good luck. She bade them good-bye as they got ready to volunteer for the service; or, for the lucky few, planned to pursue college or marriage. Everyone anticipated the worst as the word "war" tumbled out of everyone's mouths.

I, too, anticipated a very busy summer, concentrating on my girls and listening to President Roosevelt's radio addresses.

Davis and the men in town were preparing for the XIT cookout and parade festivities. Bruce had coerced me into allowing the girls to be in the parade. He asked Otto to drive a wagon, which Bruce happily decorated with bunting and the United States and Texas flags. He decided that his beautiful Elizabeth should be dressed in a vintage outfit, riding Davis's horse, and using Aunt Isabel's side saddle. Sybil followed on Otto's black stallion in cowgirl attire. It was a beautiful display with Daphne, Nancy, Margaret, and Charlotte wearing beautiful white dresses and straw hats, perched gracefully on bales of straw on the wagon and waving at the onlookers.

Davis and I received the first-prize ribbon for the "Bennett Early Pioneers" float. I was secretly pleased that we had participated. All my girls looked perfect.

Bruce ran up to us. "I told you…your girls are the hit of the parade!" He lifted Elizabeth down by her tiny 18" waist and gave her cheek a kiss right before God and everybody.

Tanner welcomed all the girls with red-and-white bouquets. He and Sybil held hands. Their affection for each other was obvious. The crowd didn't know them as a couple, but they certainly did now.

On the porch, after the colorful parade and the town's famous free cookout, Sybil announced that she would *not* go back to college. She wanted to spend every minute with her beloved Tanner. I smiled weakly when she gave me the anticipated news. Her summer had been spent with Tanner's family on numerous trips Back East to Spring Lake, New Jersey, where they partied most of the season to the sounds of big bands on lush-green, rolling mansion grounds. After they returned for the XIT, I was sure their engagement would soon follow.

Elizabeth and Bruce were a couple that entire summer. After all, she was the oldest and probably should be the first to marry. We thought that Bruce Pearson was wonderful to her and for her. He had a way of turning any occasion into a party. He was talented and smart. In his gentlemanly fashion, he wanted to honor Davis and me by asking us for Elizabeth's hand. He wanted to wait until after the XIT, but before school started again.

The Monday after the XIT, I prepared for work at the DeSoto as usual. I called out as I left, "See you later, girls."

Sybil and Elizabeth were already in the kitchen drinking their coffee. As I got ready to walk out the door, I overheard the last bits of their conversation.

Sybil was chattering with Elizabeth regarding their men. "I'd like to go down to the DeSoto to see if Tanner is having breakfast. I want to tell him that I told mother I wasn't going back to school."

"Wish I was so brave. I don't want to leave Bruce, but I feel I would disappoint Mother greatly if I quit."

"Let's get dressed and go down to the hotel. We should make sure Mother has a chance to get to work. Daddy could be there and we could say hi to him too. He meets with his men about now," Sybil said with excitement.

"Okay, be ready in 15!" responded Elizabeth.

I arrived at work to see Bruce sitting with Davis at the men's table. He coaxed me to join them.

"Bruce, I can't go to the men's table," I protested.

"Yes you can, Mrs. B. Trust me."

He took my arm and guided me to where the men sat. I sat down next to Davis.

Bruce handed Davis an envelope. The men's conversation stopped. Davis opened the envelope and we read:

May I have your daughter, Elizabeth Bennett's, hand in marriage?
Bruce Lee Pearson
August 15, 1936

Davis and I smiled, and Davis read the note out loud.

Sybil and Elizabeth came into the coffee shop and went over to the men's table.

"What are you doing here?" they chimed, almost in unison.

Bruce bent down on his knee before Elizabeth and asked, "Miss Elizabeth Bennett, will you marry me?"

Elizabeth gasped. Elizabeth shook. And Elizabeth said, "Yes."

Bruce reached into his pocket and threw confetti in the air. Everyone clapped and cheered. He kissed Elizabeth gently and pushed back a curl that had fallen onto her forehead.

Davis couldn't hold back his tears. Slaps of congratulation came from all the men. I was thrilled. I turned down my eyes so no one could see the puddles forming in them.

"Yeah! It worked," shouted Sybil.

"You scoundrel!" Elizabeth said to her. "Now, where's Tanner?"

"Oh, he's hiding, with his Kodak, behind the far booth!"

"Surprise! Congratulations to Bruce and Elizabeth," Tanner said, popping out of the booth.

"How can I work with all this excitement going on?" I exclaimed.

"You mean I really surprised you, Mrs. Bennett?" Bruce said.

"Bruce Pearson, you are really a trickster."

"How about you, honey?" he said, kissing Elizabeth's hand, which he had squeezed into a red pulp.

"I guess I'll have to get used to lots of fun surprises," Elizabeth admitted.

With that, everyone clapped again.

The couples wandered off to get the awaiting champagne Tanner had arranged in the lobby.

"Well, Davis, looks like you've got your hands *really* full these days," Mr. Pierce chuckled.

"As Davis used to say, it's far easier to manage a herd of cattle over all those girls," Mr. Huntington laughed, putting his arm around Davis's shoulders.

"Bruce has a real way of celebrating, is all I've got to say," I said. "I have to go sit down at my desk. See you gentlemen later." I winked as I exited the men's table.

"Coffee, Mrs. Bennett?" Joe called from behind the counter.

"Yes, in my office, if you don't mind. Thank you, Joe."

I sat at my desk and looked out the window. It would be a 1937 Easter Monday wedding, and no more college for Elizabeth.

10
How Do You Like 'Em—Well Done Or Over Easy?

The world seemed almost normal as I concentrated on our first family wedding. I was deeply grateful that I didn't have to deal with anything contentious. Bruce Pearson was a fine young man for our Elizabeth, even to the degree that he had agreed to convert to Catholicism. While rumors of events of unrest in Europe clouded the daily news, we moved forward with our joyous planning.

I was proud of Elizabeth. Margaret and Nancy were still at "The Mount" and I could be sure they were getting a fine education. They would have their wedding days in due time, but first things were first. Daphne continued to push through her studies with strong ambition, always grateful to be at Loretto Heights. Denver and college were her dream come true.

I certainly didn't have to bring it up, but I could clearly see the financial burden for Davis and me. "Tomorrow will take care of itself with the help of God," I repeated to myself day after day. *Maybe when Mother and the boys come for the wedding, I'll ask if they'll take Charlotte to Dallas for high school. Dallas will provide a level of education equivalent to The Mount without the expense.*

I lived, ate, and slept thinking about what was best for my girls. Poor Davis and I had many nights of long conversations about my plans for each of them. He trusted me implicitly, but I knew he hated to see girl after girl leave the house. They were his heart's expression of love. They had their flaws, but I preferred to ignore them—or fix them as best I could, then ignore them with grace and style. Davis thought each daughter was an expression of individuality and personality. In his mind, nothing needed fixing.

All this action and reaction ran through my head as I waited to help Elizabeth. She took charge and got a mail-order wedding dress from Dallas...not the handmade version of my day. She expected the dress in a week's time, but of course, the mail was late the day it was due to arrive. Somebody's cattle had wandered over the train tracks, halting all services and the mail. We still lived in a remote part of Texas, and things came in and out basically one way. It was fast some of the time, and slow when something important was coming. It was a new era, but still controlled by the Wild West. It was a funny story, though. Turned out that one of Davis's wretched cowboys had escaped jail, and the cattle blocking the tracks were part of a herd he had stolen from Mr. Motley's cattle.

"Elizabeth dear," I called to my daughter. "I thought you might want to take Bruce's car and go to Dumas to pick up the dress right off the train. I don't want to test the conductor's rules, and he might not like you taking it when Dumas wasn't the package's destination, but it might be worth a try."

"At least today isn't my wedding day and I wasn't late for the church," Elizabeth chuckled. "I imagine that would have given Bruce a taste of his own trickster medicine."

After a successful mission, Elizabeth returned home with her wedding dress.

"You want to open it now?" I asked. "The girls might be home soon."

"Let's go into your room, Mama, and close the door."

We anxiously opened the package.

"Elizabeth, it's so fashionable!" I said. I held it up and shook it out.

Elizabeth hurriedly put on the dress of her dreams.

"Sybil and her friend Irene helped me pick it out of the Neiman Marcus catalog," she said as she spun slowly in front of the mirror.

"You should have been on the cover... Turn one more time. It's just lovely with that dropped waist and short skirt."

"Mama, you don't think it's too trendy, do you?"

"Elizabeth, we have to live for today...times are changing so fast and Daddy and I want you to be happy."

"Yoo-hoo, anybody home?" shouted Sybil from the living room.

Elizabeth poked her head out the bedroom door. "It came...look! I don't want the others to see, so look quickly."

Sybil eyed her sister's dress. "You're the cat's meow, Miss Elizabeth...good job!" she enthused.

And she was. The wedding in our little Catholic church was perfect. Father Patrick presided. He grinned broadly as he welcomed Mother Connelly and Mother Bennett; a truce I thought never would be signed. Davis cried all the way down the aisle and Bruce playfully clicked his heels as he bowed to Davis while taking Elizabeth's hand.

The joyous afternoon masked the upheaval ahead.

I was so proud as the family filled the church reception tables, which were loaded with cucumber and chicken salad sandwiches, and a lovely raisin, apple, and carrot salad. Cookies, homemade butter mints, and nuts kept the youngsters occupied before the happy couple cut the two-tiered formal wedding cake. Bruce made sure it had the traditional bride and groom perched on the top. He'd had cream and peach roses brought in from Mexico. Elizabeth told me that people were constantly asking for his creative opinion and help, and the flowers were just one example of his exquisite taste.

I leaned over to him. "Bruce, you should start a business. Your details are outstanding. You are a man of many talents."

"Oh, thanks, Mrs. B, but you haven't seen me dance yet. Watch out when I grab your hand! Mr. Bennett's mother is just going to have to close her eyes!"

The lively, small band had to tone it down a bit as the celebration gave way to my brother Kerrick, who ended the party with the Irish song "When Irish Eyes Are Smiling." I noticed a small tear in my mother's eye, and in the eyes of my dear aunts, Isabel and Mary. Father Patrick grinned. He blessed us all, his pride oozing over every word. I had to giggle a bit as he turned to me and winked.

After a busy but wonderful day, Nancy tucked herself into bed that night, saying, "Elizabeth was beautiful today, but it's not fair to have a war coming. When I get married, I'm going to ask for no war that day. When will this end?"

Davis, who overheard the conversation as he passed the bedroom, said, "Wish we could have that control, to shut down war when we want to return to happy times," he said in response. "Some people are so full of greed, hate, and fear."

It was 1939. Bombs...bombs...bombs. It was relentless. The war started to shrink the economy. Davis's men's group was nervous and on edge. I decided to work part-time for the Twist Junction City office, even though they had promoted me to assistant manager at the DeSoto. The hotel's revenues were dropping. Newcomers were not as frequent, so the rooms sat empty, the café and saloon less crowded. Everyone clambered to hear Roosevelt's addresses on the Philco radio or to see the news clips at the movie house. Musicals and dancing films filled the Mission Movie Theater, lifting our hearts, if only for that hour.

That year, Elizabeth and Bruce gave us our first grandchild—a girl. A boy followed two years later.

Sybil, continuing her path of nonconformity, emphatically decided that a formal East Coast wedding was not going to be. However, I did hear her the night she left us. First, the thump of the suitcase dropping on the ground, a muffled giggle, and a "shush" to Margaret, Nancy, and Charlotte. She did her usual climb out the window, landing on the holly bush. "Oh, hell..." I could hear her swear after landing on the prickly leaves.

"I'll get you, honey," I heard Tanner say in a loud whisper.

Click, click, went her heels down the driveway pavement. I crept to the front window and watched as the Oldsmobile pulled away from the curb. I trembled. I knew this might happen one day. I wondered, had Tanner asked Davis for Sybil's hand? Had Davis decided it wasn't important to tell me, or did he think I would be upset? We knew Tanner well enough and had heard about his wealthy family. Things could have been worse. And now, it had happened...my girl was eloping.

I returned to the bedroom and slid back into bed. "Davis, they left."

"Just now?" he answered. He jumped up, hurried to the living room, and looked out the front window. The car was just turning the corner, headed northwest.

"Did you know about this? Where are they going?" I asked as my husband returned to bed. I was stiff as a board under the covers. My lips were pursed and my words were chipped with pain and betrayal.

"Well, Tanner said he wanted to marry Sybil, but was afraid they would disappoint everyone if they didn't have a big wedding. That's all I really know..."

"If they elope, it will have to be in New Mexico. Yep, that's it, Raton, New Mexico! That's where you can knock on the door of the justice of the peace, all hours of the night."

I was livid at this point.

I stared at the ceiling until morning pushed through the lace curtains. I heard a sniffle come from Davis now and again. He whispered, "She didn't even say good-bye..."

"We should be accustomed to it. She knew it would make us both cry," I said. Sadness prevailed, but I felt angry. My thoughts raced. *You didn't have to hurt your father,* kept rolling through my mind; however, I did know that Tanner and his family would take care of her. Tanner's bank account would cushion any bad times. The problem was, my knowledge of Tanner stretched even further than our front porch. Tanner, the dashing young man, had had many a girlfriend. His reputation, I only hoped, would never hurt my lovely Sybil. Most of all, I hated for her name to be added to his list of conquests.

My sharp intuition had always detected a strong spark between the two of them. True love was the driving force between them, but Tanner's addiction to women was what worried me. Sybil was clever and alluring, and there would be no question that she would prove to be a challenging wife for Tanner.

Time passed as Sybil and Tanner built their lives. We didn't see them for a very long time—I believe because Sybil regretted how she had made her departure and was afraid she had hurt her father. But

Davis and I heard about the new home that Tanner built for her, that they had a darling son, and were doing well. Every now and then the memory of how she left and the hurt she had caused Davis would pop up. She was different—a bit of a renegade—but she had that Irish heart and a soft spot for her daddy. How could she have just left in the middle of the night? Unanswered incidents of disappointment and sadness have a way of resurfacing when they're unresolved.

One morning, I awoke to find Davis up and dressed before daylight. "Davis, where are you going so early, honey?"

"Out to the ranch. Otto needs some help with a small repair job in the barn. He's not as young as he once was. The horses have kicked a hole in the feed trough and I'd like to polish up my saddle if I have time."

"Let me send Otto some of the apple pie I made last night. I hate having him out there by himself. Let him know we miss him, and especially how much Charlotte misses him."

"He keeps company with a wanderer or two now and then. Gets a little work out of them and companionship at the same time. He says there are some real sad characters out there with stories that would make your hair curl—men who have lost their sons to war, lost farms to the banks, and family to starvation. There are damn few jobs out there, Cate. We're the lucky ones. Twist Junction and my men's group have been good to me. We stick together…"

Davis's voice trailed off in thought and gratitude. My hand had slipped into my apron pocket and my fingers found my rosary. I slid it between my fingers as I dwelled on his comments.

"Oh dear, I'm going to be late for work this morning," I said to myself. I ran my coral lipstick over my top lip and pressed my lips together. My right hand fluffed my hair and smoothed my proper navy dress. I was wearing my gloves less and less, but today felt like an official day for some reason, so I pulled out my short, white cotton gloves. My steps were quick as I crossed the street to jump into the car. Davis had moved it to the street to get the pick-up out of our single-lane concrete driveway. The days of our dirt road through the iron gate of our ranch house seemed so long ago. Yes, I was grateful for a car, even though I had to sweep the leaves off the windshield from time to time. Now I had shade, a lawn, and a flower bed around my own little bungalow in town. Yes, we were the lucky ones.

As I got into the car, I waved at Mr. Johnson, the trash collector, who had his son Jason in tow. As I drove down Main Street, I saw Mr. Pearson, who was just walking into the furniture store. I saw Mr. Pierce walking into the bank. My job made me feel grateful.

My foot stepped over the threshold of the hotel and my mind immediately clicked into work mode. How was I going to evict Mr. Sperry in Room 203? He hadn't paid his room, bar, or dining room bill for two weeks. The night train had better be bringing him a bag full of money!

Just as I entered the hotel, there, standing at the front desk, was Mr. Sperry. I couldn't believe my eyes.

"Good morning, ma'am!" he eagerly extended his hand as he spoke. "Believe I have a rather large bill to settle with you folks. I'm waiting for the #105 from Chicago. Mr. Armstrong and I have been negotiating a deal and I have the legal papers and checks on that train."

I wobbled a bit as his words spilled out. I steadied myself by holding on to the counter. I took my gloves off as I responded and shook his outreached hand. *Coincidence?* I thought. My stomach flip-flopped. I was responsible for this man's unpaid bill, and my intuition was working overtime to discern his reliability.

"And what deal have you found in our fine town of Twist Junction, Mr. Sperry?"

"I don't want to disclose the particulars until I have a signature on the dotted line, if you know what I mean. Let's just say it will relieve the farmers. Those silos are pretty full these days, wouldn't you say?"

"Yes, I heard that."

"Won't do anyone any good to have all that grain just sitting there rotting."

I shook my head in visual agreement, my stomach still flopping.

"Let me see the time. The train should be coming pretty soon." His gold pocket watch caught the light of the desk lamp.

I wondered, did he want to prove he was a man of means? We had a large wall clock above our heads.

"Well, I will go now and meet the train."

With my best earnest posture, I looked him straight in the eye. "Excuse me, Mr. Sperry. You have a considerable bill here to settle. Should you not return for some reason, I'm afraid I will need some collateral. I'd be glad to hold your lovely pocket watch until you return."

"Well, Mrs.—"

"Bennett," I quickly finished his sentence. "Catherine Bennett, Assistant Manager."

"Well, Mrs. Bennett, I, uh...I guess that would only be fair."

"Thank you for understanding." I held out my hand with a thump on the desk.

He hesitated and started to unhook the timepiece from its chain.

"You may as well leave the chain, Mr. Sperry. That way it's complete. I'll keep it in my office. You must hurry along. The train is almost here."

He nodded, handed me the watch, and left. Almost shaking, I turned on my heels, watch and chain in hand, and headed back to my office. I closed the door and sank into my chair with a huge sigh. I was taken aback by what I had just accomplished. My fingers hit the desk in piano-playing rotation as I wondered...would he return?

"Joe," I called out. "Is the men's group here yet?"

"No, ma'am. Another fifteen minutes I'd say."

"Can you do me a favor? Please check Mr. Sperry's room, #203, and see if his bag is still there. Oh, and can you bring me a *strong* cup of coffee?"

Joe's face formed a worried frown.

"Tell Mr. Huntington I'd like a meeting with him after he meets with the men," I added.

Staring out my window, I saw one man, Mr. Sperry, walking briskly toward the train station; and another, Mr. Johnson, with slow, purposeful movements, taking the trash off our loading dock. One man of questionable privilege, and one man who showed genuine gratitude for a job. I sat and sat.

— ◁. ◁. ◁. —

Davis found Otto in the barn.

"Howdy, Otto, how you feelin' today?"

"To be honest, Mr. B, I couldn't throw a calf if I tried."

"That's lucky, since we're only fixing the feeding trough. I can nail it while you hold the boards. That sound okay? What happened around here? Did you run everyone off?"

"Don't seem to get as many vagrants in the warmer months. The garden is looking good so far... Think I'll have some good tomatoes and corn for us. Keeping the jackrabbits away seems to be my biggest job. How are the girls? Haven't seen anyone for some time now. Not since Sybil came by one day, way long ago. Heard from her?"

They began to replace the boards in the trough.

"Sybil came here?" Davis said, surprised. "Why didn't you tell me?"

"Yes, must have been last year or longer. Guess I forgot."

"What was she doing here?"

"Didn't pay too much attention. Thought you sent her for something."

"Hmm. Well..." Davis said, standing back and admiring their handiwork. "I think the horses are going to have to work real hard to chew these boards away this time. Think I'll tinker around a bit and polish my saddle. Get yourself some grub."

"Oh, I've gotten to be quite the cook. How about I fix you some too?"

"Sounds good, Otto. Rags...where are they?"

"Rags and mineral spirits hide under the workbench," Otto responded.

Davis found the can of mineral spirits. As he reached for it, it kicked out a pencil and a wadded-up piece of paper. Opening it, he read the word "Daddy." The rest of the page was blank. It was Sybil's writing. Davis stopped dead in his tracks. What was this? What else was it intended to say, but the words never written? He staggered to a nearby bale of hay, still holding the paper.

Otto appeared with two bowls of beans. "You okay, boss?"

Otto could tell that Davis was worried...or puzzled.

"Can you remember exactly when Sybil was here?"

"Well, it was cold. Yep, the horses were in the barn. She went directly to the barn. She didn't know I saw her. Kind of hurt me that she didn't come over to say howdy, but maybe she didn't want me to know she had come. She was in a car with a man. Could have been Tanner. Interesting filly, that one...secretive and beautiful."

"Why do you say that?"

"She kept a lot to herself, I think. She was like a horse that stands alone, always looking beyond the pasture into the wide sky." He handed Davis a bowl and Davis slurped the warm liquid.

"How d'ya like those beans?"

"Not bad, my friend. Mind if I stay out here alone for a while, Otto?"

"Oh, no sir. I reckon by the look on your face that you got some thinkin' to do."

Davis continued to sit on the hay bale. The raw straw stuck through his pants. The discomfort didn't affect him as much as his thoughts of why Sybil had come to the ranch and what she had intended to say in the unfinished note. He got up and stood in the barn doorway, looking out, wondering what Sybil might have needed that day.

Finally, he pulled down his dusty saddle. He had stopped riding the day Sadie had stumbled and practically fell on him. He and the horse were both getting old and they both knew it. Now, he just petted her and talked to her about old times.

Then...there it was, another note, wedged between the peg and the weight of the saddle. Davis grabbed it and again sat on the bale of hay.

My Dearest Daddy,

I hope you will forgive me for running away with Tanner. I couldn't say good-bye. I was afraid to tell you because I knew we

would both cry and cry. It was easier to make it an adventure. I didn't mean to hurt you. I love you too much. I knew you would understand, someday, how much I love Tanner. He makes my heart sing, like Mama makes your heart sing. The pressure of a large wedding would never have worked. Tanner's family and their friends would have made you so uncomfortable. It's not that you embarrass me or anything like that…rather the opposite. You make me so proud that I am your daughter. I hope you won't be mad at me for too long.
    I love you...
    Sybil

    After reading the note several times, Davis stayed perched on the edge of the hay bale. Then he blurted out loud, "Okay, now my heart can rest. You rascal of a girl, you. Thank you."
    Memories flooded him with each wipe of the rag on the leather saddle. So many tender moments…sitting in his rocker, playfully running his fingers over her feet, tickling her toes, smoothing her hair with his rough hands or hugging her while she was giggling and mischievous. Smiling, he admired his clean saddle, then put it away and returned to his truck, lost in thought.
    His whole being felt lighter as he drove back to town. Davis couldn't wait to share this surprise with his Cate. Without words, he knew he wasn't driving alone. His Mexican angel was there with him.
    Having been completely consumed with the note, Davis realized that he had forgotten to say good-bye to Otto. He was concerned about his friend. He was aging, too. Davis decided he would ask Cate if it was okay if Otto moved into town. They had a basement apartment Otto could use. The house would be empty soon. There was a great possibility of Charlotte going to Dallas with her grandmother to attend high school. Margaret would be at college with Daphne. *Wouldn't hurt to have a little male blood in this house for a change,* Davis thought.
    "Hey, Cate, you home?" Davis said anxiously as he came through the kitchen door.
    "Just me," shouted Charlotte. "Missed you, Daddy, at noon

dinner...everything okay at the ranch and with Otto?"

"Doing a little repair work today, but poor Otto is slowing down. What do you think about him coming to town next fall or winter and staying here?"

"Nifty. He was always my best friend next to Punky. I miss him, you know."

— ◁. ◁. ◁. —

A short while later, I returned home.

"There you are, Cate. Thought you got lost in the bowels of the DeSoto," Davis grinned.

I smiled halfheartedly as I walked over to my quizzical husband and kissed the top of his balding head. It had been a day for the record books. Such a very long day...and year. I was no longer sure I wanted to be the assistant manager at the DeSoto Hotel. Mr. Sperry's bills were much-needed revenue for the payroll and food supplies. His remaining luggage and his contact information represented a legitimate businessman. Western Union confirmed that the company he represented was General Mills. Why he was in Twist Junction was the mystery. I was determined that Mr. Sperry and the challenges of my day would remain DeSoto business. I would not bring business into our home.

"I'm sorry, Davis, I've had a very challenging day. I'd like to sit on the porch for a little spell before I go to bed early."

"But Catherine, I have so much news."

"Davis, my head can't handle anymore today. I'm sorry, dear."

"It's mostly good news, which can wait I suppose...might heal that troubled soul of yours though, Cate," he said.

"No, I can't hear or think anymore tonight."

Davis waved away Charlotte as she started out the door to join us on the front porch rockers. "Talk to you in just a minute," Davis almost whispered to her.

His patience and support, coupled with his broad, strong hands rubbing my shoulders, enabled me to almost drift effortlessly from the porch to my bed. My day's thoughts continued to nag me. Grabbing the worn rosary beads from my apron, I managed a prayer or two, asking God for the answer to my predicament. Thoughts of possible reports to the police, no paychecks on Friday, and horrible scandals being reported in the *Twist Junction Texan*...my options were far from easy. Or would the whole Sperry affair somehow be blamed on my sloppy accountability? I couldn't bear the last option. It would devastate Davis and would destroy my credibility in town. Who would hire me after such incompetent work? I did have a gold watch of unknown value...and I could make some inquiries at the granary. Perhaps I could get some clues as to whether there indeed was any big deal in the works. I wouldn't want to embarrass anyone unnecessarily. Treading carefully was all I could do until I had all the puzzle pieces. How had I become so involved?

I dozed off readily with the help of Davis's neck and shoulder rub. Then, like a light bulb had exploded, I awoke at 3:00 a.m. My mind began racing with my plan. Yes, before work I would go to the granary and ask a few questions...nothing accusatory, nothing of great substance. Practicing over and over in my head, I would say, "Good morning, Mr. Gilbert, do you have a minute? Thank you. As Assistant Manager of the Desoto, I'm trying to project what our house count might be over the next month. Are you expecting any out-of-town gentlemen for negotiations or observations of your fine mill? I realize I may be asking proprietary questions, but I too run a business and I have to make projections and reports to Mr. Huntington, my boss. I'll be checking with other prosperous businesses in town. Believe me, none of this information will be shared with the public or *The Texan*. The war is changing business on many levels, and I want to have sufficient facts." I would also say, "Like Mr. Sperry, businessmen coming for long periods of time are relevant for my staffing. You are familiar with this gentleman, I'm sure..." And I would wait for his response, then follow with, "Will he be back any time soon? Do you expect more gentlemen as well?" And I would again wait for his response.

Yes, I think this conversation will be helpful and appropriate. I'll check with the dry goods and furniture stores, and with Mr. Pierce at the bank. Are people coming to ask questions to invest, resettle, or put together grain or cattle deals? Wonder what Davis hears? After going through all my plans it was almost 5:00. I made my way to the kitchen.

"Good morning, Davis Bennett. Coffee is ready," I said when Davis came into the kitchen a short while later.

"Cate, I thought you must have run away in the middle of the night. Glad it was only to the kitchen. Five o'clock is a little early, even for you." He chuckled. "Well, now that I've got your attention...I thought I was going to have to make an appointment in your office so I could talk to you."

"Well, Davis, to be honest, I had a big problem at the hotel yesterday and I've been up all night trying to map out my strategy. I can't clog my brain with anything else this morning. That appointment idea sounds good. How about after you meet with the men?" I handed Davis his coffee. "Do you think you could ask the men if anyone knows of some big business deal that might be brewing with some out-of-towners?" I added.

"Catherine, what I have to say deserves more than a meeting in your office. These are important family matters. I think you've lost sight of what is important around here. Your job is consuming you in a way that I am not too happy about." His voice was raised by this time.

I snapped back, "Davis, the economy, the war—these are important! They affect us all! I have to go get ready. I may lose my job if I don't figure all this out soon. I have to leave early for meetings."

"Catherine, I don't like this one bit. Business is interfering with our family."

I could feel his anger.

"Maybe I'll go out to check on Otto this morning before seeing the boys..." Davis grumbled, and abruptly left.

Davis's demeanor bothered me, but I had to stay focused on my morning plans. I called the DeSoto. "Joe, I'm going to be a little late coming in this morning. Take charge, will you?"

I set breakfast out for Charlotte, woke her gently, and headed out the door. I was heading toward the closest I had ever been to a "man's world." I felt like I had painted my whole body in a coat of bright-red determination. Holding my 5'2" body as tall as it would go, I proceeded with my plan of asking questions and gathering information from each of my business stops. The men were reluctant to impart too much information at first, but when they realized others had cooperated, they opened up and gave me both real and prospective figures.

Relieved, I found Mr. Sperry and his dealings to be legitimate. His research and deals centered around an innovation in breakfast foods. A telegram addressed to me arrived later that morning, explaining that his sudden exit was not of his doing. A new market possibility and the train schedule were what had made him act so abruptly. He had wired funds to pay his bill and instructed us to put his luggage, watch, and chain on the next train north out of town. I was relieved...but now I was curious. Were all of the Twist Junction deals off? Knowing the town business seemed weighty to me, but at least I could impress Mr. Huntington with statistics regarding the viability of the hotel's services. He was to meet with me that afternoon. I was proud to be able to say that I had done my job, and the salaries and bills could now be paid.

— 4. 4. 4. —

Davis drove out to see Otto. He wanted his temper to cool a bit after the conversation he'd had with Cate that morning.

"Otto, my man, how you doing?"

Otto's body seemed frail. Davis observed his number-one man slumped in his chair, half dressed, drinking his black coffee.

"Goin' slow today, boss. Just heard one of my old range riders who had joined the Army was killed in France. A nasty war we have...a loss of a damn good life. He was a horseman and cattleman... What was he doing jumping off a raft onto a beach with a rifle? He wasn't a killer, Mr. Davis. He was an animal man...horses and cattle, that's all he knew."

His eyes dropped as he spoke, as if he were seeing his buddy's reflection in his coffee.

"Too much change, Otto," Davis said. "Even my Cate is so wrapped up with her job that she doesn't have the time or energy to talk to me. I know whatever was on her mind had to be pretty damn important, but it hurt me. Where is my wife and the girls' mother? We're being pulled by too much change."

Davis grabbed a cup of coffee. He and Otto sat in silence until the clucks of the chickens and the light rustle of the trees in the breeze brought them back to the moment. Otto finished dressing. They got up and walked out to the barn. The horses welcomed them as they anxiously awaited their oats and water. The few cattle on the ranch were close by, waiting for their morning rations. Otto had not done the minimum of his job, but Davis understood. He wasn't mad. He was concerned.

"Otto, the cattle need you and it looks like we've got some ripe vegetables. I'll take some to Cate, and some eggs too. I'll feed the horses. You take it easy. How about coming to Daphne's college graduation good-bye dinner next week? She's going to Washington, D.C., to work this summer."

"Don't you think that's dangerous, boss? How did time fly so fast? Last thing I remember, she was graduating from high school. Didn't she complete it in three years, too?"

"Yes, yes, time flew by, and now wartime and the government need all the help they can get. You know my daughters. They're determined, just like their mother! Daphne thinks it's exciting, and you know, I think she'll be a really good secretary. She'll be running her office before she knows it. She's a smart one, that girl."

"Thanks for the dinner invitation. I'll be there. Do I have to get a haircut for the occasion?"

"Suit yourself. All my girls will be in party dresses and Bruce will have his suit on. I wish I could get Sybil and Tanner to come. I think it would please Daphne, and they have to know they are forgiven for running away. They are part of our family, right?"

"Yep, Sybil is like your thumb…a part of you, boss."

"Otto, did you know she left me a note under my saddle in the barn? It sat there for almost two years, but because I never rode, I never found it."

"No kidding? She wanted you to know she loved you, didn't she?"

Davis nodded. "Go on out to the cattle. I'll do the few things here and I'll see you next week."

After Davis tended to the chores, he drove off, still worried about Otto. *Too many changes, indeed...*

Davis's meeting with his men's group reflected the same...caution, waiting for the big changes to come, and talk of a military air training base being built outside of town. His heart felt heavy as he marched into Cate's office for his appointment. He had a lot on his mind and in his heart.

— ⌐ ⌐ ⌐ —

I was happy to see my husband. "Davis dear, I'm *so* sorry about this morning but I'm so glad to see you now. Come in and sit down. Can I get you some coffee, dear?"

"No, I've had enough with the men and also with Otto."

"Otto?"

"He's not doing well, Cate. He's getting old and is very tired. Would you mind if we brought him into town to live in our basement apartment for the winter?"

"Certainly. I think he deserves that."

"I also invited him to Daphne's going-away dinner next week."

"Wonderful! Was that what you wanted to tell me last night?"

"No, something much more important. When I was working in the barn, I got my saddle down to polish it and a note fell to the ground....*a note from Sybil!* She wrote it before she eloped..." Reaching into his breast pocket, he pulled out the crumpled letter written in Sybil's handwriting. "She didn't want to hurt us."

He passed the paper to me, then got up and looked out the window as I read it. He could hear my soft sniffling as I fumbled for my bag and my favorite Irish lace hanky.

Clearing my throat, I got up and hugged Davis from behind. "As exciting as the eloping seemed, I'm sure she was sad too. She knew she wanted this man, even though it came with complications... I remember going through some rough times when we got married. Oh dear, poor Sybil. I need to write her a letter of forgiveness. We should invite them to Daphne's party."

"I thought the same thing," commented Davis as he turned to give me a gentle kiss on the forehead. In that same minute, Mr. Huntington arrived in my office.

"Oh, the lovebirds of Twist Junction are caught in action!" he exclaimed. "No wonder you have such a wonderful family, Davis, you still treat your bride like a queen. I'll come back in ten minutes, Catherine."

"Thank you, Mr. Huntington. I'll be ready for our meeting then." I looked lovingly at my husband. "Davis, I'll write to Sybil before I leave the office today. I won't be home at noon. My meeting with Mr. Huntington is what I have been so nervous about yesterday and today. I'll have lots to tell you after speaking with him."

When Mr. Huntington returned, I had papers spread out on my desk and a list of all my day's appointments. A wire of the cash lay on top. His eyes flashed as he tried to comprehend the extent of my reports, but I was certain the wire transfer was his first observation. From that moment on, he included me in every decision regarding hotel business and would ask my opinion regarding other business matters. A pay raise of $10 per week was immediate. When he left after our meeting, I had my second cry of the day. I was proud of myself and relieved that I had professionally handled the unnerving situation of Mr. Sperry. I guess I had succeeded in stepping over the threshold into a "man's world." And soon, I would see my very own girls stepping over that same threshold.

11
10,000 Men Outside My Window

My heart pounded as I stood on the train platform once again. Holding back my tears and trying to relax my shoulders, I shared my concerns with Davis. Washington, D.C., was exciting to be sure. But it was wartime. Daphne bubbled as she bounced up the steps to the train. I could see her settle into her window seat. She looked at me and mouthed, "I love you. See you at Thanksgiving." Her energetic wave reassured me that this strong girl definitely had my determination. She would be fine.

"She *will* be fine...won't she?" I blurted out to Davis.

He took my arm and patted it as we turned to walk home.

"Cate, why are you worrying so? This isn't like you."

"It's wartime, Davis. Anything could happen. She'll be so far away, and those girls don't really know anyone. I would never have let her go if her roommates weren't joining her."

"You really think we could have held her back? Not that one," Davis chuckled. "Cate, if you had been in her shoes at that age, I could see you jumping on that train with the very same enthusiasm."

"I feel like our family breaking up. Margaret, Nancy, and Charlotte are all scattered away at different schools."

Davis looked at me with a raised brow. "Isn't that what you wanted? You're a confused woman."

"Oh, Davis, I know I did it." I let out a huge sigh. "Denver, Kansas, Dallas…the price of a good education! We do have Sybil and cute little Trae back after summering in Spring Lake. That makes me happy. We're very lucky. And Elizabeth and her family are our angels."

Thanksgiving seemed to be far in the future. Admittedly, Davis and I were lonely for our girls. I attempted to fill the void by stopping by the post office every day for their letters. Reports arrived frequently, often filled with trivia concerning some interesting young man. The topic of studies rarely surfaced from Nancy; however, Mother had Charlotte toeing the line, working hard every night on her Dallas high school studies. I would read and reread every word of every note, especially the stories from Washington. Daphne's job at the War Department made her heart heavy with the war's tragedies. She described long days of accounting for the numbers of the dead and those missing in action. She would bounce back with details of Saturday activities of tea dances on the roof of the Army-Navy Country Club, the dresses she would wear, her corsages, and her hair, or the Loews Theater on F Street showing the latest Cary Grant or Marlene Dietrich films.

We received a letter from Margaret, and as I read it to Davis, he rolled his eyes.

Dear Mama and Daddy,
I'm in my science midterm class and we are to be taking Sister Josephine's test. I know you know me well enough that I cannot tell you a lie, so when you receive my grades you won't be shocked. I'm writing you this letter instead of taking the exam. I figured everyone has their head down writing, so I'd do the same. I don't understand anything about science. I wish I could have substituted this class for music or something I liked. The sky is so blue as I look out the window. Ten more minutes and I can scoot out the door. Don't think anyone will notice that I didn't turn in my blue book. I'm so sorry if I've disappointed you. Wish I could be typing this letter to you. I'm pretty good at that. Can't wait to see you at Thanksgiving!
Your loving daughter,
Margaret

I folded the letter and stared up at Davis.

"Well, Cate, they can't all be the same...smart at everything," he chuckled as his coffee jostled around in his cup. "At least she's upfront and honest. I'd give her a column of numbers to add any day...have her type my obituary or play 'Onward Christian Soldiers' on the piano. She's a sweetie."

"Davis, I've been thinking. Maybe it's time to start helping others. We've been so blessed. You know Mr. Johnson, the trash man? He has such a polite and bright son, Jason. He'll never be able to get very far in life...he has a limp and can't join the service. I've seen him help his dad from time to time and do odd jobs around town. He's a high school junior now. Think I'll approach him to see if he'd be interested in going to college."

"Catherine...Catherine..." Davis protested, holding up his hands. "It's hard enough for us to get by." He paused. "You have the biggest heart. Education is all-consuming in your head. I believe you'd send the dog to a school for tricks if there was such a thing."

"Don't make fun, Mr. Bennett. The bible says we should do unto others and help our fellow man. I want to be a good Christian woman. The new city job has me bringing in more money. I can afford to put a few dollars away each week for someone else. We only have three girls to feed, and they'll be working soon."

"Do you know what you *really* want, woman? First, you want them all away and in school, then you're down because you're lonely." Getting up from the kitchen table, Davis shook his head and proceeded into the music room, then turned on the latest baseball game being broadcast on the Philco.

"Alert, alert!" The alarming announcement pierced the airwaves. "Germans attack London. Blenheim Palace hit and the Royals barely escape."

I ran into the room to hear the latest news. "Oh, Davis, things are definitely getting worse. It's bad enough we're rationing our food. Aren't we lucky to have a garden? I'm awfully glad I was able to can some things this year. Otto did a great job keeping the plot going without those pesky rabbits getting it all."

"Yup. Otto and I debated putting in a third of our usual crops and running only thirty head of cattle. It'll be hard keeping up with things, especially with Otto's failing health, but we might be grateful for the food options."

"I'm going to write my weekly letters to the girls. If it's not too late when I'm done, I'll walk to the post office. I didn't get there yesterday. Then I can mail my letters and see if anything has arrived." I hurried to get paper and pen.

The evening wasn't too brisk for that time of year. My footsteps were deliberate as I headed for the post office. My mind raced. I felt I needed to hear news from my girls…good or bad. The mail slot swallowed my letters, all headed off in different directions. I checked for incoming mail. Sure enough, I could see a leaning envelope through the glass door of Box 613. For some strange reason, a lump in my stomach made me hesitate as I reached for the letter. It was from Daphne. I tucked it into my coat pocket, determined to read it in my lounge chair with a cup of tea. My mother's Irish ways taught me that a cup of tea soothed the soul, and she was right.

The return address was Washington, D.C. The stamp area was marked "Free," which was customary in wartime. Daphne made me slightly anxious. I never quite knew what she might be up to next.

"Davis, a letter from Daphne," I called out over the baseball broadcast.

"We're at the top of the ninth. Be there in a minute."

Dear Mama and Daddy,

Fighting has become more intense on the European front. My lists were twice as long today. By chance, I glanced at the California boys before I started typing. Mama…George's name was there. I had to run to the ladies' room. I cried and cried. Should I tell Sybil or do you want to do it? His poor parents.

Your daughter,
Daphne

"Oh, no!" I gasped. "Dear God in Heaven!" I sat like a rock. The teacup rattled in my shaking hand. Images of a vibrant young man knocking at my door, visiting my girls, and most of all, proudly telling us he was refurnishing our home after the robbery, filled my head. His tender heart and his appreciative manner now grabbed my soul. As I sat alone, the tears flowed. "God, why did you take this beautiful soul..." tumbled out of my mouth.

"What did you say?" Davis called.

I couldn't answer. I couldn't move. The tea grew cold and the napkin wetter from blotting my tears. George wasn't my son, but he was like my son, sitting with the girls at suppertime, taking care of them as they experienced their first dates, and giving them advice along the way. *God's plans are hard to understand...* I thought sadly. I set down my teacup and slowly went into the bedroom. My fingers automatically slipped into my apron pocket and the beads rolled between my fingers. I returned to the living room and handed the letter to Davis.

Davis's body slumped as he read the letter. The silence penetrated the dimly lit room. Without words, I took my cup to the kitchen. Then I returned to my room, moved the bed step close to our four-poster bed, slid in, and covered my head and entire body with the warm blankets.

Thanksgiving came with its usual flurry. The girls arrived in rapid succession. Otto, trying to be useful, greeted them at the train station to handle their bags, and herded them around like cattle. The volume of chitter-chatter in the house increased with the arrival of each daughter. Davis sat in his chair next to the roaring fire and I scuttled back and forth between the kitchen and the living room. The girls' attention went first to Davis for big hugs, then to me, standing at attention in my apron uniform. Otto whisked the luggage off to the bedroom. One by one, beds creaked as the girls flopped on them like birds coming in for a rough landing on their nests. Nancy and Charlotte joined their father for a fireside chat, while Maggie and Daphne stayed in their room. I could see them out of the corner of my eye, and listened to their conversations as I worked in the kitchen.

"I never thought I'd say this, Daphne...but I *really* missed you," Maggie said, rolling onto her side. "When I hear about soldiers, battles, and guns, I wonder if you might be in danger in Washington."

"We do have practice air raid drills, but people don't think an attack would hit D.C. There are plenty of rumors of secret shelters for the president and his cabinet. The excitement of all this intrigue is contagious. We never know what's next or who will be shipped out, so we live and play hard, so to speak."

"Do you miss Bob, your old boyfriend? Or Denver or Twist Junction?" Maggie continued.

"Not really," Daphne answered. "Did you know that I wrote Bob, and invited him to come for Thanksgiving? Mama said it was okay. He writes me practically every day. Hope he's not bringing a ring. I'm just not sure I *really* love him. Fact is, I have another beau in D.C."

"You do?" Maggie sounded surprised.

"Don't go blabbing that...promise?"

"Tell me more. Is he a soldier? Where is he from? What does he look like?"

"Oh, Maggie...Sybil saw him once when she was on the East Coast visiting Tanner's family. She took the train down to visit me. Anyway, she said she thought he was elegant. You should see him glide me around the dance floor. He won't go off to fight. He's an attaché."

"A what? Attached?"

"Sort of. He's assigned to generals to be their right-hand man. So he takes them everywhere and makes all their arrangements. You know, so they never really get in harm's way. Attached at the hip, so to speak."

"Sounds very important, if you ask me."

"Yes, he makes sure everything is perfect, and that's how he treats me, too."

I heard Daphne sigh.

"Queen Bee, huh? That suits you, all right!" Maggie snickered at her own teasing remark.

"I knew I shouldn't have told you. But remember, you made a promise, right? For God's sake, you wouldn't hint a smidgen of this to

Bob, right?"

"Well, okay, but what a story…so exciting and romantic, dancing under the stars until midnight..." Maggie said as she rolled back and stared at the ceiling in a dreamlike state, savoring Daphne's every word.

"Have you heard the Big Band sounds? They're the rage!" Daphne continued.

"The Brown, in Denver, is bringing in Benny somebody. Do you know his name?"

"Goodman?" Daphne guessed.

"You know everything, Daphy!"

"I run in a very sophisticated crowd. My friends are up on everything. Most of them come from wealthy East Coast families with prestigious military histories. That's how we got our nice rental house and our good jobs. Not sure how I fit in. I guess they think I'm from some fancy Texas ranch family."

"Daphy, you're smart and beautiful."

"Thanks, Maggie, but I wish I had your gorgeous legs and feet."

"Girls, can you come help?" I called from the kitchen. "I'm not running a sorority house!"

"See you later, alligator," Margaret whispered.

"I'll be there in a minute!" Daphne called back to me, always the one to move slowly when it came to work.

Charlotte squealed with delight as she met Otto coming up the basement stairs with boxes of my good china. She had been distracted by her sisters at the train station, and was now able to focus on her special friend now that she had time to chat.

"Good Lord, girl, I thought you saw a mouse," he teased her. "Charlotte, you're all grown-up and 'Dallasfied.' How do you like living with your grandmother and all your uncles?"

"To tell you the truth, Grandmother is very strict. She makes me study so hard…I hardly have time to go shopping with my girlfriends. I didn't know it was such a big city. Bigger than Denver, I think. Otto, I'm so glad you're living in town with us now."

"Yep," Otto said, leaning against the wall to lighten the weight of the box. "Finished up the garden, sent the last few cattle off and even had a sad day of putting Sadie and my old horse down. Poor old horses, they were good to us. One of your cousins plowed up the last crop. Your daddy says we're going to take a rest for a while. He's leased out the upper forty acres. But I'm not sitting on my backside. There's still plenty to do to keep the fences and house in good repair. I'll have to give you a paintbrush next time you go out there."

"Otto, I can't paint!"

"Time you learned something practical, little miss."

"Um, chit-chatting on the back stairs, are you?" I said, poking my head around the corner to look at them. "I need Margaret and Nancy to wash those dusty dishes. We've got work to do around here."

"Sorry, Mama, my fault. I just *had* to talk to Otto. I've missed him so much. He says he's going to take me out to the ranch...he's going to teach me how to paint."

"I'd sure like to see that day, Charlotte. Meanwhile, set the table for sixteen. Oh dear, I forgot Bob, that's seventeen. Is he still coming, Daphne?"

Calling from the bedroom, Daphne said, almost bereft of emotion, "Yes, I believe so. His train is due this afternoon at 5:00."

I thought, *Doesn't sound like a girl in love...* "That's good," I said out loud. "We'll all have time to chat about the goings-on in California before our big day tomorrow. Your daddy has left for Channing to get our turkey from Aunt Isabel. He should be back soon. Aunt Mary did chop off his head, but we still have feathers to pluck off. Cleaning him up will take a while."

"I'd be glad to help, Mrs. B," Otto said.

"I can help Otto, too, Mama," Charlotte joined in.

"Good. Now, Margaret and Nancy, please do the pies today—two pumpkins and two pecans. Daphne and I will get the biscuits and cornbread baked for the dressing. Snap the beans and peel the potatoes too, dear Charlotte. I'm sorry I couldn't find any fresh cranberries this year. Our supplies are limited these days. There were three cans, but we'll have to be frugal with one. I left the other two for the neighbors. I'm sure Mother Bennett will be looking for some, too."

"Will Aunt Polly eat with her mother, or could we have her here?" Charlotte added.

"Polly is always welcome here, but she will be with the Bennett side of the family, as usual."

"Mama, I'd like to take her a piece of my pecan pie," said Nancy. "She loves nuts."

"That's good...the nut will take the nuts to her nutty aunt," Daphne joked.

"Enough!" I said, exasperated. "Let's turn on the radio. Maybe there will be some soothing music."

"Oh, pooh, now we can't gossip. See what you did, Daphy!" Margaret stomped her foot with disappointment.

"Don't worry," I replied. "She'll be out of here soon to get all dolled up for Bob."

"Don't know why she'd do that. I don't think she even likes him," Margaret blurted deliberately in Nancy's direction, just loud enough for her to overhear.

"What?" Nancy spun around and looked at Daphne. "I thought you were getting engaged this weekend."

"What are you two talking about? What did you say? Engaged?" Daphne spat. "Who said anything about that? Honestly, I'll never learn. *Do not* talk about anything personal in this house... If you two weren't busy making pies, the gossip would be all over town. Pretty soon Phoebe Ann would be running through the front door saying she wants to be in my wedding or something. Mama, this is too much. I'm going to get ready to meet Bob's train." And with that, she stomped off to the bedroom.

I shook my head as the others teased and joked.

The pick-up's door slammed shut outside. "Want to open the back door..." Davis called from outside.

Charlotte rushed to help, practically skidding across the puddles of cooking water on the floor.

"Would you men mind plucking the turkey outside?" I pleaded.

Otto positioned himself on the steps with a circle of newspapers. "Nice-looking bird, boss!"

"Feels like a ton, but Isabel swears it's not a pound over twenty-five," Davis said. "Cate will have to get him stuffed and into the oven before we go to bed... Just teasing. How's it all coming? Would you mind if I went to the DeSoto to see if the men are still meeting today? There was to be a big discussion about some sort of secret Air Force installation outside of town."

"Air Force? That means men! Tell us all about it, Daddy, will you?" Nancy squeaked.

"That's all you think about, Nancy," Maggie remarked.

"And you, Miss Songbird?"

"Bye, Davis," I said. "Please turn that radio up a little louder, dear. I need some more soothing music."

"No teasing now, girls," Davis said on his way out the door. "If you're angry, the pies won't taste good. Food can take on bad energy, you know." He paused as Daphne came into the room. "Daphne, you are mighty gussied up. Curled your hair too, I see."

"Yes, going to meet my man."

Maggie rolled her eyes.

"How do you like my toeless heels? Got them last summer on Fifth Avenue in New York City with Sybil. They're the rage these days. My roommates wanted to borrow them every minute when they weren't on my feet. Rolland thought they were super sexy."

"Who?" I said, stopping my vegetable peeling.

Daphne's breath drew in sharply as she realized she had revealed the identity of her secret boyfriend.

"Oh, nobody but a friend...he hangs around all the girls at our row house." Trying to minimize the boyfriend fumble, she said, "Suede seems to be the most elegant. Black looks like velvet, right?"

She twirled, showing off her shoes and winsome shape. I seemed to be the only one looking, as the girls seemed to be bored with her bragging.

"Can I borrow your red coat, Nancy? Bob can spot me better in a bright color. Oops, got to run. That train is always on time."

"Hold on, I didn't say yes to the coat yet!" Nancy said. "It can be yes if I can wear the suede heels to Thanksgiving dinner."

"You're a tough negotiator, but I'm late and I'll have to agree this time."

"Yes!" Nancy whispered triumphantly to Maggie. "I beat out Daphne."

"How are those pies coming? Something smells good," I complimented them with a smile. I looked over their creations.

Margaret said, "Just perfect."

"That's my Margaret. Nancy, keep an eye on yours. Sometimes the pecans get too brown." I dipped my finger into the filling. "This is perfect, too! I'll tell everybody who made these."

It was Thanksgiving Day, 1941. Grandchildren, husbands, boyfriends, and Otto filled our table along with my dear aunts, my Davis, and my girls.

Davis's mellow voice stopped all conversation. "May we bow our heads."

I peeked out the corner of my eye to spot all those who had not lowered their heads. Sybil's little Trae fidgeted and pulled his cousin Pamela's hair. Elizabeth caught his hand before it became a full-out crying session. Daphne's eyes were down, but she and Bob only had one hand up in prayer. Her actions showed something less reverent going on.

"Amen" was the signal for food to appear on the table. Everyone gasped as Davis toted the big, twenty-five-pound bird to the table. Applause sounded as it came in for the perfect landing at his place. The knife slapped against the sharpener, which signaled the beginning of the festivities.

Bob started off the conversation, asking about the Washington parties. "Do tell us what makes them so exciting," he said.

Bruce chimed in, "What is the newest and most popular drink?

We'll have to have a 'tribute to Washington' party with all the latest. New dance steps too, Daphne!"

"Enough decadence!" Aunt Isabel wanted to balance everything with stories of married life in Dumas. "Tell us about Dumas, Sybil dear."

"I want to tell about Dallas," Charlotte piped up.

Conversations swirled around the table almost as fast as the dishes were passed from person to person.

"We have four pies for dessert, so don't hesitate to take some... pecan *and* pumpkin," I said.

Davis cleared his throat. "Girls, you put on a mighty fine spread today. We're so lucky to be together. Hard to get out-of-towners here very often. Mama and I miss you."

"Oh Daddy, you're going to make us all cry," Charlotte interrupted.

"It's a real pleasure to be with your fine family, sir," Bob added.

"Well, you should be part of it, then," Bruce joked. "That's when it really gets good... The gossip is stifling. Covers darn near the whole country these days."

"Elizabeth, do you let Bruce read our letters? If so, I'll have to be more discreet," Margaret said.

Laughter broke out.

"Daddy," Nancy said, "you haven't shared the latest Twist Junction gossip. You know...the military thing."

"It does seem to be coming. It will be an Army and Air Force training base. They claim they'll be training glider pilots, but the men about town find gliders questionable with the way the war is escalating. It likely will be single-engine planes for now."

Nancy's eyes grew wider. "Zowie! How very exciting! Will there be jobs and maybe hundreds of pilots?"

"Looks that way. Maybe you girls can all come home and not have to go so far to find work."

"Now, now, Daddy, I can't promise that. Twist Junction simply isn't Washington," Daphne said.

"You could see Bob again," Davis said.

I was certain that Bob was going to have to fight hard to get

Daphne.

"Don't worry too much, Bob. War can't last forever," Daphne said, realizing she needed to say something to his puzzled expression.

Now I was *sure* something wasn't quite right.

Sybil's husband, Tanner, changed the subject slightly. "Well, looks like Sybil and I will be sitting pretty. Those planes are going to need my fuel...and lots of it. Guess I need to start asking some questions so I'll have my production ready. That will be a swell contract to get."

"Always business, business, business," snapped Sybil, who had been quieter than usual, even though little Trae kept her occupied. She was continually chasing him out from under the table, behind the chairs, and into the kitchen.

I popped up, offering, "More pie, anyone? President Roosevelt will be on the Philco soon with his National Thanksgiving speech. I don't want to miss it. For those not interested, can you clear the table?" I smiled. "Aunt Isabel or Aunt Mary, or anyone else, will you join me for some tea or coffee?"

The elderly ladies nodded. Davis and Elizabeth had their coffee already.

"Otto? Bob, Bruce?" I asked.

The men answered with appreciative nods.

The crackle on the radio indicated that the speech was about to begin.

"My fellow Americans. Eleanor and I wish to extend to this proud nation a very Happy Thanksgiving..."

My eyes closed as I tried to concentrate on his warm, reassuring words, promising a short war and our utmost protection at all times. I knew he meant it...but was it possible?

Isabel and Mary shook their heads, and Davis sat quiet and stoic...each in their own world of worry. The young couples flirted, teased, and quietly laughed. The children ran to the music room and played with Charlotte. I wondered if they realized the severity of the world's situation, or just preferred to put it out of their heads for the moment. I was sure "it can't happen to us" was their state of mind.

Charlotte had somehow managed to get the little ones to lie on her bed, where she read Hans Christian Andersen fairy tales to them.

After the president had spoken, I felt comforted for the moment. The young men began conversing at the table again, and the girls started cleaning up in the kitchen. I felt I had a well-run machine in motion.

"Catherine, dear," Aunt Isabel said as she wobbled over to me. "We have a long drive to Channing. Better to get there before dark... You have *many* helpers. We *must* talk when we have more time and less activity. The girls are becoming lovely young women, but it's too much for an old spinster like me."

Aunt Mary smiled and hugged me. "Lovely Thanksgiving."

Davis walked them to the door and out to their car. Opening the car door, he said, "I want to thank you for the delicious, hearty bird this year."

The ladies smiled as they slipped onto the car's bench seat.

"Wonderful family you have, Davis," Aunt Mary said as she closed the weighty car door.

Sybil swooped up her curly-headed boy and announced that they too needed to head for home. I could see pain, or maybe a tear, in her eye as she touched my cheek with hers. Davis escorted her to the door, just as he had done for Aunt Isabel and Aunt Mary. He always wanted to take care of the women. He shook Tanner's hand, then turned to give Sybil a kiss on the forehead.

"I love you, sweetie," he whispered.

"Love you, too, Daddy." She had a slight shake in her voice, which seemed to puzzle Davis.

Elizabeth and Bruce followed with their children in tow. After hugs and kisses, they were out the door. Bruce turned to Bob. "If you want a drink at the bar tonight, I'll join you. You're staying at the DeSoto, right?"

"Sure enough. Meet me at 7:30 then," Bob confirmed.

Noticing that Elizabeth and Daphne were not looking too keen on the plan, I immediately suggested, "Can you find a babysitter,

Elizabeth? And stay here, perhaps? It's so rare you girls can be together. Wish Sybil and Tanner had stayed over."

"Yes, one sitter for all the children. We could split it," Elizabeth said.

"I'll help pay," I offered.

"Oh Mama, thank you so much. I'll come back when Bruce meets Bob at the DeSoto," Elizabeth enthused as she left with her family.

"Yeah, a pajama party!" enthused Nancy.

"Oh, Nancy!" I chided. Nancy, the creative one, was turning an evening together into a party. Even I had to grin. I hoped the girls would end up in the living room for storytelling. I secretly wanted to listen in on their conversation. I was convinced it would *not* be as detailed and honest if I were present, or asked for a recap after the fact.

A short while later, Elizabeth had returned. I slipped my apron on as the girls appeared in the requested pjs and robes. I brought out a tray of hot chocolate. Slowly, I passed it around as I listened to every word.

"Working at the base, wouldn't that be a dream?" Nancy said. "All those men in their flight jackets and uniforms! I'm sure the base will take a few months to complete, and by then I will have finished school."

"No college, Nancy?" I forgot to be a silent listener and bit my tongue.

"I'm not good college material, Mama."

"Mama, I am," said Margaret. "But I'd come back from Loretto Heights to work if I had to. The base is going to be very exciting."

Smiling, I sat back and enjoyed being with my girls. It was a memorable holiday.

As if overnight, the full-fledged base was built, provisioned, and activated. Margaret and Nancy had finished school and were back home. Daphne had bigger dreams to stay in Washington. Unbeknownst to us, she chose Captain Rolland Price to be her husband, I'm sure destroying Bob. News of her engagement came as a shock.

Dear Mama,

Everything is happening so fast these days, but I hope you and Daddy understand. Men are being shipped off with only a one-day notice and I felt I needed to make up my mind and listen to my heart. I am to be married to Rolland Price. We would like to be married right after Easter and I do hope you and Daddy can come. We have to have the wedding here in Washington due to the uncertainties we face day to day. I will sadly understand if this is not possible, but I will write you about every plan and detail as the time draws nearer.

Love,
Daphne

My hand shook as I read the note. *Davis and I haven't even met this chap*, I thought. It made me apprehensive. Another East Coast man! First, Tanner's roots in Pennsylvania and New Jersey and his different ways of living a fast and glamorous life…and now a captain in D.C.! I was concerned for Daphne. The breaking-up of our family to different types of men in different locations was a new concept for me. In my day, people rarely left their hometown, but these were different times. Trains and passenger planes made anything possible. Exciting and sad all at the same time, I welcomed lives of adventure for my girls, but it was hard. Letting go was not easy. I should have expected this outcome for Daphne. She was most like me, I suppose—headstrong, determined, intelligent, and very capable. And so it was, #3 in Washington, D.C.!

I pressed the letter to my heart. Running my hands over it, I rocked in the quietness of my bedroom. I closed my eyes and could see a curly-headed, naughty girl running from Davis's belt…darting in front of me to have the boiling kitchen water scald her…standing at her aunt's gate after she rode the train to Channing all by herself…dancing in Twist Junction's Dancing Darlings…and receiving her college diploma with pride and joy. Yes, I guess she was ready. Her older sisters were making their way and the younger ones, no doubt, would follow close behind. I got up off the bed and followed the radio sounds to Davis, where he was listening to the stock and grain reports.

"I got news from Daphne today," I said as I raised my voice over the radio announcer.

Davis looked up, smiled, and held his fingers to his lips.

Wandering off into the kitchen, I got myself some hot tea, slid into the banquette, and reread the letter. I could hear the silence after the broadcast. My tall, gentle man slid in beside me and pressed his hand into mine. His hazel eyes dimmed and shifted their gaze to the paper in my hand.

"Want to read it to me, Cate? Good or bad news?"

I began to read and his head nodded his approval. His grin got bigger. "Now this sounds like a girl in love! I'm going to have to talk to that scallywag Roll...Roll...Rolland guy. He's got the second liveliest pony from our lot." Davis's body shook gently as he chuckled.

"Aren't you worried about what kind of guy he might be?"

"No. The name says it all...important and most probably capable of making Daphne very happy. She knows what she wants. After all, she turned away a perfectly good guy, Bob. Roll...Roll..." He shook his head. "Rolland could only be better." He leaned back and smiled, holding my hand tighter.

I placed the letter on the table for the girls and Otto to see.

"I'm off to bed, my man. This kind of news wears me out." I started for the bedroom, then turned back to Davis. "Wish I could figure out a way to go to their wedding. The trains are so crowded with servicemen. I guess it would be very hard and expensive to get a ticket, I'm sad to say."

Not long after receiving Daphne's letter, a letter from Mr. Rolland Price arrived.

Dear Mr. and Mrs. Bennett,

Now that Daphne has seen fit to select me as her lifelong companion, my whole heart speaks with magnanimous joy; yet how futile I feel in search for words which will generate in your hearts the same enthusiasm we share.

We prayed that it might be possible for me to have the privilege of meeting you and your family so that you might have an opportunity to learn something about me before we broke the news. This war-torn world, however, seems to permit one little control over circumstances which affect their life. I do so hope that, in spite of the lack of such an opportunity, you will not find it too difficult to share Daphne with me.

About a month ago, I was selected to go abroad on a military mission. It seemed at the time, and does yet in many minds, to be quite an honor. Naturally, now I have lost all desire for this assignment. I have had my departure postponed and am concentrating on having my orders rescinded. We felt that he who plans our destiny will make it possible to have these orders canceled.

Altho' we had hoped it could be sooner, I'm elated over the date Daphne has selected, April 4; its apparent significance in your family makes it most appropriate. The announcement of our engagement I understand will be worked out between you and Daphne.

Daphne could have made a better selection in a materialistic way—she is not marrying into a wealthy family. We will, however, be comfortable and as happy as it is possible for me to make her.

Me to date: I was spoiled, had everything until 1930, when my family lost everything, including all of Father's insurance, in a Florida hurricane. Father died several years later, but my education continued. I am a college graduate from N.C. State. I became the youngest Advertising Manager of a major public utility in the United States before being called to active duty in the War Department in Washington in 1940.

The future for us: I'm due for promotion to captain this week; if we do not remain in the Army after the war, and if no better opportunity is afforded, I can undoubtedly return to the employ of the utility company. My insurance will be arranged in Daphne's interest, and we plan to live initially in an apartment of our own.

Needless to say, I'm extremely anxious that all this meets with your approval and that I will have the good fortune of receiving a note from you real soon.

Sincerely, Rolland Price
Ninth of February, 2517 39th Street N.W.

— 4 4 4 —

Margaret and Nancy returned home from their airbase dates.

"Aren't we lucky! That was great fun tonight. The band at the base was over the top," chatted Margaret as they made their way into the kitchen. "All those over-the-moon men and a good job, too. Yep. Life is good!" She spied Daphne's letter on the table. "Oh! A letter from Daphne. Look at this," she exclaimed, sliding into the banquette and perusing the letter. "I told you so!"

"Told me what?" Nancy asked while pulling a Coke from the Frigidaire. She slid in beside her sister and grabbed the letter. "Oh, oh, oh...marrying Rolland Price! In Washington? How exciting! But what about Bob?"

"I *knew* it! She really didn't love Bob. I could just tell at Thanksgiving. She was nice to him, but she never got lost when they stared into each other's eyes. Nope. There was no spark. She told me she didn't think Bob was *the one*."

"She told you when?"

"We had a special secret," Maggie smirked.

"You didn't tell me!"

"It was a *secret*," Maggie smirked again.

"Nobody tells me anything around here," Nancy pouted. "Well, I'm excited. Now all those boys at the base are ours and she won't be trying to grab the best ones away from us."

"Good thought, Nan."

"I'd better get to bed. I have a big speech to give tomorrow about bonds. I don't understand a thing about them, but my boss says I have to convince the boys to buy them. Something about maturity...or is it maternity?" She sighed. "Good night, Maggie. Sleep tight."

"Yep, I have a big delivery too, and I have to be at the base bright and early. Supplies, supplies, supplies… Can't wait for another dance at the officers' club. Guess that makes up for all the job responsibilities..." Margaret's thoughts drifted off into dreams of dancing and boys.

— 4 4 4 —

The next morning, the girls were in a frenzy as they got ready for work. I sat in the kitchen banquette, sipping my morning coffee, as they scurried around.

"Hurry, Nancy. I need to be early today," Margaret said impatiently.

"Do you like the green or yellow sweater on me? I'm making that speech, you know."

"You'll knock 'em dead no matter what color sweater you wear. Now hurry!" Margaret said, and darted out the door.

"Nancy dear, the yellow one is cheerful. Wear that," I said.

"Thanks, Mama. I'll grab some toast and juice if you don't mind."

"Margaret is already in the car. Hurry along," I prodded.

— 4. 4. 4. —

The trucks had arrived and were unloading pallet after pallet. The colonel stood at the office door, hands on his hips.

Margaret's smile quivered. "Good morning, sir. I'll be ready with the paperwork and payment before the shipment is complete, I promise." She twirled her desk chair around to the safe and cabinets behind her. She pulled out all the orders and placed them in precise order, then clicked through the numbers on the new safe. She was the only one, other than the colonel, entrusted with its combination. As she pulled out the drawer inside, she noticed two stacks of money.

That's odd, she thought.

The night before, she had counted everything and placed the money in *one* stack on the shelf. Her cheeks flushed. She quickly counted the stack, then counted it again. Something was wrong.

Margaret called to her boss, "Sir, something isn't right. Have you opened the safe and paid for any provisions? I'm short two hundred dollars. I just counted the new bills—eighteen hundred dollars, left in two stacks, not the two thousand as the amount was last night, which I left in one stack." She was mortified.

"Are you sure, Miss Bennett?"

"Yes, sir."

"This is a *big* problem, as you can imagine. Does anyone else know the combination?"

"No, not that I know of, sir."

Margaret did recall a lieutenant who had been very nosy, and had hovered near the safe when it was being installed and the combination programmed. He had asked if she needed any help. But she kept this to herself, as she did not want to accuse anyone. Nervously, she got up and walked into the personnel office.

"Where is the manifest showing the men that are being deployed?" she asked quietly.

"Here you go, Miss Bennett," said the clerk. "Is there a problem?"

"Are the men still here?"

"Oh, no ma'am. They were sent out last night at midnight."

Margaret looked over the names on the manifest. His name, that very same lieutenant, was on the roster. Her heart sank. He was gone and she was left holding the bag.

Within minutes the MPs were swarming her desk. The colonel was paying the shipping company. It was chaos. Margaret remained silent, then excused herself and went to fetch Nancy. She dragged her to the ladies' room and told her the horrible story. Margaret burst into tears.

"What can I do?" Nancy said. "I can come with you and vouch for you. I'll convince them it wasn't you. You have an alibi, remember? Last night I was with you, out dancing, and then sleeping. They'll see it wasn't you."

Nancy grabbed Margaret's hand and pulled her back to her office. Margaret blew her nose, not once but two times, right in front of her boss and the two stern MPs.

"Hello, gentlemen. I'm Nancy Bennett, Margaret's sister. I'm here to clear up this matter of missing funds," Nancy said with a clipped, professional air.

"Thank you for coming, but I am afraid we have to question Miss Margaret first. You are welcome to stay if you'd like," the senior MP replied.

"Absolutely, I'll stay. This is outrageous." Nancy plopped down on the colonel's chair.

Margaret could see her fuming. Her little sister was a powerhouse when put to the test. Nancy squirmed on Margaret's behalf, biting her tongue, trying not to be out of order as the colonel and MPs questioned her sister.

"Thank you, Miss Bennett," the senior MP said when the questioning was complete. "We will call you if we have more questions. Do you have anything else to add?"

"Not at the moment," she answered as she rose from the chair and the men left.

Colonel Lovell said, "Margaret, I believe you would never do this, but it's not looking good."

"Sir, I didn't want to say this in front of the police, but…" She described the incident with the lieutenant and told the colonel of his deployment the previous night.

"That's very coincidental, Margaret. I wish we had proof."

"Yes. Unfortunately, I wiped the safe dial before I opened it today and now there are only my fingerprints on it. I always do that, so my fingers don't slip as I dial the combination."

The colonel sighed. "I never did like that man, and I remember that he hung around this office frequently after the new safe arrived. Thought he was just interested in you."

"No, not at all, sir. We never really spoke."

"I think we need to share this info with the MPs. I'll call them back. I don't know what can be done, since he's no longer under the jurisdiction of this base. Clever man, I'd say."

"Sir," Maggie worried, "do you think this will be reported to the paper?"

"Do you *have* to use her name?" Nancy piped up. "Sir, are you aware that I was with my sister *all* night last night?"

"I will do whatever I can to clear your sister," the colonel said. "But I can't promise anything. At least you showed me the entire funds before you went home last night. That I can attest to."

"Thank you, sir," Margaret mumbled.

"Why don't you take the rest of the day off, girls?" the colonel suggested. "This has been traumatic enough." He winked. "You won't leave town now, will you?"

"Oh, not on your life, Colonel," Nancy adamantly answered for them both.

The girls thanked the colonel and left. They jumped into their car and drove directly to Main Street. They could hardly see as tears welled up in their eyes. It was as if they were being sent home from school for misbehaving—only they hadn't misbehaved.

– ⊴ ⊴ ⊴ –

The paper ran the story about the theft. The people who knew efficient and mild-mannered Margaret laughed at the thought of her stealing anything. Interviews about the situation were endless, but finally, it was determined that Margaret and our family had an excellent reputation and were beyond reproach. It only took a few weeks and the entire incident had blown over, like dust from the Dust Bowl, sweeping away the bad memories.

I shook my head as I hurt for my little Margaret, remembering well the DeSoto incident that I had experienced a few years earlier, and how despondent I had felt. People from outside our town held a threat over us, sometimes bringing their questionable ways into our honest and loyal community. We were opening ourselves to unhealthy possibilities. The good and bad went hand in hand with change and progress. I was grateful that Davis and I were able to give the girls good lessons of core values and sufficient advanced schooling. Because of this, they were able to find good jobs at the base. Their job security made Davis and I feel secure as well.

My biggest worry was Sybil. Strangely, it should have been Daphne, being so far away, planning a wedding and a life so different than the one she had lived in the Texas Panhandle. But Daphne was capable beyond the pale. Sybil, on the other hand, was more sensitive behind her mask of glamour and humor. She had shown hints of sadness when she and Tanner had come for Thanksgiving, and now she wrote of his extended absences. I wouldn't have been surprised if something brought her back to Twist Junction. I knew Tanner, or of Tanner, before they married, from his DeSoto Hotel days, so nothing surprised me. But I knew that these secrets must be kept to myself.

Davis found me in the living room and interrupted my thoughts. "Cate, what are you so deep in thought about? I came up here to report on Otto, and here you are, sitting here looking glum, too." His firm hands grabbed the lounge chair arms and he filled the chair with his muscled body. "I'm worried. Otto just sits staring out the window or sleeping in bed, day after day, no enthusiasm and no conversation to offer. Maybe I should walk him up to the hotel and get him some coffee."

"Maybe he misses the land and the animals...the old times...his old friends. Where is Jeb? Has anyone heard from him? Maybe a visit would do his soul good."

"At Mr. Motley's, I reckon. I think you're right. We'll have noon dinner and I'll drive him on over to Dumas."

— ⊲. ⊲. ⊲. —

Davis descended the basement steps to Otto's room to tell him about his great new idea.

"Hey, Otto," he greeted his friend. "I'm going over to Dumas. Want to come with me and see Jeb? I suppose I'll be ready about noontime. It won't hurt to have a little something in our stomachs for the trip. What do you say?"

"Pretty good idea, Mr. Davis. I'll be ready." He propped himself up on the side of the bed, bent over with a little groan, pulled some holey socks off, and started to unbutton his long johns. "Guess a shower won't hurt neither," he grinned.

The ham steaks, sweet potatoes, collard greens, and biscuits disappeared quickly, and they were off like two little boys on a special adventure.

The pick-up seemed to have extra zip as the forty miles whizzed by. As they arrived in into Dumas, Davis caught sight of Tanner, a suitcase in each hand, standing on the train platform across the street. He slowed down and started to give Tanner a wave, but at the last minute thought better of it.

Otto said, "Isn't that Sybil's Tanner? He sure has a lot of luggage. I reckon he's running away," he laughed.

"Funny you should say that. Cate has been really worried about Sybil and Tanner. I always thought he was just a pretty face. Hope I'm wrong... Otto, I don't meddle in my girls' lives, but do you think we should drive by Sybil's?"

"Boss, this trip is becoming more than we bargained for. We ought to just think on this whole bag of worms we might have discovered."

"You're right," Davis agreed. "Jeb will be surprised to see us, and that's what we should stay focused on—*our* adventure. All this other stuff is Sybil's business, not ours."

About five miles beyond the other side of town, an arched iron gate loomed by the roadside. The "Motley's Cattle Company" sign was forged from the same iron.

"I'll push open the gate," Otto said.

Cattle grazed to their right as Davis headed down the road.

"Good-looking herd, Mr. B," spoke Otto.

Far in the distance, they spied a man unloading hay bales. His pitchfork moved slow but steady. Sure enough, it was Jeb. His kinky white hair peeked out from under his cowboy hat, showing great contrast to his shining, satin-black skin.

Davis stopped the truck. He and Otto waited for several minutes before Jeb saw them and a smile covered his face.

"You boys are looking at me like you're jealous. Get out here and help," he teased.

Davis looked at Otto. Smiling, they both jumped out of the truck. There were extra pitchforks and they immediately began to open the bales, spreading the feed for the cattle. Davis and Otto smiled as they worked in silence, side by side, like in the old days. They could hear a soft hymn coming from Jeb. Davis joined in, then Otto, and soon all of them were singing as they worked. After about an hour, Davis felt his muscles begin to stiffen. He jammed his pitchfork into the ground and walked over to shake the hand of his old partner, Jeb. Jeb looked at Davis with a small tear in his eye and threw his arms around his friend.

"Sure have missed you guys. Funny, there are days I look out, see the cattle, and think I see you on ol' Sadie..."

"She's gone, Jeb. Had to put her down last spring."

Jeb shook his head in sorrow. "And you, Mr. Otto? How you been doing?"

"Just growin' old, I reckon. Moved into town at Catherine's and Davis's. The ranch was gettin' to be too much for me, but I had an over-the-top garden last summer."

"I'm leasing out the land this year," Davis said. "But can't say we're too happy about it. Right, Otto? Miss the dirt." Davis kicked up the ground beneath his boots. "I miss that big sky..." He raised his head and felt the sun on his cheeks. "I miss the animals..." He walked over and patted the head of one of the cows eating nearby. "We don't belong in town every day. Otto here has become a hermit."

Otto laughed.

"Well, you can help in the busy season if you'd like," Jeb offered with a twinkle in his eye.

"Got a coffee shop in these parts?" Davis asked.

"Sure."

"Jump in. Let's get some pie and coffee," Davis said, motioning to the truck.

The afternoon passed with long, long stories, some soft moments, and many laughs. When they dropped off Jeb, he slapped the side of the truck.

"You boys come back any time. I got room in my bunkhouse."

As Davis and Otto drove away, Davis looked in the rearview mirror. Jeb's silhouette was stunning as the sun set behind him—a notable, strong, tall figure with a wide-brimmed hat against the flat land and the vibrant, colorful sky. Davis and Otto were quiet, as if saying a silent "amen" at the end of a prayer.

Davis's truck made a sharp left as he came back through Dumas. At the end of the last street stood a lovely home. A car was in the driveway, and in the driveway stood a girl loading an open trunk. He pulled up and said gently, "May I help?"

Sybil ran to the pick-up, flung open the door, and threw herself at Davis, sobbing.

"Oh, Daddy..."

He hugged her until her tears subsided.

Eventually, Davis and Otto slid out of the cab of the pick-up. Davis walked over to Sybil's car, followed by Otto. They began loading boxes and bags into the car. Little Trae stood by, watching. A small dog paced anxiously around the boy's legs. Sybil put them both in the front seat, smooshed between blankets and pillows stacked on the seat and floor.

"Goin' my way?" Davis asked her.

"Uh-huh," she nodded.

Her Buick followed Davis and Otto up the road.

"Never know what you're going to find on the side of the road these days," Davis said to Otto, his gaze alternating between the road ahead and his rearview mirror.

12

Beyond Rainbows

Sybil, Trae, and their dog set up house down the street from us. The Mercer family were decent people and provided a lovely little house for Sybil and our grandson. Little Trae came over to our house on a regular basis, but the hollow look in that little boy's eyes broke my heart. Sybil had lost her giddy sense of humor and rarely left her house. I often brought her leftovers, as she was too ashamed to join us at our daily suppers. After all, what could she say to her inquisitive sisters? I understood and could only imagine her pain.

Davis took daily walks, stopping by to talk with his grandson and to take him for walks in the park or in town. They were like Mutt and Jeff, strolling with Trae's shaggy dog behind them. When they visited me at my office, I detected a twinkle in Davis's eye when Trae played with the buttons on the office adding machine.

One day, looking down proudly, Davis held my hand and whispered, "John Howard?" and we both laughed, remembering the name we said we'd give to a son if we ever had one.

"I like this outcome better. I couldn't have raised another child," I said.

"It's not over yet, my dear," Davis smirked.

"I'll never get you to Daphne's wedding now that you have a new sidekick," I teased. "It upsets me, Davis. I know we can't go. Just wish she could have come home for the ceremony."

"I would like to meet that Rolland rascal," Davis commented.

The adding machine tape was curling all over the floor and the dog was pouncing on it.

"Oh, Trae!" I said.

"Can't take our eyes off these youngsters for one minute," responded Davis, like a responsible babysitter. "Hey, boy, how would you like supper at the big table today with your cousins and aunts? Let's get goin', little man!" He began to pick up the adding machine paper. "Christmas is coming. See all the lights and pictures of Santa?" Davis pointed to the Main Street stores outside my office window.

"Santa brings presents, right Daddy Davis?" Trae said.

"If a little boy or girl is good," Davis said.

"I wanna be good! What do you say, Daddy Davis?"

"Well, we can work on that for ya," Davis chuckled.

"What do good little boys do?"

"Let me see…"

I could hardly stop myself from laughing as Davis counted off about ten things only good little boys do. "I must ask your mother if there's more, and..." he looked over at me, "your grandmother too."

Good as gold, Trae hardly moved or spoke at supper that evening.

On Sunday, when I returned from Mass and Davis was home from the Baptist service, we had a big pre-Christmas gathering with my aunts to discuss our holiday plans. Afterward, Aunt Isabel and Aunt Mary left for their drive back to Channing, promising the usual turkey and coconut cake for our holiday. I had just sat down to read and listen to classical music on the radio, and Davis had gone downstairs to visit our ailing Otto.

Beep...beep...beep! screeched the radio.

"Alert! Alert!" interrupted the violin concerto being broadcast. "Up-to-the-minute news..."

The girls came running into the living room as the beeping continued. Davis sensed something was wrong. He gently threw Otto's arm over his shoulder and they climbed the basement stairs.

"Mama, Mama, what is happening?" squealed the girls in unison.

"This is your president..." came the words from the radio—words that I knew forecasted bad news. The room became dead silent. The front door flung open and Sybil, carrying Trae, joined our grim group.

"Moments ago, Pearl Harbor was bombed in its waking hours.

Casualties are widespread with sinking ships and hundreds of civilians gunned down in cold blood. We have verified the Japanese to be the attackers. The extent of the damage is unknown." The announcer followed with, "We will interrupt any further broadcasts as news comes in."

The girls began to cry. I gritted my teeth as I slipped my hand into my apron pocket and slid rosary bead after rosary bead through my fingers.

Davis and Otto remained quiet, motionless.

"Well, somebody say something!" Sybil said with exasperation.

"What can we do?" I answered.

People ran into the street. Everyone looked up as if they might see a Japanese plane at any moment. I trembled as thoughts of Daphne in Washington, D.C., swirled in my mind.

"Cate, we're okay here," Davis said. "We have a minor air training base. They're after our ships, our East Asian fleet...the big boys."

"Davis, what about Washington? Is it next? Is Daphne in danger?"

"I suppose anything can happen, but surveillance will probably be at its highest after today."

Neighbors began to come over, all hugging each other, shaking their heads, and offering their thoughts about the state of the nation. Many of them were worried about Daphne's safety.

A military truck from the base circled the streets, its loudspeaker announcing up-to-the-minute reports from Washington and the president. The announcer said *The Free World* would air at our movie theater Wednesday and Thursday, and would run three times each day. Public safety would be one of the main topics. The young driver winked and waved to Margaret and Nancy. Huddled together, they barely noticed, but managed a timid wave in return. Within the next hour, more reports came over our radio. People slowly returned inside their homes.

The next day came with the president's radio address.

"Yesterday, December 7, 1941—a date which will live in infamy—the United States of America was suddenly and deliberately attacked by naval and air forces of the Empire of Japan..."

We listened in shock as President Roosevelt spoke of the numerous attacks Japan had made, and of the loss of American lives. I so wanted to call or hear from Daphne, but the telephone lines remained busy into the night. I could only imagine being by myself in such a place as Washington at her age. Regardless of how many friends you have, being with your family is your only real comfort in times of crisis. Rolland would have to jump in with both feet. He was to be her new family.

Daphne wrote later that Rolland had to walk several miles to be with her that afternoon, as Washington was under strict lockdown. He arrived only to be called up in the next moment. She also wrote that the city's blackout created an eerie sight.

Dear Mama and Daddy,
The nearby Cathedral bells that usually toll hourly remained in a cautious, respectful silence. Security offices opened on Sunday and remained open all through the night. In an effort to accept the anticipated additional workload, I arrived two hours early to my office. People were jammed on the buses with no seats or standing room. Cabs had six or more people...so crowded, you could feel or hear each person breathing. In shock, Mama, we didn't quite know how we felt, we just had to get back behind our desks and begin to help out. Before the attack, my wedding, hair, and dress had been on my mind daily; now, I barely think about what I'm wearing or how I look. Rolland has been so consumed with his job, I haven't heard but a quick "I'm okay" about every other day. I'd like to say don't worry, Mama and Daddy, but I do worry.

Daphne's words made everything more intense. Margaret and Nancy spoke very little about the base's activities, most of which I assumed were high security. Nancy was a slave to her forms and typewriter as she interviewed each airman for contact information and next of kin, should he be lost in combat.

As I walked to work each day, more and more of the houses and businesses displayed American flags in their windows. The third page of the Twist Junction newspaper listed an ever-increasing column of killed or missing-in-action locals.

"Davis," I said one morning, "this paper is getting to be too sad to read. As we've said numerous times, we were very lucky to have only girls. Look at all your friends who have lost sons..."

"The morning coffee group sometimes just sits in silence. We don't know what to say, as each man shares the sadness. Our creative minds and aging bodies don't have so many answers these days. We see more and more hobos jumping off the freight cars outside of town, then walking in to see what food or shelter can be found here. Men line up at the back door of the DeSoto. Mr. Huntington feeds fifty men a day with leftovers, and still they go through the trash and rotten food at Swearingen Grocery. We're just a small version of what the big cities are experiencing. I've heard that some of the Mexican families give out free enchiladas. You can see streetlight poles marked with 'hobo stop' in front of their houses. Times are going to be changing when we get food rationing stamps, restricting how much we're allowed to buy per week."

"Davis, where do you get all these stories? I only hear about how many hours a day we can have lights and gas."

"The men's conversations aren't pretty. We're mighty lucky compared to so many people across this country. We can still survive."

Our conversation continued as we sat in our living room beside the fire.

"Thanks be to God, Davis, but just think what our mothers have had to endure through their lifetimes. How is your mother?"

He sighed. "Polly says she's frail and worries about her lasting through the year. I don't even know if she understands about the war. She barely knows my name when I stop by." Then he chuckled. "But funny, she always asks about you... 'Sweet Catherine' is what she calls you. Think she'd be hard-pressed to name all the girls though. I've never told her Daphne is in Washington. I'd hear her long opinion if I did. She'd shake her head and wag her finger, I'm sure. She's hardly left Twist Junction her whole married life, and doesn't understand why anyone else would leave."

"She's probably wise enough to know that you can experience most things right here...after a while, anyway. Life has been good to her and your family, thanks to all the opportunities Twist Junction has to offer. The advancement of women here still remains behind progress in the big cities. Twist Junction doesn't encourage giving a man's job to a woman, but the war has adjusted their thinking somewhat. I'm just lucky that they hired a woman in the city office. Eleanor Roosevelt has spoken out about women's support of our war and troops. She has established many ideas for how women can help the cause. Women are working in factories and wrapping bandages as part of the war effort. We're all to be commended now." I turned to the girls as they listened to our conversation and flipped through the latest magazines. "Girls, I'm so proud that our family has three of you in war-related jobs. I know you're growing up in a difficult time, but I don't want you to dwell on negativity. Tonight I bought us movie tickets to see the newest musical starring Gene Kelly. He's one of our greatest singers and dancers, next to my favorite, Fred Astaire. Davis, I assume you're going to choir practice, and wouldn't be interested since the movie isn't about cattle and horses."

"You're right about that, Cate. Seeing my girls dance on stage is all I need to see. They're prettier than Gene Kelly, anyway."

"Oh, Daddy," Nancy blushed.

"Do you want to ask Sybil? I'll take care of Trae and take him to my choir practice, and bring him home to bed," Davis offered.

"Yes! I'll run down and ask her," Maggie spoke up. "We only have a few minutes before the next show."

Margaret bolted out the door and returned a few minutes later.

"She's on her way! Let's get our coats."

Sybil came through the door a moment later, followed by Trae.

"Here she is," Davis said. "Hi, Sybil. Hi, Mr. Cuteness."

"We're off, Daddy. Thanks!" Sybil said, and ran over to give Davis a big kiss and a hug.

"Sorry we have to walk, girls," I said.

"Oh, it's okay. We love to walk and I know you have to save your gas," Maggie piped up.

In no time, we were downtown at the theater.

"Can you imagine...our mother asking us to a movie?" teased Nancy.

"I think I've gone to Heaven. All my favorite things, singing and dancing!" Margaret rolled her eyes up at the beaming ticket taker and grinned.

"Come on, kewpie doll." Sybil grabbed her arm as Maggie stood dreaming about what was to come next...music, music, music.

The traumatic newsreel featuring the events of the war faded fast as the Big Band sounds filled the theater with gaiety.

Maggie leaned over to Nancy. "My husband has to be a good dancer. Maybe not a stage dancer, but someone I can glide over the dance floor with, just like Daphne seems to be doing with Rolland."

"Shush." I leaned over. "Save the chitchat till we get home."

Maggie squirmed in her seat and settled back into her dream world. Her head tilted just so as she studied Gene Kelly's every move. She was awestruck. Transfixed. I could see Nancy wrapping her arms around herself and closing her eyes from time to time. Sybil tapped her foot, swaying right and left with the music. The smile on her face made the outing the perfect idea in my mind. The film provided tunes the girls hummed on their walk home.

I walked to work the next day. Having left a few minutes early, I was able to check the post office for letters from Daphne and Charlotte. The Washington postmark leaped out of the box.

Mama and Daddy,

A short note before my big day next Monday. We have had to make several changes to our wedding party. The men are being called up right and left. I'm going to the florist today to see what is still going to be available. Scarcity there too. Cross your fingers that I get my white lilies. Better yet, pull out your rosary beads! I can't bear to have all my plans change. I will miss all of you desperately.

Your daughter,
Daphne

The thought of Daphne being all alone for her wedding day broke my heart. I couldn't mention it to Davis again, as he felt guilty enough. I had a strong inclination that missing a daughter's wedding was not going to happen again. If only I could get on the 5:30 train today or Friday, I could be in Washington by Sunday night. My mind continued to dream about how it was possible. But it was wartime. I could only dream.

Time flew by, as it had a habit of doing. A lovely Easter weekend came and went. We had a joyous Mass at Father Patrick's service. Songs bellowed from Davis's church. After services, we had a more meager than usual Easter dinner, with all the family minus Daphne.

On Monday, my mind wandered constantly as I tried to think about what Daphne might be doing each minute. I carried a lump in my throat all day, fearful that I would break down if anyone mentioned the word "wedding."

Finally, Wednesday's early morning mail delivery brought a long letter from Daphne. I was pleased that she could get one off before her honeymoon trip to Natural Bridge, Virginia.

Rushing home, I read and reread the endearing letter with Davis.

Dearest Daddy and Mother,
I will try to think of everything...and the parts I miss will have to be told in another edition. You can let me know if this description doesn't meet with your approval and I will see what can be done about it. My wedding day...I went to eight o'clock Mass and Communion and then to town to do some last-minute shopping. Everyone thought I was nuts—downtown shopping until it was time for me to begin getting ready—but I couldn't see the sense of wasting the day just because I was to be married. The girls were all home to

help the bride and we had such a gay time getting me dressed. I had them scrubbing my back, giving me facials, fixing my nails, and a hundred and one other things.

My dress…really, it's lovely…white satin, and I was so proud of it. I bought it at the famous Trousseau Salon in Philadelphia. I'm sending pictures of it under separate cover and hope that you can see the details of the dress, such as all of the buttons, the sleeves, the bracelet Rolland gave me, the cross which he gave me, the bow in the front and back of the skirt, my bouquet, and such. It will make into a very pretty formal—but after looking at the pictures, if you think that you would like to save it for the other girls, let me know and I'll send it home for you to keep. The veil is borrowed, but I had the white satin halo made for it, so that is mine.

Vernon Todd drove Rolland's uncle's big black Buick and came for me at a quarter to four. I wasn't the least bit excited, but very happy. Jane looked so pretty in her blue taffeta dress with a matching blue halo and veil just like mine. You can see the details of that in the pictures also. I had asked both Harry and Paul Kilday to give me away, but neither was able to be in Washington, so I asked Lieutenant Nikora to give me away. He is so nice and both he and Mrs. Nikora have been so good to me, trying to help any way they could. Father Phelan read the vows. It was quite an impressive setting and one I was proud of. I really have no idea what the organist played, but I faintly remember hearing the melody "Here Comes the Bride" while I walked down the aisle. It is said that he's the third best organist in the world, so I'm sure that he did his part well.

There were about seventy at the church to witness our wedding—those from the office whom we had invited and Rolland's relatives in Washington. Incidentally, it seems that I have always forgotten to tell you—Rolland is an Episcopalian but has been to Mass with me every Sunday since our engagement.

The reception was at Rolland's apartment. We had the florist decorate everything and it really looked lovely. The caterer fixed the table and all of the refreshments—punch, wedding cake (all white—

you can see the pictures we have of it), little sandwiches, ice cream, little cakes and cookies, mints, nuts, etc. I wish you could have been there in the receiving line. Everything turned out beautifully, and the strangest thing was...I didn't worry about one single thing! I have never been so calm about anything, not even one of our Sunday dinners, and I'm sure you would have enjoyed seeing me in that role for a change. We had only thirty for the reception.

A friend of Rolland's took moving pictures in Technicolor of the wedding. He has been out of town since we've returned, so we are anxious to know how they turned out. He took pictures of me going into the church, going up the aisle, parts of the service, leaving the church, the people coming to the reception, our going away on our honeymoon, and anything else which he had enough light to photograph. I do hope that you will be able to see them too.

My going-away outfit—a suit of light blue, an orchid, white gloves, luggage-tan shoes, bag, and a luggage-tan-and-white hat with a luggage-tan veil. I only have one picture of the outfit now, but really I'm sure that I looked better than that, or Rolland wouldn't have taken me! It will at least give you an idea of what I wore.

I'm enclosing the snapshots Kitty took at the reception and am sending the other pictures in another envelope. Some of these pictures didn't turn out at all well—Rolland just doesn't take a good picture at all. The one that you have really looks like him, but in all of our wedding pictures he doesn't look at all natural. The pictures (in the other envelope) were taken by a photographer. The ones of me alone were taken about an hour before the wedding and those of the group were taken immediately afterward.

Will write you about our gifts, honeymoon, etc., later. I'm enclosing clippings which appeared in the Washington and the Hagerstown papers. They aren't such good write-ups as neither of us had the time to tell the society editor all about everything. Again, let me say—I am not in the least ashamed of Twist Junction, but we listed Amarillo in the paper, as the majority of people around here really haven't heard of Twist Junction and this at least gives them a vague idea of what part of the country I am from.

I am also enclosing a view of our apartment. We're going to live here until May 15th. Rolland's mother and Mr. Irving are moving Wednesday. We should keep this one, as it is really lovely—but it is far too expensive. How do you like the view of ours? Can you imagine spending sixty-five dollars, unfurnished, for an apartment of that size?

I'm so happy about Daddy's new job—it really sounds nice and I'm sure that he will enjoy it. I am to begin my new one in about a week, but I haven't anything to report until then.

My love to you both—really missed you on the 4th. More later but must quit now.

Daphne

After I had absorbed every word, I shared the letter with the girls. They read it again three times each. Breakfast conversation centered on every detail of the ivory satin dress and the men in their dress uniforms. Nancy was so absorbed with the romance of it all that Maggie had to honk the horn to remind her that it was time to leave for work.

"You're going to make me late, dream girl!" Maggie snapped as I rushed Nancy out the door. She jumped into the car, and Maggie gunned it all the way down Route 54 to the base.

— ⊲⊦ ⊲⊦ ⊲⊦ —

"Sorry, Maggie, I couldn't help myself, thinking of Daphne's day. She did a good job of telling us about every detail, don't you think? I couldn't help thinking that I'll be getting married to Harry when he gets home after his next tour. It could happen any day, you know!"

"Well, he'd better get over to the house and ask Daddy for your hand if you all are serious."

"He's giving me a ring very soon. He's just divine, don't you think? Wish I could meet his family. They're all in Massachusetts... I have so many family survival records to do today. Seems a big group is shipping out soon."

"Hope not before the big Valentine's dance this weekend. We're getting a Big Band from Amarillo at the Officers' Club."

"Oh yeah, Harry mentioned that."

"Maybe that cute Roger will take me. He's been hinting all week. All these men and only a few days to date them."

They arrived at the base and pulled up alongside the curb in front of the main building.

"Here we are," Maggie said. "Jump out before I park. Have a good day, Nan!"

— ◁. ◁. ◁. —

The door slammed after Davis as he left for work and I finished my last cup of tea. I moved slowly, still remorseful that I had missed my daughter's wedding. It was a guilt I would live with for the rest of my life. I jumped up so as not to be late for work and felt a little dizzy. I held on to the table to balance myself, and shook my head while inhaling deep breaths. "Wonder what that was," I said out loud to myself. "Well, never mind, it's gone now," I continued with my one-sided conversation.

Looking into my mother's oval mirror brought back memories of my mother on my wedding day. I had looked in that very mirror as she placed my Irish lace veil on my head. My heart was heavy as I left the house and walked slowly down the street.

My little dizzy spell made me think that I should pay more attention to my mother and Mrs. Bennett. *I shall share Daphne's wedding letter with them. They'll enjoy that,* I thought. I hadn't stopped by to see Mrs. Bennett in a long while, and I needed to send a letter off to Mother in Dallas.

— ◁. ◁. ◁. —

The base is a flurry today, thought Nancy.

Men were lined up at her desk as she arrived. "Think I'm having a sale here, boys? What's going on?"

"We're shippin' out, miss, and have to get our paperwork in order," said one of the men.

"Anybody know if Harry Rogers is one of those going?" Nancy asked.

"Oh yes, I think so," answered another soldier.

"When did you say you're going?"

"Not quite sure yet. Maybe tonight or tomorrow."

Nancy gasped as she picked up the papers and held them in her shaking hands. She then asked the questions required on the forms. "Name? Serial number? Date of birth? Home address? Marital status?"

She looked up when she called out Joe Slatter's name. Margaret had dated him on and off over the past month. He didn't know Nancy was Margaret's sister. Nancy went through the questions with him, and when it came to marital status, he said "married" and followed with his wife's name.

Well, well, Nancy said to herself. *That sneaky little bad boy. I can't wait to tell Maggie.*

Anxiously, she kept waiting to see Harry, but thought maybe he was in another line. She thought he would certainly try to find her to say good-bye.

At the end of the day, Nancy was exhausted as she leaned against Maggie's car. The setting sun made her close her eyes for a minute. A pair of warm hands slipped around her waist.

"There you are!" Harry said. "I was terrified I had missed you. We've been in classes, lines, and packing all day. I didn't get to take you out to a fancy place when I gave you this, and for that I am sorry, Nancy." He knelt down and said, "Will you marry me when I get back?" He slid a small diamond solitaire ring on the finger of her shaking hand.

Sobbing, Nancy nodded. "Yes! Oh, Harry!"

He kissed her so hard she felt plastered against the side of the car.

"What am I interrupting?" Maggie said with a smile.

Nancy's hand flew in Maggie's direction. "Look!"

"Oh, Nancy!"

"You didn't even get to meet my parents!" Nancy said to Harry.

"When I get back, doll!"

"Sergeant!" came a strict call from the barracks. With that, off Harry ran, throwing kisses across the parking lot.

"Write, Harry!" Nancy called after him. Trembling, she continued to lean against the car, trying her best to get her breath back. "I'm not sure what just happened—it was so fast! That's *not* the way I pictured it would play out. *Not* in a parking lot next to your car!"

"Life is full of surprises, huh Nan? You're going to give Mama and Daddy a heart attack."

— ⚐ ⚐ ⚐ —

Nancy came running into the kitchen with her hand extended like a flat plate.

"Oh, Heavenly Father!" I shrieked.

"Well, I wasn't sure who would have you," Davis joked. "Cate, I feel like someone opened the pasture gate and all the fillies are running away!" Davis laughed and laughed.

"Oh, Daddy. He was very, very sorry not to ask your permission and meet you and Mama, but since it's wartime, things are happening so fast. He just got his orders last night and that's only a twenty-four-hour notice!"

"Do you know anything about him, dear?" I quizzed.

"Oh, yes. He comes from a big family just like ours. They're Catholic and live in a small New England town. He promised to take me there when he gets back. And Mama, I promise my wedding will be right here in Twist Junction. After all, that's where we met and where my family is."

"Good, Nancy, because I still can't get over missing Daphne's wedding."

"Can I be in it?" Maggie interrupted.

"Of course, silly. You're really the only one who knows him. I don't want to make many plans. It might be bad luck."

"Good idea," I said. "You really don't know when or where he will return, for that matter."

"Life is too, too uncertain," Nancy answered with a muffled voice.

Pulling off her cardigan, she headed into the girls' room. Shortly, she had piled up pillows and had started to write in her journal...the one she used only for special occasions.

All of a sudden, almost holding her breath, she called out, "Maggie! I forgot to tell you something I found out today. You know that guy Joe that flirts with you and always wants you to go dancing? Well...he's married and has a baby."

Maggie's head appeared in the doorway. "What?"

"Yep. He had to tell me when he was filling out his paperwork today."

"Well, that scoundrel! I should give him a piece of my mind... No, better yet, next time he asks me out I'll just respond with, 'What would your wife think?' Some men! They think they can get away with anything. When the cat's away, the mice will play...that saying really is true!"

— ⊲ ⊲ ⊲ —

Just before dawn, we heard a loud thump. Davis and I were still in bed and looked at each other.

"What was that?" Maggie met us in the hall.

"Everyone okay?" I asked.

"Yes, we think so," said Maggie.

"Oh...Otto!" Davis said, snapping his fingers. "Let me check on Otto."

He ran down the basement steps as fast as his limp would let him.

"Cate, Cate, come quick!" he called from the basement. "I think Otto hit his head on the bedside table. He's breathing, but his head is bleeding. I need some help. I don't think you or the girls can lift him. The stairs are too hard. Someone call my brother Owen! And hurry!"

Maggie scrambled for the phone, and within moments of the phone call, Uncle Owen arrived.

"Uncle Owen's here, Daddy!" Nancy shouted as she opened the back door and directed her uncle to the stairs.

"Easy does it, Davis," said Owen. "I have my neighbor on the way too. Let's try to get him into my car. Your pick-up cab is too high."

"He doesn't like fancy. Would rather be in the pick-up or on a horse," Davis responded.

I brought them some towels.

"Thanks," Davis said. "I think the bleeding is slowing." He looked at his old friend as he dabbed the blood from his forehead. "Can you hear me, Otto? You're going to be okay."

"Uh-huh..." came the faint reply, and with those two words, Otto's eyes rolled back in his head.

"Think he's in shock," Owen said. "Let's get a move on."

The neighbor showed up and they managed to get Otto into the car.

I called the hospital and told them to expect them. The girls and I watched through the living room window as the car sped off.

"Will he die?" Charlotte whispered. She wasn't used to so much drama after her years living in Dallas with Mother Connelly in her quiet household.

"No, dear," I answered. "It was just a little fall out of bed."

Little did I know that complications had set in. His heartbeat was irregular and the head injury bled extensively. Otto was too weak, too tired, and too ready to go. Davis held his hand and sobbed and sobbed until it was over.

The hospital called me with the sad news.

"Oh, no! God in Heaven," I exclaimed. I slumped on the nearby kitchen table.

The girls, hearing my reaction, ran in.

"It's not good news. Otto just died. Hurry, let's get dressed and go down to be with your father," I said, trying to gather my thoughts.

"Mama, I can't bear to go," Charlotte said. She began to cry. "He was my best friend, my very best friend when I was growing up. I can't see him like this."

I came over to her, held her chin, and looked into her eyes. "I'm sorry this is so hard on you. I guess I didn't realize how special he was to you. You pray for him here in your own way. We'll be home soon."

Charlotte turned away. I watched her shoulders move up and down with her sobs. It broke my heart too.

Margaret drove us to the hospital and let me out to run to the emergency room before she parked. She and Nancy raced into the hospital to join me. The morning was a blur of questions by police and doctors, asking about Otto's next of kin, his full name, and his date and place of birth. Davis couldn't do anything but hold Otto's cold, stiffening hand. Owen had called Jeb, the only other person who knew Otto. I answered the questions as best I could, but no one really knew much about him.

The girls stood by their father with their hands resting on his broad shoulders. It was like a boxcar of sorrow. The girls were lined up next to each other, swaying slightly to and fro. Otto had been a part of our family for so long. He was always by Davis's side, through thick and thin, and had shared all of our holidays and weddings. The more recollecting I did, the sadder it all became. California...the ranch...we never could have survived without Otto. I slid into a corner and pulled out my hankie. I let the tears flow.

An hour passed. The emergency room curtain slid open with a powerful *swish*. There stood Jeb, his head lowered. I motioned to the girls that it was time for us to leave.

— 4. 4. 4. —

Jeb came over to Davis and Otto. Immediately, he lowered himself on one leg to kneel next to Otto and, in a very soft voice, he started to sing an old cowboy song. Davis joined in, and they cried together over the loss of their friend.

Jeb's arm went around Davis's shoulders as he led Davis out to his pick-up. They drove out to the ranch in silence and ended up sitting under the cottonwood tree, staring at the land for the rest of the day. As the sun began to set, Jeb got out a shovel and began digging. Finally, he said, "I think Otto would like this spot under the old cottonwood."

"Yep, think so..." Davis said. "He used to push Charlotte on the swing most afternoons. You know, he built the swing for our girls when Elizabeth was born. First thing he did besides making the fence rails closer together...yep..."

"Don't think I'm going to finish this grave tonight. Mind if I stay in the bunkhouse?"

"Golly, Jeb. That place is almost falling down. Come home with me," Davis offered.

"I've stayed in worse, Davis. This was Otto's home. Don't forget… they're not too friendly to me back in town."

"You're right about those townies. How soon I forget. Jeb, I'd like to stay too. What do you say?"

"That's a great way for us to honor our old friend. I'll see if there are any cans of grub for us."

As darkness settled in, Jeb and Davis found some kerosene lanterns in the house and lit them.

A pick-up came through the gate. Owen jumped out. "Catherine thought you boys would be here. See you've been busy," he said as he glanced over at the beginnings of the grave. He continued around to the other side of the truck. When he opened the door, Davis and Jeb could smell warm biscuits, fried chicken, and green beans. "Beulah thought you might need this. She said this was a cowboy favorite too…coffee in a thermos and chocolate cake."

"I'd give Beulah a squeeze if she were here," Davis said, slightly shaking from all the emotion.

"You take it easy, little brother. This has been a rough day. We'll catch up tomorrow. Hey, I think I have some nice pine for a casket. I'll get on it right away." With a wave, Owen left.

"Let's get some grub and sleep. I'll shake off the mattresses and dust off the plates and spoons," Davis said.

— 4. 4. 4. —

Bruce's family's funeral home had Otto looking swell. They waited for the casket Owen was making to be completed, then a few rogue cowboys who knew Otto helped take the casket out to the gravesite. We all gathered there at sunrise a couple of days later. I was so proud of our family and the community. Otto would have been surprised to see all those who loved him. Someone had cleaned out the old ranch house and we served food brought by the womenfolk. Elizabeth and Bruce picked wildflowers for the top of the casket. A groomed horse and an empty saddle, shined to the nines, stood by the gravesite.

Davis and I approached Otto's final resting place, followed by the girls. Charlotte stayed in the car. I understood. Jeb and the other cowboys fell into line behind us, followed by Mr. Huntington and the other men from Davis's group, who honored this fine man. Father Patrick spoke personally, without the Catholic traditions. Davis and his friends from the Baptist church sang. The early morning breeze picked up enough to make the old rope swing sway. I looked at it and smiled.

After the service, I looked out the window of the house and saw Charlotte sneak to the grave and pat the horse. She stood for several minutes weeping. Slowly, I came out with a plate of food. I stood at a distance, waiting for the perfect moment to approach her. She looked at the swing rope, the bunkhouse, the barn and the house. She saw me by the old garden and clothesline. She approached me slowly and mouthed, "I'm sorry."

"Don't worry, dear," I responded softly. "Here's some food. I truly understand."

— ⊣ ⊣ ⊣ —

Charlotte went into the bunkhouse. To her surprise, she found Jeb and a few of the cowboys inside.

"Oh...oh, I'm sorry. I thought nobody was here." She quickly wiped her tearful face while juggling her plate.

Jeb spoke up immediately. "You must be Charlotte! Otto would speak about you when we were out around the campfires. He said you liked to swing, ride Punky, and watch him while he worked. Right?"

"Yes, he was a special friend to me," she sniffed. "Can I get you all some food?"

"Your mother is bringing us some. Thanks."

"I'll help her. Be right back."

After the food was delivered, Charlotte wandered into the barn...a haven, a quiet place, except for her "un-friends," the mice. She had so many memories of playing in straw-bale castles.

This was Daddy's and Otto's world. Horse stalls, saddles, feed… everything to run the ranch. She placed her hand on the branding iron, surprised by how heavy it was, and smiled.

"Charlotte, Charlotte..." Nancy and Maggie called out. "Time to go..."

"Coming," she answered. "Good-bye, barn memories…good-bye, Otto…" she said and turned to leave.

— 4 4 4 —

Ours was a somber house for the next few months. It saddened me to see the emptiness in Davis's eyes. Otto was like a brother to him. In fact, Davis was closer to Otto than he was with most of his real brothers. I did some deep contemplating, to try to think of a way to cheer him up. Our choices were slim, what with very little travel being allowed during the war. The crops and cattle were both risky business at this time. We talked of starting a hardware store, which seemed to be a promising idea. Davis could be kept busy seeing the public daily. I hoped that being consumed enough in another type of business might help put past memories in the back of his mind. It was definitely something I thought we should pursue, and I brought it up often.

"Davis, dear, I've been worried about you. What would you say about the idea of starting the hardware store, like we talked about?"

"I don't know much about business, but I could be helpful, showing and selling tools and farming supplies. Cate, I'm going to continue to lease the land. Bringing in the income and keeping the land fertile will help us in the long run. I'm sure of that."

"I'll look into the available downtown buildings during my lunch break. It would be nice to have you nearby." I winked at him.

With a lot of hard work, a few months later the business opened with support from the community. I could detect a certain cheerfulness in my old Davis; a cheerfulness I hadn't seen in a long time. His hugs and kisses on my forehead returned with more frequency. I saw him walk his customers to the door and give them a friendly wave good-bye. When the doors were open and the breeze was just right, from my office I could hear his deep voice bellow, "Thanks for coming," or "Don't worry, you can pay me later."

Life seemed to return to a good place. My girls thrived. Elizabeth and Bruce were happily growing their floral business and buying their first home. Sybil was dating, raising her son, and painting. Daphne and Rolland were settled for the moment in Washington, D.C., and were expecting their first baby. Margaret and Nancy, while finding their jobs at the base less exciting, had steady incomes. Charlotte was back in Twist Junction, in school, studying and enjoying her friends. Most folks struggled and experienced rough times, but not so much for us.

It was clear to me that *some* people would *always* have to work hard, with little opportunity to make a comfortable life. I used to smile at the trash man's son, Jason. He was a sharp youngster, always offering to help me if I needed something. He would come by with his dad before or after school. I'd ask what he was studying, and he would grin and explain with excitement his favorite class and his interest in things. I became enamored with him.

"Morning, Mrs. Bennett," he said to me one day, poking his head into my office. "Got anything for me to do for you today? I'm not busy after school."

"What about your homework, Jason?"

"Oh, I wouldn't forget that. My grades are almost all B's and one A. I'm surprising my mom and dad. Thanks to your encouragement, I enjoyed that last library book you suggested. What are your girls up to? What books did they like?"

I ignored his question for the moment. "What are you going to do after you finish high school? The war will hopefully be over by then. You've got only one more year."

"I'll still help my daddy and I'll look for a job, I suppose. Don't worry, I'll continue going to the library and reading, just like you've told me."

"Did you ever think of going to college?" I asked.

"Oh, yes ma'am." His blue eyes lit up. "My folks have agreed it would be good, but they don't see any way they can afford to send me." His head dropped. "They have more kids besides me and I help them a lot," he almost whispered.

"Couldn't you help more if you had a fine education?"

"Oh yes, but I'd have to pay for it."

"Well, what if someone loaned you the money? Like me?"

"What an idea!" He seemed excited by the notion. "I'll have to think about it. I'm a hard worker and I could pay it back. Wow, Mrs. Bennett, I'll give that some thought. Have a good day!"

"Oh, Jason," I called after him. "Stop by the new hardware store. Maybe Mr. Bennett has some work for you today."

"Thanks, Mrs. Bennett. You always have so many ideas!"

He ran to catch up with the trash truck down the street.

After Jason bounded out of my office, Elizabeth poked her head through the door.

"Morning, Mother," she greeted me.

Surprised, I said, "What brings you here, Elizabeth?"

"It was coffee break time and I thought I'd come down to chat a minute."

"Sit here, by my desk. I have an extra chair here somewhere," I said. "What can I do for you?"

"Well…one of Grandmother Bennett's friends came by the shop today. She wanted to buy one flower. I asked what she was going to do with just one flower. She said she had a friend who was feeling badly… then said it was Grandmother Bennett. Guess she didn't remember I was her granddaughter. I know she didn't have any money to speak of, so I told her to pick something and I'd give her a customer appreciation discount."

"Oh Elizabeth, you're so generous."

"It gave me joy to see that little old lady so happy. I wrapped it in a tissue with a bow. I charged her a nickel. Do you think that was okay?"

"Of course it was. I'll be right over for one of those customer appreciation discounts!" I smiled and patted her hand.

"Well, while I'm here...do you know if Grandmother Bennett is sick or anything? Has Daddy said anything? I'd go over with the children, but I wasn't sure if that would be too much for her."

"You know, dear, she keeps to herself and never complains. Polly said she's getting weak because of her age and hasn't been feeling well. But other than that, I can't really say."

"Oh, this family is so private sometimes, it's maddening! I never know anything!" Elizabeth started to get up.

"Now, don't be upset."

"But she's my grandmother..." Elizabeth blurted.

"I'll have Daddy check on her and let you know tomorrow if she's up for visitors. How's that?"

"Thanks, Mama." Elizabeth leaned over and gave me a kiss on my cheek.

I looked out and watched my neatly dressed, elegant daughter move down the sidewalk with a clip in her gait. I was proud.

A lovely note came from Daphne.

> *Dear Mother and Daddy,*
>
> *After reading your most recent letter, I'm thrilled you are excited about my pregnancy. I thought this news would be ho-hum after three grandchildren already. I am also a bit nervous and might have to tap into all your experience, Mama, even though times have changed drastically.*

And there was more news from Washington.

> *Rolland has been promoted to major. He has two new location options: Canada and Chicago. We have chosen Chicago so I can be nearer to family. Seems our little one will be from Chicago, since we're moving next month and the baby is due in October.*
>
> *I never would have dreamed I could live in two exciting cities. While this post will be temporary, I'm excited about the experience.*
>
> *Maybe you can come visit me. I know I will be able to come home and visit you sooner than I thought. It would be possible from*

Chicago.
Missing you tremendously,
Daphne

"Davis, look at this!" I waved my letter. "Daphne is moving to Chicago!"

"Daggum! It's about time she's closer to us again."

As we climbed into bed that night, Davis said, "Saw my mother today. Elizabeth was good to report a rumor. She isn't good, Cate. She's getting worse. I don't think she or Polly wanted to worry us with our busy lives, so they didn't tell me how bad it really was. Polly has her hands full. Can we drop some food to them? Maybe I should start visiting from time to time, too. I don't know if I'm strong enough to lose my best friend and now maybe my mother."

I took his hand and raised it to my trembling lips. It hurt me to see my brave, strong man become so fragile with sorrow. I felt the weight of his burden in my heart.

Mrs. Bennett died. My father-in-law, her husband, was already gone. Three of her fourteen children were also gone. Her death drained Davis. He closed his store for her funeral. Elizabeth put up a wreath along with Mrs. Bennett's picture at the store's entrance, in honor of Davis's mother. Davis needed to do something extra to honor his mother, so he said he wanted to sing at the funeral. The rest of his siblings, our family and their families, and friends came by the hundreds, filling the church. Mrs. Bennett commanded great respect in life, as well as in death. As a tribute, a parade of people and cars held up the town's roads for twenty minutes, even though it was only a few blocks to her gravesite on the other side of town.

— ♩ ♩ ♩ —

Davis's heart was not in his business after his mother's passing. Mr. Huntington could detect a difference in Davis's demeanor. As the men analyzed the town's direction and economy, he said to Davis, "How's your business, young man?"

He always referred to Davis as "young man," even though Davis had aged and his hair was graying.

"Up and down, I guess. People come, some pay, others say they'll pay later. Later never becomes now. I want to give everyone a chance...I didn't expect them to take advantage of me as they have. Don't seem to be making money."

"Let me take a look at your books for you," Mr. Huntington responded.

"Oh no, that's not necessary, sir," Davis protested.

"Yes, it is. I insist."

Davis conceded, and Mr. Huntington said, "You can't extend any more credit. You have to take a paycheck and pay your bills or you're going to lose everything. And you're *very close*, Davis, to losing everything! You have to be less of a nice guy."

Davis responded, "It's not my temperament, Mr. Huntington. I don't like being hard on people. We all have our hard times."

"People know that you're too kind for your own good," Mr. Huntington said. "You need to decide whether this venture is a good one for you, or change your credit policies. I don't want to see you or the business fail."

"Thanks, as usual, Mr. Huntington."

—4. 4. 4.—

As always, I kept track of what my girls were up to. One afternoon, as Davis and I sat in the living room and I had his attention, I said, "I don't think Charlotte is being challenged enough at our Twist Junction high school. She often says she's far beyond the other students. Daphne and I have been passing an idea back and forth. She and Rolland will have two bedrooms in Chicago. Daphne would be glad to have a babysitter in exchange for Charlotte living with them for her senior year. I've been reading about a lovely girls' school near Daphne's apartment. I think I can swing one year's tuition, especially if Charlotte could get an academic scholarship. Charlotte was very excited about the possibility.

Rolland and Daphne are being very generous. Do you think a change from this small town would help Charlotte and her reclusive tendencies? Remember how sending Margaret and Nancy to school did a world of good for them? Nancy just blossomed."

"Cate, seems like you're dead set that this is a perfect solution. Right?"

"Well…" I answered.

"We're sending off our last one. Doesn't that make you concerned or nervous...or sad?"

"I suppose. I hadn't really thought about how it would affect me or you. I'm sorry, Davis."

"It's all right, Cate. I just want you to be sure that this is what you want."

I put my hands in my lap and gave a big sigh. "I want them all to be the best they can be—successful, beautiful, popular, and perfect. I want to give them every opportunity…opportunities I never had. Do you understand that, dear?"

Davis left the cocoon of his large lounge chair and sat next to me on the sofa, placing his hands on mine. "You're ruthless, my wonderful wife. You want everyone to live your dreams, and you won't give up until they have it all."

I turned away from him. My sentimental Irish tears were coming faster than I could have imagined. "Is that what I'm doing?"

"Yes, Cate, you're trying your very best to take care of each and every one of us, one by one."

At the end of the summer, Charlotte was boarding the Chicago and Rock Island train. Her tan leather bag banged its way up the stairs to the sleeping car. I detected tears running down her face on either side of her broad smile, and the train lurched as she feverishly waved good-bye. I blew kisses and Davis held me up by my shaking elbow.

"Let's drive by the cemetery," Davis said quietly as we got into the car and closed the doors.

"By all means, whatever you want."

I waited in the car as my husband knelt by his mother's grave. My heart seemed to be beating faster than usual. I closed my eyes and tried to calm myself.

13
Roller Coaster Rides

In the years that followed Mrs. Bennett's death, I thought I was making sense of my life. We would ultimately have five grandchildren, four weddings, and five graduations during the decade of the '40s. But the core of my spiritual support system was gone. My mother had died, too, leaving a hole in my heart.

Radio stories from our strong national leader faded one spring afternoon. Now, the stories were not *from* him, but *about* him. FDR had died suddenly at his country home in Georgia. The radio's crackle and *beep, beep, beep* caused the hair to rise on my neck. We were still at war in 1945, and this represented a severe national crisis. President Roosevelt's strength, and how he inspired us and held our country together, would be impossible to follow.

Movie newsreels showed people and trucks lining the road from Georgia to Washington, D.C., in a gesture of deep respect.

Daphne wrote:

> *Dear Mama and Daddy,*
>
> *We certainly are grateful to be back in Washington. Rolland and I joined what seemed to be the whole rest of the city to watch the funeral procession of our beloved president, FDR. The silence, or very low conversations, permeated the feeling of the crowd. I will never forget the sight of Eleanor Roosevelt and the magnificent caisson as it crept past us. We could only hear the clop, clop, clop of the horses' hooves. Sniffling was the only other sound that pierced the moment. Mama, I don't think I will ever, ever forget this experience. I suppose these times are the glue that makes us want to be here in our capital.*
>
> *With much sadness,*
> *Daphne*

Davis was quieter than usual. Reading Daphne's note made the news of the last few days a reality—a reality we didn't want to believe.

My only solace had been seeing my newest granddaughter a few weeks earlier, before she went back to the East Coast with Daphne and Rolland. My mother had seen her too, a short time before she died. My healing came from these thoughts and feelings...a granddaughter replacing an elder. The evolution of change sobered me. I was the matriarch now, and the responsibility of guiding my family rested in my lap. Gratefully, I was only in charge of my six girls and a cowboy, and not the entire country, as had been thrust upon our new leader, President Truman.

Nancy received letters from her fiancé, Harry, through all those rough times. And then...a knock at our door. A uniformed officer held out the dreaded yellow envelope. I left the room so that Nancy could have a private moment. Harry had been killed in action.

I felt like my consolation for this weeping child had little effect, but Davis's calm and warmth seemed to take away some of the sting. I felt as if I were holding a Mixmaster, and my children were being tossed into different parts of the country, emotion to emotion. My only solace was Elizabeth, who was happily married here in Twist Junction. Charlotte had gone to Loretto Heights, in Denver, for college after Daphne and Rolland left Chicago for reassignment to Washington. Nancy decided she wanted to work in Washington too, and would live with Daphne and Rolland there. Sybil was back and forth with little Trae to see Tanner's family in New Jersey, and now Margaret had decided Albuquerque would be an intriguing place to work. Not too close and not too far from home. Promises from dear friends to watch out for Margaret's best interests calmed my reaction to her plan.

Thinking that my life was becoming too complicated, I decided to go for a rest. I retreated to the bedroom, slipping my hand into my apron pocket.

"Dear God, this is in Your hands. Father, protect my girls," I said as my fingers flew around the rosary beads.

In Albuquerque, indeed, our friends the Elliotts arranged an apartment for Margaret under their watchful eye. I heard that Margaret thrived, working again for the government on a military base.

> *Dear Mama,*
> *We're busy morning till nightfall. My own apartment is the best. I do a lot of the cleaning here, but I love it. I'm seeing a wonderful young man, a friend of the Elliotts. We go out dancing or just take walks most evenings. Things aren't serious, but I sure think he's swell.*
> *Love,*
> *Margaret*

Letters from my girls flew across the country. Nancy's stories won the prize for most entertaining—everything from her experiences as a notary in a downtown government office to sharing a room with Daphne's darling daughter, Abby, which topped the cake.

> *Dear Mama and Daddy,*
> *Who would have ever thought I would become a notary? Such a responsible job. I much prefer exciting office work to my year at college, with schoolteachers blabbing about some boring subject. I know you tried, but school was not for me.*
> *As Daphne has told you, everyone here in Washington is in a hurry. Starry-eyed couples get married day and night. Sometimes, I wonder if some of this coupling is based on love or the moment. I wonder what it would feel like to be one of them...I wonder if the men will return. I get teary when I can tell that they really love each other. It makes me think of Harry, my lost love, and it hurts my heart.*
> *Daphne and Rolland are the <u>most</u> romantic couple. I <u>love</u> living in their new house. Did she tell you about the large trees lining the street, and her backyard of gardens, and her patio for drinks and cookouts? But Mama, I had a real setback with their little girl, Abby. She has a great imagination and is very precocious, to the point that, while we were relaxing one night after dinner, I had put her to bed...and I thought things were a little too quiet. Opening the door to our room just a crack, I discovered a circus scene. My lipstick was*

smeared on her face like a clown, and wiggly circles were drawn around the roses on the wallpaper. Dusting powder was everywhere, even on my best new black suit. It looked like a Dalmatian dog! I admit that I shrieked. Daphne ran upstairs, and do you know what that little brat said? "You don't have to get so mad about it, honey!"

Oh, Mama, I was madder than a wet hen. Don't know that I have been so mad since I caught your grandsons Trae and Ben striking matches in the back alley behind your house. I never told you, but those boys will never forget it! I was beet red that day when I shouted at them...making them get right in the house, no dinner and straight to bed! They were dirty and very hungry. The boys were so upset. I did hear Ben quietly say, "Do you like Nancy?" And Trae said, "Not even the Devil would like her!" I'm getting quite the "mean aunt" reputation.

Daddy, I have thought...could I ever have children? Like you, I'd probably run into the next room and laugh at my naughty kids. How do I get into these situations? I'm still shaking powder out of the bed and chair and I have to go to work early...so good night.

Love,
Nancy

Davis loved the "bad kids" letter, and before I knew it, another Nancy incident had occurred, this time requiring her father's expertise.

Nancy was working late one night. She picked up a ringing phone as she was running out the door to catch the bus. A man's voice asked for John Peters Jones.

"I'm sorry, he does not work in this department," Nancy said politely.

The voice *insisted* that she check again, and the same answer came from Nancy in reply.

This time the voice said, "This is Lyndon B. Johnson from Austin, Texas, and I want to speak to John Peters Jones."

Nancy promptly replied, "*Well*, this is Nancy Bennett from Twist Junction, Texas, and Mr. Jones does *not* work here."

With that, Senator Johnson slammed down the phone. Nancy went home in tears, worried that she would lose her job the next day. Upset, she called her daddy, recalling every detail.

Davis said, "Lyndon Johnson, huh? He's the biggest crook in town. Wonder what he wanted? Don't you worry…"

The next day, with a shaky voice, Nancy repeated the details of the telephone incident to the stern general in charge. Nancy said she could hardly breathe as she waited for his response.

"Oh, don't pay any attention to that blowhard," he said. "Just go back to work."

Stunned, Nancy resumed her seat behind her desk. She told us she didn't think she'd ever understand that place or those people.

Propriety was always foremost on my mind, and Davis found the girls to be pure entertainment. The balance of the two of us kept the family on track through my working years. On occasion, I'd look into my mirror. My long, raven hair had become a salt-and-pepper bob. My lake-blue eyes were a cloudy version of grayish blue. I found myself watching my life fly by and yearned to travel to Europe or some other exotic destination.

"Davis, would you go to Europe with me?" I asked one evening as I stared at my aging, 50-year-old reflection in the mirror.

Teasing, Davis responded, "Tomorrow, or did you have next year in mind? We still have a war going on, Cate. To be honest, I don't have to travel. Maybe we could travel around our own country when the time is right. That would be good enough for me."

"I see our bodies moving more slowly and our hair graying," I said. "We need to go while we can. I'm about ready to retire. Maybe we can build a cabin in the mountains or something…Cimarron is beautiful. We could fish and watch the aspens turn gold. Would you like that?"

"Cate, wish I had a dime for all your dreams. Your mind never stops."

I turned from my midlife image in the mirror and walked over to hug my ever-adoring cowboy. Aching to do something or go somewhere, I said, "Want to drive out to the ranch and see how our tenant farmers are doing?"

Davis jumped to his feet. "Now you're talking. I'll get my cowboy hat."

He held my hand as we drove down the highway. Cattle looked up at him as we slowly passed the pastures. Their faces seemed to say, "Who are you?" as they watched us drive by.

When we arrived at the ranch, Davis got out and leaned on one of the fence posts.

"Those were good days," he said, turning to me in his pick-up.

I could feel that he was missing the animals and the land he loved so. They were his babies. He stood in profile, hat cocked just so. I saw a sadness fall over his rugged face. My eyes were full. Yes, he was at home…content to be right there, leaning on the fence post, the sun setting behind him. He didn't need to travel. He was where he wanted to be.

I was torn. Seeing him so fulfilled was beautiful, but I needed to see what else was out there to make my soul content.

Our moments of quiet reflection, dreaming, and planning constantly took a back seat to the changing lives of the girls. Nancy concluded that she wanted to join Margaret in Albuquerque; Sybil wanted to find a husband, a partner, to share a happier life.

Sybil dropped by one afternoon. "Mama, I am so sorry for the divorce. I am so sorry for any embarrassment I have caused the family. I appreciate you not talking about it. It must have been hard."

"I'm glad for you, dear, that you have a house and money to support yourself. The Mercers are decent and generous people. And little Trae is a dear."

"It isn't easy being beautiful and glamorous," Sybil sighed. "I think I intimidate most men. I want to get out and have fun again. I think I'll join Elizabeth and Bruce at one of their parties sometime. Do you think that's okay?"

"Yes, dear, that would do you good."

"Elizabeth called and is having a Big Band party tonight. She said Trae and Ben can play together and sleep there. My response was a little arrogant. 'Got any good-looking cowboys coming?' I said when she invited me. All she could say to me was, 'Haven't you had enough for a while?' Guess I'm off the blue-eyed, blond type, but I miss someone calling me 'honey girl' or 'sweetie pie.' Do you understand, Mama?"

Thinking, I commented, "Someone said the Boyd boy is in town again."

"He's too young and lives way out Colorado way."

"Yes, but his daddy's ranch, Sand Dune Shadows, is the best and most beautiful land in the southeastern part of the state. Some say it is 500,000 acres...runs beside the sand dunes. Wonder how many head that much land would hold?"

Sybil retorted, "I am so tired of cattle and oil talk. I just want a little fun for a change... If the Mercer in-laws had their way, Trae would have a full-time nanny and we would be living at Spring Lake, and I'd have nothing and nobody. I believe they're genuinely embarrassed by that philandering son of theirs. If Tanner had let me get more involved with the business, none of this would have happened and there would have been no travel without me. We could have had real fun!" She paused. "Mama...why wasn't I enough?"

"Sybil, women are like trophies for him. He did love you, but he loved himself more, sort of like an addiction—an addiction to women. Come on, let Elizabeth see if the Boyd boy will come to the party tonight," I encouraged.

"Okay," she said hesitantly. "Maybe she should have Bruce ask him. If anything happens, I'll tell you all about it!"

And off she went, her spirits lifted and excited about the prospects. I was happy to see a spring in my daughter's step once again.

The next day, Sybil told me the whole story.

"Well, we gathered to full-volume music. The girls wore flirty, flowery dresses and gossiped in the patio corner...most likely about me. I leaned against a tall iron chair and shook my hair, pretending not to care. I wore my coral cross-bodice dress, which has the slightest flounce at the bottom. Sure enough, Mama, he came to the party. Garland Boyd is now a tall, handsome man with chiseled features. He came through the garden gate and his calm presence almost made him seem invisible. He's someone different. If he had a braid in his black hair, he could have been mistaken for an Indian. He's polished, though...almost shy... When Bruce called to welcome him, it changed his demeanor. He's the type that responds with a mild, soft-spoken voice. 'Howdy' was all he said...or had to, for that matter. You know, this is the first time I've seen Garland in years. He stands straight as a fence post and fills his boots proudly. There was no mistaking him. He's a born-and-bred cowboy. I didn't know...but he told me that he had been trying to meet me, even before Tanner. I guess I hadn't paid much attention to him because he was just a younger hometown boy."

To my surprise, she looked up and swooned a bit.

"When he glanced my way, it was as if he was putting himself in second gear. Slowly, Mama, he headed through the others to my spot at the chair. My dimples must have been showing because he responded with a warm smile." Sybil grew silent in thought. "Yes, everything was deliberate and slow. I could tell that this guy wasn't going to kick up his heels in public...he's not a dancer or a party boy, but he does like to pour a hefty drink. His conversation seemed so smooth and effortless. He says he has seen Trae playing on the wall outside your house, and he seemed to know Tanner through business. He seemed to be all business, but I did learn that he loves to get out of Twist Junction and off his ranch near Alamosa. He said the Brown Palace in Denver or the Broadmoor in Colorado Springs are some of his favorite places. Mama, he said they almost have a permanent spot for him at the bar and know him by name. I imagine he has a good eye and a love for beautiful things...must have included me." She giggled. "What do you think, Mama?" Sybil paused and giggled some more. "Don't get tired of me asking for a babysitter as Garland and I become an item. I know Daddy won't much like Garland's drinking, but what's a man to do out there all alone? A half-million acres is indeed 'way out there.'"

A short time later, after my daughter and her new beau had been dating for a while, Sybil told me, "Mama! Garland wants to show me off to his parents. We'll have to travel before the snows start in late fall. Much of the ranch becomes impassible then, with the snow erasing any signs of the road. He says if we were to get stuck, the mud is so thick it would take two men and two horses to pull a pick-up out of the muck."

And with that, Sybil planned her trip to meet his family. As soon as they were home again, my daughter began regaling me with every detail of the week.

"As we rumbled over the cattle guards at the Sand Dune Shadows gate, Garland became very relaxed. Big Garland met us at their rough-hewn front door. It was so beautiful. Inside, Arameta, Garland's mother, sat in her chair. She had a long, gray braid down her back. She was finishing the last stitch of a stunning appliquéd, sequined sweater. I thought she seemed kind of stoic at first. She handed me the sweater, and shocked, I said, 'Oh, Mrs. Boyd, I can't accept this!' She said, 'Oh, yes you can, my dear. This is only the first of many. I am extremely delighted to think that we might have another woman for our bridge and luncheon group, or perhaps a bride for my only son.' Mama, Mrs. Boyd seemed pleased with me. I was on my very best behavior—no joking at the dinner table, if you know what I mean. She quizzed me... Do I cook, ride, play bridge, and could I live out there so far from town? I can tell she's the type to be self-sufficient and is a strong partner for Garland's father. I'm sure she could rope a horse and brand the cattle if she had to. They have a lovely house, but she wasn't about the frills of life. But Mama, have you ever seen her beadwork? It should be in a museum. She looks a bit Indian...is she? You can almost feel the power of the past Indians on that land... Such strong, scenic color paints the sky at sunrise and sunset. It was magical. I'd never seen the sand dunes, either."

"The Boyds are a very fine family whom we have known through the years," I said. "Big Garland has a reputation as a significant rancher and businessman. Some say he has a bull worth over a million dollars. Sybil, you certainly attract the cream of the crop. Do you think Garland could ever make you happy?"

"What is happy, Mama? Sometimes, I really feel I don't know...or maybe I'm scared. I don't want to be left again, or feel so 'inside out' again. We smile at the same time and seem to appreciate nice things. He never refuses me anything, and more often than not offers before I ask. He doesn't have to be the life of the party, like Tanner. One pretty girl seems to satisfy him. Maybe, if I'm lucky, it will be just me."

"Sybil, you're a lot to handle and he's smart enough to know it." I gave a little laugh. "Daddy thinks he'll take good care of you. He can't tie you down or you won't be happy. At least he likes places beyond the fence posts of his land."

"Yes, he even says he likes the sun in California during the winter and doesn't mind leaving the snow at the ranch. Minimally, I could wear beautiful clothes when we travel to the Broadmoor, the Brown, or to Palm Springs."

She was quiet for a moment. I could tell that she was thinking.

"Am I talking myself into this marriage, or the *things* of this marriage? I don't want *only* that," she said thoughtfully.

Happen as it did, in April of 1947, in our home on Main Street, Sybil wore a chocolate, floor-length dress and a wired, large-brimmed hat that was the latest style. Her bridesmaids looked like a lineup of the best models from New York City's Ford Agency. Davis joked that he finally got to give away 'Little Miss Mischievous.' He knew it was for *real* this go around...no eloping. I thought that the country club must have a special account by now called "Bennett Weddings." Eventually, we would have three country club receptions in all.

Chicken salad sandwiches, deviled eggs, cucumber sandwiches, thin slices of Texas beef with horseradish, Randy's Rootin' Tootin' band... Things were looser with the Baptist side of the family by now. Sybil wanted something different, so she had a cowboy and cowgirl topper on the cake, and a rope between the layers. Bruce and Elizabeth created pale-green and white blossoms in all the bouquets. Sybil was thrilled that her flowers had come from California and Mexico. They were hard to gather, but nothing was too good for her or too hard for her.

After the ceremony, Davis leaned over to Garland. "Son, I think you got the wildest filly."

"Yes, sir. Something like that in her makes me love her. They're always the ones that challenge you."

"Don't try to tame her or she'll kick you away," Davis cautioned.

"I understand, sir."

That night as we got ready for bed, Davis said, "Cate, I told Garland he shouldn't try to tame Sybil. I hope he takes me seriously. Just won't work if he doesn't. She's her own woman. *That* we know from experience."

My bed took me into its open arms that night. It relaxed me, and all the tension and excitement of the wedding melted me into the mattress. Davis had spoken his piece about the day and his new son-in-law. Now all was still and quiet, except for his heavy breaths and heaving chest. I continued to experience shortness of breath, but my guarded concerns were mine alone. Racing thoughts kept my sleep away. My best friend, who lay beside me, would have been glad to share in my thoughts, but he was tired beyond any conversation and I didn't want to disturb him.

My anxiety seems to be getting the best of me these days, I thought as I rested my hand over my heart. *But I'm not alarming anyone about this. It's my secret. But what will my purpose be after the weddings and my job? Certainly, Margaret will be on the coattails of Sybil's wedding. A suitor is after Nancy...it will all happen too fast, I'm afraid. Then there's Charlotte, who has promises of European travel after graduation next year. The chicks will have flown the coop before I know it. And me and Davis? My desires for travel have to happen soon. One never knows...too many mysteries around the corner, I always say. Should we get a cabin in the mountains near a stream for fishing? Davis would like that. A trip down South to see his old homestead? He'd like that and I'd like that too. Why do I feel so anxious? Life feels so short to me!*

No sooner had I rolled over in bed and shut my eyes, did I indeed have another wedding to plan.

A week after Sybil and Garland's honeymoon, Margaret and Clark arrived from Albuquerque; a long, four-hour drive. I answered the front door and there stood my Albuquerque daughter.

"Margaret, what are you and Clark doing here?" I said, surprised.

"You're just in time for Sunday supper. Elizabeth and Bruce and the children will be here soon. This will be our last dinner with Sybil and Garland before they permanently move up to the ranch."

Margaret walked through the door. We hugged.

"I'm so glad to have you both," I said.

Davis was getting dressed in the bedroom.

"Davis, come see who just arrived!" I called out to him.

Davis burst through the bedroom door, still in his Sunday suit pants and starched white shirt. He picked up tiny Margaret and gave her a fatherly kiss on the cheek. He immediately went over to Clark and welcomed him with a warm handshake.

"I need to check the oven," I said, and headed into the kitchen.

Davis's excitement was endearing. He loved his little Maggie. "Maggie, we've missed you. How's the job going since you've been back? I know those old Army buzzards have been tough to work for, but Clark, you seem to be making her glow!"

"Well, sir, that's why we're here," Clark spoke up." I'd like your permission to make Margaret my wife."

"Cate!" Davis called into the kitchen. "We're having a celebration this afternoon!"

"Celebration?" Elizabeth caught the word as she opened the front door. The living room became chaotic as it filled with laughing children and shrills of excitement.

"No matter how many weddings or births we have, this house always sings with electricity," I said, smiling broadly as I stood next to Davis.

The girls vanished into the kitchen to do last-minute stirring and to get the biscuits out of the oven. The men retreated outside for a last smoke before eating.

I heard Sybil and Garland as they arrived, and peeked out the window to see Trae running ahead of them on the Main Street sidewalk. At the front porch of our house, he caught the men laughing and blowing their smoke into the wind.

"Daddy Davis, Daddy Davis! I thought you had a fire. There's so much smoke! Can I try to make smoke too?"

Realizing their bad example, the men immediately smudged out their cigarettes in the nearby concrete planter. Clark stood silently, waiting for Davis to answer Trae.

Sybil came up the walkway, arm in arm with Garland, and yelled, "Yoo-hoo!" breaking the awkward moment.

The news about Margaret and Clark was shared, and the silence was broken.

Later that evening, when the household had resumed its calm and quiet, Davis, still troubled by the cigarette incident, shared his concerns with me.

"Cate, I forget how vulnerable these children are. I never thought about how they might want to be like us. Boys are much more impressionable than our girls ever were. Trae snuggled up to me the other day and said 'Daddy Davis, I love you so much I want my name to be Bennett, just like you.'" Davis closed his eyes, shook his head, and said, "I know, I know," as if someone was talking to him. Then he continued, "I've got to watch my ways from here on out."

In the middle of the night, Davis's body jerked. He grabbed my hand and sat up. Startled, I too sat up and stared at my handsome cowboy in the darkness.

"The Mexican came," Davis whispered. "He explained how I was a *very* important figure in my grandsons' lives. This is to become my new role. Cate, it took my breath away..." Tears of truth rolled down his face.

"I have a feeling this will become a big job for you, Davis," I said. "The boys will be a little more difficult than those calves and the girls, you know."

I could see the moonlight shining on his damp cheeks, but a smile began to form. He squeezed my hand.

We slept so soundly that I was almost late for work the next morning. I jumped out of bed, realizing that my reputation for promptness was about to be compromised.

"Davis Bennett, I'm going to be late, and all because of you and your Mexican angel. Wish you'd keep your messages to yourself till morning," I said. Drinking the fresh coffee Davis had just brewed, I winked as I teased him. Off I ran with a piece of toast in one hand and my pocketbook flying off my arm in the other.

Davis's message weighed on him. He had always considered himself to be the kindest, fairest, most loving of grandfathers. He sang to the grandchildren. He read to them and played with them, especially Ben and Trae. He kicked himself for not seeing the smoking thing as being a bad example, even though everyone smoked and everyone's parents smoked. But he held himself to a higher standard; not consciously, but he wanted to be the perfect grandfather. He wanted to be the one they would confide in and look up to. He had the time and the open heart for them, as their parents were busy with their lives and businesses. Our own grandfathers had passed and had not been part of our lives or our girls' lives, so I wasn't sure that Davis fully understood the impact of this role. So many things were changing. People lived longer and their roles were different. Our world was a world of girls. Our desire for a boy had skipped a generation, and now we had grandsons to raise.

A September wedding was upon us before we knew it. It would be held in our small, home-like Catholic church, which reduced my stress level. Even though Father Patrick was getting to be quite elderly, he agreed to marry Margaret. Clark was a Catholic, and Father Patrick delighted in this solid union. Margaret's dress was on loan from Daphne, and I felt I needed to add something special, just for her. Asking a friend for her silver punch bowl made Margaret feel like this was *her* day alone. Davis was given permission to walk her down the aisle. The rigid Catholic rule of a non-Catholic participating in a sacred sacrament had been overlooked...at least by Father Patrick. I could see

Davis whisper to Margaret before they passed by the simple white pews to the music "Here comes the Bride."

Later, Davis told me he'd said, "I love you, little Maggie" and nibbled on her ear just to make them both do a "love laugh."

Seeing elegant Clark in his double-breasted tuxedo as he whisked my daughter off in his shiny black car made my eyes glisten behind my mother's Irish linen hankie. In the end, laughs erupted as we saw a "just married" sign sprayed on the back window. Clark was so proud, not even he had the desire to wipe it off during their driving honeymoon.

Not long after the wedding, I received a note from Margaret, in which she shared about the honeymoon and arriving in Albuquerque.

> *Dear Mama,*
>
> *People from the Harrington Hotel in Amarillo to Westward Ho in Gallop, New Mexico, cheered and welcomed us like movie stars wherever we went. I felt so important and so married. And Mama, did you know that Nancy had Clark's apartment all cleaned and dinner on the table when we got back to Albuquerque? I thought I would cry. Mama, just watch, we are going to be so happy and have a wonderful life!*
>
> *Thanks to you and Daddy for a perfect wedding.*
>
> *Love,*
>
> *Maggie*

We all had great plans for the future. The war had ended two years earlier, so travel abroad was safe. I was anxious to make Charlotte's plans for travel to Europe a reality.

"Charlotte," I said to her one day. "You have graduated from college. You have worked while going to school and saved your money. I have saved a bit as well, so Daddy and I have agreed that you should take your dream trip to Europe. I have researched a travel group that will leave on the ship *Kotainten* in June. And how about if we come and meet your ship when you return to Hoboken?"

Charlotte looked puzzled. "Hoboken? Is that a place or a game? Oh yes, that's where Frank Sinatra is from." She giggled, realizing what we had offered. She then squealed and ran to throw her arms around us. None of the other girls had ever gone to Europe!

On September 1, 1948, we helped her board the train to experience her lifelong love, travel.

Charlotte wrote home describing a gray Europe, with city after city full of rubble. She saw people picking up the pieces of their lives, as well as their belongings. Shocked, it made her ashamed of any complaints about the inconveniences of war stateside that she and her friends had ever expressed.

> *Dear Mama,*
> *The children's clothes are so worn...stitched and restitched. Men worked humbly, sometimes dragging a war-damaged leg or arm. Yet, I do see some flowers blooming and hear talk of a better future. These will be forever memories. I had studied the history of the great cities of London and Paris, and now they are coming alive for me. I actually saw the Mona Lisa at the Louvre. I cannot wait to bring home all my presents and more stories to you all.*
> *Love,*
> *Charlotte*

I read Charlotte's European letters multiple times, until the paper was wrinkled and the ink smudged. Davis laughed as I devoured every description.

"Cate, we're not going to give you a test. You don't have to study every word!"

"Davis, this is *my* trip, too. I want to be there...except I would have gone to Ireland. I want to see where it all began...with my relatives, that is. Daddy's home, the pubs, the young girl weavers, Mother's school and the church that she loved so dearly...Daddy's university in Dublin... Someday, Davis Bennett, I'll be on a ship and will go...maybe with one of my girls."

"Hope you do, dear Cate. And I'll be waiting right here for you to come back. You can tell me all about the sights and the sound of people speaking your mother's brogue."

"Wonder how Nancy is getting along with her new job in the jewelry and silver business? Guess I was a little hard on her when I told her I didn't want her to leave government work."

"She held her own, just like you would have done, Cate. I've learned long ago that you Bennett women know your own minds. And now, aren't you proud that she's making good money and being sent to all those silver companies back East?"

"Some man from Connecticut has taken a liking to her. I hate to lose her to the East, like we did Daphne."

"Not likely, I'd say, but what does a father know?"

I had an idea. "Maybe she can get her boss to send her to New York City, and we'll go too. Then we can all meet Charlotte when her ship comes in. Hoboken isn't far from there."

I decided to ask her about it and soon got a note in reply.

> *Dear Mama,*
>
> *I asked my boss if he would give me time off or send me on assignment to New York. It seems he promised one of his best customers a twelve-piece set of sterling flatware before the end of the year. He's having a hard time keeping his promise. We have a silver shortage after the war it seems. Now, he wants me to ask Mr. Dickson, the salesman for Wallace Sterling in Connecticut, if he would help me out... Sure enough, Mr. Dickson agreed and I'm being sent to New York to pick up the order! Guess I'll be able to go with you and Daddy. Talk soon.*
>
> *Love,*
> *Nancy*

I was ecstatic to read this news. "Davis, Nancy can talk anybody into anything. Can you believe it? We're all going to New York together!"

"Uh-huh. She can do anything..." Davis said with a twinkle in his eye. "Let's go! I know this will be exciting for you, Cate."

"Oh, Davis. Imagine us in New York City! Do you think we'll be able to meet Mr. Dickson?"

"We're just getting silver, I thought."

"Well, he seems like he would do *anything* for Nancy and I just want to meet him."

Davis raised his eyebrows.

"Okay," I admitted, "I'm a *little* nosy."

"Uh-huh..."

The promised silver was waiting for us as we checked into our hotel...sadly, no Mr. Dickson, but he had left a lovely note for Nancy.

Dear Miss Bennett,

I apologize I could not bring you this order in person, but I had a last-minute business trip that the company scheduled for me. I am disappointed not to see you, but perhaps we could have dinner on my next trip to Albuquerque.

With fond regards,
Wallace Dickson

"Well, I didn't want to see him...this trip, anyway," Nancy pouted in self-defense.

I sensed a little more remorse than she was willing to admit, but we were in New York City together, and we were all very excited to meet Charlotte, whose ship would dock the next morning.

Bright and early, we were headed to the boat docks on the other side of the Hudson River.

"Hurry, Daddy. I can see the ship already in its berth. Hope Charlotte isn't down the plank yet," Nancy chattered on. She spied a flower stand full of colorful bouquets. "Let's stop and get her flowers. How about these yellow roses? You know, for the yellow rose of Texas!"

"Hurry dear," I said. "We'll keep walking."

The looming ship rocked back and forth. Men were yelling and ropes were being thrown to the hands on the docks. People crowded the rails on each level of the *Volendam,* trying to see their families and friends. Such commotion. With a *bang, clang,* the gangplank lowered.

"I see her, Davis, the one with the gray hat," I said. "She's waving. She sees us too."

Charlotte wriggled down the gangplank and burst into our arms. Her feet dangled as Davis lifted her off the concrete. Nancy, squealing with excitement, asked question after question as we made our way back to the hotel. Charlotte threw open her bag and handed us each a surprise treasure. Afterward, we headed to our celebration dinner in the elegant Ritz dining room.

As dinner progressed, Davis could see me retreat mentally as I thought back to my father's travel stories and his memories. Charlotte continued with her tales, watching Nancy's fascination. She never noted my silence, only my smile. I would never have thought that Charlotte's trip could bring back memories of my father's recollections from such depths within me. I was conflicted; happy and sad simultaneously. I had never seen a large ocean liner in person. This too made me picture the long journey my family had endured so many years ago. Charlotte could take that long trip for reasons of pleasure, but these people had done it for survival and the hope for a better life. A contrast in times sobered me as I sat in deep thought, even after we returned to our room.

"Davis, I had no idea I would have such sad feelings about my daddy upon hearing Charlotte speak of her travels."

"We never know when a sleeping emotion will come back to haunt us, Cate. You could never have predicted sadness today."

"What's the matter with me? I'm so happy and excited for Charlotte. I didn't realize this trip was as much for me."

"Yes, you do live through your girls from time to time. No harm in it. They play out your hopes and dreams, I'd say, but it's always good for *them* too, sweetheart."

As our visit to New York City drew to a close, Davis and I sat in our room drinking coffee and reading the newspaper.

"Charlotte will most likely be leaving us soon," I said, flipping through the pages. "What girl could stay in Twist Junction after seeing

Paris, Rome, and London? Television is the new industry—they say so right here," I tapped the paper with my finger, "in the *New York Times*. I love reading such an important paper. It will be difficult for even me to go home this afternoon..." Glancing further at the paper, I said, "Oh Davis, look at all the shows we could have seen. Broadway is like no other place to erase your woes and challenge your imagination! I imagine you would have liked one of the musicals...look, *Lend an Ear,* starring Carol Channing and Dennis Nelson! And the smash hit *Mister Roberts* is playing too... Charlotte will have a lot of big-city choices for her next adventure. I wonder if New York City, or maybe Denver or Chicago, will win out."

"Slow down, Cate, let's all get home first," Davis chuckled.

Our conversation was interrupted by three rapid knocks on our door.

"The girls are at the door. You'd think there was a house on fire!" Davis said as he went to open it for them.

"What a glorious day!" Nancy twirled through the hall into our room.

"We're going out for a New York cup of coffee at one of the little delis, and then we want to find some of the swanky shops that Sybil and Daphne were always talking about. What do you say? Want to come?"

"Davis, you'd love the coffee shop. Why don't you go? I'd like to sit in the lovely lobby and read my paper...I'm just a little tired today..."

"Daddy, get your hat and let's go, go, go!" enthused Nancy.

"Everyone meet back here at 3:00. Our train leaves at 4:30 on the dot," I said.

I felt like my voice fell on deaf ears as they laughed down the hall, dragging Davis behind them like a puppy. I was satisfied with my choice of a continental breakfast and reading downstairs, where I could watch the parade of sleek clothes. After finishing my paper, I meandered out to see the carriages lined up for Central Park tours. I thought, *Now that looks like a romantic idea that Wallace Dickson might think of for Nancy someday. He's the dashing and romantic type, I understand.* I turned to see my Davis headed in my direction, his head above the masses of people, slowly navigating the pushy crowd, smoking his favorite Pall Mall cigarettes. He smoked less since the incident with the grandchildren, but nonetheless, I feared it would remain his lifelong bad habit.

"Good day, cowboy," I commented as he got closer.

"Am I that obvious?" he responded.

I nodded and took his arm as I breathed in the crisp fall air.

"And how was breakfast?" I asked.

"Those girls!" Davis said, shaking his head. "Men scrambled to offer their stools to them. I must say, I got a chuckle as they sashayed over to them, leaving me in the dust. I managed to get a seat because Nancy got two people to move over so I could sit next to them. She's a born negotiator, all right. The waitress must have poured us three cups of coffee each. Thought they were going to go all over the counter, but it was like a dance as she paraded back and forth. And Cate, the scrumptious buns were as big as saucers! I'm ready to go, though...too much hustle and bustle for me."

Our train arrived with punctual purpose, and soon we had left New York City and our glorious few days of memories behind. During the trip home, Davis spent most of his time in the smoker car or the dining car having coffee. I tried to write my weekly letters and read while being jostled from side to side. The girls enjoyed walking from car to car, checking out all of the eligible young bachelors.

"Mama...thought we'd stop in to check on you. Shall we all have dinner together in the dining car tonight?" Charlotte asked.

"That will be lovely, but are you sure? You looked like you were having great fun last night when you were on your own."

Nancy piped up, "We want to be together. It's harder and harder to be together these days. Albuquerque isn't far, but my weekends seem to fly by. I'll have a real change to my social schedule now that Maggie is married. Who knows? Maybe Wallace Dickson will start coming around more often. I know he felt like a third wheel with Maggie and me when he would ask us out for dinner. Now we can be a foursome with Clark and Maggie. I'm just dreaming, but wouldn't that be fun?"

"Nancy, you're just like Mother, always planning ahead," Charlotte said.

Dinner in the dining car had Davis quizzing the waiter about all the selections.

"Meat and potatoes, that's all I want. What do you have that is plain old food?"

"Well, Mr. Bennett, we can make something special for you. Sir, how about steak and mashed potatoes?"

"That's more like it. None of this veee-shee-swaa stuff...you know, that damn cold potato soup."

The girls blushed and we placed our orders.

"Daddy, you should try it. You love potatoes," Charlotte said.

"Soup should be hot. That's all there is to it. I'm a country cowboy with simple tastes. And where are the biscuits, anyway?"

"Here come some nice hot Parker House rolls," I said.

"Whose house?"

"Oh, Davis, that's a kind of dinner roll," I chided. "We're having such fun. You'll be home to my cooking soon enough."

"Yes, Daddy. I'll be there for a while to help while I look for a job. I can cook up a storm for you—even a pie or two," Charlotte guaranteed.

Twist Junction looked like it was bustling when the train pulled in two mornings later. Bruce met us to carry our bags.

"Howdy! How was the trip? I see Europe didn't keep you, Charlotte. Was it fun?"

"We've had a gangbuster time! I brought Elizabeth some perfume from Paris. I can't wait to give it to her."

"Come to the flower shop. We're so proud of our new adventure. Business is wildly busy. Lots of deaths and new babies..." He turned to me and Davis. "Davis, bet you and Mrs. B are glad to be home."

"Yes, and I had lots of time to think. I'm going to get another herd and have the tenants run them on my land. I can go out and check on them, and not have all the work Otto and I used to have. The economy is good and it doesn't hurt to make a little extra money. I have no regrets about closing the hardware store. Not my cup of tea. I miss the land and the animals."

"That would do you good," I agreed. "I've been thinking too. What do you think about us using some of that cattle money and my salary, and finding a spot at Cimarron Canyon to build a little cabin? I've been thinking a lot about slowing down. It could be a nice experience for the grandchildren, too."

"Cate, your mind is like the train—always going fast. Fast to the next stop, so to speak!"

"Guess I do like to think of the future. I don't want to work too much longer... Who knows where Charlotte will end up?" I giggled. "I heard they wanted a social reporter for WXIT local radio. That would be perfect for her."

"Daddy, Mama," Charlotte interrupted. "I was just talking to Elizabeth. She said there was a broadcasting job on the radio."

We laughed.

"We were just talking about that," I said.

"Why are you smiling and looking at each other? Do you think that's a dumb job?"

"No, dear. It could be interesting. You might like that industry. Maybe it will be a stepping stone. You did a good job at Loretto Heights, being the liaison for all their VIP celebrity guests. Didn't Ann Blythe write you a thank you note? You have a real talent for dealing with high society."

"Well, I know we're not a high-society town, but I could get my feet wet. Do you think it would be okay to try out tomorrow? You wouldn't be embarrassed if I was talking about gossip, parties, and local news?"

"No, dear. See how they like your voice on the air and go from there."

The next morning, Charlotte shot out of the house before I left for work.

"Looks like you want that job more than I thought," I said before the front door slammed shut.

"Good luck, honey," Davis called after her. "I'll be at the DeSoto coffee shop if you want to stop by later."

"What a day," I said. "I think I'll stop by the post office before I go to the office. I'm anxious to see if the girls wrote while we were gone."

Smiling, Davis shook his head.

I pulled on my gloves, adjusted my hat, and slid my pocketbook over my arm. My pace was moderately quick, but I glanced into the flower shop window and stopped abruptly. It was beautifully filled with fall chrysanthemums. Rust, yellow, and burgundy potted plants were stacked on hay bales among pumpkins. Bruce was so talented. I could see Elizabeth, neat as a pin, organizing her cash register and waving as I caught her eye. It took me the next few blocks to get over how perfectly proud I was of all my different girls. They were settling successfully into life. My eyes glistened with more pride than I ever expected I could feel.

14
Cabin Fever

I was so distracted that I almost forgot to stop by the old brick post office. The stone steps were worn from people checking their mail two times a day. The postmaster always said I was his favorite customer because I would quietly emote when I saw a tilted white envelope behind the scratched glass window of our box. Today was no exception. I twirled the dial to release the combination numbers and opened the etched door to find two letters, one from Daphne and one from Margaret.

As I walked down the pavement toward my office, I could hardly hold back and tore open Daphne's letter. Pausing for a moment, I read...

> *Dear Mama,*
>
> *I had so hoped you and Daddy could have come to Washington when you went to meet Charlotte; however, I understand you only had a short vacation and Daddy can only take so much train travel. Nonetheless, I know it must have been fun to be with Nancy. Did you meet Mr. Dickson? He's all she talks about these days. I can only imagine how exciting it was to meet Charlotte's ship, too. I'll be on one sometime...someday...I've promised myself!*
>
> *Well, I have good news. I'll be bringing the children to see you next summer. Rolland continues to work hard and hopes for time off as well. Perhaps we can drive our new burgundy Plymouth. It's quite smart... My hair continues to be long and I work daily to keep slim and trim... Baby crying, naptime over.*
>
> *Love,*
> *Daphne*

News of Daphne and Rolland's upcoming trip to see us had me giddy. I had to hold off reading the letter from Margaret. When I arrived at the town office, there were people lined up at my office door. It was the first of the month and everyone wanted to pay their utilities on time.

"Morning, morning, morning," I said as I excused myself through the line. After flipping the light switch on, sharpening my pencil, and pulling out the records book, I was ready.

The day dragged on as I calculated late payments from the previous month and processed numbers. I barely had time to take my coffee break. I was glad when it was time to go home for noontime dinner, which Charlotte had fixed for us. I took a deep, relaxing breath and closed my eyes as I walked through the front door. My house smelled of pot roast and gravy.

Charlotte seemed to be distracted in her own world and barely heard me come in. She was cheery, humming as she poured herself some iced tea.

"Oh, hi Mama. I'll pour you some tea. Something to eat?"

"In a minute. How did your interview go, dear?"

"Mama, I was shocked. They only asked me to talk into the mike two times, and then said, 'Done!' They offered me the social news broadcast, which airs two times a week. If they find the program popular and need more show time, they will increase it. They offered me the opportunity to name the show. What do you think of that? And it pays $5 per hour!"

"Did you accept?"

"I told them I would be back in touch in the morning. I wanted to know what you thought and I want some time, if I'm to do it, to think of a clever title. What do you think?"

"Well, why not, if you think it sounds like fun. What harm can it do?"

"I can just imagine what my sisters will say…what a tease I'll be, for sure."

"Here, I got a letter from Daphne and I haven't had a minute to read Margaret's."

I heard Davis at the back door.

"Hello, sweetheart," I said as he came into the house. "Smells good, doesn't it? Lots of news. Sit down... Things are busy as usual. Letters, news, jobs...and you *must* go by the flower shop. It's just beautiful!"

The phone rang so loudly it seemed to jump off the wall.

"Now, who can that be?" I said as I answered the call. "Sybil! Well, how is the ranch, dear? No, but we're about to sit down... That would be better, when I have more time... But what is the *big* surprise?" I strained to hear my daughter as the words tumbled through the phone. "A baby! When? I'm so happy!" I waved at Davis. "Davis, come talk to Sybil." I handed him the receiver.

"Don't have enough to do up there, huh, but make babies?" her dad teased. "Well, that's the best news of the day... Yes, sweetie, we'll talk later..." He hung up. "Daggum it, Cate, I thought we had a big family now, but look what possibilities all these girls can give us down the road."

"Wonder if she'll have her baby in a barn?" Charlotte commented.

"Now Charlotte, be kind," I admonished as we sat down at the table.

"She's certainly far from any doctor, hospital, or much of anything," Charlotte added. "I'd be scared."

"I'll ask her, but she'll probably come down here or Albuquerque to have the baby. Pass the beans to your father, dear."

"Mighty good, Charlotte," Davis said.

"Thanks, Daddy."

I hurried through my dinner, then gathered my purse. "I have to get back to the office. Let's talk about the letters, Charlotte's job, and talk more to Sybil tonight." I had the door half open when I said, "Davis, have you talked with your tenants about the herd?"

"Gonna go out and do it this afternoon."

"See you later, then," I said, and headed out.

It seemed like a long day. Everything I wanted to do was at home, but I was stuck at the office collecting fees. My mind wandered. Everything under the sun came into my head. I was beginning to lose interest in my work. A career was not as exciting these days. I took the backside of the throw-away copy of my receipts and began making several lists, then opened my purse and slit open Margaret's letter. She told how she and Clark were talking about opening their own men's clothing store...in Twist Junction. It would mean a big economic step from Albuquerque. Perhaps living with us could be a chance for them to save money. A son-in-law in the house might be interesting. We'd never had that experience. As Davis said, our family size seemed to be exploding. I had to make charts to see who was where and what they were doing.

And Nancy had no sooner gotten back to Albuquerque than Mr. Dickson started visiting with regularity. The phone became the preferred mode of communication. It seemed that since Nancy was quite busy with her gentleman, her weekly letters became weekly phone calls, often rushed and with little time for conversation. One such call went like this:

"Hello, Mama! This is Nancy. I only have a minute, but I wanted you to know I think I'm falling for that East Coast guy! He is one of the most elegant and funniest men I have ever known. Can you believe it—I almost refused to go to dinner with him only a few months ago? Can I bring him home when he comes back to this area? I'd like to see what Daddy thinks of him... Margaret's Clark gets on with him *really* well and we've had some gay times together... Think he wants me to meet him in San Francisco next month. Oh, it's *too* exciting! Here he comes. We're going out to dinner at the country club. He has special permission to use it. Gotta go. Good-bye, Mama!"

"Good-bye!" I said. With a laugh, I turned to my husband. "Do you know, Davis Bennett, I was on the phone all that time with Nancy, and she didn't give me a chance to say one word. And *then* she hung up!"

"That's love for you."

"She wants to bring her beau here to meet us."

"Well, that's a good sign," he chuckled.

"Charlotte will have enough to talk about on her radio show just covering the Bennett girls. People think we're fascinating for some reason. I think we need to take a trip next weekend, before we're into more babies and weddings. Want to go look at land in the New Mexico canyons for our cabin spot?"

My three-day holiday weekends were treasured. I knew Davis and I would enjoy the wide-open spaces of New Mexico. As we passed our land, I patted Davis's knee and watched him glancing at his newest white-faced Herefords. His heart was so drawn to that ranch and the beautiful cattle grazing on it. Seeing him happy like that always reminded me of why I loved my cowboy so much. A few hours down the road we could see the Springer Hotel just over the state line in New Mexico.

"I'm looking forward to a nice meal and a feather bed tonight, Mr. B," I said.

"Sounds good to me, Mrs. B. Tomorrow morning we'll head to the canyons and the lake at Eagle's Nest. Sorry we're missing Aspen time, but any time is God's time up there…pure air, blue skies, crystal-clear water," Davis said.

The next morning, we were on the road early. We soon saw the road snaking by a stream. In the distance, we could see dots of cabins tucked in between the looming pines.

"Where's the real estate office around here? Looks like the perfect place for the cabin," Davis said.

"Let's stop at the local café," I suggested. "They will know about land for sale."

We spotted a nearby, derelict truck stop and went inside.

Davis spoke up, "Afternoon, folks!"

A waitress approached.

"One black coffee and a chilled Coca-Cola with ice, please, ma'am. I can almost see the deer rustling in the bushes over there. Must be some pretty good huntin' in these parts."

"Oh, yes sir. We get lots of hunters and fishermen," the waitress replied.

"Who is selling some land back in the canyon?"

"Mr. Green owns most of it," the waitress said.

"Is he selling off parcels these days?"

"You interested in some? My husband and I were looking at a piece on the creek up there, but we have to save our money. My car broke down last week. No cabin for us now," the waitress said as she slid the drinks onto the Formica table.

"How can we get in touch with Mr. Green?"

"He's out of town today and tomorrow. Would you like my husband to show it to ya? He doesn't have a car, though."

"We'd be glad to drive if it isn't too much trouble for him to show us around."

She hurried to the crank phone. "Hey, Jim Bob, I'm at the café and two fine people want to see the lot we looked at, you know, the one by the creek." She nodded at us. "Sure, I'll feed them some pie."

Davis nodded an "okay" and she hung up the earpiece. She brought us two pieces of cherry pie while we waited.

"Should have given me this first, miss. Best daggum cherry pie I've ever had," Davis said.

"Yep, we make it right here in the back. I always make my crust with lard."

"Another cup of coffee, if you will," Davis said.

As they conversed, I sipped my Coke and thought, *This is going really well. Thank you, God. When Davis's tummy is happy, he'll be willing to do anything.*

A short while later, a stout man in overalls moseyed into the café.

"Hey there, I'm Jim Bob Davenport."

He pulled up a metal chair, which squealed as it dragged on the red-and-white checkered linoleum floor.

"Some coffee, Suzie, please," he said to the waitress. "So, you like our area, do ya? Peaceful, ain't it? Joe Green doesn't give away his property, but I think he needs some money these days... Only so much land on that pretty little stream up there...good fishin' and good sunsets too. We wanted it, Suzie and I...going to build our dream house...but I'd be glad to show it to ya. I do favors for Joe now and then. We all help each other out around here." He got up. "Don't mind driving, do ya, Mr....ah..." He paused. "What was your name?"

"Bennett, Davis and Catherine."

We paid Suzie for the pie, then went out to the car. Jim Bob paused as we opened the car doors.

"You first, Miss Catherine," he said, opening the door to the back seat.

He sat up front, directing Davis over dirt, rocks, and gravel, until finally he said, "Can't go much further. Gonna have to walk from here."

"No problem," Davis said. "How far?"

"Just over the crest on the right. Here's the stream, down here, and the property goes to the meadow below. You're up pretty high for the views, too."

Davis held my elbow as I navigated the loose earth and rocks. I turned around and saw a spectacular vista of pines, aspens, and pinion trees. It was so different from the flat, treeless Panhandle. I glanced up to see two eagles circling above us. The men talked. I stood silently in my own world, in unison with nature, imagining the wildflowers of the spring and the golden-yellow aspens of the fall.

Finally, I said, "Is the fishing good here?"

"Ma'am, the best. You can have a look at the stream...a mountain trout will practically jump on your line. You can have it cooked and on your table in ten minutes." He smiled a toothless smile.

He was gentle, kind, and honest. Clearly, he loved this spot. I felt guilty that I did too.

"When is Mr. Green back?" Davis asked.

"Don't know for sure."

"How much do you think he wants?" I asked.

"Can't really say, but maybe three to five hundred dollars."

"Oh, I see," I said, gulping and clearing my throat. "Guess we've taken enough of your time, sir."

The wind rustled the branches in the pines as we descended the hillside. I hesitated as we headed back to the car. I didn't want to leave that beautiful place.

"Is there a rooming house or motel near here?" Davis said,

breaking my "thinking time" as we made our way back into town.

Jim Bob motioned for Davis to stop the car.

"Go round the next curve in the road and hang a left. Go round the lake. There's a small place there. Mr. Jenkins should have a room for you folks. Good to meet ya," he mumbled as he jumped out in front of a modest shack.

"Thank you. I'll leave my name and number on a napkin up at the café if we have any further questions. Anything else, Cate?"

"We just have to talk, I suppose."

The car seemed to drive itself to the log cabin inn. Completely chilled, I immediately went over to the pinion log fire and sat down in a chair beside it. Davis registered, gathered our bags, then joined me. With our room set and dinner plans made, we could finally relax.

"Want to go up to our room before we eat? Do you need to freshen up?" Davis asked me.

"Yes, dear. That's a nice idea," I said, and reached for the key he held out for me.

I found room #3. A crackled mirror hung over the sink. The toilet and shower were down the hall. The bed was puffy. It looked so inviting that I wanted to lie down, but feeling I would sleep till breakfast if I did, I resisted the temptation. I looked into the mirror. The reflection of my porcelain skin showed lines, and the eyes looking back at me had layered eyelids. The image took me by surprise. *It must be the crackled glass*, I theorized. Davis was waiting. There was nothing to do but pinch my cheeks and fluff my hair. I looked down at my dusty, dirty shoes...wouldn't hurt to change them, either, I decided. Remembering I had packed perfume, I gave a squirt of Lily of the Valley behind each ear.

In the lobby, Davis was almost asleep in the chair beside the fireplace. The flames crackled and sent a nice warmth out into the room. His body jerked as he heard my footsteps.

"And here comes my lovely Cate!"

"Oh, Davis, stop."

The cozy dining room was through a set of rough, oak, double doors. We joined a few tables of visitors under an antler chandelier. Another fireplace was immediately next to our table.

I nestled up against the massive stone front, which seemed to hold the heat like a blanket. My body was thinner now, and I felt the chill. Davis reached across the table with his strong, heavy hand...a hand worn from many years of holding down a calf to brand, from mending fences or grabbing a rope. He had worked hard—often, I thought, too hard. His smile was still engaging. I could feel his love passing to me across the rough linen tablecloth. I sighed blissfully. *My cowboy...*

A skinny waitress greeted us. "What'cha gonna have tonight, folks?"

I smiled, thinking she really needed a hug instead of just a passing stranger's smile. "Are you having a special tonight?" I asked.

"Chicken fried steak or pork chops with gravy."

"Hmm, that's a difficult choice. I think I'll have chicken fried steak. Davis?"

"Sounds like a good idea. One for me too."

"Be right back," she said, and was off to the kitchen.

"What did you think about the site on the mountain?" I said eagerly to Davis. "Could you picture a big porch looking out over all those pines and the blue sky?"

I wanted to engage him before dinner had come and gone, and we were off to bed. The mountain air made us hungry and sleepy. I wanted to leave the table with some sense of Davis's thinking, but the cozy, relaxed elements around us made his thoughts harder to pull out of him.

"Davis, this place is so relaxing. I think we could eat and rest for a week. Maybe that's exactly why we need our own retreat."

"Hmm..."

I let him have his quiet as he gazed into the orange-red flames. The color and light on his rough, square face still had a power over me. God forbid he should ever know what I was really thinking. *We need that mountain lot...don't let it go, Davis! Please, please!*

Large oval plates arrived stacked with several pieces of the most tender chicken fried steak, creamy mashed potatoes, and white gravy. Davis nodded with approval. We ate silently, the only sound being the crackling fire and the muted conversations around us.

"Pretty daggum good, I'd say," Davis finally said, wiping his mouth with his napkin. "Not as good as your Irish stew, but they can make some mean gravy. Miss," he said to the waitress as she passed by, "you have any cornbread?"

"Oh, yes sir, be right out!"

"Now life will be perfect," Davis sighed blissfully.

"Pie tonight? Maybe coffee?" the waitress asked.

"What kind?" Davis said.

She rattled off a list. I just gazed into the fireplace.

"Could you bring me some chocolate ice cream, please?" Davis asked.

"Well, well. We really *are* on vacation. You must think this is a special occasion!" I said.

"It is. I want to buy you the mountain lot for your cabin, Cate."

I was speechless. I could barely think! As the waitress brought Davis his bowl of ice cream, I said, "Davis Bennett, you really can surprise me, even after all these years. I think we'll just love it! Thank you so much! I had no idea...no idea! Guess we'll have to leave our number on the café napkin, after all. Davis, you don't even know how much it will cost yet! I'll help with the building materials. I have a full teapot again." I knew I was babbling, but I didn't care. I was so excited.

"Can't be that much money. That old guy probably just needs cash. I'd say anything is better than nothing, and we have just what he needs."

My man of few words and generous actions ate the last of his ice cream, got up, leaned over, and kissed my toasty forehead. He pulled out my chair and we proceeded up the hewn-log stairs.

Our news and excitement paled when we arrived home. Charlotte had been bitten by the live communication bug and had decided to go for an interview in Chicago with a talent scouting company for the newest venue, television. And Nancy called to announce her engagement. Unbeknownst to me, Davis had gotten a phone call from Mr. Dickson before our trip, asking for her hand, and had kept it secret from me. I just shook my head. *Lots of secrets in a big family,* I thought.

The excitement was electric—building plans and wedding plans, all at once...and just when I thought that life was getting simpler! One lesson I seemed to be learning was "one step at a time." Nothing stayed the same, and as it all flew by, I hardly had time to worry, agree, or disagree with anything happening at any one time. Diapers were easy to change, but to guide our girls' lives in a certain direction was quite another kettle of fish. At my age, I just had to sit back and relax. Life would take care of itself and the girls. I felt I had raised them with high goals and expectations, so they would have to take it from there, and I would have to trust that they knew what they were doing. The mother heifer has to let go of her calf, as Davis always reminded me. They learn to get up and walk, despite their mother's nudging. Some days I wished I had sat out there on the plains, learning from nature as Davis had done. Life is really pretty basic. Everything happens in its own time. His patience always "allowed" life's path, whereas I worried and prodded.

Charlotte boarded the train north. I couldn't help but wonder if this was a forever move. She was aglow with excitement, even though we were fighting off the good-bye tears. Davis stood next to me, holding me—and I'm sure himself—up. Our baby was off to another big-city adventure and a very different way of life.

Charlotte's letters and phone calls allowed me many vicarious experiences. In fact, through my girls, I experienced so much. I ran my own business through Elizabeth's flower shop. I lived on the largest ranch west of the Rio Grande through Sybil's half-million-acre ranch in Colorado. I experienced political life up close in our nation's capital through Daphne's days in Washington, D.C. I experienced my dashing son-in-law dressing all the gentry of up-and-coming Albuquerque through Margaret's husband's job at prestigious Stromberg's. And she became his happy working wife, putting her secretarial and accounting skills to good use. Now I would experience life in New England through Nancy's stories of her elegant life as the beautiful young wife of Wallace Dickson, an older executive in the silver industry. And finally,

Charlotte's short-lived radio show led to a new job in Chicago, and I would now witness the rise of the new industry, television, and its stars. How could I have asked for a more stimulating life, all from the lounge chair in my own living room?

So, now my retirement was near. The cabin's log walls would be up soon, and the wide pine-planked floors and stone-faced fireplace would follow shortly. Visions of sitting and looking out over the mountain land and the meandering stream below the front porch filled me with contentment. Imagining it was like watching dreams for the girls trickle past the rocks as the water carried them on their way downstream. The thought of throwing a line into its crystal-clear water and finding our breakfast wriggling on the end of the rod evoked a smile. Questions zipped through my mind, like would we have a phone, or would our time there always be peacefully quiet? *I'll have Bruce bring some charming furnishings,* I thought, *and a radio so Davis can hear his baseball games, and rockers for the porch...*

I found it almost impossible to keep my mind on my job. I would plan for our project and try my best to concentrate on my tasks for each day. Difficult as it was, I cheerily greeted all my customers. Often they would ask about our cabin project or the family, and I would fall back into stories and thoughts of Daphne coming east with her children, visiting the cabin, seeing Sybil at the ranch, or enjoying Albuquerque with Margaret while eating Mexican food at La Fonda in Old Town. Yes, we had so much to do and see without a job to encumber me.

"Perhaps we can take the whole family up to the Taos Inn," I said one day, planning ahead one more time. I stood next to Davis, who sat rocking on the front porch. "Would you like that?" I continued, and leaned against the porch pillar.

"Oh Cate, I've seen my share of Indians, pueblos, and their dances."

"But you always like our trips once we get there. Well...maybe I'll ask my brothers to join me in Taos sometime. I think our grandchildren need to see these places."

"I agree, sweetheart, but I'll like hearing your stories when you get back just as much, without ever leaving Twist Junction."

"What about if I plan a trip for just you and your sister Polly? Say, back to Ft. Deposit in Alabama...to where you were born?"

"Um...let me think about it."

"Surely you would like that, and Polly would be thrilled. She could show you everything."

"Cate, you just can't sit still. Come sit with me here on the porch. Summer will be here before you know it and our lives will be topsy-turvy again. Enjoy the flowers coming up and our peace together. Let's drive out to the ranch and see the green of the wheat in the fields."

I left the porch pillar and sat next to him. I let his words sink in. "I can't let my middle years of life go by. I want to do *everything*, while I can. *And* I want to do them with you, my dear, sweet man."

Davis reached for my hand. "You're right, Cate. I know you have to do everything. I don't want to hold you back. With all our new grandchildren, we'll be outnumbered soon and we won't be able to get away as much as you'd like. I understand. I'll come with you. And the cabin...I'm anxious to enjoy that with you, too."

He squeezed my hand and brought it slowly up to his lips, then touched it to his cheek. He was such a gentle man who showed his tenderness outwardly. It was a trait I never mastered, which bothered me from time to time; however, being his solid rock of a wife must have satisfied Davis over our forty years of marriage.

We heard the screen door squeak open at 5:30 the next morning. Wrapping his robe around his stiff body, Davis came out of the bedroom to spot the shadow of Elizabeth in the early morning light. I followed, tying my robe with haste and rubbing my sleepy eyes. Elizabeth stood rigid, like she had seen a ghost.

"Elizabeth!" he said.

We ran to her and held her. She felt lifeless as she stood in silence.

"Davis, make us some coffee please," I said.

Taking her hand, I guided her to the kitchen banquette. Her eyes were red and glazed over, her hair uncombed, her starched blouse wrinkled and buttoned wrong.

I waited. Davis waited.

"He's dead," were the words that she managed to get out of her quivering mouth. "On the Dumas highway...crashed into a culvert...they found him about 4:00 a.m. Drinking again. Oh, Mama! Oh, Daddy!"

Shaking, Davis could barely bring over the coffee. He spilled it with every step. He put the wet saucers and cups on the table. I wiped the spills and he hugged his eldest daughter with all his might.

"Did you know he was a drinker, Mama? He never hurt me, but he was a drinker...went to Amarillo one or two times a week...so no one here could see his drinking. He always came back, but there were many times I had to dress the kids and open the shop while he slept it off. All that, but I loved him, Mama. So much life, so much fun...so much talent..." Her words trailed off.

We held her in silence. Then she got up slowly and walked out the screen door just as she had come in.

Almost in a whisper, I said, "What pain and fear she must be suffering. What should we do?"

At that point, Davis had tears rolling down his face. Grabbing the coffee-stained napkins, he sobbed. Bruce was his first son-in-law. His coffee shop buddy. He loved the prankster, who had once thrown him into the horse trough at XIT for not dressing in Western attire. Bruce had also made his eldest daughter softer and made her smile.

A few hours passed. I got up, picked up the wall phone, and dialed Elizabeth. The phone rang and rang. Finally, Elizabeth's sister-in-law answered.

"This is Catherine," I said. "Are the children in school? Do they know?"

"Hello, Catherine. Elizabeth is lying down. The children are at school and they do not know yet," answered Helen, speaking in a low tone of voice. "We are all in shock..."

"Would it be helpful for me to call Father Patrick and arrange to hold the church for the funeral? Perhaps I can get the children from school and give them dinner. It might give Elizabeth a little more time."

"That sounds generous. I will stay with her," Helen agreed.

I hung up the phone. "I think I'll wait to call the girls until tonight, after the children leave. I don't want to spoil everyone's day. Father Patrick might have an idea for the funeral date by then..." I said to myself aloud. Looking at Davis, I suggested. "Let's not breathe a word of this...you know how rumors fly. And this is an ugly one."

Davis was still staring at the kitchen table as I called Father Patrick, then got dressed to go pick up the grandchildren. Before I went out to the car, I asked him, "Are you okay? Do I need to stay with you?"

Funny that I said that to him. I was ignoring my own stress and the slight chest pains that were radiating across my ribcage.

"No, no. I think I'll take a drive out to the land and see the cattle," he answered quietly.

— ⊲⊦ ⊲⊦ ⊲⊦ —

When Davis slid into his old pick-up, the Mexican was already there, waiting. They rode for miles but he didn't speak. Finally, the old Mexican in the straw hat gently said, "It is only the beginning, Mr. Davis. You must be brave. Treasure your good times. Life will continue as it has been, but sadness and loss start now."

Davis's eyes were glued straight ahead. He pulled over, got out of the truck, and came around to the passenger's side to let his Mexican angel out...but he was gone. Davis leaned against the truck, his heavy chest heaving and his heart breaking. He turned and rested his forehead against the dusty window, his tan hat tilted back. He sobbed like he had never done before. Somehow, he knew deep inside that life's last cycle would be very, very difficult for him. Could he lessen the impact? Protect his wife and family? He sighed. No, life had its own path. He knew that all too well. Reminiscing, Davis recalled how he could never save struggling calves in the field, as much as he tried, many, many times. Life had its own way. Suddenly, he turned his face to the sky, drew in a deep breath, and yelled, "God, help me!"

The nearby herd looked up for a moment, startled...then all was calm. Davis could see the old Mexican walking up the road. The sun broke through a luminous cloud and Davis felt his strength returning.

— 4. 4. 4. —

I felt I had no sooner hung up with the girls when the door opened a few hours after midnight. Sybil, Garland, and two sleeping children arrived quietly. Maggie and Clark followed shortly. Together we sat in the living room all night, speechless.

Breaking the long hours of silence, Margaret finally said, "Coffee anyone?"

We obviously weren't going back to bed.

Sybil, who had been in shock since she sat down, got up and announced, "I'm going over to Elizabeth's to see if she's awake..." Her words followed her out the door in midsentence.

We reminisced, occasionally catching ourselves laughing over the entertaining young man we were grieving.

Maggie, almost emotionless, all of a sudden announced, "I almost forgot to tell you, Mama and Daddy...I heard from Charlotte before we left and she should be on the next train from Chicago."

"Clark, would you check the schedule later today? I'll be making the funeral arrangements with Elizabeth and Father Patrick at about 9:00," I said.

Solemn, Margaret spoke up once again. "I guess we need to get to the flower shop and help out. I can't imagine Elizabeth making bouquets for her own dead husband. Sybil is very good at that sort of thing, so maybe I can help grab what they might need, maybe clean and sweep a bit."

Still in my dazed state, I said, "Daphne and Nancy are beside themselves that they're not here, but they both said they would like to visit with everybody when things aren't so fresh and they can bring the children. I know Daphne will go to Mass and pray for Bruce on his funeral day. You girls are so good to be here..." I said gratefully.

"Mama, we couldn't sleep, we had to come. Elizabeth needs us," Maggie concluded.

— 4. 4. 4. —

Sybil tiptoed to the back window of Elizabeth's bedroom. She could see that her sister's small bed light was on. Her head had slumped over to the side on the pillow, and she clutched a rosary that was spread out on her stomach. Sybil tapped the window pane lightly and Elizabeth's head snapped over to see her sister at the window. Sybil ran to the front door and back down the tiny hall to her sister's bedroom. She grabbed her sister's limp body and held it. She gently rocked her back and forth.

"I'm here, Elizabeth. I'm here for you."

Their bodies quivered together in unison. Gasping for air, they sobbed in each other's arms.

Elizabeth stood and looked at their wedding picture on the dresser, almost talking to herself. "I'll never forgive him. I've had enough! I stayed in this town after college just to be the responsible daughter. My husband, Mr. Charisma, Mr. Creative, Mr. Drunk, did himself in while out on one of his drinking spells in the next town!" Her voice was full of anger and disappointment. "My life as a partner and working wife is in limbo. Here I will sit, night after night, with two children to raise and a business to run. I'm only thirty-nine! How can I arrange all the funeral flower orders by myself, or numerous weddings, for that matter? Bruce was the creative one. Bruce was the town's favorite joker and best dancer around. I feel hollow, inside and out..."

Sybil sat in silence, listening to her ranting sister.

Elizabeth's thoughts led her. "I can't stay in this house; the memories are too strong. I deserve something better after all these years. The best house in town, or maybe a move. Start over somewhere where nobody knows us or about all of the embarrassing stories of Bruce's drinking or long nights of partying. Where did I fail? The only thing I felt I really did right was to have a grandson for poor Daddy. Remember how Daddy's wonderful, apple-round cheeks were glowing the day he was born? And Momma, well, she always quietly approved. If it weren't for these children, I would be in that Buick of mine, heading down the biggest highway out of town. Doing things of duty can cause your heart to ache, and mine does on all levels. If it weren't for Mrs. Farwell's funeral coming up, I probably would have gone into hiding myself...in Santa Fe, sipping margaritas, sleeping till noon in the soothing adobe walls of a La Posada casita. Or, heck, taking the train across country to the next ship to Ireland. I could visit great-granddaddy's grave and our great-grandmother's house." Weeping, she continued, "It is too much sadness for me right now. I gotta go! Somebody else can do Mrs. Farwell's damn flowers."

Sybil got up from the corner of the bed and went over to hug Elizabeth's turned back. She cried with her sister as she leaned her head on Elizabeth's heaving shoulders.

Then they heard, "Mommy, why are you crying?"

And at that moment, Elizabeth knew she had to stay. She had to answer the questions, take care of her children, and do the damn flowers. She knew there were many questions and no answers. She was lost to her sadness, remembering the other time of great uncertainty in her life, the Great Depression, when people would jump out of fifty-story buildings, unable to handle their financial losses. *I'm not jumping out of any building. We don't have anything over three stories, and no mountains for miles and miles to throw myself off of. Not many choices,* she thought. "Go back to sleep now. I'll come in to be with you in a minute," she voiced in a whisper to little Ben.

Sybil gathered her words together. "Elizabeth, I remember the feeling of being alone...the responsibility of being alone with Trae. Those were hard, hard days for me. Divorce is somewhat like a death... the end of a chapter...but I am *always* available for you. I can come visit you, or you can send the children to me up at the ranch. We have plenty of room, and the boys can catch the kittens in the barn or ride, or watch the ranch hands rope the calves...but for now, how about having me open up the shop for you and get some arrangements going? Maggie can answer the phone and help a bit till you get there. You need to get yourself dressed and get the children settled. I don't think their father's death has really sunk into their little heads."

"Don't think into mine, either," Elizabeth responded.

"Good thing Mama told them the sad story. Falling asleep at the wheel is a little softer version... Take your time, sweetie, the shop will be fine between your helpers, Maggie, and me. One step at a time," Sybil said. She walked down the hall and opened the front door.

Charlotte stepped off the train, tears already running down her cheeks. At the funeral the following day, there were more tears. The burial…more tears. And then it was over. Nothing would be the same from that point on.

15

My Boots Are Tight And I Don't See The Sunrise Anymore

Change came quickly to our house on Main Street. Just as I was beginning my retirement, here came Margaret and Clark to fill the quiet. A new baby boy was born and the piano resonated wonderful music once again. Margaret's talent for making us delicious suppers, and Clark's enthusiasm as he opened an exciting men's store for all Twist Junction to brag on, made the house alive once again. Somehow, I found the time to plan our upcoming trips and for our move into our cozy cabin in the mountains.

Davis smiled broadly. "Cate, we did it. The cabin is ready for our escape! Now, what is cookin' in that mind of yours regarding our trip to Alabama with Polly? You know, she has asked me about it every time I see her. She is truly excited. We'll be providing a much-deserved gift for her."

"Davis, don't have a date. I agree, she really deserves this trip and so do you...even though you don't realize it. When you see your homestead it will bring back memories galore. Just watch. You and Polly can laugh and chat for hours! The drive alone will be like watching a movie from our car seat. Think of all the beautiful roads, gardens, and plantations we'll be seeing, and you can see what kind of cattle they raise down there. We'll let you have coffee with the locals each morning. You'll have fun, believe you me! Oops, the baby is crying..."

"I'll get him. He's a cute little fella." Davis got up. "I got the baby, Maggie," he called to her as she cleaned up the supper dishes. "Holding little boys is different, they are so wiggly," he said after a minute. "Think Maggie will let me take him to the cabin?"

"Now, Davis!"

He snickered and smiled.

With our car packed, soon Twist Junction was in the distance and a hot orange sunset greeted us as we headed west. Several hours out, we stopped at Springer, New Mexico, for the night. We then headed west the next morning, on the road to Taos and Cimarron, where we would experience a white that blanketed everything in its path. The regular occurrence of snow in March did not come as a surprise, but we had never owned property on a mountain slope before.

Davis's silence was deafening the closer we got. A new Olds on an old mountain road...would it make it? I was sure he was calculating all his options as I chattered on about the lacy beauty of the low boughs on the pines. Three-quarters of the road had been cleared sometime during the day, but an undetected rock caught the undercarriage of the car. We would go no further.

We took what we could manage to carry—a pot of Irish stew, some light baggage, and a box of family memorabilia. Davis forged the trail and I tried to be stoic. It reminded me of the long, arduous walk we'd made many years ago, when my family was moving from New Braunfels to Twist Junction. *What is a little snow, only up to my boot tops, at this point?* I thought as we trudged toward our cabin.

The new key worked, and firewood had been stacked by the thoughtful Mr. Davenport and his café waitress wife. Knowing we were to arrive that day, she had baked Davis's favorite pie and had covered it with an upside-down plate.

"People are so kind in these parts. They must know what we are made of too, to drive so far and then walk in the snow to get here!"

Davis turned on a dime to start the fire. I lit the gas stove and set the stew on top. We sat in our coats for the next hour. I glanced out the window to see the snow thicken. It started to block my favorite view.

"Guess the stream is frozen and we won't be catching any trout for breakfast," I observed.

"Yep, guess its biscuits and gravy at the diner. But...I can still use my 'round-up' coffee pot before we forge out. A good cup of coffee out of this old thing will remind me of Otto and Jeb. Those were the good ol' days for me, Cate. You know, I *do* miss Otto..."

I nodded as I moved around a bit to put out my transported treasures. I had just lugged up the mountain way too much memorabilia, but I convinced myself that these were the things that made the cabin our home. Silently, I hid my heavy heart and tears as I thought of our devoted Otto.

"There," I said, "it's beginning to look like the Bennetts live here... Davis, the kerosene lamps are perfect. I'll get out the dishes Bruce gave me." A lump in my throat caught me off guard. My mouth quivered. "There have been so many angels in our lives...wonderful people who have made our lives better. Bruce, and our Otto..."

I stirred the stew and wandered into the bedroom. There I turned down the flannel sheets. Glancing out to the living room, I could see Davis staring into the flames. His eyes had pooled too. Quietly, I joined him, staring at the flames until my eyes closed with fatigue.

Mr. Davenport arrived early with a shovel and began to cut a path. A foot of snow had fallen the night before. Davis opened the door to motion him in for his special "cowboy coffee."

"Howdy," Davenport said after stomping the snow off his boots. "We wanted you two to have a romantic welcome last night. Well, Mrs. Bennett, your decorating went a little overboard, but it sure is pretty!" he said as he walked over to the table.

I nodded and said a quick good morning, then headed for the shower. I could hear the men talking as I waited patiently for warm water.

Davis immediately poured him some coffee. "Young man, let me warm you! You have been so thoughtful. What do I owe you for the wood? Tell your wife I couldn't have been happier with the delicious pie, too. What a friendly gesture!"

"We aim to please, sir. God put us all here together."

"Thought we'd go down to the café and get more of that good food. The stream is sleeping under a snow blanket, hiding our fresh-fish breakfast," Davis said with a grin.

"I'll wait for you, Mr. Bennett. I think you might need some help getting your car out. I saw it a-ways down the road."

"Shoulda brought my old pick-up, but it just isn't that comfy for the missus on a long trip."

"I'll go on down to the car and figure out a plan. See ya soon. Great coffee! Thanks."

"Cate, how ya doin' in the shower? Glad the pipes didn't freeze... did you get enough water?"

"Good enough, thanks. Guess it's back to my travel wools. A spring dress won't do with this weather. Let's go."

In hindsight, I suppose I had to have *some* stories to accompany our first visit to our beloved cabin. Lesson learned. Use it only in May or June to mid-September.

A month later, loading our car for the much-anticipated trip south seemed more promising. At least, Polly was excited. I don't believe she cared *where* she was going, she was just *going!*

We oohed and aahed past so much Southern beauty. Davis was hysterical as he listened to the high-school-girlish shrieks of joy coming from Polly. Kodaking all the way, Polly eventually found and identified their childhood home. She stood for what seemed like hours at the end of the walkway, staring up at her old home—the home where she had once played dolls and bounced her baby brother, Davis, on her lap. Davis stood by her with his arm around her fragile shoulders. Their bodies began to lean on each other. They hugged in a long embrace, and with one step in front of the other, slowly got back into our car.

After driving several blocks, she said, "They've kept it up so well. I'm so proud. Weren't you Davis? Our home...our beautiful home..."

I could feel my heart speeding and slowing...speeding and slowing. *Something's not quite right,* I thought. Not wanting to be the center of attention, I said nothing and just listened to Polly's stories. *I'll look into this strange feeling when I get home,* I thought.

Home only presented more excitement with Daphne, her children, and Nancy and her children coming to visit. Margaret's son was more active than ever and Davis jumped into his role as grandfather wholeheartedly.

My chest pains came and went.

I planned our summer trips and activities, which I enjoyed even without my husband in tow. Davis chose to sing at church every week—choir practice on Tuesday and service on Sunday. He saw to his cattle and got up later and later each day.

Realizing that entertainment in Twist Junction was limited, I planned a loop tour for the East Coast grandchildren. Where else could they ride horses bareback like Indians, or play in the corrals in the animal muck, but at Sybil's Colorado ranch? The ranch where Sybil would smoosh her face into a silk stocking and scare the ranch hands at night by scratching on the windows, then popping her head up in the open screen. She would story-tell and we would laugh for hours at her antics. Here the children could see the cowboys cook, cut the meat, stir the huge steel pots, and whip up a tale or two for good measure. The cook's heavily lined face was always slathered in her famous beauty cream, Crisco, which made her appear like a shiny waxed figure. Nothing was more spectacular than the thick AA Grade steaks straight from the herd, or the fuchsia and tangerine sunsets over the sand dunes through the enormous living room picture window that framed the breathtaking vista. Yes, it was a perfect setting.

I will always remember beautiful Sybil, surviving way out there, lonely—or better yet, bored—until the next big boxes of clothes would be shipped from Montaldo's. Her closets were brimming with the latest fashions. Long and lean, she wore them with perfect elegance and grace. Her body was the perfect mannequin. The girls would have fashion shows while their children played.

Soon we discovered that if we wore the youngsters out enough, we could have a peaceful car ride to New Mexico. My long-planned family trip to the famous Taos Inn was our next stop. I had arranged that we would meet my brothers, who had come from Dallas, and Elizabeth and the children from Twist Junction. Seventeen of us rode horses, watched Indians dance around the fire pit, and ate enough enchiladas to last us the rest of our lives. Oh, how I missed my Davis.

I told him later that it was nice to see Elizabeth drinking margaritas, laughing and smiling. She even took the youngsters up to the Taos Pueblo while we strolled leisurely through town and visited the Taos Hotel, where we stopped to sip their famous turquoise margaritas.

It was a time when the small Indian children would run up to tourists' cars, begging for a penny. It was a time for me to indulge my grandchildren with arrowheads or small, beaded calfskin purses. The inequality was just a way of life. We never gave a thought to their harsh conditions. There was no running water, and poor schools were prevalent, even in the 1950s. The Indians were tough and lived off the land like their ancestors, steeped in storytelling, craft making, as well as creating collectible pottery.

The trip included a stop at the cabin that Davis and I were so proud of. Chasing away any visiting mice made us all a little uncomfortable, but the thrill of catching our trout breakfast made a fond memory. I was the first to nab a big fish, and thank the Lord my brothers were there to clean it. Even I wasn't adept at cleaning them yet. I got the girls going and heating up coffee with Davis's campfire coffee pot. More fish, more scaling...we ate all morning.

After a couple of days on the road, and knowing that Daphne and Maggie were anxious to see each other, we headed back to Twist Junction. You could tell when everyone had had enough. Their eyes glazed over and they became cranky or really quiet. I preferred the really quiet. After all, the Twist Junction highlight, XIT, was to be in a few days.

I was glad to have Daphne driving with me. I realized that my stamina was waning, not that I would ever let on. I was grateful for the hot meal that Margaret had ready for us when we got home. It was a perfect ending to our adventures. Daphne cleaned up and I sat rocking on the porch with Davis.

"Was it what you hoped for, Cate...the trip, that is?" Davis asked me.

I nodded, with little energy to story-tell at that point.

Then Davis said, "Did they like the cabin?"

"Oh honey, yes, I'm sorry. I meant to tell you right off. We lit the fire, chased the mice, and ate trout till they were coming out of our ears. I caught the first one, and even the children hooked some fish. It was so exciting. It's going to be a really restful place for everyone. I'm anxious to go again sometime, before the cold."

"Uh-huh..."

"Davis, I'm a little weary. Think I'll slide off to bed early." I went inside. "Girls, I'd love to chat, but I'll leave the stories and putting the children down in your capable hands."

"Do you and Daddy mind if Elizabeth comes over this evening?" Margaret asked.

"Not at all. I'm glad you can be together."

As soon as Davis and I were out of sight, I could hear them as they all giggled late into the night.

At one point, I heard Margaret ask, "How is Mother? Does she seem all right?"

"Oh sure, just tired from our long trip," Daphne replied, then jumped right back into more Sybil stories.

Not much conversation came from Elizabeth. She seemed to be quiet. I knew she was thinking more about me lately and was worried about me and Davis, but chose to let the subject drop at this time of laughter and gaiety. She'd had enough sadness for a while. She didn't need more worry in her life.

Fall was a welcome breath of fresh air. The temperatures had dropped and the sun wasn't as intense. The XIT parade of horses and waving Texas beauties, and the barbeques with thousands of strangers, had passed.

Clark's shop was not as successful as they had hoped. Sadly, and reluctantly, Margaret and Clark returned to their familiar home and clientele in Albuquerque. Margaret was pregnant once again and Clark resumed his work at Strombergs.

I could sense Davis's disappointment as he watched their green Plymouth drive away. He had rather liked his new job, babysitting his youngest grandson, Glenn. He enjoyed his daughter's piano music every night and having another man in the house. The idea of being alone with me was fine, but he and I both realized that we missed our family being around. We did make lovely trips to the mountains often, stopping in Albuquerque on the way home, but this caused Davis to miss too much of his church singing, which seemed to be so very important to him. His voice was strong, and his body worn, but he could still maintain his self-esteem with his singing.

I wanted to see Davis happy. After all, he had contributed for so many years, making sure I was happy as the time passed. I filled my days painting. I read my weekly letters from the girls and wrote back to them. But secretly, I felt the tightness in my chest occurring more often. I didn't want to say anything or alarm anyone, so I kept the pace of a more leisurely life. I smiled as usual, not really knowing whether I was fooling Davis or myself. He could see my color fading and would question me from time to time, and I would give him my responsive smile.

Then one day, I scared myself. I drove myself to the doctor. Thoughts raced through my mind. My life was full. I had been the driver of my team of horses, the girls and Davis. I don't know just when my energy began to fade. All I know is it was approximately when the girls' energy began to pick up. I never really wanted to let go of the reins completely, but sometimes it felt like too much...everyone was so scattered. I was glad that I had been so determined to see where each girl had settled. Had those girls learned anything? Did they know how to set up and run a household? How to cook? How to be perfect ladies, wives, and mothers? My thoughts were certainly more settled after I actually put eyes on the reality of their situations.

As much as I tried to keep everyone together, my idea of building a mountain cabin in Cimarron, where we could all enjoy togetherness and nature, didn't work. The truth was, everyone wanted to come home to Twist Junction, and short vacation times limited travel to other places.

Their personalities much preferred destinations with more town activity. The natural beauty of the outdoors was too much like the outdoor activities I had tried to discourage in my girls as youngsters. I didn't think through the consequences of them being "perfect ladies." Two sides of the coin, or perfect balance, is often too hard to achieve.

Many times I would try to recall whether I had taught the girls all the things I wanted them to be and do. Each one of those girls was to be responsible for the next generation, my grandchildren. Had I done my job well?

Davis, on the other hand, took it upon himself to instill memories of tender moments, moments of unconditional love, and the utmost respect for others. Valuable, to be sure. Beyond belief was his true devotion to God. I held tight to my Catholic Irish upbringing. Church had become a pivotal part of our lives, during good times and bad.

I knew I would always be there for my family, even from the other side. Hopefully, I had instilled in the girls the idea of a closeness to their angels, their ancestors, their protectors. The times of difficult childbirths, or certainly the frightening Dust Bowl, and Davis's tractor accident...God and angels were the ones that gave us the added strength to survive. I was always the first to believe in teamwork, no matter which side it came from—the heavens above or the neighbors next door.

Then, I would relapse with questions of what would happen after I was gone. Times of stress and sadness had weakened me and left me fragile. Becoming a woman of fortitude, like my mother, was an expected reality. I grew up knowing that women have to have a determined will to survive in challenging times. Thinking back, I realized that each incident had affected my heart, which was beating only to help me survive the very hardest of times. The toll it took was its ultimate demise.

I wasn't accustomed to being the focus of anything, but I felt weaker than usual. Dr. Dawson sat me down and reminded me of all the responsibilities I'd had, my busy life, and the number of children and grandchildren I held so dear. How could this *not* be a constant job of caretaking? He said I was suffering from exhaustion. Dr. Dawson recommended a little hospital rest; time for me to finally slow down.

Had I not had a wonderful life, and done everything I wanted? Well, almost. Elizabeth wanted to take me back to Ireland to see the roots of our family. I so wanted this time with my wonderful eldest daughter. She, too, needed time with her mother. With the support needed so desperately after her husband's death, the recent widow anticipated the adventure as much as I did. It was a trip I didn't realize would never come. Crossing the ocean, seeing only water for days, and then arriving on a launch to the vibrant, green soil of Ireland was an experience I would only dream about.

As I rested in the hospital, I could feel myself weakening. I became quiet and inactive—feelings previously unknown to me. Even though it was March, Nancy and her children were out west while Wallace had business. Daphne knew the others were all together or nearby, and not wanting to be without her family, she arranged a reunion trip. My brothers secretly expressed concern and came to Twist Junction also. I had some wonderful moments with the precious ones in my life.

Davis, unsure what to do or where to be, sat quietly in a self-imposed fog. Never did he imagine not being with me, his Catherine. Hospitals made him uncomfortable, and he left the hours of visitation mainly to the girls. One by one, each girl would bring him to see me as I shriveled away, becoming colorless by the day. Weeks melted into sleepless nights—memories, memories, and more memories flashed back and forth all day and night. My years weren't many, only 56, but my job as a determined daughter, wife, mother, and grandmother had been played out. My life and the lives of my family were to be the best of the best. I had insisted on perfection. I would leave this world being the matriarch of six daughters and twelve grandchildren.

— ⊲⊦ ⊲⊦ ⊲⊦ —

Davis sat for a while in our empty home, in his chair with his chin resting on his chest and his eyes closed.

Out of nowhere, he heard a voice in the darkness. "Señor, it's me. How you doing?"

It was his Mexican angel. Davis was not startled. He sighed gently and opened his eyes.

"We getting to be two old men. We suffered many tears. Cate is coming with me tonight. Is that okay with you, señor? I promise to take real good care of her. And someday you can come with us, too."

Davis had had many visits from the old Mexican, but not with a message so real and personal. His heart heaved in his chest and his eyes blurred with tears. The inevitable was coming that night. He knew the words were true; the words he never wanted to hear. He said to himself, "Men rarely outlast women. Why does it have to be different this time?"

He wiped his eyes and turned to say something to the Mexican... but he was gone. Exhausted, Davis went to bed and fell into a deep, deep sleep.

— ⊰ ⊰ ⊰ —

I knew I was still lying in a stiff hospital bed...but only my body was left. Just then, Davis's old Mexican man appeared at the foot of my bed. I had never seen him, but I knew him instantly. He greeted me with a warm smile.

"Hello, Miss Catherine," he said, and tipped his straw hat politely.

The girls had left for a quick coffee break at the hospitality station down the hall. No one was there—just the Mexican and me.

He asked, "Are you ready to come with me now?"

My mind allowed him a silent "yes." He approached me ever so gently and scooped me up into his powerful arms. Before I knew it, I could feel that we were leaving the hospital. My mind allowed him to carry me away, knowing that this was what Davis would want.

At the same time, my Davis was startled awake with a jolt, as if someone had shaken his body. He knew what it meant. He closed his eyes again. In his mind's eye, he could see the backs of the old Mexican and me, his dear Cate, as we walked arm in arm down a long path through arbors of white roses.

Davis's world had crashed around him only a few times in his life. The night of my death followed a day of cold winds and clouds that had raced across the sky. A calm of deep intensity had settled in at sunrise. Somewhat blinded, a stunned Davis went to the funeral home with Elizabeth at his side, to begin making arrangements. Afterward, as they headed for home, Elizabeth held his arm to steady him. His thoughts were swimming in his head and his feet didn't seem to settle him onto the sidewalk. The years of taking care of me, the children, and nature's treasures, the animals and the land, were coming to a close. He felt disconnected. I was going away and he wanted to go too. His eyes and mouth drooped in sadness.

Our Elizabeth spoke up. "You're going to be okay; maybe not this minute, but you'll see. All the family will always love you and want to be with you. All your choir and church friends and Aunt Polly will be even closer to you now. Mama's resting now...and I'm going to fix you pork chops and stewed tomatoes tonight."

"Elizabeth, I don't know if I'll be able to taste them. Maybe I just need to sit awhile."

"Daddy, you're coming home to my house, aren't you? All the family is going to be there."

"After a while. I just want to go home for now."

"Okay, Daddy. I'll take you home."

Charlotte, Nancy, and Margaret arrived at Elizabeth's just as she pulled into her driveway. Everyone gathered in the living room.

"I drove Daddy to the funeral parlor and then back home," Elizabeth said quietly.

Sobbing conversations of memories and love filled the living room.

Maggie paused, drying her eyes. "Would anyone like to join me for prayers at the church?"

Shaking silhouettes left the house and climbed into the car.

Daphne broke the silence. "I'd like to go to the cemetery today and look at the plot before the burial."

The afternoon dragged on. Soon the girls had returned home, and the smell of browned pork chops and stewed tomatoes filled the house.

"I think I need a drink," Sybil announced as she flopped onto the nearest lounge chair.

Maggie followed. "Got some soft music on one of your records, Elizabeth?"

Conversations diverted to children, married life, and the future.

Later that day, our grandson Ben dropped by our home with a piping hot plate for two. He sat with his grandfather in silent camaraderie. They stared down at their plates as they slowly ate their supper. They both sat in pain; the pain of memories and the pain that fear projects for the future. Ben was my Davis's buddy. He had been through a tough time too, with the sudden death of his father. That alone was a tough pill for a young boy to swallow.

A horn honked and Ben heard his buddies laughing and talking outside. Without a moment's hesitation, Davis said, "Son, your friends are waiting for you. Go have some fun tonight. You deserve it."

"I don't want to leave you, Daddy Davis. Are you doing okay?"

"Yes, son. A little quiet before Margaret and the girls come home later this evening will be just what I need."

Young Ben jumped up, but turned when he got to the door. In his slow drawl, he tenderly said, "I'll be back to see you and catch up tomorrow. See ya, Daddy Davis."

Exhausted, the girls returned later that evening, checked on their sleeping father, and took claim to their old "growing-up" beds.

In the early morning hours, Maggie quietly came into our bedroom. "Daddy? Are you awake?" she whispered. She sat on the edge of the bed, her hand gentle on his shoulder. She pulled the sheets up to cover his broad chest. "We're all headed back over to Elizabeth's. Can I help get you up? Would you like a cup of coffee?"

"No coffee now. I'll get it at Elizabeth's. You might help me get to the front steps. I feel a little shaky."

She leaned over as he sat on the edge of the bed, making sure that his hands were on each side of his body to steady the heaviness within him. She gave him a gentle kiss on his forehead, but secretly wished it could be the other way around—that it could have been the playful nibble on her ear from her daddy, which she remembered so well from her childhood—from carefree and happier times.

The adults gathered at Elizabeth's home, letting the children remain asleep a few more hours before daybreak came. Surely, they wouldn't go to school that day. Each girl seemed to automatically take on a job without conversation. Elizabeth made sure the coffee was ready as each one came in the door. Eggs, biscuits with gravy, and bacon were ready to be prepared. Maggie sat Davis down on the sofa next to Daphne, who put her arm around him. Sybil, on the other side, held his hand. Maggie joined Elizabeth in the kitchen, where Elizabeth told her what she wanted her to do.

Charlotte, sitting quietly across from her father, had tears rolling down her cheeks. Nancy sat beside her. Nobody knew what to say.

Sybil could feel little life in Davis's cold hand. Daphne noticed that holding him was like holding a lifeless bag of oats. She laid her head against his shoulder, realizing for the first time that he was a frame of dwindling muscle. "Oh Daddy, we need to feed you. You're getting to be too skinny."

He nodded like a puppet.

Sybil squeezed his hand, and his other hand patted her hand with mutual comfort. Her deep love for her daddy tore her apart as she observed his total sadness that morning.

The focus eventually shifted away from me to Davis and his fragile state. He hadn't ever been alone in hard times—never without me. I was gone, that was that, and each girl rushed in to take over. Weeks later, in their own private, quiet times, they would cry, reminisce, and miss me. But right now they had to be strong for their daddy. Phone calls to relatives and friends had to be made. Funeral arrangements had to be made. What flowers would I have liked? What coffin? What dress should I wear? Should I hold rosary beads?

I tried to answer them from the other side, supporting their intuition. With the efforts of my brothers, the Connelly boys, and the Bennett girls, Davis could slowly recover from the fog of sadness and not have to deal with too many decisions.

However diminished Davis was, after a short while, still overwhelmed with responsibilities, he decided to sell the New Mexico cabin. He told Margaret, "I've sold the cabin. Nobody goes anymore, anyway."

"Daddy, how could you do such a thing without talking to any of us?" Margaret said, shocked.

Surprised by her reaction, Davis said, "I guess I don't know how to behave when your mother isn't here to share in the decision making." Within the blink of an eye, he called the purchaser and told him he had changed his mind.

"Thank you, Daddy," Margaret whispered.

Sometimes at night, my Davis would talk to me in his pre-sleep hours. I had a way of answering his questions and even confirming some of his thoughts and decisions.

"Davis, the cabin was a place of joy for us, but times have indeed changed," I told him. "You don't feel up to going as often, and Clark is certainly too busy and quite honestly, isn't the type to like it much anyway. The mice are always an issue with the girls. You made the right decision. You were right to sell the cabin. Margaret just wasn't ready, that's all. Hanging on to old times and memories takes a lot out of a person."

Just before falling asleep, Davis said, "Thank you, Cate."

He did wait six more months, then asked Margaret and the girls, "Mind if we sell the cabin now?"

This time, everyone was ready.

Davis wondered what was going to happen to him. He had never been alone, and I didn't think he could do it. Davis knew Polly had her ways and her house, and didn't need him. Elizabeth had children and a business to occupy her time. Davis knew he was not going away to Sybil's ranch to sit alone, or to any big city with the others. He thought, *Mary Louise, the lady who eyes me at the church, is nice enough. Maybe she could take care of my aching bones and throbbing feet.* But he worried about what our girls would think.

That evening I spoke to Davis. "I never expected you to be alone after I left you. I know you love me deeply, and will forever. I don't want you to be alone. It's okay. Eventually, the girls will understand too."

Davis was startled. "Cate?" he whispered. He sat up and rubbed his eyes. It was dark and chilly. No one was there. At one point, he wondered where he was. Somewhere deep inside he had a knowing that what happened was true—unexplainable, but true. He knew I had spoken to him and had given my approval. But how could he consider such a thing, even though I seemed to encourage it? I was at peace with it. I knew he would always love me, his little blue-eyed partner.

Shortly thereafter, Davis halfheartedly made a decision to take Mary Louise for his second wife. Behind this decision was coping with the scrutiny that would come from the girls…not understanding, not compassionate. He knew them too well and respected their loyalty to me. But Davis was doing this for the girls too. He didn't want them to have to take care of him. Fear of not having their love did significantly alter his thinking. Without his girls and family, Davis thought he had nothing.

Mary Louise and Davis knew the girls' strong wills and opinions. The only way for them to marry would be quietly. The pastor of the Baptist church, on Christmas afternoon, would perform the private ceremony. But complications arose.

Sybil and Garland said they wanted to come for Christmas…a rare event. Because of the guilt from years of exclusion, because of my death, or whatever the reason was, this was the year they wanted to come. They were late arriving at the house, then very late, and then very, very late. Davis was beside himself, thinking maybe he would have to sneak out of the house during the holiday festivities to make it to the church on time. He looked at his watch ten times. He kept Mary Louise and the pastor updated, but the frustration grew. No one knew what was about to happen but Davis.

Finally, the Boyds arrived, the presents were opened, and supper had been eaten. Davis slipped out the back door and across the street to the Baptist church. Once the ceremony was completed, he brought his new bride back through the front door and stood before his family. He made his announcement. Shock prevailed without many words. In hindsight, this would be seen as the most inconsiderate action of Davis's life, but years later, it would eventually be understood after the hurt wore off. Mary Louise and Davis left for a Broadmoor honeymoon, leaving the entire family in stunned silence.

Furious, the girls pulled back. My plan for Davis's remarriage was not going as I wished. Time did heal things, but slowly...very slowly. A trauma only second to this marriage was the family discussion to sell or keep our treasured ranch land. A tortured time of reality set in for Davis, who had no sons, sons-in-law, or grandsons interested in raising cattle or growing crops.

It was a tearful day when the deed was signed over to the new owner. I was there by Davis's side. Davis heard my words, and they seemed to make him feel better. "I always dreaded this day too," I told him. "It's okay, I love and support you always..."

After the signing, a kind family friend cut blocks of fence posts and pieces of barbed wire from the ranch's fence line. He mounted gold plaques on them, and each girl was presented with one of the treasured gifts. They were also handed a beautiful copy of Davis's "open 4" branding iron.

Years passed. The wind blew old dirt away and new grasses appeared. The next generation made memories with their version of appreciation and love, perfection and determination.

And so was the legacy of a man's heart and a woman's drive. In 1973, eighteen years after I died, the Mexican and I visited Davis to bring him home.

About the Author

Penne Poole is a first-time novelist. Her lifetime experiences draw from travels around the world, living in Washington, D.C.; Sonoma, California; Santa Fe, New Mexico; the Northern Neck of Virginia; and Hanoi, Vietnam. Her summers growing up included visits to Cape Cod, Massachusetts; the shores of Chesapeake Bay, the Panhandle of Texas, New Mexico, and the ranchlands of Colorado. Educated in interior design and world travel, Miss Poole draws on her love of all peoples, their cultures, and all things of beauty as a basis for all of her writings.

Miss Poole is a member of the Marin Branch of the California Writer's Club, and a New Mexico Book Association member. She is also an amateur poet.

Miss Poole's career spans over 40 years as a nationally known interior designer.